'It makes a gripping read, complete with adventure, a little magic, vivid characters and a turbulent background.' *The Bookseller*

'Like *A Tale of Two Cities* rewritten by Angela Carter, this is a tale steeped in wickedness of a ferociously enjoyable kind . . . Perhaps the biggest surprise is the power of her prose.'

Amanda Craig, *The Times*

'This book absorbs the reader from the word go. We are plunged straight into a world of secrecy, pomp, poverty and evil . . . Sally Gardner's style of writing is unique; she tells a fresh, imaginative tale that leaps from character to character with unhindered ease to convey a story which is thrilling, humorous and moving, with real depth, verve and style.' *Undercover*

'Brilliantly rich and complex' *Independent on Sunday*

'so beautiful, so elegantly printed and tastefully done . . . An exciting and magical story . . . Gardner writes with much brio and zing . . . a rattling good story.' Adèle Geras, *Guardian*

THE RED NECKLACE & THE SILVER BLADE

SALLY GARDNER

Orion
Children's Books

This omnibus edition first published in Great Britain in 2012
by Orion Children's Books
Originally published as two separate volumes:
The Red Necklace
First published in Great Britain in 2007
by Orion Children's Books
The Silver Blade
First published in Great Britain in 2009
by Orion Children's Books
a division of the Orion Publishing Group Ltd
Orion House
5 Upper St Martin's Lane
London WC2H 9EA
An Hachette UK Company

1 3 5 7 9 10 8 6 4 2

The Orion Publishing Group's policy is to use papers that
are natural, renewable and recyclable products and made
from wood grown in sustainable forests. The logging and
manufacturing processes are expected to conform to the
environmental regulations of the country of origin.

A catalogue record for this book is available
from the British Library

ISBN 978 1 4440 0627 8

Printed in Great Britain by
CPI Group (UK) Ltd, Croydon, CR0 4YY

www.orionbooks.co.uk

CONTENTS

THE RED NECKLACE

To Weavel

my darling brother Stephen, the first
person
I ever told my stories to.
This is for you. I hope you enjoy it.
  With all my love
    Turtle

Prologue

This is Paris; here the winds of change are blowing, whispering their discontent into the very hearts of her citizens. A Paris waiting for the first slow turn of a wheel that will bring with it a revolution the like of which Europe has never known. In the coming year the people will be called upon to play their part in the tearing down of the Bastille, in the destruction of the old regime, in the stopping of the clocks.

This is where the devil goes walking, looking with interest in at the window of Dr Guillotin, who works night and day to perfect the humane killing machine, sharpening his angled blade on the innocent necks of sheep. Little does the earnest doctor know that his new design will be centre stage, a bloody altarpiece in the drama that is about to unfold.

But wait, not so fast. King Louis XVI and his Queen, Marie Antoinette, are still outside Paris, at Versailles. This is the winter of 1789, one of the worst in living memory. Jack Frost has dug his fingers deep into the

heart of this frozen city, so that it looks almost unrecognisable under its thick blanket of snow.

All still appears as it should be. All has yet to break ...

Chapter One

Here, then, is where our story starts, in a run-down theatre on the rue du Temple, with a boy called Yann Margoza, who was born with a gift for knowing what people were thinking, and an uncanny ability to throw his voice.

Yann had a sharp, intelligent face, olive skin, a mop of jet-black hair, and eyes dark as midnight, with two stars shining in them. He was a solitary boy who enjoyed nothing better than being left alone to explore whatever city or town he was in, until it felt to him like a second skin.

For the past few months the theatre had been home to Yann and his friend and mentor, the dwarf Têtu.

Têtu acted as assistant to his old friend Topolain the magician, and together they travelled all over France, performing. Without ever appearing on stage, he could

1

move objects at will like a sorcerer, while Topolain fronted the show and did tricks of his own. Yann was fourteen now, and still didn't understand how Têtu did it, even though he had helped behind the scenes since he was small.

Têtu's age was anyone's guess and, as he would say, no one's business. He compensated for his small size and his strange high-pitched voice with a fierce intelligence. Nothing missed his canny eye, nobody made a fool of him. He could speak many languages, but would not say where he came from.

It had been Têtu's idea to invest their savings in the making of the wooden Pierrot.

The clown was built to designs carefully worked out by Têtu; it had a white-painted face and glass eyes, and was dressed in a baggy blue top and trousers.

Topolain had not been sure that he wanted to perform with a doll.

'A doll!' exclaimed Têtu, throwing his arms up in disgust. 'This is no doll! This is an automaton! It will make our fortunes. I tell you, no one will be able to fathom its secret, and you, my dear friend, will never tell.'

Topolain rose to the challenge. The result had been a sensation. Monsieur Aulard, manager of the Théâtre du Temple, had taken them on and for the past four months they had played to full houses. Monsieur Aulard couldn't remember a show being sold out like this before. In these dark times, it struck him as nothing short of a miracle.

The Pierrot had caught people's imaginations. There were many different opinions going around the neighbourhood cafés of the Marais as to what strange alchemy had created it. Some thought that it was controlled by magic. More practical minds wondered if it was clockwork, or if there was someone hidden inside. This theory was soon dismissed, as every night Topolain would invite a member of the audience up on stage to look for himself. All who saw it were agreed that it was made from solid wood. Even if it had been hollow, there was no space inside for anyone to hide.

Yet not only could the Pierrot walk and talk, it could also, as Topolain told the astonished audience every night, see into the heart of every man and woman there, and know their darkest secrets. It understood their plight even better than the King of France.

For the grand finale, Topolain would perform the trick he was best known for – the magic bullet. He would ask a member of the audience to come up on stage and fire a pistol at him. To much rolling of drums, he would catch the bullet in his hand, proclaiming that he had drunk from the cup of everlasting life. After seeing what he could do with the automaton, the audience did not doubt him. Maybe such a great magician as this could indeed trick the Grim Reaper.

Every evening after the final curtain had fallen and the applause had died away, Yann would wait in the wings until the theatre was empty. His job then was to remove the small table on which had been placed the pistol and the bullet.

Tonight the stage felt bitterly cold. Yann heard a noise as a blast of wind howled its mournful way into the stalls, and peered out into the darkened auditorium. It was eerily deserted, yet he could have sworn he heard someone whispering in the shadows.

'Hello?' he called out.

'You all right?' asked Didier the caretaker, walking on to the stage. He was a giant of a man with a deep, gravelly voice and a vacant moonlike face. He had worked so long at the theatre that he had become part of the building.

'I thought I heard someone in the stalls,' said Yann.

Didier stood by the edge of the proscenium arch and glared menacingly into the gloom. He reminded Yann of a statue that had come to life and wasn't on quite the same scale as the rest of humanity.

'There's no one there. More than likely it's a rat. Don't worry, I'll get the blighter.'

He disappeared into the wings, humming as he went, leaving Yann alone. Yann felt strangely uneasy. The sooner he was gone from here the better, he thought to himself.

There! The whispering was louder this time.

'Who's there?' shouted Yann. 'Show yourself.'

Then he heard a woman's soft voice, whispering to him in Romany, the language he and Tetu spoke privately together. He nearly jumped out of his skin, for it felt as if she was standing right next to him. He could see no one, yet he could almost feel her breath like a gentle breeze upon his neck.

4

She was saying, 'The devil's own is on your trail. Run like the wind.'

———◆———

Topolain's dressing room was at the end of the corridor on the first floor. They had been moved down to what Monsieur Aulard grandly called a dressing room for superior actors. It was as shabby as all the other dressing rooms, but it was a little larger and had the decided privilege of having a fireplace. The log basket was all but empty and the fire near defeated by the cold. The room was lit with tallow candles that let drifts of black smoke rise from the wick, turning the ceiling dark brown in colour.

Topolain was sitting looking at his painted face in a mirror. He was a stout man with doughy features.

'How did you know the shoemaker had a snuffbox in his pocket, Yann?' he asked.

Yann shrugged. 'I could hear his thoughts loud and clear,' he said.

Têtu, who was kneeling on the floor carefully packing away the wooden Pierrot, listened and smiled, knowing that Yann's abilities were still unpredictable. Sometimes, without being aware of it, he could read people's minds; sometimes he could even see into the future.

Yann went over to where Têtu was kneeling.

'I need to talk to you.'

Topolain put his head to one side and listened. Someone was coming up the stairs. 'Shhh.'

A pair of heavy boots could be heard on the bare

wooden boards, coming towards the dressing room. There was a rap at the door. Topolain jumped up in surprise, spilling his wine on to the calico cloth on the dressing table so that it turned dark red.

A huge man stood imposingly in the doorway, his smart black tailored coat emphasising his bulk and standing out against the shabbiness of his surroundings. Yet it was his face, not his garments, which caught Yann's attention. It was covered in scars like the map of a city you would never wish to visit. His left eye was the colour of rancid milk. The pupil, dead and black, could be seen beneath its curdled surface. His other eye was bloodshot. He was a terrifying apparition.

The man handed Topolain a card. The magician took it, careful to wipe the sweat from his hands before he did so. As he read the name Count Kalliovski he felt a quiver of excitement. He knew that Count Kalliovski was one of the wealthiest men in Paris, and that he was famed for having the finest collection of automata in Europe.

'This is an honour indeed,' said Topolain.

'I am steward to Count Kalliovski. I am known as Milkeye,' said the man. He held out a leather purse before him as one might hold a bone out to a dog.

'My master wants you to entertain his friends tonight at the château of the Marquis de Villeduval. If Count Kalliovski is pleased with your performance' – here he jangled the purse – 'this will be your reward. The carriage is waiting. We would ask for haste.'

Yann knew exactly what Topolain was going to say next.

'I shall be delighted. I shall be with you just as fast as I can get myself and my assistants together.'

'Haste,' Milkeye repeated sharply. 'I don't want our horses freezing to death out there. They are valuable.'

The door closed behind him with a thud, so that the thin walls shook.

As soon as they were alone, Topolain lifted Têtu off his feet and danced him around the room.

'This is what we have been dreaming of! With this invitation the doors of grand society will be open to us. We will each have a new wig, the finest silk waistcoats from Lyon, and rings the size of gulls' eggs!'

He looked at his reflection in the mirror, added a touch of rouge to his cheeks, and picked up his hat and the box that contained the pistol.

'Are we ready to amaze, astound and bewilder?'

'Wait, wait!' pleaded Yann. He pulled Têtu aside and said quietly, 'When I went to clear up this evening I heard a voice speaking Romany, saying, "The devil's own is on your trail. Run like the wind."'

'What are you whispering about?' asked Topolain. 'Come on, we'll be late.'

Yann said desperately, 'Please, let's not go. I have a bad feeling.'

'Wait, not so fast, Topolain,' said Têtu. 'The boy may be right.'

'Come on, the two of you!' said Topolain. 'This is our destiny calling. Greatness lies ahead of us! I've waited a lifetime for this. Stop worrying. Tonight we will be princes.'

7

Yann and Têtu knew that it was useless to say more. They carried the long box with the Pierrot in it down the steep stairs, Yann trying to chase away the image of a coffin from his mind.

At the bottom, fixed to the wall, was what looked like a sentry box. In it sat old Madame Manou, whose task it was to guard the stage door.

'Well,' she said, leaning out and seeing that they had the Pierrot with them, 'so you're going off in that grand carriage, are you? I suppose it belongs to some fine aristocrat who has more money than sense. Dragging you off on a night like this when all good men should be making for their beds!'

'Tell Monsieur Aulard where we're going,' said Têtu, and he handed her the card that Milkeye had given Topolain.

All Topolain was thinking was that maybe the King and Queen would be there. The thought was like a fur coat against the cold, which wrapped itself around him as he walked out into the bitter night, Yann's and Têtu's anxieties forgotten.

The carriage, lacquered beetle-black, with six fine white horses, stood waiting, shiny bright against the grey of the old snow, which was now being gently covered by a fresh muslin layer of snowflakes. This carriage looked to Yann as if it had been sent from another world.

Each of them was given foot and hand warmers and a fur rug for the journey ahead. Topolain lay back enveloped in the red velvet upholstery, with its perfume of expensive sandalwood.

'This is the life, eh?' he said, smiling at Têtu. He looked up at the ceiling. 'Oh to be rich, to have the open sky painted inside your carriage!'

Effortlessly the coach made its way down the rue du Temple and past the Conciergerie, and crossed the Pont Neuf. Yann looked along the frozen River Seine out towards the spires of Notre Dame outlined against a blue-black sky. He loved this city with its tall lopsided houses, stained with the grime of centuries, stitched together by narrow alleyways.

The thoroughfares were not paved: they were nothing more than open sewers clogged with manure, blood and guts. There was a constant clamour, the clang of the blacksmith's anvil, the shouts of the street criers, the confusion of beasts as they were led to slaughter. Yet in amongst this rabbit warren of streets stood the great houses, the pearls of Paris, whose pomp and grandeur were a constant reminder of the absolute power, the absolute wealth of the King.

The inhabitants, for the most part, were crammed into small apartments with no sanitation. Here sunlight was always a stranger. Candles were needed to see anything at all. For that the tallow factories belched out their stinking dragon's breath which hung tonight and every night in a menacing cloud above the smoking chimneys. It was not hard to imagine that the devil himself might take up residence here, or that in this filth of poverty and hunger grew the seeds of revolution.

On they went, out towards St Germain, along the rue

de Sèvres where the houses began to give way to snowy woods that looked as if they had been covered in a delicate lace.

Topolain had fallen asleep, his mouth open, a dribble of saliva running down his chin. Têtu had his eyes closed as well. Only Yann was wide awake. The further away from Paris they went, the more apprehensive he became. Try as he might, he could not shake off a deep sense of foreboding. He wished he had never heard the whispering voice.

'The devil's own is on your trail.'

The Marquis de Villeduval's debts were alarming. He took no notice of his financial advisers, who told him that he was on the verge of bankruptcy. He believed there would always be money. It was his birthright. He had been born with expensive tastes and the privileges of nobility. What matter if funds were low? He would simply raise the rents on his estate. This time next year all his problems would be over. In the meantime he would just have to borrow more from Count Kalliovski, who never blinked an eye at the outrageous sums the Marquis requested.

This was how he had financed the building of his newest property, a small château halfway between Paris and Versailles, which allowed him easy access to the court and the capital. When he tired of both, he was to be found at the château on the family estate in Normandy. All that he owned was effortlessly perfect; his taste was superb, the bills always shocking.

That evening the Marquis was holding a supper party to thank Count Kalliovski for his continuing generosity. The guest list included the great and the good of French society, dukes, princes, counts, cardinals and bishops. Like the Marquis, they all had good reason to be grateful to the Count.

But why such generosity? What was there to be gained from it? Count Kalliovski was extremely rich, that was true, a well-travelled, cultivated and entertaining man. His little black book contained most of the important names and addresses in French society. He was often to be seen out hunting with the King's party, and was rumoured to have helped the Queen with one of her more embarrassing gambling debts. In return for his constant generosity, he simply asked for those tiny little secrets, the kind of thing you wouldn't even say in the confessional box. All you had to do was whisper them to him and absolution was guaranteed, the money given. He kept his friends like pampered lapdogs. They never suspected that the hand that fed them had also bought their souls.

Many rumours circulated about Kalliovski, which he encouraged. When asked his age he would say he was as old as Charlemagne. When asked about his great black wolfhound Balthazar he would say that he had never been without the dog. One thing, though, was certain: many were his mistresses and no one was his wife.

The secret of his success lay in the absence of emotion. Over the years he had learnt how to empty himself of sentiment, to keep himself free of passion. Love he considered to be a blind spot on the map of the soul.

He had an iron-clad heart. His motto was one that should have warned all who knew him of his true nature, but a greedy man only sees the purse of gold before him. Count Kalliovski's motto was simple: have no mercy, show no mercy.

For the Marquis's part, he was in awe of the Count, fascinated by him. If he was honest with himself, something he avoided at all costs, he was more than a little jealous of him. Tonight, though, he wanted to impress the Count. Nothing had been spared to make the celebration a success. Only the finest ingredients were to be used for the banquet. The country might well be starving, but here in his kitchens there was food enough to waste.

He had even gone to the trouble of having his daughter brought home from her convent to satisfy a whim of the Count, who had asked to see her. Why, he could not imagine. He thought little of his only child, and might well have forgotten all about her if it hadn't been for

Kalliovski's request. For the Marquis considered Sido to be a mark of imperfection upon his otherwise perfect existence.

The Marquis's splendid new château stood testament to his secretive nature and his sophisticated taste. Each of its many salons was different. Some were painted with scenes of the Elysian Fields, where nymphs picnicked with the gods. In others, there were gilded rococo mirrors that reflected the many crystal chandeliers. On the first floor all the salons opened up into one another through double doors with marble columns. The effect was a giddy vista of rooms, each one more opulent than the last, and each complemented by sumptuous arrangements of flowers, their colours matching the decoration, all grown in the Marquis's hothouses. It might be winter outside, but here the Marquis could create spring with narcissi, mimosa, tulips and lilacs, lit by a thousand candles.

But behind the grand façade of smokescreens and mirrors lay what no eye saw, the narrow, dark, poky corridors that formed the unseen and unsightly varicose veins of the house. They were for the servants' use only. The Marquis liked to fancy that an invisible hand served him. And so his army of footmen and maids performed their tasks quietly in felted slippers, like mice behind the skirting boards.

On the day of the party, the Mother Superior told Sido that she was wanted at her father's new château near Paris.

It had been two years since she had last seen him and for a moment she wondered if he had been taken ill. Her memory of her father was of a cold, unloving man who had little time for his daughter. Sido had grown into a shy, awkward-looking girl who walked with a limp, an unforgivable impediment which reflected badly on the great name of Villeduval. She had lost her mother when she was only three, and for most of her twelve years she had been brought up away from her father at the convent. The Marquis had handed her over to the Mother Superior at the tender age of five, with instructions to teach the girl to be less clumsy and to walk without limping, if such a thing were possible.

Sido's surprise at finding that she was going to the château just for a supper party filled her with excitement and trepidation. As the coach drove away, and the convent doors closed behind her, she hoped passionately that she would never have to see the place again, that this might be the start of a new life where her father would love her at last.

Sido's happiness soon vanished as the coach made its way along the country roads. Peering out of the frosty carriage window, she could hardly recognise the landscape they were driving through. In the thin blue watery light figures seemed to rise out of the snow like ghosts, given shape only by the rags they were wearing. They trudged silently along the side of the road with grim determination. Faces stared at her, registering no hope, all resigned to their fate. Old men, young men, women carrying babies, grandmothers, small weary children, all were ill-equipped for the bitter winter weather as they slowly and painfully made their way towards Paris.

Sido stared at this terrible vision. She knocked on the roof of the carriage, her words sounding hollow and useless. 'We should stop and help,' she called to Bernard, her father's coachman.

The coach kept on moving.

'Please,' Sido called again. 'We must help them.'

'The whole of France needs help,' came the answer. 'If we stop for these, there are a hundred more ahead. Best not to look, mademoiselle.' But how was it possible to turn your eyes away from such a sea of sadness?

T his was the first time that Sido had seen the château. The carriage made its way up a drive bordered by trees. The road was being swept clear of snow by men who stopped to let the coach pass, doffing their hats, the bitter cold making their breath look like dragon smoke. Others were up in the snow-laden branches of the trees, hanging little lanterns that were to be lit later that evening.

Her father's new château looked like a fairytale castle, complete with towers and turrets, floating free of the formal gardens which surrounded it.

The coach went round to the servants' entrance where it came to a halt. The Marquis's valet came out to greet her.

'How are you, Luc?' asked Sido, pleased to see a face she recognised.

'Well, mademoiselle.' Then, feeling some explanation was due, he went on, 'I have been instructed to take you up the back way to your chamber. The Marquis does not wish to be disturbed.'

Sido followed the valet up a set of cold stone stairs and through a plain wooden door into a long dark corridor. Luc lit one of the candles. It shone a shy light down what seemed a never-ending passageway.

'Where are we going?' asked Sido.

The valet turned round with a finger to his lips. 'No talking, mademoiselle.'

Sido followed in silence. Every now and again cat's cradles of light shone from one wall to the other, through peepholes. Luc opened a door.

'This will be your bedchamber. The Marquis will call you when he is ready.'

'What are the corridors for?'

'The Marquis does not like to see his servants,' said the valet, his face expressionless, and with that he closed the door behind him. It disappeared perfectly into the painted panels so that if you didn't know it was there it would be impossible to tell.

This was a plain room, panelled in powder blue. The four-poster bed had thick dark blue velvet drapes, a fabric screen stood near a dressing table, and above the fireplace hung a painting of an Italian masked ball. There were no flowers to welcome her, no bowls of fruits, no sweetmeats, though these were given to all the other guests.

For her part, Sido was just grateful to be away from the convent. She stared out of the window. The sky was snow-laden, her breath a shadow on the window-pane, and it saddened her that she could not recall her mother's face.

Hours passed, so that she was wondering if she had been forgotten when the valet reappeared. 'The Marquis wants to see you now, mademoiselle.'

Sido straightened her skirt, took a deep breath and concentrated with all her might on not limping as she was taken downstairs. Through an open door she glimpsed the dining room with its seven tall windows and polished parquet floor, its walls painted with exotic birds and vistas of undiscovered lands. The long table, with its silver, china and cut glass, looked abundant and welcoming, waiting for the fever of conversation, the rustle of silk to bring it to life. Sido felt a shiver of excitement. Tonight she would be sitting at this very table.

The Marquis was waiting in his study. He had a large, needy, greedy face that gathered itself into a weak, undefined chin and had about it the promise of per-petual disappointment. He stared down his aristocratic nose at his daughter as if summing up a work of art and finding it wanting.

'I see, Sidonie, that you are not much changed since

last we met. A little taller, maybe? Unfortunate. Tallness is unattractive in a girl.'

The abruptness of the criticism and the use of her full name made all Sido's skills of navigation abandon her. She felt clumsy and out of place in the Marquis's study, which was panelled with gold leaf and filled with valuable objects. She was so fearful of putting a foot wrong that she stepped back, narrowly avoiding a table displaying the Marquis's latest acquisition, a collection of scientific instruments.

'Look where you're going!' His voice was sharp and cold, his lips pursed together as if they had just tasted something sour.

Sido felt herself blush. Blown backwards by his words, she bumped into another table, sending its arrangement of leather-bound books crashing to the floor. The noise was shocking in the quiet room.

'In heaven's name, are you as stupid as you appear? And I see you still have that unpleasant limp. It seems not to have improved in the slightest,' said the Marquis irritably.

Sido stood there wishing with all her heart that the floor would open and swallow her up.

At that moment Count Kalliovski was shown into the chamber. At his heels was a large black wolfhound, his famous dog, Balthazar.

Sido had not seen him since she was small, and her first impression was that she would not like to be left alone with either the man or his dog. She dropped her gaze and curtsied as she felt his sharp inquisitive eyes upon her. Glancing up quickly now and then for a discreet look, she saw a tall thin man, elegantly dressed, his skin smooth and ageless, without lines, as if it had been preserved in aspic. He had the perfume of wealth about him.

'That,' said the Marquis abruptly, 'is my daughter. Why I went to the expense and inconvenience of bringing her back here, I cannot imagine.'

'To humour me, I do believe,' said Count Kalliovski, setting the table to rights but leaving the books where they had fallen. He sat himself in a chair and stretched his long legs out before him, placing his hands together to form a steeple in front of his mouth. They were large, ugly hands that somehow didn't seem to go with the rest of him. The dog settled near his master. Sido saw that the pattern on the Count's embroidered silk waistcoat was of little black skulls intertwined with ivy leaves.

'Charming,' said the Count, studying Sido with an expert eye. 'But is there no food at your convent?'

'Not much, sir,' Sido replied.

The Count smiled. 'Tell me then, are the nuns all as pale and thin as you?'

'No, sir.'

'I thought not. Do they eat at their own table?'

Sido nodded.

'And which convent is this?'

When Sido told him, the Count laughed out loud.

'I know the Cardinal. I have lent him money in the past to settle his gambling debts.'

The Marquis looked most uncomfortable.

'My dear friend, I may not have your eye for art, or the finer details of architecture, but I do consider myself to be a connoisseur of women. Your daughter has the most bewitching blue eyes. Give her a few more years and you will find her to be ravishing.'

The Marquis stared at Sido. He looked like a spoilt overgrown child who is being asked to play nicely. 'With respect, my dear Count, plain she is and plain she will remain. I fear you have been taken in by the beauty of my study and the afternoon light.'

'Not in the slightest. I am just concerned to hear that your daughter has been sent to such an indifferent school. Tell me, Marquis, what use is a dull and charmless wife? No, to make the most of your daughter I suggest that from now on she should be educated at home.'

Sido stood there, surprised to find that she had an ally in the Count.

The Marquis rang for his valet.

'The girl is to be bathed and the dressmaker summoned,' he said grudgingly. 'She will be dining with us this evening.'

It took Sido a moment to realise what her father had just said. Perhaps she might be allowed to stay here after all. She wondered if just for once fate was smiling kindly on her.

I t was eleven-thirty, and the guests had just finished eating. It had been a feast to be savoured, and glasses clinked as the wine flowed. Upstairs the gaming tables had been laid out and a group of musicians played in the long sitting room.

On their arrival, Topolain, Têtu and Yann had been shown into the library, where a small stage had been erected, with a makeshift curtain. The only light in the room came from the fire and the candles on the mantelpiece. When the candles blazed up you could see that this was a large semicircular room. The walls were lined from floor to ceiling with bookshelves, divided halfway down by a wooden walkway. At each end was a spiral staircase. It was hard to fathom where the ceiling began or ended; the books looked as though they might go on to eternity.

Topolain was not in a good mood. When they reached the house he had been in a deep sleep and he had stumbled badly as he got out of the coach, making a fool of himself in front of the footman.

'Shouldn't have let me nod off,' he snapped at Têtu, who deliberately ignored him. He stood near the fire doing his best to get some warmth back into his frozen limbs, for in spite of all the fur rugs in the coach, he still felt chilled to the marrow.

Only Yann was alert and excited enough to explore. He moved away from the fire into the dark recesses of the library. He had never seen so many books. He took one out of the shelf. It was brand new, some of its pages still uncut. He put it back and took out another, smiling to himself. Whoever owned the château used this room more to impress than for the knowledge it held.

It seemed extraordinary to Yann that a château should be owned by one man, and it made him feel insect-small. Still, for all its grandeur, there was something uncomfortable about the place, as if the foundations were having an argument with the earth. A bad omen, he thought, for tonight's show.

The large double doors at the end of the room opened and in the draught that followed, the candles flared up. Yann turned to see a tall man enter the library. He was dressed in black, his hair powdered white, and he walked with an assured step, the red heels of his shiny buckled shoes clicking loudly on the parquet floor. A black wolfhound followed him. He was holding something that Yann couldn't quite make out. Now in the firelight he saw clearly what it was, a human skull carved in wood.

The sight of it made Yann move further back into the darkness of the bookshelves. There was something sinister about this man. He supposed him to be the Marquis de Villeduval.

Count Kalliovski ignored Topolain and Têtu, and he hadn't seen the boy. Turning his back on the fire, he put the wooden skull on the table, opening it up to reveal a magnificent timepiece. On its face was the image of the Grim Reaper.

Topolain rushed forward, accidentally tripping and making nonsense of his low bow. Balthazar growled, showing a perfect set of sharp, pointed fangs. Topolain hastily moved back. Kalliovski didn't look up.

'It is an honour, Count Kalliovski, to be called to your splendid residence,' said Topolain. 'May I congratulate you on your fine taste?'

'This is not my residence. It belongs to the Marquis de Villeduval. Let us hope your magic shows more skill than your words do.'

Topolain was still not fully awake. How could he have forgotten what he had already been told? He attempted some more toe-curling flattery, making matters worse. Balthazar snarled again, a low menacing rumble of a sound like the coming of thunder, his ears pinned back, his eyes shining yellow, watching every move the magician made, longing for one word from his master to tear him to pieces. Topolain took another step backwards. He was terrified of dogs.

Têtu, watching this, had a sense of rising panic. His mind whirled as he tried to remember exactly where and when it was he had last seen this man.

It was the sight of the Count's hands that finally loosened Têtu's memory. He knew now with a dreadful certainty that they were all cursed. For all Kalliovski's airs and graces he still had the hands of a butcher, the hands of a murderer. How could he ever forget them? Here before him was a ghost from his past, the enemy he had hoped never to see again. How he wished that he had paid more attention to what Yann had been saying. Yann! Where was the boy? Têtu's mouth felt dry. He was relieved to see him in the shadows. All he could hope for now was that Topolain would for once keep his mouth shut.

Yann had never been able to read Têtu's mind, though tonight that didn't stop him from realising that something was wrong with the dwarf, and it wasn't just his usual tiredness after the show: it was something altogether more worrying. He listened as the Count began to speak.

'I called you here tonight because I was impressed by your performance at the Théâtre du Temple. I too have a great interest in automata,' said the Count.

Topolain smiled feebly. He was only half listening. He was positive he had met this man before, though where, for the life of him he couldn't remember.

'Do you know who first came up with the idea of man as a living machine?' said the Count. 'It was the philosopher Descartes. It might interest you to know that he even had a replica of his dead daughter Francine constructed for him.'

'I didn't know that,' said Topolain. He realised with a start that Kalliovski was staring at him intently. He had never heard of Descartes, and knew nothing of philosophy. Nervously, he took out his handkerchief and blew his nose.

'And then there was Jacques de Vaucanson,' continued the Count musingly. 'You may remember that he came up with that wonder of the world, the defecating duck.'

Now Topolain felt safer. Everyone in France knew about the defecating duck. He coughed and drew himself up.

'I never had the privilege of seeing the duck. It must have been most amusing to see it take the grain from your hand, appear to eat it and then expel it just like a real duck.'

'Quite,' said Count Kalliovski dryly. His face was expressionless. 'And do you know that it was nothing more than a clockwork toy? The Age of Enlightenment, and all it brings us is a defecating duck! I trust your Pierrot holds more magic than that.'

'Oh yes, sir, much more,' said Topolain. Then, without thinking, he enquired, 'Forgive me for asking, but haven't we met before? I never forget a face and yours is one that ...' He stopped, realising too late that his tongue had run away with itself. He knew it was a fatal mistake.

Kalliovski's eyes narrowed to scrutinise the man in

front of him. He turned to look at the dwarf, a spark of recognition showing on his face. Only then did the poor magician remember when and where he had last seen the Count. Under his blotched white makeup all the colour drained from his face.

The Count smiled inwardly. He turned on his red heels and left the room. Têtu and Topolain listened to his footsteps retreat into the distance. They were well and truly trapped.

'What have I done?' said Topolain.

Yann could suddenly feel Topolain's fear, though his thoughts were jumbled together and made no sense at all.

'Quiet,' Têtu grunted. 'The boy is here. You'd better leave the pistol out of the show.'

Topolain poured himself a generous glass of cognac from a decanter, his hands shaking. He drained the cognac in one gulp. 'No pistol. I think that's wise. But we're dead, aren't we?'

The memory of the voice carly that evening began to haunt Yann again. There must, he thought, be a way to escape.

Above him on the wooden walkway came the sound of footsteps. A footman appeared as if from nowhere, and started to walk down the spiral staircase with a dish of sweetmeats. Quickly Yann made for the staircase at the opposite end of the room. He watched the footman leave the dish beside the decanters on the table before returning the same way he had come, through an invisible door in the bookshelves. Yann, catlike, went up the stairs after him and caught hold of the door before it fully closed.

'See if you can find a way out of here. I'll keep the door open. Go!' hissed Têtu.

Yann found himself standing in a dark, musty-smelling passageway. Up ahead he could see the flicker of candle-light as the footman disappeared down the rabbit warren of corridors. It reminded him of walking between the painted flats in the theatre. But why did the château have this hidden labyrinth of corridors? What was it trying to hide? What illusion was it hoping to create?

◆

Sido had been dressed and ready for hours, but no one had come for her. She could hear music and laughter wafting up the stairs as doors down below opened and closed. It was late. Supper must be over. She had been forgotten. Hungry and disappointed with waiting, she lay down on the four-poster bed and closed her eyes.

This was how Yann first saw her. He had discovered that there were peepholes in all the doors, and by looking through them he had a good idea by now of the layout of the château. It was like watching different scenes from a play, with guests getting ready and putting the final touches to their finery. He felt drawn to this girl, certain that she wouldn't cry out if he were to venture in. He pushed against the door and it opened silently. Not wishing to wake the girl up, he sat down and waited for her to stir.

There was something about her that fascinated him, and he was curious to know why she had been left up here all alone. She reminded him of a china doll, with long eyelashes that fluttered like a butterfly's wings, and an abundance of dark hair that cascaded across the pillows.

Sido woke up with a start, then, seeing the boy, sat bolt upright in bed.

'Who are you? What are you doing here?'

She pulled the curtains around her and peeped out, wondering if she should call for help.

'Even if you did, no one would come,' said Yann.

This was very unsettling. Had she been talking aloud and not known it?

'What is your name?' she asked.

'Yann Margoza. What's yours?'

'Sido de Villeduval. Why are you here?'

'I am with the magician. We are doing the show tonight, downstairs in the room with all the books.'

'The library?'

'Whoever it belongs to hasn't read any of them. They are all new.'

'Everything in the house is new. My father has only just built it.'

'Are you a princess?'

'No,' Sido laughed, 'I am not.'

'I couldn't live like this,' said Yann. 'The walls would close in on me. It would become a pretty prison.'

The boy shouldn't be here, Sido thought, yet the strange thing was that she had no desire for him to leave.

29

He made her feel less forgotten and less hungry. She tried hard to think what she knew about boys, which was very little. Unlike the other girls at the convent, she had no brothers or cousins to help her out. Now there was a strange boy in her bedchamber. If she were caught with him, she would be sent back to the convent to be forgotten again.

'You won't be, not now you are here.'

'How do you do that, know what I am thinking?'

Yann picked up a book and said, 'It's all the same, thinking and saying. Can you read?'

Sido nodded.

'Are you sure I won't be sent back to the convent?' she asked.

'You will stay here.'

His words thrilled her.

'I would like to read words. Thoughts can be so confusing. Why does this house have secret corridors?'

'My father had the corridors built because he doesn't like to see the servants. Thank you for what you said. Still, I think you should leave.'

Yann knew he should, but there was something intriguing about this girl that made him forget the reason he had gone off exploring.

He smiled at her. 'There's no need to worry. No one will come for you until the show begins.'

This was a strange boy indeed. It was like being in church and feeling that you were opened up and all of you could be seen.

'The doors have peepholes. I looked through one.

That's how I saw you. Would you like to see?'

Sido nodded.

'Come on, leave your shoes.'

In her dress of watered silk that rustled as she moved, she followed Yann through the hidden door and down the secret passages. Together they took turns looking through the peepholes. A lady in a boudoir adjusted her impossibly tall wig, complaining to her maid that it was too heavy and that she had a headache. In another room, a man was kissing a lady on the neck. She was blushing and Sido saw her step quickly aside, fanning herself as her husband appeared at the door. Ladies and gentlemen were sitting in a sumptuous salon, and the scene looked almost golden in the glow of so much candlelight.

She felt Yann touch her arm lightly.

'We must go back,' he said.

They retraced their steps. Sido quickly straightened out the bed and put her shoes back on. When there was a sharp knock on the door her heart nearly missed a beat.

Then she realised that the boy with the all-seeing eyes had vanished.

Chapter Four

So it was that on the last stroke of midnight the scene was set. All that was keeping the performance from beginning was the late arrival of the Marquis. The guests were waiting as an argument broke out between two of their party, a cardinal and an intensely earnest-looking young man called Louis de Jonquières.

'The clergy are the First Estate of France, the nobility are the Second, and the Third Estate are the rest of the country. We're seriously outnumbered. It is imperative that we question our role,' said the young man.

'I suppose you think the Third Estate should have a voice. Are we expected to give a say to every peasant? Have you thought through the consequences?' asked the Cardinal with distaste.

'You are a man of the Church. The Bible commands us to consider the poor,' replied Louis de Jonquières, warming to his theme. 'In my view, if their lot is to be improved, they should have a say in the way things are run. Come, you must agree that at present our society leaves much to be desired.'

The Cardinal looked pained. He cleared his throat to make his point.

'My ancestors fought to make this country what it is. We are a great nation, the envy of the world. You surely do not imagine that this has been achieved by the people? It is our duty to retain our position and lead the way.'

'But the nobility cannot be relied upon,' said Louis de Jonquières. 'We are not going to change our ways in order to put bread on the tables of the starving. Look what has happened in America! The people rid themselves of English sovereignty and now, with our help, it is a republic. Many of my friends would argue that absolute monarchy is dead.'

The Cardinal's cheeks were now as red as his silk gown.

'Society,' he said haughtily, 'will have to evolve, and that, monsieur, will take time. Nothing is going to be achieved in a day.'

'But why should the poor pay for the privileges of the rich? They are so many, and we are so few,' said Louis de Jonquières passionately.

Count Kalliovski, who was enjoying watching the Cardinal's discomfiture, interrupted with a laugh.

'Enough, enough,' he said. 'For tonight, my friends, let's leave politics alone. The subject makes dreary companions of us all.'

Now, with the timing of a great actor, the Marquis entered the room, accompanied by Sido. He took his seat at the front of the makeshift stage. Sido sat down beside him.

Her attention was caught by the Duchesse de Lamantes, with her fashionably tall coiffure. On top, amongst an assortment of ribbons and flowers, sat a coach made out of gold thread, drawn by six dapple-grey horses of blown glass. This brittle design sat oddly with the sour face of its wearer, who looked as if one smile might crack the piecrust of her makeup.

'Who,' enquired the Duchess, lifting up her spy-glass, 'is that plain-looking creature? Can it be the Marquis's daughter? What a disappointment for him.'

The Marquis silenced the company. 'I hope I haven't missed any of this intriguing little performance of yours, Count Kalliovski.'

'Not at all, my dear friend,' said the Count. 'As you can see, the curtain has not yet been drawn.' He clapped his hands for silence.

———◆———

'Messieurs et mesdames, to thank the Marquis for this splendid evening I have brought him a show from the theatre at the rue du Temple – a show so popular that it has been sold out for the past four months. I give you the People's Pierrot.'

There was a round of applause as the curtain was pulled back and Topolain brought the Pierrot to the front of the stage.

The magician started as always by demonstrating to the audience the working of its wooden limbs and its lack of strings.

'Monsieur le Marquis, Count Kalliovski, my lords and ladies,' he announced with a flourish, 'I have here the wonder of Paris. He can walk! He can talk! Moreover, he can look into the future, see into the depths of your hearts, and know your darkest secrets.'

'Why would it want to do that?' interrupted the Marquis. 'It seems most impertinent.'

A titter of laughter echoed round the room.

Topolain stopped, uncertain whether he should continue or wait.

'My dear Count,' said the Marquis, who in truth was irritated that it hadn't been his own idea to bring this show here, 'these are mere street entertainers. I am surprised that you have brought them here.'

'Be patient. I can assure you that this little notion of mine is going to prove most entertaining.'

Topolain was so put out by all the delay that he found himself tongue-tied, unable to remember the questions that he usually asked the Pierrot. To his relief, the Pierrot stood up and opened its steely glass eyes. It stretched out its wooden fingers and moved its wooden limbs. There was complete silence.

Topolain recovered himself and began to work his audience. With care, he lifted up the Pierrot's baggy blue top to show the carved wooden torso. He tapped it with his hand; it made a pleasingly solid sound.

'Bravo! An artful mystery indeed,' said the Marquis.

Count Kalliovski stared fixedly at the wooden Pierrot; he too was intrigued to know how the strange doll worked.

Topolain, his voice no longer faltering, said, 'Ask the Pierrot a question. Any question will do. I promise you the answer will not disappoint.'

Yann, from his vantage point hidden in the shadows, could see the stage and the audience clearly. Têtu, standing beside him, was working the Pierrot, though how he did it remained to Yann a profound mystery. It was their combined talents that made the show the success it was.

'Tell me then, what kind of dog have I got?' said a lady with face patches and a painted fan.

This was what Yann could do, read minds and throw his voice so that it sounded as if the Pierrot was talking.

'A spaniel. She had puppies three days ago.'

The lady laughed. 'How charming, and how clever.'

Now it started just as it had done in the theatre earlier that evening, a ribbon of silly questions neatly tied up and answered to everyone's satisfaction. Yann felt pleased that nothing more taxing had been asked of him. Two shows a night was hard work, especially for Têtu.

Just then Louis de Jonquières remarked, 'If the Pierrot is right about small things, things of no importance, then maybe he can inform us on the bigger questions of the day.'

36

'Really, monsieur!' said the Duchesse de Lamantes. 'Why do you insist on being so disagreeable? Why not save your talk for the coffeehouses of Paris instead of asking a wooden doll to take part in your idiotic debate? Let it rest. It is most inappropriate.'

'Forgive me,' said Louis de Jonquières, 'but I am curious. Tell me, Pierrot, will the present regime fall?'

With this question the room changed. Yann saw in the slipstream of his mind an audience of headless people, blood running down their fine clothes. He heard the Pierrot say, as if from many miles away, 'A thousand years of French kings are coming to an end.'

The audience began to shift on their chairs. Topolain rushed towards the front of the stage. 'The doll jests,' he cried. 'Please now ask him a question he can answer.'

Louis de Jonquières pushed back his chair and stood up.

'Without wishing to make a dull fellow of a wooden doll, perhaps he would care to give us his candid opinion as to whether France will evolve itself into a con- stitutional monarchy.'

'Please, monsieur,' interrupted Topolain, 'my doll is no political fortune-teller.'

'But you said, sir, that he can see into the future, into the minds of men. I am merely asking what he sees.'

'Watches, snuffboxes, trinkets, bonbons and the like,' said Topolain. He felt he was losing his grip. What on earth had come over Yann, that he would say something so dangerous?

'Humour me,' the young man persisted.

Yann looked out at all the fine ladies and gentlemen, at the emeralds, rubies and diamonds that glittered on wilted flesh. Louis de Jonquières appeared to be holding his blood-soaked head under his arm. Yann blinked, hoping the vision would go away, only to see Death walk into the room. He wanted to keep silent, but it was as if he were possessed.

He heard the Pierrot say, 'I see you all drowning in blood.'

This remark was so unexpected and so shocking that Topolain burst out laughing. 'As you see, messieurs and mesdames, on the question of politics the Pierrot is but a wooden doll.'

None of the guests were laughing. Instead their faces were grave and the atmosphere in the room became uneasy.

'A doll indeed,' said the Marquis solemnly. He turned to his guests. 'I can assure you, my dear friends, that such a thing would never happen here. It must be an English doll!' There was a ripple of nervous laughter. 'In England, that country of barbarians, yes, maybe. Look at what they did to their King Charles the First – chopped off his head! We would never fall so low.'

There was a murmur of approval. Everyone applauded.

Count Kalliovski watched with interest. He had sat there, judge and jury on the fate of Topolain and Têtu, and had come to his verdict. This would be their last ever performance. After tonight the old fool and his friend would be dead.

'Thank you, that will be all,' said the Marquis, dismissing Topolain. 'I believe the entertainment, if you can call it that, is over. We will adjourn.'

'Not quite yet,' said the Count. 'The show is not finished. I believe Monsieur Topolain is celebrated for a trick that he does with a pistol. Monsieur Topolain is the only man in Europe who claims that no bullet can harm him.'

'Impossible!' said the Marquis.

'Well then, let us see for ourselves,' said the Count.

Topolain was on his own. In his mind's eye he saw the Grim Reaper climb out of the wooden skull, grow in size and stand there watching him, just like Kalliovski. For one moment he contemplated escaping, but he could see Milkeye standing guard at the library doors. If he ran, it would be the end for all of them. He took a long, deep gulp of air. He who thought himself a coward now showed the bravery of a lion. Always the showman, he brought out the pistol and a bullet and showed them to the audience.

'I will prove to you that I am invincible. This bullet will be fired at my very heart, and yet I will live to tell the tale. Now, I require an assistant.'

He looked out into the audience, knowing full well who would stand up.

'You need someone with an accurate eye. I flatter myself that I am that man,' said Count Kalliovski.

Topolain wished that he had at least drunk more of the Marquis's very fine cognac. He loaded the pistol and handed it to the Count, who took his time inspecting it.

Only Topolain saw that with sleight of hand he had interfered with the weapon.

'When I raise my handkerchief, you will fire.'

'Wait,' said the Count. 'Have you forgotten? Should you not say some magic words to keep you safe?'

Oh, Topolain remembered all right, but he knew there were no words to keep him safe.

The Count's voice broke through his memories. 'No bullet . . .'

'No bullet,' repeated Topolain, 'can harm me. I have drunk from the cup of everlasting life.'

With these words he walked away bravely as if he were about to fight a duel, though, unlike Kalliovski, he was unarmed. He looked his murderer straight in the eyes as he lifted his white handkerchief.

'Fire!'

The Count pulled the trigger. There was a loud retort, followed by the acrid smell of gunpowder and scorched flesh. Topolain stumbled and the audience gasped as they watched the handkerchief he was holding turn bright red.

Topolain stood up. In his sweating palm he held up the bullet and showed it to the audience. He staggered forwards to take a final bow.

The curtains were drawn and the audience clapped politely. By now they had lost interest.

'Most peculiar,' said the Marquis. 'Come, I think we are all in need of champagne. Let us go upstairs, where the card tables demand our attention.'

The great library doors were opened and music filtered into the room. The Marquis led the way out, quite forgetting his daughter, who stood staring transfixed at the curtains as the other guests filed past her. All seemed unaware of the drama unfolding behind the velvet drapes. None of them turned round as there was a thud from backstage. None of them saw Topolain slumped down on the chair.

Death had made his entrance upon the small stage. He was all too visible to the magician. As a trickle of blood ran down his chin, he had the strangest sensation of becoming detached from his body, connected only by spider threads of silver memory. Now he was floating up over the guests, past the crowded bookshelves towards the bright painted ceiling with its angels and cherubs.

The silver threads snapped and he was free. Caught in a gust of wind, he was blown out of the library into the hall with its marble busts and winged statues, where the doors had been opened to let in a latecomer. The snow flurried in as Jacques Topolain, the magician, glided out into the dark night. He saw no more, he heard no more, he was no more.

Yann had rushed with Têtu to help. He had taken one look at Topolain and seen Death's black gown trail across the stage. Sido too had witnessed Topolain's end, but the Count had turned her round and led her from the room, locking the doors behind him. The candles flickered in the draught.

Têtu put his head to Topolain's chest, listening for a

heartbeat. He shook his head. There was nothing to be done.

'It has never gone wrong before. Why now?' cried Yann.

Têtu was examining the weapon. 'It didn't go wrong this time either,' he said. 'The pistol has been tampered with. Topolain didn't stand a chance. He was murdered.'

Yann had never before stared death in the face as he did now. It looked to him so absolute, a final curtain fallen. The essence of Topolain had gone, snuffed out like a candle. Only the body that housed him was left lying on the stage in a pool of congealing blood, with Têtu kneeling beside him, tears rolling down his cheeks, rocking back and forth on his heels and sobbing.

'I should have listened to you. We shouldn't have come. Then this would never have happened,' he said defeatedly.

Yann put a gentle hand on the dwarf's shoulder and bent down to whisper to him. 'We have to leave.'

Têtu was silent. In the dim light of the room Yann could see him shaking. He was in a bad way. He was already exhausted from doing two performances in one night, and now the shock of losing such a dear friend had taken all his strength away and robbed him of his senses.

All Yann could think was that they must somehow get out of here.

Out in the hall, the guests were making their way up the grand staircase to where the Marquis de Villeduval stood, champagne glass in hand. Sido felt perplexed by their indifference. Surely they realised that the magician wasn't acting, surely they realised he had been seriously hurt. Why did no one summon a surgeon to help?

She turned in desperation to the Duchess. 'I think the magician has been wounded.'

'Nonsense, child! It was just play-acting.'

Could these people not see what had taken place? Sido wondered. Did they not care? She felt she had arrived in a foreign land, where the language seemed twisted and words possessed double meanings.

'There is really no need to alarm yourself, my dear child,' said the Duchess, hardly glancing down at Sido. Her eyes searched the room for more distinguished company. 'I can assure you that your magician will live to work another day.' She walked away, leaving Sido alone.

'I don't want to grow up to be like that,' thought Sido. She looked up at Count Kalliovski, who was surrounded by ladies. They reminded her of hens bobbing up and down, preening their feathers, all vying for his attention, all hoping to be first in the pecking order.

Sido would have liked to go back into the library to see for herself what had happened to the magician, but one of the Count's men was standing guard outside and she knew that if she moved any closer she might attract unwanted attention. She moved behind a pillar and watched with a sense of relief as Kalliovski escorted two ladies up towards the card room and out of sight.

Beside her on the first step of the staircase stood a young lady in an elaborate pink silk dress, with a hawk-nosed gentleman.

'Do you remember the time the Marquis brought in a fortune-teller?' the young lady was asking.

Her admirer shook his head. 'Alas, I was not invited. I suppose it was Count Kalliovski's doing.'

'The Count was not even there. The Marquis sent his gamekeeper out into the countryside and he brought back this old gypsy. She refused to tell our fortunes, no matter how much gold she was given. She would only speak to the Marquis and no one else.'

'What did she say?'

'It was so ridiculous it made us all laugh. She told the Marquis he would lose everything to the king of the gypsies.'

Sido, who had been half listening to this and half looking about her, caught a glimpse of light coming from under the staircase. A door opened and a footman came through, carrying a tray of champagne glasses.

Behind him Sido could just see the beginnings of a passageway. She knew then what she was going to do. Without giving it a second thought she slipped over to the door and found herself at the bottom of a flight of stone stairs. She knew there must be a way through the secret corridors to the library. It was just a matter of finding the right door.

Gently, Yann helped Têtu to stand and with difficulty guided him up the spiral staircase and along the wooden gantry to the concealed door in the bookshelves. By now all the colour in Têtu's face had drained away. Yann knew that it was up to him to save the dwarf. His exhaustion had robbed him of his instinct to survive. What surprised Yann was that although he himself was well aware of the danger they were in, he felt no fear. His vision was clear, colours were electric, and everything seemed sharper. Every nerve of him felt completely alive.

But the concealed door was shut fast.

'Don't worry, I'll get you out of here,' he said soothingly, knowing full well that the shutters of Têtu's mind had closed down. He heard the library door open and then close with a firm click, and pulled Têtu back into the shadows.

Count Kalliovski called out, 'I know you're both there. My man tells me there is a boy as well. There's no point hiding. Listen to me carefully. If you don't want to go the same way as Topolain, you'd better tell me how the Pierrot works.'

He waited for an answer. Yann kept quiet. He could hear the Count walking to and fro, trying to determine where they were.

'I have examined the doll. It is a piece of solid wood: it could not have been worked from the inside. I am a man of science. Come now, tell me its secret.'

'Why did you murder Topolain?' shouted Yann.

'Quiet, boy. Dwarf, answer my question. Tell me the secret of the automaton and I will protect you. If you refuse me I tell you this, no matter what you do, no matter where you hide, I will find you. Think carefully before you answer, for I never make an offer twice.'

Têtu's small legs had started to shudder as if caught in a trap. Yann heard the scrabble of Balthazar's claws up the spiral staircase and there was the dog staring at them with its yellow eyes, its mouth snarled back, its fangs shining bright with saliva. Balthazar growled.

'Bring them to me,' commanded the Count.

Têtu's legs twitched all the more as the dog's shadow was thrown large against the bookshelves. Yann stood up. Holding his hands out in front of his body, he pointed his fingers directly at the dog's eyes and spoke softly in a language that Balthazar seemed to understand. The beast dropped on all fours as if the firm hand of a giant had suddenly crushed him.

Yann did not blink or break his stare. Defeated, Balthazar, his tail between his legs, went back down the stairs whimpering to his master.

'What have you done to him, Têtu? What gypsy sorcery is this?' demanded Count Kalliovski angrily.

Yann said nothing but moved silently towards the banister rail. To his despair he saw Milkeye enter the room. The Count spoke to him. Yann couldn't hear the words, but knew what he was saying. Quickly, he moved back to the darkness of the bookshelves and tried again to push with all his strength upon the concealed door. He could hear the Count below as he walked with Balthazar towards the library doors. The dog's clicking claws told him they were leaving.

'I want the dwarf and I want that boy,' said the Count. 'Don't let them get away.'

'Yes, master.' Milkeye was already at the bottom of the staircase.

For the last time Yann tried the door, feeling it desperately with his hands for hidden locks or latches. He could hear Milkeye getting closer. He was near the top of the staircase and still the door wouldn't give. Yann could almost see the top of his head. It was no use. He would have to stand and fight: that was all that was left to him.

Suddenly the door opened. Standing in the darkness of the passageway he could see the girl.

'Help me,' he whispered, and together they pulled Têtu through.

By the time Milkeye had taken the last few steps to the top of the gantry, there was nobody there.

It wasn't easy to drag Têtu along the narrow passageways. He was heavy, as if his bones had turned to stone. Only when they were in Sido's chamber with the screen moved to block off the peephole did Yann finally feel safe, safe enough to say, 'We must lie him down.'

'Of course,' said Sido, pulling back the bedcovers.

'He'll be better once he's slept,' said Yann.

It took all his strength to get Têtu's heavy body up on the bed. He was an alarming sight, with all the colour drained from his face. Hastily he covered the dwarf with a quilt, his anger subsiding a touch when he saw Sido standing there anxiously watching. By some twist of fate she had become unwittingly involved in what was happening. The only hope he had of escaping lay with her.

If she lost her nerve, he and Têtu wouldn't stand a chance of getting out alive.

'Who is he?' she asked.

'His name is Têtu. He's looked after me since I was born. We work together, with Topolain.'

'Will he be all right?'

'Yes, but he should stay hidden. If anyone comes in, it just looks as if the bed has been turned down.'

'What about the magician?' asked Sido. 'Is he dead?'

'His heart gave out,' said Yann.

'I don't believe that.' She said it so bluntly that he knew she couldn't be fooled.

'No, it isn't true, but there's no time to explain. We have to get out of here. I need your help.'

'But what can I do?'

'Be brave.'

'I don't think I am brave.'

He smiled at her. 'I know you are. Will you stay here with Têtu while I search for a way out?'

The thought of being alone in the room with the sleeping dwarf terrifed Sido. With a sickening feeling in her stomach she nodded, hoping that Yann could not read her mind. She wanted to scream no, I am not brave, but when she looked into his dark eyes she knew she would do as he asked.

'I'm not good at lying,' she said, hoping that this might make him change his mind.

'I know that too.'

The silence after he had gone felt almost solid, as if it were pressing down on her chest, squeezing the air out of her. She sat on a chair by the bed and told herself again and again to be calm.

A few minutes later there was a knock on the door. Sido felt every nerve in her body tighten. Checking that Têtu was completely covered, she stood up, took a deep breath, and said, 'Come in.'

Count Kalliovski stood in the doorway, Balthazar at his side.

'I came to see if you were all right. You vanished so quickly after the little show.' He entered the room, closing the door behind him. 'Why, my dear child, how pale you are. You look as if you've seen a ghost.'

Sido moved towards the bed.

'It was only an illusion, you know. No harm was done.'

Despite herself she began to shiver, and as if in response, Balthazar started to growl softly. Count Kalliovski looked around him suspiciously.

'I was feeling very tired, sir,' said Sido hastily. 'I came up to my chamber to lie down. I have not eaten since early this morning and there has been more excitement than I am used to.'

'Your life at the convent is, I imagine, a quiet one,' said the Count. He looked around the bedchamber again. His gaze fell upon the screen before returning to the bed. 'I suppose by now you would be fast asleep?'

Sido nodded and wondered if her legs would continue to support her. They felt like hollow reeds shaking under her petticoats. The Count stood facing her, his shadow casting a monstrous figure on the wall behind him, one that appeared to possess a multitude of hands, all poking

51

and prodding into the dark recesses of the bedchamber.

The bed with the sleeping body of the dwarf was only three steps away. Balthazar had begun to edge closer, his growling becoming more insistent.

'You are alone, of course?' asked the Count.

'Why, yes, sir.'

'Do you mind if I see what has caught Balthazar's fancy?' The Count moved forward. Now only two steps separated him from the dwarf.

'Please, sir,' pleaded Sido. 'I am frightened of dogs, and it is clear that yours does not like me.'

'You have no need to fear Balthazar,' said the Count with a smile. 'He will not harm you. He only growls at strangers.'

If Count Kalliovski moved one more step, it would all be over. Everything would be discovered. She would be sent back to the convent in disgrace. As for the boy and the dwarf, she hardly dared think about it.

'Please, sir, it is not right or proper for a man to visit a girl's chamber. The Mother Superior would be shocked to hear of such a thing.' She found to her surprise that she had tears in her eyes. 'Please,' she begged again, 'don't let your dog come any nearer.'

The room began to spin and a metallic taste filled Sido's mouth. She thought she was about to faint. She grabbed at the four-poster bed, holding on to consciousness with all her might.

The Count's voice softened. 'My dear child,' he said, 'I had no desire to alarm you. You must be faint for lack of food. I will see that some supper is brought up to you straight away. It is outrageous that you should be so neglected.'

He gave a deep bow and called for Balthazar. 'Forgive the intrusion,' he said, closing the door softly behind him.

Sido leaned her head on the bedpost, trying to stop the room from spinning. She remained statue-still, listening to the scratching of claws and the clicking of heels as they retreated into the distance. Only then did she loosen her grip. She sank to the floor, resting her head in her hands, and prayed that Yann would hurry.

———◆———

Carefully and soundlessly, Yann made his way along the secret passages to the stone staircase and looked over the wrought-iron banister. He caught a glimpse of the kitchens below, saw the doors swing open and shut, heard the clatter of pans and the murmur of voices. A man stood in the stairwell and stamped snow from his boots before disappearing from sight. There must be a door to the outside world there.

He was returning the way he had come when a pin-prick of light caught his attention. He looked through the peephole into a grand bedchamber, with huge displays of white tulips and black roses on the table. Maybe it was the flowers, maybe it was the lavishness of the decor, more likely it was the large dog bowl sitting on the floor that told Yann that this was where Count Kalliovski slept.

If nothing else, they were owed the blood money that

had been promised to them at the beginning of this nightmare. How would they get back to Paris without a sou to their name?

Yann pushed against the door and slipped inside. An eerie red light shone from the coals in the grate. The walls were painted with hunting scenes that in the spit and hiss of the firelight appeared to be moving. The wooden skull sat on the table beside the vase. It might have been valuable, but he knew also that it was cursed, and would bring whoever took it nothing but bad luck. Next to it was a necklace – a blood-red ribbon with seven crimson stones set into it. Without thinking, he put it in his pocket. It would be something to show Têtu.

He began to search the room for money.

This is what Yann knew, what he had always known: that all objects, great and small, have a spirit. Sometimes, if you listen carefully, you can almost hear the sound they make.

Hidden deep in among the drapes of the bed was a purse. Yann picked it up and put it in his pocket, where it felt pleasingly heavy. Now he had to get out of here as fast as he could.

* * *

Sido hadn't dared move since the Count had left. Yann found her still sitting on the floor, her head in her hands. She looked up at him.

'Where have you been? Count Kalliovski was here.'

'It took longer than I thought. We'll be gone in a minute.' He went straight to the bed and pulled back the covers. 'Wake up,' he said gently, shaking Têtu back into life as he helped him to his feet. He was pleased to see that the dwarf's eyes were purple-black once more and his skin no longer pale.

'Where am I?' said Têtu, who for a moment thought that he must have woken from a bad dream. Yann said something to him in a language Sido had never heard before. Têtu gulped as the memory of what had happened came back to him.

Yann turned back to look at Sido, sitting crumpled and abandoned on the floor, and for a moment he had an overwhelming desire to take her with them, to save her from being one of the headless ones.

There was a knock at the door. Sido scrambled to her feet. Quickly Yann and the dwarf disappeared behind the screen and through the panel, sliding it back into place just as the Count entered, followed by a footman carrying a tray with Sido's supper. This time the dog at the Count's heels was silent. The tray was laid before her. The sight of the food made her mouth water. Eat slowly, she said to herself. Don't rush.

The Count's eyes darted round the room as he ordered the footman to straighten out the bed.

'There is no need,' said Sido quickly.

'Continue,' said the Count smoothly, addressing the footman. Balthazar had begun sniffing the air.

'I hope you don't mind if I keep you company while you dine?'

Sido knew that the longer he stayed, the longer the dwarf and the boy had to make their escape.

'I would like that,' she said.

Count Kalliovski sat down on a chair by the bed. The dog at his feet let out a heavy sigh and, putting its head on its outstretched paws, closed its eyes.

'I think your dog is more used to me now,' said Sido.

'So it seems. When you have finished, I will take you down to see the fireworks. Your father assures me that they will be magnificent.'

Sido watched the Count as with hooded eyes he searched the room once more, looking for evidence to confirm his suspicions. In the quicksilver candlelight he made a menacing figure, and she knew then that he was no friend. Her instinct told her that there was no escape: this dark spider was waiting patiently to catch her in his gold-spun web.

The kitchens of the château were busy. Even after the main banquet had been served there was more than enough to do. The gambling tables demanded a constant supply of drinks and *petits fours*. Jean Rollet, the chef, and his staff would be working all night until the very last guest had left or retired. The arrival of two more in the kitchen went almost unnoticed except as extra pairs of hands to help.

'Hey, you there, lackey,' a valet shouted at Yann, 'the Viscount needs this tray taken up to him at once.'

Yann shook his head. 'We are the entertainers, hired for the Count's show. We need to get back to Paris tonight.'

The valet threw up his hands in disgust. 'What are you doing in here, then?'

Yann felt bewildered. He had never been in such a large kitchen before, with servants running backwards and forwards, the chef swearing and stamping his foot, bells ringing, the noise, the smells, the heat. It was like a furnace.

Têtu started to sway. He was going to fall over if he didn't sit down. Yann grabbed a stool.

'No you don't,' said one of the cooks, snatching it back and lifting her wooden spoon as if it were a weapon. 'Away with you, gypsies.'

'We have to get back to Paris.'

'Well, what are you doing asking me? Do I look as if I have a magic carpet?' Then, seeing the state of Têtu, she softened. 'You'd better go and ask the coachmen in there.'

Yann helped Têtu through the kitchen to a small antechamber where a group of men were sitting at a table, their plates wiped clean, their glasses full.

'My friend needs to sit down,' said Yann, and one of the men pulled out a chair for him.

'He don't look too perky. What's wrong with him?'

'We need help. Are any of you Paris bound tonight?'

'Not if I can help it,' said one of the men, pushing his chair back and lighting his pipe. 'With luck, they'll be playing cards till dawn and then some.'

Suddenly Yann felt as if he had hit a wall. He had got this far without being discovered, and now, just when there seemed hope that they might escape, all was lost.

Time was slipping away from him; he knew it would not be long before the Count found out about the secret passages.

'Here,' said a man with a shining bald head, pouring some wine from a large clay pitcher into a glass. 'Give this to Titch. He looks as he could do with it.'

'Thank you,' said Yann, helping Têtu with the wine. Slowly he began to look more like his old self.

'Has he always been that small or will he grow?' asked the bald-headed man, laughing.

If Yann had been given a gold coin every time he had heard Têtu insulted they would be rich by now. Still, it riled him as it always did to hear his friend slighted, though he knew better than to react.

A footman opened the door and poked his head round. 'The Viscomtesse de Lisle will be staying.'

'Good to know it,' said her coachman. 'First sensible thing the old bat's done in ages.'

'You think so?' laughed the footman. 'Well, she wants her pet monkey brought back from Paris. She thinks it'll be lonely. It's not your night, Dufort my old friend.'

'Hasn't she seen the snow outside?' said Dufort, gesturing towards the window.

'That's why she wants her monkey.'

'Oh well,' sighed Dufort, 'here we go again. Doubt I'll make it back before tomorrow. Tell you this much,' he muttered into the last dregs of his wine, 'one day I'll be my own master. No more of this come here, go there, lucky-to-have-a-job nonsense.'

All the men laughed. 'You know what you can do?'

said the bald-headed one. 'Write all your grievances out and send them to the King.'

'That's a good one,' said his friend, slapping him on the back. 'Maybe the King will be able to get her to behave.'

Everyone burst out laughing, everyone except Dufort, who looked furious as he pulled on his heavy coat, loath to be leaving the warmth and comfort of the kitchens.

'To make matters worse, the roads aren't safe these days, what with all the bandits and brigands, and she's too mean to pay for a lackey to help,' he grumbled.

Yann seized his chance. 'We will keep you company,' he said.

'What, take a couple of gypsies like you? Forget it.'

Têtu, now able to walk unaided, followed Yann back through the kitchens past a rack of freshly baked bread that was cooling from the ovens. With the swiftness of hand that takes a lifetime to master, he took two of the loaves and hid them in his topcoat before making his way out into the snowy courtyard.

'It's no good you two following me,' said Dufort. 'I'm not taking you and that's final.'

'Would money change your mind?' asked Yann.

'Would the man in the moon giving me a silver eye make me think different? Of course it would. It ain't going to happen, though.'

Yann, as if from thin air, conjured up five coins and handed one of them to Dufort. He looked at it carefully, then put it in his mouth and gave it a good bite to check its worth. He didn't know what to make of this strange pair, the street urchin and the little fellow with the girly, squeaky voice.

'Where did you get this kind of money?' he said.

'We were brought here from a Paris theatre to entertain the guests. We're magicians. We were paid handsomely for our trouble,' said Têtu.

'Then where's your driver, Titch?'

'We can't find him. He must have left earlier to avoid the worst of the weather.'

'We were held up,' added Yann quickly, 'because my friend was feeling unwell.' He knew that Dufort was wavering between doubt and the certainty of the coins that he held in his hand. 'I'll give you this now and as much again when we reach the city. Is that fair?'

'All right,' said Dufort reluctantly, 'as long as you don't tell anyone. The old bat's most particular about who is allowed in her carriage. Monkeys yes, dwarves and dogs no.'

The coachman led the way across the yard to the Marquis's stables. They were the height of luxury. He might not have cared much for his servants or his daughter, but the Marquis's horses were a different matter altogether. He liked them to be well looked after. He had a notion that after his death he might be born again as a fine stallion, in which case the Marquis wanted to be housed here with crystal chandeliers to illuminate his hay and underground heating to warm his hooves.

'Look at that,' said Dufort. 'His tenants live in hovels with barely enough to eat and the horses live like lords. It makes my blood boil, it does.'

He opened the door of the carriage and let Têtu in. 'If you don't mind, I'd like the boy to ride with me and keep an eye out for thieves. When we're near Paris, I'll lock you both into the carriage. Don't want the riff-raff trying to hitch a ride, do we?'

He handed Yann a heavy coat to wear. It nearly drowned him. 'Always keep two handy, in case of rain.'

It was a small carriage with two young horses to pull it, both of whom seemed highly strung and reluctant to leave the warmth of the stable. Finally, with much urging, they made their way down the avenue of trees whose branches were full of little lights that twinkled like stars. Beyond the estate lay a vast black abyss, waiting to swallow them up.

'I hate driving at night,' said Dufort miserably, his breath coming out of him in a foggy mist. 'It gives me the creeps.'

The darkness had never bothered Yann, especially not tonight. There was safety in a starless sky.

'We may be less than four leagues from the city, and this may well be the best road France has to offer, but with no moon ... Ah, what's that?' The coachman flinched as the sky above the château erupted with the sound of fireworks. They exploded into the darkness, painting patterns of light in the shape of stars, serpents, comets, and chrysanthemums. It was an astounding sight in this landscape of ice and snow.

Terrified by the noise, the horses reared up. Dufort, distracted by the fireworks, lost control of the reins, grabbing at the sides of the carriage to stop himself from being thrown to the ground. The horses, now wild with fear, were galloping. Up ahead the road turned, and Yann could see that at this speed the coach would skid on the ice. Inside he could hear Têtu shouting as he was thrown from side to side. With difficulty he scrambled down from the coachman's seat.

'You're mad!' yelled Dufort, as with one measured leap Yann managed to mount the first horse. Holding on to its neck for all he was worth, he leant forward and whispered into its pinned-back ears. At the sound of his soft voice both horses became calmer and slowed down until they finally came to a halt, steam rising from their glossy coats. Yann climbed down and stroked their muzzles, talking to them in a language that the startled coachman was sure he had heard before.

'You're a brave one and no mistake,' said Dufort, wiping the sweat from his forehead. 'I thought I was a goner back there.' He handed Yann his flask as they set off again. 'There's a thing! What did you say to them?'

Yann shrugged, looking back to see the last of the fireworks as they illuminated the château before it too disappeared altogether.

'The only other person I've seen talk to horses like that was a gypsy man. I had a feeling you two had gypsy blood.'

Yann wasn't listening. He was wondering if Sido had been allowed to see the fireworks, or if she was still locked in her chamber. He smiled as he stared at the road in front of him. The thought of how angry the

Count would be to discover that the purse and the red necklace were missing warmed him.

Dufort shivered. 'I always think them forests are full of eyes, all watching and waiting.' He laughed. 'Tell you this, boy, I'll be glad when I see the lights of Paris.'

Yann looked into the woods of beech trees, their silvery barks catching the reflection of the carriage's lights. An owl hooted, and its haunting cry followed them as they made their way down the icy road. An hour and a half later he was allowed into the carriage where, half frozen, he quickly fell asleep.

———◆———

Têtu woke him just before dawn. The coach had reached the gates of Paris. Through a gap in the curtains Yann could see crowds of people all waiting to be let into the city in the hope of earning the price of a loaf of bread. The carts that had food to sell were being heavily guarded by police and soldiers. They were the first to be let in, while the begging and pleading from the crowd rose in volume.

'Get away with you,' bellowed the gatekeeper. 'There's no work in the city. It's frozen solid like the rest of this blasted country.'

Groups of starving people were being forcibly turned back, while others yelled that they had papers.

At last the carriage came to a standstill.

'How are you, Dufort?' they heard the gatekeeper enquire.

'Why, Monsieur Gaspard!' said Dufort with genuine

surprise. 'What are you doing here? A new job, I see, and a good one.'

'A good one, this, dealing with the rabble every day? You must be joking! I only got it because the old chap had a heart attack. They say one man's misfortune is another man's misfortune.' They both started to laugh.

'Is the Viscountess with you?' asked the gatekeeper.

'No, thank the Lord.'

'So why did she send you back empty?'

'She wants me to fetch her monkey. I'll be back this way as soon as I've got the little beast.'

'A monkey,' chuckled the gatekeeper. 'I've heard it all now. Away with you.'

The carriage set off again, lurching from side to side as it made its way over the cobbles and over the Pont Neuf and then they were on the right bank of the Seine. There, in a narrow side street, Dufort stopped, climbed down and unlocked the door.

'You did well, my friend,' said Têtu.

Yann was too tired to do anything other than take some coins from the purse and hand them to Dufort.

'This is too much,' said Dufort, looking longingly at the money in his hand.

'Keep it,' said Têtu.

'Very decent of you. You're good people,' said Dufort, climbing up again and taking hold of the reins. 'I reckon it's me who should be thanking you for saving the coach. I owe you one.'

The snow had started to fall again. Yann put his hands deep in his pockets. He could feel the purse and the weight of it reassured him that they had money left over; but the red necklace had vanished.

'Come on,' said Têtu.

With heads bowed, coats pulled tight around tired, cold bodies, they walked towards Monsieur Henri Aulard's apartment in the Marais, knowing they had the unpleasant task of breaking the news of Topolain's death to him.

———◆———

Count Kalliovski, returning to his chamber in the early hours of the morning, looked into the heart of the fire. It had been a good night. He had watched as more money was lost than won on the gaming tables. The little black leather-bound notebook that he privately called the Book of Tears was full of I.O.U.s with the trembling signatures of desperate souls longing to borrow more, sure that their luck would change.

Men's morals were as insubstantial as tissue, and about as transparent, he thought. Oh yes. He had bought himself more foolish-minded men and women, who would soon be asked to pay him back with interest.

He put the Book of Tears on the desk. It was only then that he noticed the absence of the red necklace. A cold fury overtook him. Balthazar made a low growl, and he spun round.

'Who's there?' he said to an empty room.

The Count went over to the bed, felt in the drapes for the purse, and cursed out loud when he found it gone. With rising anger he summoned Milkeye.

'Where are they?'

'We're still looking, master.'

'Why haven't you found them?'

They could be anywhere in the labyrinth of secret passages behind the walls,' said Milkeye. For such a big man he seemed to have shrunk in size.

'Show me,' said the Count coldly.

Milkeye opened the hidden door.

The Count took a candle and disappeared into the passage. Coming back into the room, he turned his icy gaze upon his servant, and pinned him up against the wall.

'I made you and I can destroy you, and I will. I want both of them. Do you understand?'

'Alive, master?'

'No, dead.'

M onsieur Aulard was not a morning person. The previous night he had been out drinking with some actors. Now, red-faced and snoring, he was fast asleep.

It took him a few minutes to realise that the terrible banging sound was not coming from the inside of his head, that it was something quite detached from him.

His parrot Iago, who was sitting on his usual perch shipwrecked amongst the shambles of the bedchamber, joined in the commotion by screeching, 'Wake up, naughty boy, wake up!' In a desperate attempt to silence the noise Monsieur Aulard threw his wig at the parrot. The knocking just kept on, getting louder and more urgent.

Finally, barefoot and shivering, Monsieur Aulard dragged himself out of his warm bed. His head felt like a rotten apple. His apartment looked as bad as he felt. The source of the noise was coming from the front door.

He fumbled with the lock until he finally managed to open it. Two Yanns and two Têtus floated before him. They were swaying back and forth, overlapping each other.

Something was missing from this unsettling picture. There should be a third person.

'Where's Topolain?'

Têtu walked into the apartment, followed by Yann. Even half awake and with a thumping headache, Monsieur Aulard could see that Têtu was in a bad way.

'My dear friend, are you unwell?' He looked back at the door, expecting to see Topolain come panting up the stairs behind.

'Topolain's dead,' said Têtu with a sob.

'Dead!' repeated Monsieur Aulard. 'Dead? Not Topolain! He was larger than life. How can he be dead?'

'A bullet,' said Têtu, his face collapsing as tears appeared in his watery red eyes. 'He was shot like a dog.'

'No, no, no! *Mort bleu!* Yann, speak to me, tell me this is a nightmare!' He grabbed hold of the boy's flimsy coat so that the sleeve came away from the armhole with an unforgiving ripping sound.

'Count Kalliovski shot him,' said Yann.

'But why would Count Kalliovski kill Topolain?' His teeth were beginning to chatter. He pulled his housecoat tight around him and abstractedly went over to the fireplace, throwing a few wet coals on to the burning cinders. It had the immediate effect of puffing clouds of smoke back into the chamber and he started to cough as Yann opened the window.

The bitter coldness of the air cleared the smoke and Monsieur Aulard's head too, long enough at least for him to realise that he was in deep trouble. He sat down heavily on an armchair whose horsehair insides were spilling out. It creaked alarmingly under the weight of his hangover.

'The trick must have gone wrong. It must have been an accident.'

'It was no accident,' said Têtu. 'The Count knew exactly what he was doing. He tampered with the pistol.'

'But why would Count Kalliovski, who is famous and respected, murder a mere magician?'

It was the question Yann had been asking himself all the way back to Paris, a question Têtu up to now had refused to answer.

'Because,' said Têtu wearily, 'Topolain recognised Kalliovski, and instead of keeping quiet he let his tongue get the better of him. Topolain knew him from a long time ago, when he was called by another name.' He spoke so quietly that Monsieur Aulard was not sure that he had heard him correctly.

Yann could see that if Kalliovski was a fraud he would want no one knowing it. Still, Têtu's explanation raised more questions than it answered. He put a half-frozen pan of wine on the fire to boil, searched through the mess to find some glasses, and cleared the table as Têtu took one of the loaves from out of his jacket, where it sat before them like a golden brown sun.

At the sight of the loaf, Monsieur Aulard's attention

wavered from his immediate grief. 'Where did you get that?' he asked.

'From the Marquis de Villeduval's kitchen.' Têtu broke off a piece and handed it to him.

The hot wine and bread worked their magic on Monsieur Aulard. With a huge sigh he went to get dressed, reappearing with his wig placed lopsidedly on his head, his waistcoat buttons done up wrongly and his shirt hanging out.

'I have a full house, all tickets sold and no performer!'

'You'll have to find someone else,' said Têtu.

'*Mort bleu*,' said Monsieur Aulard. 'I tell you, if I weren't so kindhearted, I would have you two thrown on to the streets for your failure to protect Topolain. Why, he was one of the greatest magicians France has ever seen!' He wiped his eyes and, putting on his heavy outer coat and muffler, opened the front door, letting in a blast of icy wind from the stone stairwell. 'You can't stay here, you know.'

'Don't worry, we'll soon be gone,' said Têtu. 'Count Kalliovski is after us, too. We had trouble getting out of the château alive.'

Monsieur Aulard stopped in his tracks and turned round.

'*Mort bleu*! You know who he is too, don't you?'

'Yes, for my sins, I do.'

'Who is he, then?'

'That,' said Têtu, closing his eyes, 'would not be worth my life to tell you.'

M onsieur Aulard arrived at the theatre and started to make enquiries to see who could fill Topolain's place for the evening performance. He sat at his desk and opened the bottom drawer where he found what he was looking for, a none-too-clean glass and a bottle of wine. He pulled out the cork and poured himself a drink. It tasted good. He closed his eyes, taking another sip.

He opened his eyes with a start. There, sitting in the chair before him, was someone he had never seen before, but whom he knew at once was Count Kalliovski. It was as if the devil himself had appeared from nowhere.

The shock made him choke on his wine, spraying it over his desk. Desperately he tried to recover himself.

'*Mort bleu*, you gave me the fright of my life,' he gasped. Pulling out an over-used handkerchief, he wiped his mouth and then the desk. 'I didn't hear you, monsieur!'

'Where are they?' demanded the Count.

'Where are who?' said Monsieur Aulard, hurriedly refilling his glass.

The Count's hand in its black leather glove moved effortlessly towards the stem. With his fingers spread, he pinned the glass firmly to the table. 'You know very well who I am after. The boy and the dwarf.'

'I know no such thing,' said Monsieur Aulard, trying to summon up much-needed indignation. 'Perhaps you would be kind enough to tell me where Topolain is.'

'Topolain is dead. I'll wager you've been told as much by the dwarf. It was I who pulled the trigger. A most unfortunate *accident*,' said the Count with emphasis.

Sweat was beginning to form on Monsieur Aulard's forehead. The room felt uncomfortably hot.

Kalliovski leaned forward and stared menacingly at him. 'I need information.'

Monsieur Aulard felt an icy trickle of sweat creep down his back.

'You will tell me where they are hiding. I know you know where they are,' said the Count, standing up.

'I assure you I do not. I haven't seen them,' said Monsieur Aulard. Each word he spoke sounded shakier than the last.

'You have until the curtain goes up at seven to tell me,' said the Count. 'If you fail' – here he gave a mean, thin-lipped smile – 'if you fail, I hope for your sake that you have made peace with your Maker.'

The door closed behind him as poor Monsieur Aulard waited to make sure that he had gone. Then, grabbing hold of the bottle, he drank what was left.

———◆———

It was three o'clock and still snowing when Monsieur Aulard trudged up the stone stairs to the front door of his apartment. It swung alarmingly back and forth on its hinges.

'Hello,' called Monsieur Aulard, his heart beating so fast that he thought it might give out altogether. There was no answer.

'You been popular,' said his neighbour, a lady with a face like a ferret, sticking her head out of her front door. 'A big man with a cloudy eye came looking for you and your friends.'

'What friends?' said Monsieur Aulard.

'The boy and that there dwarf. He said he knew them.'

Monsieur Aulard took out his wine-stained handkerchief and wiped away the snow.

'He said he knew where to find you.'

Monsieur Aulard, dry-mouthed and terrified, pushed open the door. The apartment looked worse than it had this morning. His possessions had been thrown across the room, papers scattered, the table knocked over, and glasses smashed. Even his mattress had been pulled from the bed. Iago, his feathers all ruffled, was hiding in a cupboard. He looked wretched. Monsieur Aulard stroked the parrot's head and put him back on his perch. Then he sat down in his armchair, and, feeling a piece of paper beneath him, pulled it out to see that it was a poster for the greatest show on earth, with Topolain and the People's Pierrot, the first walking, talking, all-knowing automaton.

'I am ruined,' wept Monsieur Aulard. 'The only time I have a success in my theatre, it vanishes in a puff of smoke.'

Finally, exhaustion overcame him and he fell fast asleep. He woke with a start, changed, and made his way miserably back to the theatre, terrified of telling the Count that this time he truly did not know the whereabouts of the boy and the dwarf.

Monsieur Aulard arrived at the theatre just before seven to be told that he had had no visitors and that no one had asked after him. He went up the stairs to his office and opened the door. The room was dark. Why had no one bothered to light the lamp? he thought irritably, fumbling for the tinderbox. He stumbled, steadying himself on his desk. In the dark he could see an unfamiliar shape.

'Who's there?' he called.

He lit the wick.

Slowly and terribly, the dead body of Topolain was revealed, sitting in his chair. Around his neck was a thin line of dried beads of blood. In his lap was the sawn-off head of the Pierrot, its glass eyes glinting in the lamplight.

Monsieur Aulard's scream could be heard all the way through the theatre and out on the rue du Temple.

Chapter Nine

Têtu and Yann had left the apartment earlier that morning, not long after Monsieur Aulard, for they knew that was the first place Milkeye would look for them.

The apartment block was never quiet. The lives of its inhabitants seemed to spill out on to the landing rather like the stuffing of Monsieur Aulard's chair. A terrible row was taking place between a husband and wife on the floor below, witnessed and commented on by the other tenants. There was a cacophony of sounds: shouting, screaming, babies crying, dogs barking, the background noise of lives lived on the edge of existence. In such chaos Yann and Têtu went down the stairs almost unnoticed.

At the bottom sat a child of about seven, who looked older than his years, thin and half frozen.

'Best you go inside, *mon petit.*'

The boy stared at the dwarf, terrified. He didn't know

what to make of the strange fellow who conjured up a loaf of bread from out of his coat. He looked at it in disbelief before grabbing it and running up the stairs. Only when safely out of reach did he lean down over the wrought-iron banister and shout, 'Thank you, monsieur.'

It had been one of those twilight days when the gloom of night still lingers on. The sky was so heavy with snow that it appeared to have collapsed under its own weight on to the buildings below. It was not a day for having your sleeve come adrift from your coat. Even the church bells had a muffled half-heard sound. No one was out by choice in these icy streets, with the snow piled high against the sides of the buildings, so that the walkways were narrow and treacherous.

The months of December and January had produced a bitter harvest, a crop of starved and frozen corpses, the money it brought in lining the pockets of the coffin-makers.

The lights and smoky warmth of Moet's Tavern seemed like a slice of heaven in this frozen city. As usual, it was full of hot-headed youths and men arguing over the state of the kingdom. Têtu found a table tucked away in the corner out of sight. Here he ordered the dish of the day for himself and Yann. Only when his fingers finally felt that they belonged to him again did he begin to sew the sleeve back on to the boy's coat.

Yann felt not only that his coat had come apart but

that his world had been torn to pieces. Everything had changed the minute the pistol had gone off, killing Topolain.

What he knew about the past amounted to no more than a few facts, bright beads from an unthreaded necklace, reluctantly given to him by Têtu, who refused to join them together. He had no father that he knew of; his mother had been a dancer in a circus, and had died soon after he was born; Margoza was the name of a village of which Têtu had fond memories. His survival had been due to Têtu, and Têtu alone.

What he knew about the dwarf was not much more. He had once been a jester to a king; which king, he wouldn't say. He had travelled the world with a dancing bear. All that had happened a long time before he had found himself with a baby to care for. Never once had he mentioned Count Kalliovski, or who he might be. So why now had the Count tampered with the pistol? What exactly was it that Topolain and Têtu knew?

The more Yann thought about it, the more certain he was that there was one question which, if answered truthfully, might string together all the beads on the necklace.

'Who is Count Kalliovski?'

Têtu shrugged his shoulders.

'One day I will tell you,' he said finally, cutting the threads with his teeth. He shook out the coat and handed it back to Yann.

'I'm old enough to know right away.'

Some secrets are best kept, Têtu thought to himself.

'Yannick, you know I love you as if you were my son. Don't you trust me?'

'I do.'

'Then believe me, I will answer all your questions, but not now. Now is not the time. Now is not the place.'

The food arrived and they set to eating.

Three tables away sat a group of young men, one of whom had a nose that looked as if it been in an argument with a fist. His skin was pock-marked and he was talking loudly about the rights of citizens. He had no doubt drunk more than a skinful of wine, for he kept standing up and shouting out: 'Citizens, the wind is changing! The old regime will be blown away. All is dust, all is dust!'

His friends quickly pulled him back down on to his seat.

'I have the right to say what I damn well please,' he shouted, glaring at another man sitting alone at a table. 'Don't you agree, citizen?'

Yann had been watching all this intently and did not at first notice Têtu wrapping his muffler about him and putting on his hat.

'Where are you going?'

'I have someone to see. I'll be back in a couple of hours. You are to wait here for me. If Milkeye comes looking for us, make yourself scarce.'

Têtu set off purposefully, walking away from the Marais across the Pont Marie towards the left bank, where he stopped as he had done several times before to make sure that no one was following him.

He knew that he had to get the boy out of Paris. It was

too dangerous for him to stay. The only hope of doing so lay with a friend of his, the English banker Charles Cordell. He walked on, remembering the night all those years ago at the theatre in Le Havre, a memorable evening all round, for it was the first time that Topolain had successfully performed the bullet trick and the first time Têtu had met Cordell. The two of them had struck up an unlikely friendship. Their mutual interest, to begin with at least, was magic, for Cordell fancied himself something of an amateur conjurer.

Cordell soon realised that prejudice made people underestimate the dwarf. Têtu was not taken seriously, so he was told things other men would never have heard. Ladies confided in him, young men spouted their views. The dwarf listened to the gossip of the coffee-houses, the prittle-prattle of the salons and the oratory of the clubs. Cordell, like Têtu, knew that these places were where the real intrigue lay.

The two would meet regularly at the Café Royal, where Têtu would tell Cordell all he had heard and seen. This information gave the banker a clearer idea of what was going on and how best to advise his clients.

The snow was still falling as Têtu made his way towards the rue du Dragon, with its grand, imposing houses. They had a smug quality, as if they had folded their arms across their frilled façades, and looked down judgmentally from tall disapproving windows on to the tree-lined boulevard below.

Têtu stood waiting for what felt like a lifetime before a housekeeper came hurrying out, carrying a lantern.

'Is Monsieur Cordell in?'

'Is he expecting you?'

'No, I came on the off-chance. I need to see him urgently. Will you say that Têtu is here?'

The housekeeper went inside, closing the door behind her. Têtu stood waiting, stamping his feet and blowing on his frozen hands. The door opened again and he was shown into the hall. His teeth were chattering as the housekeeper took his coat, hat and muffler. The snow that had formed itself into frozen clumps on his stockings was melting on to the wooden floor. He stamped the rest off his shoes as he heard the door above him open, and looked up the stairwell at Charles Cordell.

Têtu had never been more pleased to see his friend's grave, bespectacled face staring down at him, and for the first time since the murder the night before he felt a glimmer of hope.

'Why, my dear friend, you look half frozen,' said Cordell, coming forward with his hand outstretched.

'I need your help. I am in a great deal of trouble,' said Têtu. And before he had even been taken into the elegant drawing room he had told Cordell the story of Topolain's death.

'He is a great loss,' said Cordell, taking Têtu over to the fire and bringing out a bottle of cognac. 'So ... Kalliovski ...'

Têtu nodded. 'I have been a complete idiot,' he said angrily. 'I let my guard down, believed we were safe after all these years. Fool, fool that I am not to have known who he was. I, of all people, should have suspected. I walked straight into a trap.'

Têtu got to his feet as if sitting still was impossible, and started to walk up and down the room. 'I knew he was a master of disguise, yet I too was nearly taken in by him. Do you know what gave him away? His hands, his large ugly hands.'

He made a sound that could have been mistaken for a laugh, though Cordell heard it as pent-up fury.

'Yes, his face may be smooth and ageless but you can never change your hands, they never lie.'

'May I ask why you are so afraid of Kalliovski?'

'Sometimes you meet someone you know is touched by evil. Kalliovski is such a man. I believe he came originally from Transylvania. We met when Topolain and I were working in St Petersburg, where he made his money by cheating at the card tables. He was a cheap trickster, a gambler. He was interested in us because of the magic; we didn't much like him, stayed out of his way. But he became obsessed with a friend of ours, a young dancer. In the end, in fear of her life, she ran away from him and we went with her. The idea was that we would protect her, for we had seen what he was like when he didn't get what he wanted.'

'What happened?'

'He followed us to France. He found us, and he killed her with his bare hands. I could do nothing to save her. After that he was wanted for murder, and he disappeared. Later I heard that he had made his way back east towards Transylvania, and had married. I believed –

or rather I wanted to believe – that no good would have come to him. I first heard the name Kalliovski shortly after I met you, but I had no inkling that it was the same man. The Count Kalliovski I learned about was a mysterious figure, who claimed to be on the verge of creating an automaton that could pass as a human. From all accounts, he was a man who would sell his soul to the devil to learn the secret of creating life.'

'My dear friend,' said Cordell, 'it seems to me that you have unwittingly turned over a stone and found there a deadly creature.'

'There is one other thing you should know,' said Têtu, and he pulled from his pocket the red necklace. 'This is what Yann found in Kalliovski's room.' He handed it to Cordell, a thin red ribbon with seven crimson garnets set into it like drops of blood.

'If this were to be worn round the neck,' said Cordell, examining it, 'it would look as if your throat had been cut.'

'Precisely,' said Têtu. 'The only people who have ever been found wearing such a thing, so I have been told, are dead. I am sure that Kalliovski is in some way involved. This being found in his chamber proves it.'

'Têtu, my dear friend, I can't bear to see you in such a state. What can I do to help?'

'I need to disappear. I can't take the boy with me, it would be impossible. I want him out of the way for a while at least. I want him to go to London, be given a chance to learn to read and write. Just a few months, that's all, then he can come back.'

'I am sure Henry Laxton, my colleague in London, wouldn't mind looking after the boy until things are back to normal. Coincidentally, Laxton has some knowledge of Kalliovski,' said Cordell, refilling Têtu's glass. 'Laxton has a French wife, whose sister was married to the Marquis de Villeduval. Some years ago, when Mrs Laxton's sister was killed in an accident, he went to Normandy, to the château of the Villeduvals. It was very odd. The Marquis appeared to have no interest in his wife's death, or in what would happen to their only daughter, Sido.'

'We met the Marquis's daughter,' said Têtu. 'She helped us escape.'

'What small circles we all travel in. It was Kalliovski who stopped Henry Laxton from bringing Sido back to London to be brought up by his wife. The Marquis didn't care one way or another about his daughter, yet for some peculiar reason Kalliovski did. Tell me one thing,' Cordell went on, going over to his desk. 'What part did the boy play with the Pierrot?'

'He was the voice, and he read people's minds.'

'Interesting,' said Cordell, handing Têtu an envelope. 'Now, here is enough money to pay for your expenses.'

'No, I don't need it.'

'My dear friend, take it. I know the proprietor at the Hôtel d'Angleterre, a Madame Saltaire. You'll be safe there. I take it that the boy has no passport?'

'No.'

'Then I will have to get that organised. It will take a

84

day. You must stay in your room until you hear from me. By the way, how old is the boy?'

'Fourteen. He is like a son to me. I love him as if he were my own flesh and blood.'

Charles Cordell smiled. 'I will let Henry Laxton know to expect him.'

The two men shook hands.

———————◆———————

Têtu sat in Charles Cordell's carriage, grateful for the lift back to Moet's Tavern, and thinking to himself about what he hadn't told his friend. A secret that Têtu hoped to take to his grave, for some words can do as much damage to the living as a shot fired from a pistol.

It was at about the same time as the carriage pulled up outside the tavern that Monsieur Aulard lit his lantern.

Chapter Ten

Yann had waited in Moet's Tavern until it had grown dark. He was beginning to think that Têtu was never coming back when, to his great relief, he saw the dwarf's small shape push and jostle its way to where he was sitting.

'Everything is arranged,' said Têtu. 'Come, we must get out of here.'

They walked swiftly away from the Palais Royal and down a tangle of narrow streets.

'Where are we going?' asked Yann.

'To a hotel. We'll stay there for the night, and then you'll get the coach to Calais and go to London,' said Têtu.

'London!' said Yann, stunned.

'Come on, keep up.' Têtu was now walking as fast as his legs would allow him. He looked anxiously around him. 'Don't dawdle. The sooner we're off these streets the better.'

The entrance to the Hôtel d'Angleterre was a wooden door that opened into a courtyard overlooked by two other apartment blocks. At the far end, under a stone arch, stood a narrow door that led out on to the rue de Richelieu, a two-minute walk from the Palais Royal.

Here Têtu, as Cordell had suggested, took a room for the night.

'Why are we going to London?' asked Yann, the minute they were alone.

'Not we; you. You are going to London.'

'No!' said Yann. 'I'm not going anywhere without you.'

'Paris is not safe. Kalliovski wants us both dead. I can disappear – I've done it all my life.'

Yann started to interrupt.

'Wait, wait. Before you say anything, listen. I have a great friend, an Englishman called Charles Cordell, who is a banker based in Paris. He has agreed to send you to London and put you in the care of his partner, Henry Laxton, who will teach you to read and write and speak English.'

'I'm not leaving you.'

Têtu's face looked as hard as ever Yann had seen it.

'Listen to me. You are not a baby. It will only be for a few months. You will do this and that is the end of it.'

Yann was too exhausted to argue any more, too angry to sleep. He lay face down on the bed, furious, only to find that when he woke up it was morning.

Whether or not Têtu had slept, Yann couldn't tell. The dwarf was pacing to and fro, mumbling to himself. On a table sat a bottle of wine and a loaf of bread.

Yann sat up and said, 'I still don't understand why I have to go away.'

'I'm going to explain. I'm going to tell you things you want to know. Will you listen, or are you going to block up your ears with anger, so that you won't hear anything but your own thunder?'

Yann shrugged.

'You've often asked me about your mother, and now I will tell you,' said Têtu. 'Your mother loved you dearly. She wanted no harm to come to you, and I promised her I would keep your gypsy origins quiet.'

'Gypsy!' said Yann. It was a word like an old tin mug that had followed them wherever they went ... a swearword, a figure of speech, an insult. It confirmed what he already knew, that he and Têtu were misfits, outcasts living on the edges of society. He had never imagined it to be the truth. He and Têtu spoke Romany for their own protection, Têtu had told him, because few people understood it or knew where it came from. Now he could see that these roots went far deeper than he had ever thought, and he wished with all his heart that it were not so.

'Yannick, we are an ancient and noble people,' said Têtu. 'Take from this what is good, and learn from it. I regret that you couldn't grow up in a gypsy world where you would have known our ways and secrets.'

'I've asked you so often if we were gypsies, and you've always shrugged your shoulders and said no,' said Yann.

'It was for your own safety. You know there is a price on every gypsy's head. The gallows and the huntsman's gun wait for us.'

The seriousness of what Têtu was saying took away all Yann's anger. Maybe this explained why they were not like other people. Maybe it at last explained why he could read minds and see into the future.

'I have done my best by you, Yannick,' said Têtu. 'I have given you a piece of your gypsy origins by teaching you our language. Your mother didn't even want me to do that, for fear that you would be taken away from me, that I would be branded like cattle and sent away to sea. It was for the best that I kept silent.'

Yann sat down on the edge of the bed. 'Go on.'

Here Têtu stopped, as if reconsidering all he had said so far.

'Your mother was called Anis, and she was beautiful. She had your eyes, dark as ebony and deep as a well. When I met her at the circus in St Petersburg I knew straight away that she was Romany, like me. She told me that each year her people followed the ancient routes, wintering in caves, and when the snows passed they travelled deep into the forests, keeping away from the house-dwellers.

'Anis's mother was the keeper of the arts of sorcery among her tribe. She had extraordinary powers. She could move objects without touching them. Her daughter could do it too.'

'And so can you.'

Têtu continued. 'All objects have threads of light coming from them. Living objects have the brightest threads of light, energy that flashes like lightning. Lifeless objects, such as cups, jugs, or beds, have dull threads of light. If you can see this light, then you can become a master, able to move things at your will. Think, Yann, what power that would give you.'

'Is that how you work the Pierrot? Is it? Tell me.'

Têtu said nothing.

'All right,' said Yann. 'If you won't answer that, tell me how my mother ended up in a circus.'

'Something terrible happened. It was Anis's wedding day. She was fourteen and the boy was sixteen. She believed that they were one soul divided into two bodies, and that only when they were together were they whole.

'The ceremony started at daybreak round the campfire, when the marriage was sealed with a cut made on the bride's right wrist and the groom's left wrist; then their hands were bound together and they took an oath to free one another when love had left their hearts.

'There was singing and dancing to celebrate – and then the huntsmen came to kill the gypsies. Anis's mother saw them sitting on their fine horses watching, waiting. She ordered her people to carry on dancing, shouting out "Life is life!" in Romany. The gypsies went on playing their fiddles and singing their songs. They didn't run. Until the shooting started.'

'But my mother must have managed to get away,' said Yann.

'Anis said she never knew how. It was as if her mother had made her invisible. But she remembered the last thing her bridegroom said to her: "In death they will never catch us, my beloved one. We are birds, we are free."

'She remembered nothing more. When she woke up she found herself in the hollow of a tree. It was getting dark. She stood in the middle of that clearing and saw them all hanging in the trees like songbirds, colourful but lifeless: her bridegroom, her mother, every one of her tribe. Even the babies had been slaughtered. Blood dripped from the oak leaves. That day, her wedding day, she lost everything.

'She ran far away and joined a circus, never speaking of her gypsy roots, though her dark hair and eyes told the truth of it. She never spoke of it, that is, until I met her.'

Yann was very quiet. Of all the things he had imagined about his mother, he had never once imagined this.

It was Têtu who broke the silence.

'It is nothing to be ashamed of. Far from it – it is a source of pride.'

'Are you a French gypsy?'

'No, I come from Romania. It is another story for another time. I have told you how I met your mother. That is enough.'

'So am I half gypsy?'

'No.'

'You know that for certain?'

'Yes.'

'My father was the gypsy boy my mother married?'

'No, Yannick, he was killed some seven years before you were born. Who your real father was, I do not know, but Anis believed you were a gift from the spirit of her one true love. We gypsies know and understand things that those attached to houses and land will never comprehend. We have outlived and outwitted great civilisations.'

'Do you think I have inherited those gifts?'

'You are a natural. You have an exceptional talent already.'

'Will you teach me to work the Pierrot like you do?'

Têtu laughed. 'In time, Yann, in time.'

There was a knock at the door. On Cordell's instructions, Madame Saltaire had brought a package up to Têtu. It contained Yann's travel documents and a passport.

'You leave tonight,' said Têtu after she had gone. 'I'll take you to the coach at seven. A man called Tull, an Englishman, will escort you to Calais, where there will be a boat waiting to take you to Dover. We must hurry, so as not to miss the tide.'

Yann wanted to say again that he didn't want to go. This time, though, he knew it was useless. Instead he made up his mind that in this new country he would let no one know of his gypsy origins. There he would have a fresh start. For once in his life he would be like everyone else.

As they left, Têtu had pulled Yann's coat about him and buttoned it up as if he were a child. Yann had then an image of his mother, and a terrible sense of loss rushed in upon him.

'I can do that,' he had said.

Still Têtu insisted, standing on tiptoe to put the muffler round Yann's neck and tucking it carefully into his coat.

The hall of the hotel was empty. The lantern outside was shining on the snow, making it look blue. A cat came meowing across the courtyard, lifting its paws in disgust at the depth of the snow and curling itself round their legs before going into the warmth.

Têtu seized Yann's hand. 'Now. We'll make a run for it.'

Far too late did Yann sense the menace in the general silence. The windows of the building overlooking the courtyard were shuttered as if they had closed their eyes against what was about to happen.

'Here goes,' said Têtu.

A shot rang out, and suddenly Yann realised he was dragging a dead weight behind him. He stopped and stared down at Têtu, who was lying crumpled in the snow.

'Get up! Get up!'

The dwarf's eyes were closed. His skin had already started looking translucent.

'No!' shouted Yann. 'No!' He tried with all his strength to lift Têtu.

At that moment he saw the red necklace lying there in the blood.

'It's no good,' whispered the dwarf. 'Go, run like the wind. Life is life, Yannick.'

Yann felt a cold leather-gloved hand come down hard on his shoulder.

'Got you!' said a voice as the shadow of Milkeye fell over him. 'There's no escaping.'

Yann could feel the burning heat of the pistol butt as it was pushed into the side of his head. Suddenly everything both slowed down and speeded up. Yann shut his eyes. In that second, when life and death hung in the balance, the trigger clicked, the barrel jammed. Yann opened his eyes to see Milkeye staring ferociously at his weapon.

Madame Saltaire ran out of the hotel screaming, hands flying. Yann twisted himself free, conscious of nothing but escape. He was already at the street door when the second bullet ricocheted off the stone wall. He ran as fast as he could, soon to be lost from view in the maze of streets.

The sharp air rasped his throat painfully but still he ran, and soon the sound of the city enveloped him, calming him. Near exhausted, he stopped, and checking that no one was following him backtracked towards the Palais Royal. He could hear the clocks chiming the hour. Seven o'clock.

A coach was waiting, its driver huddled against the icy

wind in a great cape, his groom beside him.

The coach door opened and a man with an English accent asked, 'Are you Yann Margoza? Where's the gentleman who was supposed to bring you here?'

'Dead.'

'Too bad. Get in,' said the man. 'There's no time to lose if we're to catch the tide.'

Stunned and grief-stricken, Yann climbed in. The man, the coach, all became a blur. He looked out of the window as the terrifying reality overwhelmed him. Topolain had performed the ultimate trick. He had taken with him Yann's world, the theatre, the actors, the scenery – all vanished, all gone, in a wisp of smoke from a pistol.

The coach rattled and shook. He could hear the horses snorting, their bridles jangling; and he could hear too the unmistakable voice of Têtu as he whispered to him, 'Life is life.'

Chapter Eleven

H ere, in London's fashionable Bloomsbury, is a newly built town house that
faces a tree-lined square, with streets leading
to Piccadilly and Whitehall. To the back its
windows look out to the rolling hills of Hampstead and beyond. The house, which is decorated in the French style, is charming,
comfortable, welcoming. It is the home of
Henry and Juliette Laxton.

Henry Laxton could not be described as handsome.
He had, though, an engaging face with undistinguished
features made attractive by the fact that he was a rich
banker, who had the good fortune to be married to a
beautiful woman.

This morning he was to be found in his study. A letter
from Charles Cordell had just been delivered. It should

have reached him two days ago, but the messenger had been held up by bad weather and a lame horse. He now read with increasing alarm that a boy called Yann Margoza was due at the Boar Inn, Fleet Street at three o'clock that very afternoon, giving him no time to prepare for his arrival.

Henry Laxton stood by the fire lost in thought. Taking on such a boy would, he knew, be a challenge, especially as he and his wife had no children of their own.

He rang the bell and his valet entered the room. 'Is my wife still in her boudoir?'

'I believe so, sir.'

'And does she have any visitors with her?'

'One, sir, Lady Faulkner.'

Henry Laxton smiled inwardly. He knew how bored his wife would be. Lady Faulkner's sole aim in visiting her friends was to pick up the latest tittle-tattle and add it to her cauldron of malicious small talk. He went up the stairs to his wife's boudoir.

Juliette Laxton was the younger sister of Isabelle Gautier, who had married the Marquis de Villeduval. Their father, a widower, was a wealthy bourgeois businessman, and the marriage was seen as beneficial to both sides. The Villeduvals would have an injection of much-needed money and land, and Monsieur Gautier would see at least one of his daughters settled with a title, and could claim an aristocrat as a son-in-law.

Only Juliette had had any idea of the depths of

Isabelle's misery, married to a much older man who cared only for himself.

Then, shortly after the death of Monsieur Gautier, Isabelle was killed in an accident when a coach was overturned. The only survivor was three-year-old Sido, whose leg had been badly broken.

After his wife's death the Marquis did something so strange, so out of character, that the only rational explanation was surely insanity brought on by grief. For it had turned out a double tragedy: his half-brother Armand, his father's favourite, had gone missing at the same time. All attempts to find him had failed.

Isabelle was not buried in the family vault in Normandy. Instead, her coffin was taken to a small church by the sea. There were no mourners and little ceremony. She was placed in a simple grave and the headstone merely recorded her name, Isabelle Gautier, without title, inscription or date.

The Marquis was never to speak of his wife again, and his half-brother's disappearance proved to be the death of his father.

Juliette had never got over the loss of her beloved sister. Her only consolation had been the hope that she might be allowed to bring up Isabelle's daughter Sido, but it was not to be. For reasons Juliette had never understood, Sido's father, the Marquis, had written to say that he wanted nothing more to do with the Gautier family.

For Juliette it had been a double bereavement. Not only had she lost her sister and her closest friend, but shortly after this she had had a miscarriage and been told that there was little hope of her conceiving again. It had been her greatest sadness, for she had always imagined herself surrounded by a large and noisy family.

She sat now in front of her dressing table mirror, wishing her visitor would leave. Not for the first time, Lady Faulkner was giving Juliette the benefit of her advice.

'My formula for looking perpetually young is to avoid laughter and excessive use of the facial muscles. That, I can assure you, leads to wrinkles and the falling of the flesh. Best by far to keep one's face emotionless. Only by such a means can one hold back time's cruel hand—'

She was interrupted by a knock at the door. Juliette's face lit up with a charming smile when she saw her husband enter the room, while Lady Faulkner's remained mask-like and rigid.

'I trust your family is well?' said Henry Laxton with a bow.

'Quite well,' replied Lady Faulkner stiffly.

'And does your son still spend all his time at the theatre, sporting with pretty actresses?' The question was designed to speed the guest's departure.

Lady Faulkner's features knew not quite how to react to this. Her lips longed to purse themselves together in disgust at such a suggestion, but lines, as she had just informed Mrs Laxton, must be avoided at all costs.

'I have no idea what you mean, Mr Laxton,' she said,

standing up and waving her fan vigorously. 'Jack is at Oxford, where he is studying diligently. Now, I must leave you. I have other calls to make where I will, I know, be very welcome.' And with great indignation she swept out of the room.

The Laxtons waited until they heard the front door being closed, then both burst out laughing.

'She seems more absurd every time I see her,' said Henry Laxton, pouring himself a cup of tea. 'Jack hasn't been near Oxford all term, from what I can gather. The woman is a fool.'

Juliette sighed. '*Mon chéri*, please remind me to laugh and smile and to use every muscle my face might possess, lest I end up looking as sour and miserable as that woman.'

'That would be an impossibility. Now, on a more serious note, I have had a letter this morning from Charles Cordell, and I have news that will hearten you. It relates to Sido de Villeduval.'

'To Sido? What is it?' asked Juliette urgently.

'Apparently Sido was brought home from her convent for a party that her father was giving in honour of Count Kalliovski.'

'That odious man!'

'Quite. That odious man had a whim to see her, and has persuaded the Marquis not to send her back to the convent.'

'How do you know all this? It's incredible!'

Henry Laxton grinned. 'I have my spies.'

'No, don't joke. Tell me. I know! You heard it from a client of the bank.'

'Not quite, but tonight you will be able to ask after Sido yourself. You will meet someone who spoke to her only a few days ago.'

'You're talking in riddles! Who is it?'

Henry Laxton walked towards the window and then turned back.

'Cordell has asked if we would be willing to take in a boy for a few months. He is fourteen years old, an orphan, brought up by a contact of Cordell's in Paris, a man called Têtu.'

'But what has this boy to do with Sido?'

'Aha!' said Laxton. 'I am coming to that. Têtu and the boy are travelling entertainers—'

'Travelling entertainers! What strange company Mr Cordell keeps,' Juliette exclaimed.

'—and a couple of days ago they were invited, with a magician called Topolain, to perform at a party the Marquis was giving.'

'The same party that Sido was at?'

'Precisely. And at this private performance the magician Topolain performed the bullet trick for which he was famous in Paris. It was Kalliovski who fired the pistol, and he shot the magician dead.'

'But why?'

'Why indeed? He claims it was an accident, a trick gone wrong, though neither Cordell nor Têtu believes that. Têtu is certain that it was because both he and Topolain knew something about his past. Whatever the reason, Têtu is now terrified that Kalliovski will come after him and the boy. He went to Cordell for help. Cordell has asked that we look after the boy for a few months.'

'And this boy met Sido?'

'Yes. Evidently she helped them escape.'

'And what is the boy called?'

'Yann Margoza. He hasn't had many advantages in life. Maybe we can help him, give him some education. If we are true to the principles of enlightenment, then a pauper is fit to be a king, and there is no reason why this boy cannot live on equal terms with us and learn to be a gentleman.'

Juliette's face lit up with excitement. 'There's no question of it. This boy met Sido! He will live with us as a part of the family, not in the servants' quarters.'

Henry Laxton came over and kissed the nape of his wife's very white neck.

The carriage bringing Yann to this rough dark diamond of a city made its way over Blackfriars Bridge. Mr Tull, whose job it had been to transport the boy here, had one last stop to make, at the inn on Fleet Street where he had been instructed to wait for Mr Laxton's carriage.

The courtyard of the Boar Inn was full of stagecoaches and horses, ladies and gentlemen, assorted parcels and trunks, all taken up with the hectic business of arriving or leaving. Mr Tull decided upon a well-earned breakfast. He stopped at the door of the inn and looked woefully at the boy. It struck Mr Tull as nothing short of an insult to have to take a foreign ragamuffin into this decent God-fearing place. He sighed. Orders were orders. He was to hand the boy over to Mr Laxton. Until that was done, he would have to keep him close by, for the boy had the look of one who might scarper. He took Yann by the scruff of the neck and steered him, as one would a dog, into a seat by the window.

Yann shook himself free of Mr Tull's clutches and sat huddled up in the corner. The journey had been a blur of misery and grief. He didn't like his jailer, for that was how he had come to think of Mr Tull, a bulldog of a man who had made it quite clear that the feeling was mutual. He had said as much in very bad French. '*Stupide garçon*. All this trouble! For what? For you?'

After that they had travelled in silence. It suited them both, for Yann needed time to think about what had happened. Never had he felt more alone and wretched than he did now. He regretted that he had ever agreed to come to this country, brought here by a man he didn't like and didn't trust, to stay with a man he had never met.

The inn with its low wooden beams was panelled and stained near black by tobacco. Smoke filled the air as well as the sharp smell of burnt fat and stale ale. It was full of hungry people, travellers' appetites demanding constant satisfaction.

'Bring me a tankard of the finest ale, a steak and a dozen oysters,' said Mr Tull to the innkeeper.

The innkeeper looked at Yann as he might look at a dirty plate. 'The same for him?'

Mr Tull reluctantly nodded his head. 'Only a small beer for him, mind you.'

When the innkeeper had gone Mr Tull said angrily, 'I don't know why a gentleman like Mr Laxton would be wanting to give a scallywag like you a roof over your head. If you were to turn up on my doorstep, I'd have you taken down to the workhouse without a second thought. I wouldn't want one of your kind near me or my kin.'

Yann might not have understood the language, but he got the gist of what Mr Tull was saying all too clearly.

Mr Tull fidgeted impatiently as he waited for his ale, tapping his short stubby fingers on the table.

They ate in silence. Mr Tull mopped his plate clean with the last of his bread, finished his ale, and burped loudly.

'I would say "Excuse me, Your Honour," if I were in *good* company,' he said, emphasising the word good, 'which I ain't, so I won't be saying nothing.'

He stood up and shook himself.

'Now you stay put while I see if the carriage has arrived.' He leaned across the table, grasping the lapels of Yann's coat. 'If you so much as move one of them there miserable muscles of yours, you'll be in for it and no mistake. Do you get my drift?'

Yann watched as Mr Tull wove his way across the courtyard and in that instant he decided to take his chance. His one aim was to get back to Paris to find where Têtu had been buried, and kill Kalliovski. The idea of doing away with the Count was all that had kept him together on the long journey here.

In his haste to leave, he ran into the innkeeper.

'Hey, where do you think you're going, you blasted scallywag?' the man shouted as the tray he was carrying went flying. There was a loud crash as pewter tumblers and plates of food fell to the floor. For a moment the whole room fell silent, and heads turned to see a boy running for the door as if his life depended on it.

Yann didn't stop to look back at the mess he had caused. Quickly, he swerved past a coach driver who made a desperate attempt to catch him. He ducked and dived round horses and carriages. Turning back he ran straight into a well-dressed man who firmly but kindly put his hand on his shoulder.

'Yann Margoza, I take it?' said Henry Laxton in flawless French.

Mr Tull came panting and puffing after him, shaking his fist.

'Where's that ruddy boy? That little heathen, I'll wring his scrawny neck, I will. He's been nothing but trouble since I first clapped eyes on him.'

'You will do no such thing,' said Mr Laxton, still holding firmly on to Yann. Pushing him into his carriage and climbing in after him, he nodded to his coachman, who handed Mr Tull an envelope with his money in it.

Mr Tull started counting.

'It is the agreed sum,' said Mr Laxton.

By now the carriage was making its way out through

the arch, disappearing into the main thoroughfare.

'Wait a minute! Not so ruddy fast!' shouted Mr Tull to the disappearing wheels. 'I need money for the breakages.'

Mr Tull was not in a good mood as he walked towards the Fleet River and the Red Lion Inn, a tavern renowned for the company of rogues.

If you couldn't make an honest penny by hard work, then perhaps it would be more worthwhile to make a dishonest pound instead. 'Where is the justice?' said Mr Tull to himself. 'The rich get everything and do nothing for it, and all the while they expect the likes of me to risk life and limb for them. And they don't even pay for breakages.'

He had heard the talk of clever people in Paris and in the London coffee-houses, people who knew what the tomorrows of life had in store. Civil war, that was what they were predicting. As far as he was concerned it couldn't come soon enough. There was money to be made in upheavals.

Chapter Twelve

The savagery of grief tore at Yann, filled him with rage, stripped him of his gift for reading people's minds. All that was left was the silence of heartache. His past and his future had vanished, had been gobbled up and spat out again as if the very marrow had been sucked from his soul with the murder of Têtu.

Lost in the fury of his thoughts, he hadn't heard one word Mr Laxton had been saying, until finally, standing in the hall of the house in Queen Square, he realised that by some twist of fate he had entered another world, and he didn't want to be here.

Henry Laxton's valet, Vane, had been with his master for many years and spoke tolerable French. He took Yann upstairs and showed him a large bedchamber, dominated by a four-poster bed and smelling of oranges. They reminded Yann of hot summers and journeys with Têtu. Behind a screen at the far end was another door that led to a small antechamber and there by the fire sat a bath filled with steaming hot water. What it was doing in the room Yann wasn't sure until Vane started solemnly rolling up his sleeves and said that sir was to take a bath.

Yann stared at him in disbelief and then, seeing that this was no idle threat, made for the door, but to no avail. Vane was dog-like in his determination, with a wiry strength that took Yann by surprise. Finally, defeated by exhaustion and the lack of sleep, he resigned himself to drowning.

He was washed and scrubbed until the water was as filthy as the Seine and his skin tingled all over. Wrapped in a large housecoat, he sat in front of the fire while a barber set about cutting off his long black locks and vigorously rubbing a lotion into his scalp, for the express reason, so he said, of ridding Yann of fleas.

From an assortment of shirts and breeches, Vane then set about dressing Yann as if he were a tailor's dummy. Finally, he tied a cravat round his neck and set a looking-glass before him. What Yann saw there was a stranger. If it hadn't been for the anger in his face he would have said he was staring at someone else.

Vane inspected his handiwork and took Yann down to the sitting room on the first floor to present him to Mr and Mrs Laxton.

'Well, look at you, sir,' said Mr Laxton in his perfect French. 'To the manner born, I would say.'

Yann, not knowing what was expected of him, bowed stiffly. All this felt as if it were happening to someone else, that he was simply an actor upon the stage.

'You have met my niece, Sido de Villeduval, I gather,' said Mrs Laxton.

Yann looked at her. Was he dreaming, or did she look like Sido?

'Yes.'

'And was she well?'

Was she well? He had to think what he was being asked. Was this the reason he had been brought here, to answer this one question – was Sido well?

Finally he said, 'She is unhappy.'

After an awkward supper that seemed to go on and on, with many courses and unanswered questions, Mr Laxton took him into his study. On hearing of Têtu's death, he told Yann that this was to be his new home. What he meant by this, Yann had no idea. The only family he had ever known was Têtu. Home couldn't be counted in candlesticks and cutlery, of that much he was sure. Home for him had been simple. Home was Têtu.

That night he lay awake, finding the soft mattress worrying, the smell of oranges unsettling. Finally he got out of bed and fell asleep in front of the fire, like a cat.

The days that followed were encompassed by ticking clocks and dull, meaningless routine. Time dragged its weary feet for Yann in this grand house. The long, empty momentum of the minutes and the passing hours was something he had never been aware of before.

A tutor had been employed for Yann, a Mr Rose. He

was as thin as a sheet of paper left flattened and forgotten in a book, and had about him the smell of dried-up ink. Knowledge had been beaten into him and he saw no reason why it shouldn't be beaten into every other child. His philosophy of education was not one he had shared with Mr Laxton.

On the first day of his employment, what appeared before Mr Rose was a well-dressed, intelligent-looking young gentleman.

'Appearances can be deceptive,' Mr Rose was to grumble three weeks later. 'The boy is nothing more than a savage. No tailored garment is going to alter that fact.'

This cutting remark had been his first complaint, followed by, 'The boy has no aptitude for learning.'

Mr Laxton had spoken firmly to Yann, who stood in his study and said nothing.

Another two weeks passed, by which time Yann felt as if his very life was beginning to be drummed out of him by this wizened leaf of a tutor. He would gaze out of the window, longing to be down in the street where life went on, until he could take it no longer.

One day Mr Rose, in a fit of temper, threw a book at Yann, hitting him on the head. Yann got up and calmly took the cane from his terrified tutor, breaking it across his leg before delivering a knock-out blow. Mr Rose almost flew across the room. He lay stretched out cold on the wooden floor, his nose bleeding profusely.

Yann went down the stairs to Mr Laxton's study and told him exactly what he had done and why.

There was a general commotion, a doctor was called for, and Mr Rose, regaining consciousness, demanded that the boy be brought before a magistrate and sent to the clink for the savage he was. Then, seeing that Mr Laxton was going to do nothing of the sort, he left, appalled, holding his handkerchief to his very sore nose.

Immediately he went hurrying round to Lady Faulkner, whose son Jack had benefited greatly from his tutoring. For her part she had swiftly and delightedly passed on the news that the Laxtons, for want of a child, had taken in an alleycat. The scandal kept many a lady happy over her morning coffee and many a gentleman at his club wondering what the respectable banker was thinking of.

The Laxtons took no notice whatsoever of the gossip, and employed another tutor who had no more control over Yann than the dreadful Mr Rose. He lasted only a month before storming out of the house, announcing that the boy was unteachable.

Finally free of his tutors, Yann took to leaving the house without permission and going off by himself to explore London. The vulgar tongue of the streets began to intrigue him: it was a stewpot of words and sounds that he was hungry to taste. It took him no time to speak these earthy words with a near-perfect cockney accent.

All attempts at keeping him at home failed. Locked doors and high windows were no barrier to him. He would frequently climb down the side of the house at night without being noticed by the night-watchman. He had always found the darkness friendly: it was like a huge overcoat, one he was well used to wearing. He could see almost as clearly in the dark as in the day, and had never understood people's fear of it.

For all the trouble Yann caused the Laxtons, they could not help liking the boy. There was nothing timid in his nature. He was fearless, stood up and fought, despised injustice and cared little about the injuries he received. Mr Rose was an ass of a man for not seeing how clever the boy was. Anyone who had a tongue that could master English this quickly was no fool. Têtu had been right when he told Cordell the boy had talent. The problem lay in how to make him see the opportunities he was merrily throwing away.

Mrs Laxton understood better than her husband what Yann felt. She too had been sent near mad by grief, and it was the memory of what she had gone through that made her brave.

Late one foggy March night she waited in Yann's room for him to come back from one of his escapades. He looked sheepish as he climbed through the window to see her sitting there in the dark. He was certain he was going to be punished. Instead she lit a candle and invited him to sit down.

'What is it you want?' she asked.

'To go back to Paris.'

'Why?'

'I want to find out what happened to Têtu.'

'You know what happened, he was shot. It was a terrible tragedy for you. Why do you think he sent you here?'

Yann shrugged his shoulders.

'No, that won't do,' she said sharply. 'You are a clever boy. Now, tell me again.'

'To learn to speak English, and I can now.'

'You have the accent of the street and the manners of a ruffian. Your friend Têtu went to Mr Cordell and told him you were talented, that you deserved to be given an opportunity, that there was a lot more to you than meets the eye. What I have seen is a stubborn, unhappy gypsy who is too wrapped up in himself to see what his friend sacrificed for him.'

'I am a gypsy,' said Yann through gritted teeth, realising that he was about to break down. 'I don't belong here, not in your world. Not in all this softness. Not imprisoned by walls . . .'

'When I was nine my mother died,' Mrs Laxton interrupted. 'She was very pious, and I believed that the only reason she had left me was because I had been naughty. I was lucky; I had a loving older sister who helped me to understand that she hadn't left me behind for anything I had done.' She leant forward and touched Yann's hand. 'It's not your fault Têtu died. You couldn't have caught the bullet; you are not a magician.'

Yann felt burning hot tears sting the corners of his eyes.

'I should have stayed with him – I shouldn't have run.'

He was suddenly aware that Mr Laxton was standing in the doorway, listening.

'Stayed to be killed,' Mr Laxton said. 'That would have been a waste.'

'We are here to help you,' said his wife softly, 'but you refuse to let even a chink of light into that dark space in your head.'

'I don't want anything from you. I don't want your help. I never wanted to come here!' Yann was shouting now, so angry at the tears that wouldn't stop rolling down his face, joining together under his chin. 'Save your money and save your pity. I want none of it!'

Blast the goddamn tears, why didn't they stop?

'The door is open. If you want to go back to Paris, go,' said Henry Laxton. 'I am not your jailer. You are not a slave, you are a free man.'

Yann bolted down the stairs two at a time. He pushed past the startled doorman and out into the foggy night air.

Henry Laxton leaned over the banisters and watched him go.

'Well, that's that. What a fine mess we've made.'

His wife put her arms around him. '*Mon chéri*,' she said, 'don't despair. I promise you, this is not the end. It is just the beginning.'

Chapter Thirteen

Yann only stopped running when he reached Seven Dials. The sound of his feet on the pavement was the drumbeat that finally calmed him down. Gasping for breath he leant against the corner of a building, grateful for the thick fog, and laughed out loud at his own stupidity. 'Well,' he thought bitterly, 'I can't go back there again.'

He felt certain that the Laxtons would be mighty pleased to be rid of him. Mrs Laxton had called him a gypsy! He *was* a gypsy. What did any of it matter now? He pulled the collar of his coat up, the biting cold tickling its way through the seams. He could hear around him the distorted voices of people sounding as if they were under water, their words swimming before them, their owners following, appearing out of the fog like phantoms before disappearing again.

Sido didn't answer.

'As I thought,' said the Marquis. 'A ghost. Away with you.'

———◆———

The news of what had happened that night at Versailles spread to Paris and beyond like a forest fire on a hot summer's day, but it was not until three days later that the full impact of that disastrous banquet was felt.

It started in the afternoon when Michel Floret, one of the few gardeners who had not left the Marquis's employment, had come into the kitchen to take shelter from the rain. He was warming himself by the stove, for these days the kitchen had become a meeting place for all the remaining staff.

Bernard, the coachman, was sitting there too.

'I've been thinking,' he said gloomily.

'Well, don't,' said Jean Rollet, the chef, who with one look could reduce a cabbage to compost. 'Thinking isn't going to get you anywhere.'

'Go on, Bernard, take no notice,' said Michel. 'You have the right to think. Cooks aren't kings yet.'

'That's it. That's what I think. If the King had agreed to the declaration of human rights, we'd all love him, wouldn't we?'

Jean sniffed. 'You might. I have a more discerning palate myself. You can't change an old cockerel into a spring chicken. Anyway, he doesn't believe in human rights. He's made that clear enough.'

As the cold found its way into his bones it dawned on him exactly how alone he was. Like a small pebble on a stony beach.

He shook his head. He had been a complete fool. What did he have? Nothing, just the clothes he stood up in, not a penny to his name. He looked down at his coat. In the morning he would pawn it. That should give him some money, at least enough for a day or so. For the time being he would just have to keep on walking.

He made his way towards Covent Garden where the audiences were spilling out of the theatres. All those people, eager to be home! Sedan chairs vying for business, boasting how fast they went. Carriages lined up, horses snorting.

Maybe he should try and find work in the theatre, though he wondered quite what he had to offer. The ability to throw his voice was surely not enough, not now that he couldn't read minds. That gift had abandoned him. It belonged to another time.

The bells of St Martin's were chiming eleven o'clock as he walked away from the Piazza. It was going to be a long, cold night.

On the last stroke he heard someone call out for help. It was a sharp, urgent cry that was strangled the minute it had found a voice.

Yann stopped and listened. It was the cry of a desperate man. The fog made it hard to work out where he was. He heard nothing more.

Then he caught the growl of voices coming from down an alleyway that smelled worse than the River

Seine on a hot day. Through the fog a little way ahead of him he could make out two men who seemed to have a third man held hostage against the wall.

Yann moved quickly out of sight. The men didn't notice him.

From what he could see the one nearest him looked like a fish-eyed monster, his hand as wide as a shovel covering the third man's mouth, while the second, a rat-like creature, egged him on.

'What have we got here, Sam?' said the fish-eyed monster.

'A gentleman in a fine coat!' leered Sam. 'With shiny buckles on his shoes! Hey, Joe, I reckon we've caught ourselves a plum pudding of a gent!'

'Go on, take it off,' said Joe, taking his hand away from the gentleman's mouth and pulling at the coat.

'Please, my dear commodious sirs,' cried the gentleman, 'I am but a poor thespian and this is my humble costume. I wear it to trip the light fantastic and earn my meagre bread and cheese. The buckles are nothing more than paste, for I am but a poor Malvolio whose yellow stockings are thus gartered.'

'You what?' said Sam.

'Let's take him to Doctor Death,' said Joe. 'He'll shut him up. He pays handsome for a good healthy body, he does.'

All this was too much for the actor, who let out a muffled moan. 'My stars above, no I beg thee, let not my night's candle be so rudely snuffed out. I implore you, gallant gentlemen, to spare me!'

Sam was now rifling through his pockets. 'Nothing,' he said despairingly. 'He ain't got nothing, not even a penny.'

'*Must* be a bleeding actor, then.'

'My dear sir, my name is Mr Trippen of Drury Lane. You aren't going to kill the famous Touchstone the Clown, are you? Think what the papers will say.'

Joe burst out laughing. 'Nothing,' he said. He put his hand to his face and pulled out his glass eye. 'Like to hold it, would you?'

He was about to put the glass eye back when he heard a young girl's voice calling him by his name. He spun round to see where she could be.

'Did you hear that?' said Joe. 'She was calling me.'

Then the sweet voice called again. They had no idea what she was saying, except that this time it was Sam who recognised his name.

'How about that? She's calling me too. She sounds French, she does.'

Yann called out, '*Mon ami*. If you understand what I am saying just answer *oui*.'

'Yes,' mumbled the actor.

'*N'ayez pas peur*. Don't be afraid. Just tell them I am keen to meet them. When the moment's right, try and get free. I will say *Allez!* When you hear that, move.'

'What's she saying?' said Sam in a state of great excitement.

'I can tell you, good sirs, if you would do me the honour of removing the knife from my neck.'

Joe put down his weapon. 'Tell us then, in as few words as possible.'

'My French is a little rusty, but surprising as it seems she sounds mighty keen to meet you gentlemen,' said the actor.

'Hey, hey!' said Sam. 'What else is she saying?'

'She says she's lonely and would like some kind gentleman to keep her company and buy her a drink.'

'We're in luck,' said Joe.

'I tell you she's mine. I heard her first,' said Sam.

His friend spat on his glass eye and polished it on his sleeve. 'Give me a chance to get my looks back in, and then, when she sees us, she can take her pick.'

The girl spoke again. 'Are you ready?'

At that moment, apparently out of nowhere, Yann appeared. The two rogues were so startled that Yann was able to snatch Joe's looks from him before disappearing into the fog again.

'Hey, give that back unless you want me to wring your wretched little neck,' cried Joe.

The sweet-voiced girl suddenly spoke again. 'When I throw the glass eye, you are to make a run for it.'

'What's she saying now?' asked Sam.

'She's asking what keeps you so long,' said the actor, hardly believing that the gods could have been so kind as to send this angel.

At that moment Yann shouted '*Allez!*' and threw the glass eye up into the air. Both men together made to catch it, as Mr Trippen, free of their clutches, ran for his life, swiftly followed by Yann. Once back in the main

Piazza they both stopped, the actor holding a pillar and gasping for breath.

'My dear young sir, I cannot thank you enough for your bravery in the face of such terrifying and, may I add, murderous villains. May I ask the name of my saviour?'

'Yann Margoza.'

'I have to report,' Mr Trippen carried on, standing up, 'I have to report that I felt my dying moment upon life's tentative stage had come. Its drama in its myriad forms rushed before my misty eyes, my courage slipping from me like a shadow when I thought of my darling Mrs Trippen and the young Trippens all left fatherless.'

'Do you always use so many words?' asked Yann, smiling.

'They are like bonbons for the tongue, my young friend.' He took out his hanky and mopped his brow. 'Lucky, weren't we, about the young girl being there. I can't imagine what she saw in those two rogues. But I can assure you that the fairer sex is one of life's mysteries, a folly of Mother Nature's creation, for never has there been anything more delightfully irrational and tantalising upon the face of the earth than woman. If it were not for Delilah, Samson and the temples would still have stood; if it were not for Cleopatra, Caesar . . .'

''*Allo!*' came a voice. 'Why did you run away so quickly?'

Mr Trippen spun round, his face pale. 'Alas, my young man, she has followed us. Those two ruffians will be here in a moment. I tell thee, young sir, we are undone!'

'Didn't you realise?' said Yann. He began to laugh. 'That was me pretending to be a woman.'

'No! That is incredible,' said Mr Trippen. 'Why, my dear sir, I had no idea I was talking to a fellow thespian.' He looked earnestly at Yann. 'I see now a touch of the Hamlet about you. A noble yet tragic face. Where did you learn to speak such excellent French?'

'In France,' said Yann.

'You are French?' said Mr Trippen, surprised.

Yann nodded.

'And English is not, I take it, your native language?'

'No. I have just started to exercise my tongue with it,' said Yann with a chuckle.

'A natural, a born natural.'

'Thank you, sir,' said Yann. 'I wish you a safe journey home. Goodnight.'

'Wait, wait my dear young friend, not so fast. Mrs Trippen would never pardon me if I didn't bring my saviour home for supper.'

'At this hour?' asked Yann.

'Why, this is the hour, sir, when the Trippens gather after the curtain has fallen on the day, to mull over an actor's life, to reminisce of days gone by, helped in no small part by a good port wine. My wife, having danced the Fairy Queen tonight at Sadlers Wells, will, I believe, have a chicken simmering in its juices on the fire, the bottle, ruby red, breathing in the air.'

Up to that moment Yann had forgotten quite how hungry he was. The thought of the chicken simmering away was enough to make him say yes.

They walked towards the Strand together.

Mr Trippen looked as pleased as punch with himself and did not stop singing:

> 'Hey ho the wind and the rain,
> For the rain it raineth every day'

all the way home.

———◆———

The Trippens lived in a ramshackle house in Maiden Lane, a cul-de-sac that ran parallel to the Strand. Mrs Trippen was a little sparrow of a woman, and the four Trippen children ranged in age from nine downwards. The youngest was screaming at the top of his lungs in a crib made out of a box on which the words 'Seville Oranges' were written. Clothes hung halfway across the room, but apart from the orange box and a few baskets, it appeared empty of all furniture. Mrs Trippen, standing over the range stirring a pot, looked as if she had been crying, while the three older Trippens were standing in the doorway in descending height with tragic looks printed across their small faces.

'Why, love of my life, the apple of my eye, the rosebud of my bosom. Where are the table and chairs? Where is the cupboard?'

Yann didn't wait to be introduced. He went over to where the baby lay red and near hoarse with screaming and picked the little thing up, rocking it back and forth until peace was restored.

'The bailiffs,' said Mrs Trippen, when at last she could be heard above the din, 'have taken the beds and all the furnishings of our humble lives.'

'Not the chicken! Pray tell me they did not take the chicken, or for that matter the ruby wine.'

'No,' wept Mrs Trippen, 'but the shadow of the debtors' prison once more looms over our heads.'

'We are not to despair,' said Mr Trippen firmly. 'Tonight could have ended in tragedy. Mrs Trippen, you could have been widowed and our children left fatherless if it hadn't been for that young Hamlet there holding the baby.'

At this momentous news Mrs Trippen threw herself into her husband's arms and swooned, reviving when smelling salts were administered. The children, obviously well-used to walking furniture and late-night meals, fetched more boxes while their father went outside and brought in a spare door, laying it across the crates to make a table. A sheet was thrown over that, and with the children and adults perching at various heights on a mixture of crates and baskets, the family sat down to eat. At one o'clock the meal was finished and the three Trippen children had fallen fast asleep in the next room while the baby slept contented in its orange box.

Yann lay on the floor by the burning embers of the fire, stretched out on his back, his head on his hands, and thought how strange that one event can change a life. One stupid mistake and another path is closed.

The bells rang out on the hour, every hour, in the quietness of the night. In that topsy-turvy house he came to regret bitterly the opportunities that had been given him and not taken.

The next morning Henry Laxton was to be found in his study in Queen Square, looking tired and anxious. He had been out half the night searching for Yann and now, washed and shaved, he was staring out of the window and drinking his black coffee.

Vane, the valet, who had also been out looking, brought in a bundle tied up with string.

'Any news?'

'I have just retrieved this, sir,' he said, unrolling Yann's coat.

'Dear God, don't tell me you found that lying in the gutter?'

'No, sir, in a pawnshop. It appears that young Master Margoza managed to get a fair sum for it this morning.'

Henry Laxton laughed out loud with relief. 'Then at least the boy hasn't been robbed or knifed, or worse. Do you know where he is?'

'This, sir, is the address he gave the pawnbroker. Maiden Lane.'

Henry Laxton arrived at the house to find Mr Trippen sitting on an upturned crate. A fire was blazing away and the room had a pleasing aroma of hot buttered toast; Yann, having got up early to pawn his coat, had bought provisions. Mr Trippen was flabbergasted to see such a fine gentleman standing in the doorway and regretted much that he hadn't, as planned, got dressed, but was still to be found in his battered housecoat and cap.

'You find me at a disadvantage, sir,' he said, bowing.

Mr Laxton handed him his card and Mr Trippen read it with interest. The word banker danced before him.

'I believe that you have a young man staying with you who goes by the name of Yann Margoza.'

'I have that privilege, sir, and a finer and more talented young person I have yet to meet.'

'I take it, then, he is not here?'

'No sir, he has taken the young Trippens out for the benefits of fresh air and—'

Mr Laxton interrupted him. 'The young man is in my charge.'

'Of course, sir. I am in no way kidnapping him, I can assure you of that. By Jupiter, sir, he saved my life! A brave one is that boy, sir, a young Hamlet, indeed a Henry the Fifth on the battlefield of Agincourt.'

With many theatrical gestures that near exhausted him, Mr Trippen related what had happened in Covent Garden. Henry Laxton found himself warming to the actor, and an idea came to him.

'I am unfortunate, Mr Trippen, in that unlike you I am not a father.'

'Three girls, and one son and heir.'

'You are a lucky man indeed. I wish my wife and I had been so blessed. I wonder, sir, if I might confide in you?'

'By all means! Discretion is my second name.'

Mr Laxton told the actor as much as he thought he needed to know about Yann's background and the death of Têtu.

'He was placed in my care. I found him a tutor, a Mr Rose, who, unknown to me, saw fit to try and beat the spirit out of him.'

'A rose by any other name would smell as sweet, hmmn? I should think his petals were sent flying.'

'Knocked out cold,' said Mr Laxton, smiling at the memory of all the chaos Yann had caused.

Mr Trippen clapped his hands with delight. 'In my humble experience, the cane only teaches the child to loathe the tutor, despise the lesson, and scorn all the benefits that education might bring.'

'I entirely agree,' said Mr Laxton. 'Tell me, how would you go about teaching such a boy as Yann?'

'I would never keep him tied to a desk. That way nothing would be learnt. No, I would show him London, take him to galleries, the theatre; fire his imagination. Then when it caught I would tell him about the magic of books. Never let him become bored, sir.'

Mr Laxton listened while taking in the lack of any furniture.

'Forgive me,' said Mr Trippen, suddenly changing the subject and looking dejected. 'You catch the great Touchstone at a considerable embarrassment.' He waved his hand around the room by way of explanation.

'Have you just moved here, and are waiting for your possessions to arrive, or are you in the process of leaving?' asked Mr Laxton.

'Neither, sir,' said Mr Trippen. 'I am between tides, so to speak. You know the expression, "There is a tide in the affairs of men". In my case the tide was not taken. I was recently given the opportunity to be a full-time tutor. I turned it down, believing the stage to be my one and only true calling. A foolish moment. Now, alas, debt's dagger hangs over me.'

'I have a proposition to put to you,' said Mr Laxton, 'and if the idea suits it may be one way out of your little difficulty with the debt and may help me with the boy.'

'Sir,' said Mr Trippen, sitting bolt upright, 'I am all ears.'

<hr>

Yann returned with the little Trippens to find the house remarkably quiet. The girls ran upstairs giggling, followed by Yann carrying the sleeping baby, and entered the room to see their parents seated on boxes, both looking solemnly ahead of them as if they were in church on Sunday, their attention held by a gentleman who was leaning on the mantelpiece. It was Mr Laxton.

Yann stood there feeling stupid and embarrassed, as Mr Trippen ushered his little family out of the room and left them together. He was thinking so hard about what to say that it took him a moment to realise that Mr Laxton was already talking.

'I owe you an apology, Yann. I underestimated you. I didn't understand what Mr Cordell meant when he said Têtu had told him you were talented. It was my stupidity not to see that straight away.'

Whatever Yann had been expecting to hear, this was most definitely not it. Mr Laxton's kindness floored him. He looked up and was amazed to see genuine concern in his tired face.

Finally Yann said what he had thought he would never admit to anyone, least of all to Mr Laxton.

'I bitterly regret leaving as I did. My only excuse is that I thought you would be better off without me.'

Mr Laxton sat down on an upturned box with his feet spread out before him. He leaned on his gold-topped cane.

'You could not be more mistaken if you tried. I have been out all night looking for you.'

'Mrs Laxton called me a gypsy.'

'She meant no harm by it. She is as desperate as I am for you to come home.'

'What did Mr Cordell tell you about me?'

'Just that you were brought up by a dwarf called Têtu, travelling round France and working in theatres.'

Yann nodded. 'So you know nothing more?'

'I know nothing about your parentage. I wrote to Cordell asking for more information, and had a letter from him describing how he saw the show you performed with Topolain and the People's Pierrot. He was fascinated by the way the Pierrot could walk and talk, and particularly by the way it could read people's minds. He said that Têtu had told him the success of the performance was all due to your talent.'

'That was nothing,' said Yann. 'Têtu did most of the work. But I used to be able to read minds. The gift left me the day Têtu died. Now all I can do is throw my voice and perform a few simple magic tricks.'

'Grief can strip one of all sorts of powers. I am sure it will come back in time.'

'I feel it's gone for ever,' said Yann.

'Let's hope not. I think you should know that Têtu's body was never found.'

'But I left him lying in the snow, in the courtyard where he was shot!'

'Yes, the proprietor of the hotel said as much. She went to get help and when she returned she found only a bloodstain where the body had been.'

'It doesn't make sense. Maybe . . . maybe he's not dead after all.'

'I doubt it. The man who shot him must have removed the body.'

'But he just might still be alive. I must go back and find out what happened,' said Yann.

'If that's what you want then I will, of course, make the arrangements. But before you decide, I must tell you this. Têtu risked a great deal to get you here. If he is alive, his survival will only be assured by no one finding him, especially not you.'

Yann felt as if he stood at a crossroads. One path he knew well, and one appeared too dimly lit for him to see where it led. Looking at the two of them he knew which one he was going to take. 'I will try my best not to let you down, sir.'

'Good, that's all anyone can do,' said Mr Laxton,

looking mightily relieved. 'Then we have an understanding.'

Before Yann could say another word, the door burst open and Mr Trippen entered, his arms spread out wide.

'At last the tide has turned! A wise decision, sir,' he said, violently shaking Yann's hand, 'a wise decision.'

Yann looked baffled.

And Mr Laxton said, 'I took the opportunity of asking Mr Trippen to be one of your tutors.'

'Will that suit, sir?' said Mr Trippen, looking anxiously at Yann. 'If it won't, I will not force the point. It would gladden the heart of Touchstone to be of help to a fellow thespian. Clowns are often wiser than the cleverest of men. Not for nothing do jesters keep kings company.'

Yann burst out laughing. 'And you can get the furniture back.'

'It's already settled,' said Mr Laxton.

'Yes,' said Yann, 'then it will suit very well indeed.'

Chapter Fourteen

T he Marquis de Villeduval's response to the growing political turmoil in France was to build a garden surrounded by a high wall. The garden was designed to enhance the beauty of his new château. He had employed numerous draughtsmen, architects and gardeners, and insisted that all his tenant farmers abandon their work in the fields to bring the elaborate project to life.

As part of the grand plan the Marquis ordered the removal of a small, inconvenient hill that blocked the view from the château. The farmers, whose wheat fields he had confiscated, came cap in hand to beg him to leave it be. It was a sacred mound. To disturb it would mean spoiled crops, diseased animals, ruin and starvation.

This was not the first time a peasant delegation had annoyed him with saints and superstitions. The same thing had happened when he cleared the forest round his château in Normandy to make way for a park. That time they had warned him not to touch the ancient trees that belonged to the spirits of the earth and were guarded by the gypsies. They said that misfortune would overtake him if he cut down a single one.

The Marquis was determined to clear his land of the gypsies, whom he held solely responsible for these nonsensical and irrational ideas, so one winter's day he set off in pursuit of them, with a group that included Count Kalliovski.

The party soon came across a gypsy family fleeing through the woods. The Marquis had thought to have them rounded up and transported. The Count, however, had an altogether more immediate solution. The Marquis, who had not quite the Count's taste for blood, watched from a respectable distance, and the servants looked on in horror, as Kalliovski personally killed each and every one with less mercy than he would have shown a fox.

The dead bodies were left hanging in the trees like grotesque baubles, an example to all those who put store in old wives' tales instead of having a proper respect for reason and authority.

The small hill was duly removed. A long line of horses and carts went plodding back and forth, ant-like in their industry. Then a lake was dug out and filled with water diverted from the surrounding irrigation ditches. When one of the farmers asked how they were now supposed to water the crops, the Marquis replied irritably that he expected them to solve agricultural problems themselves, not bother him.

At one end of the lake a Grecian pavilion was constructed, and from it grassy paths led to fountains and fishponds. The Marquis imagined himself wandering through groves of linden trees, where birdsong followed his every step and flowers complemented the colours of his clothes. Oh, here he would be in perfect harmony with nature, in a paradise entirely of his own making. That the cost of this paradise would bring him to financial ruin was something he chose to ignore.

The task of telling him the true state of his financial affairs fell to the long-suffering Maître Tardieu, trusted adviser to the Villeduval family for over thirty years. In that time he had served both father and son, and after the old Marquis's death he had watched with growing dismay as the family's fortune was mercilessly squandered.

Every time Maître Tardieu brought up the question of monies owed, the Marquis's solution was to raise rents, regardless of the ability of his tenants to pay them. And if that did not bring in the required sums, he simply borrowed more from the Count. In vain did Maître Tardieu try to explain that there would come a time when the Count would want something in return.

And now it seemed that the day of reckoning had arrived. On the morning of the fourteenth of July, Maître Tardieu received a letter from the Count for the attention of the Marquis. It was written in white ink on black paper with three words inscribed in red at the bottom and embossed with a deep red seal. Maître Tardieu knew that he must inform the Marquis of its contents immediately.

The elderly lawyer looked not unlike a mole with his thick round spectacles stuck firmly on the end of his nose. They were besmeared with the grime of ages, and gave everything he viewed a tinge of grey. His waistcoat and breeches were of mole-like black velvet and to complete the picture he lived in a small house down a covered passageway where candles were needed both night and day.

He called for his carriage while Madame Tardieu, terrified by the idea of her husband travelling when Paris was in such turmoil, pleaded with him not to go.

'*Chéri*, please,' she begged. 'Look at what happened yesterday. The people are arming themselves. What if the King's soldiers come into the city while you are away? There will be fighting on the streets. We shall all be killed.' She crossed herself.

'Stay calm, my dear,' said Maître Tardieu. 'I shall be back before nightfall. You are to stay indoors and not set foot outside, my pet.'

She watched from the safety of the front door, her small, anxious face peering out to see her husband make his way out of the passage into the bright alarming sunlight as an angry crowd grudgingly let him climb into his carriage.

With the curtains drawn, Maître Tardieu sat back in

his seat as the carriage rumbled through Paris. Twice, men with cockades in their hats and brandishing pitchforks stopped the carriage and demanded that Maître Tardieu get out while they searched it for firearms. It was with a great sigh of relief that he finally arrived outside the wall that encircled Paris, and set out on the road to Versailles.

The journey gave Maître Tardieu time to reflect on the past, and he felt a profound sadness when he thought of the late Marquis. He had lost his adored younger son, Armand. His elder son, mean-spirited and extravagant, had always been a trial to him. He would turn in his grave to know of the present Marquis's current debts. Maître Tardieu remembered how appalled the old Marquis had been to see the indifference with which his son greeted the news of his wife's death.

When Maître Tardieu finally arrived, he was greeted by a valet and shown into an antechamber. Here he was made to wait for a further hour and a half, without refreshment, before the Marquis deigned to receive him. Even then he refused to talk business until he had first shown the lawyer around his grounds. The Marquis, parasol in hand, sauntered lazily along the grassy avenues, stepping with care to avoid getting the silk bows on his shoes dirty.

If there was beauty here it was lost on Maître Tardieu, who was limping by the time they reached the Grecian pavilion that overlooked the lake. He saw it as a mournful place, the afternoon sun casting a leaden light over the water.

Maître Tardieu tried to raise the question of the letter but the Marquis strolled on, put out that the lawyer seemed so unappreciative of his enterprise and the beauties on offer.

'Have you noticed that the flowers match the colours of the bows on my shoes?'

To the tired eyes of Maître Tardieu, all looked grey and dead.

The Marquis now said that he never discussed business in the afternoon, but was prepared to listen to the lawyer's concerns over supper. With a sigh Maître Tardieu resigned himself to having to spend the night at the château, and sent the coachman back to Paris with a message for his wife.

While the Marquis was resting, Maître Tardieu took the opportunity to talk to the steward and to examine the household accounts. He was appalled to discover just how much money the Marquis had spent on the garden. Not only had there been the designers, the hot-houses, and the rare flowers and shrubs to pay for, but the Marquis had had a network of secret tunnels built under the flowerbeds so that the gardeners could crawl down them each morning and discreetly change the flowers to match his outfit. The birdsong that followed his every step came from aviaries strategically hidden behind the greenery. Such folly came at a high price.

What shocked Maître Tardieu even more was what he learned about Sido. Apparently she had been confined to her chamber for the past seven months: why, he could not fathom. The Marquis's valet, by way of explanation, said his master viewed her as an inconvenience. Maybe it was this, and the remembrance of what she had meant to her grandfather, that finally made him decide to throw caution to the winds and to speak his mind, whatever the outcome.

At last the lawyer and the Marquis sat down to dine, the Marquis at the head of the long table. Maître Tardieu was used to plain food and was quite overcome by the pomp and ceremony of this meal and the many dishes on offer. Five footmen stood in attendance. The room was ablaze with candles, even though it was still light outside.

'Sir,' said Maître Tardieu, 'as you know, I have come at some considerable inconvenience—'

'If you have come here to tell me any more ridiculous tales about the disturbances in Paris,' the Marquis interrupted, 'I am not interested. The whole situation has been grossly exaggerated.'

At the word "exaggerated", a candle blew out and a footman came forward to relight it.

'No, no, no!' shouted the Marquis, bringing down his bejewelled hand on the table. 'How many times must I tell you? Always use a new candle, never relight an old one.'

Again Maître Tardieu tried to speak. Again his host interrupted him. 'Did I tell you that very amusing story about the Duchess and the writing desk?'

Maître Tardieu sighed. 'Please, sir, I beg you, we must talk.'

'I see,' said the Marquis, 'that you are determined to

be dull. In that case, let us have some champagne.' He snapped his fingers at a footman. 'Politics is such a flat affair.'

In desperation Maître Tardieu decided to bring his employer up sharp. He took the letter from his waistcoat pocket and handed it to one of the footmen to give to the Marquis.

'What is this?' said the Marquis, waving the letter away. 'Do you intend to ruin my digestion?'

'It is from Count Kalliovski.'

'Oh, I see. Well, read it to me if you must.'

'Perhaps, sir, it would be better if the letter were read in private.'

'We are in private.'

'Forgive me, but we have in this room a butler and five footmen who can hear every word I am about to say.'

'Don't be absurd, man. They are merely there to serve me and have no opinions of their own. They are less important than the furniture and definitely less valuable.'

'Very well,' said Maître Tardieu. He took the letter and began to read slowly and carefully so that master and servants could hear every word.

'What does he mean?' said the Marquis.

'Exactly what he says. He wants his money back with interest and he wants it before the end of the month.'

'That is ridiculous. What has got into him? I think the best course of action is to take none. Kindly acknowledge the letter and point out that there seems to have been a misunderstanding.'

Maître Tardieu had reached the end of his tether. Throwing diplomacy and caution aside, he said, 'Sir. You are near bankrupt. There is no money left. I have warned you on many occasions, but you have refused to take my advice. Now I fear it is too late.'

'What! You sit at my table and have the impudence to talk to me so? How dare you!'

Maître Tardieu brought out a bundle of household accounts. 'Mindless extravagance,' he said flatly. 'Thousands of candles squandered, over a hundred suits a year, half of which are never worn, not to speak of the expenditure on your garden.'

The Marquis, red in the face, tried to interrupt again, but Maître Tardieu silenced him.

'There is more, and it is of even more consequence.'

He returned to the letter and read the last paragraph, in which the Count enquired after Sido's health and asked for reassurance that she was being well cared for.

At this the Marquis looked most uncomfortable. The champagne, combined with his gold lace and silk embroidered suit, was making him hot and the powder from his hair and the make-up on his face were beginning to run.

'The Count ends his letter by saying that he is looking for a wife. He believes your daughter could well be suitable. If that is the case and you agree to the marriage, all your debts will be cancelled. He says that an engagement at fourteen and a marriage at fifteen is what he has in mind.'

It had never occurred to the Marquis that the Count of all people would desire his daughter, and the idea of the man being even more closely linked to the ancient and noble family of the Villeduvals worried him. On the other hand, when he thought of his financial situation, the proposal had some merit.

'She will, of course, be married into an aristocratic family. That goes without saying,' he said flatly.

One redeeming sentence, thought Maître Tardieu. Still, he was sure it had more to do with the Marquis's pride than his daughter's well-being.

'And for how long do you intend to keep her imprisoned in her chamber?' asked the lawyer as his glass was filled, this time with fine claret.

'What? Do you expect me to dine with the child and have her run around under my feet? She is well cared for and out of sight.' The Marquis dusted his thin, mean lips with a napkin. 'I regret to say that she is most decidedly plain. Then there is her limp. She is, in my view, a broken vase, never to be made whole.'

Tardieu's dislike of this man was growing with every remark he made and he said, not without a touch of irony, 'I agree that for Mademoiselle Sido to marry the Count is not ideal. His title is unfamiliar and his lineage does not, I am sure, stretch back as far as the grand and honourable name of Villeduval. But that aside, are you aware of what such a marriage would mean?'

'If you mean she will be off my hands, all well and

good. Let some other soul suffer her. I have had more than enough.'

'Your father's will—'

'What of it?' said the Marquis with a dismissive wave of his hand. 'The subject bores me.'

'I take it, then, that you have no objection to the fact that once the marriage takes place your daughter comes into her inheritance from her grandfather's will, which of course her new husband will have at his disposal.'

Maître Tardieu could see that for the first time this evening he had rattled the man. Relishing the moment, he said, 'Shall I read again what he says at the bottom of the letter?' He leaned forward into the light of the candles. '"Your daughter is your greatest asset." Think about it, sir. She is twelve years old, so that gives you two years to find your way out of your debts and therefore be free to marry her to an aristocratic family worthy of the connection.'

The Marquis looked thunderous. In all his previous dealings with Maître Tardieu, the lawyer had never spoken to him in such a manner.

'I still have my estates in Normandy,' he said loudly.

'No,' said the lawyer, 'you have the right to take all the income from the land and the tenants until your daughter is married. On her wedding day they will become her property and that of her husband, Count Kalliovski.'

'Impossible! I will not allow it!' said the Marquis. 'How much do the estates bring in?'

'Not as much as they should. I have been reliably

informed,' the lawyer continued, 'that your tenants have taken flight without paying their rents. The crops have failed. Your barns have been ransacked by starving peasants. Instead of attending to these matters you have remained here and built a garden and a wall. In short, there is no money to pay off your debts, if that is what you were hoping.'

Finally the Marquis understood. Of course Kalliovski would be paid back in full with this marriage. The thought was intolerable.

'I don't want to hear any more,' he said, putting his hands over his ears. 'Your sermons are putting me out of humour.'

Maître Tardieu had no intention of stopping. 'There is something written at the very bottom of the letter, not in white ink but in red. Three words only. "Remember your wife."'

Through the grime of his spectacles the lawyer hardly noticed the deathly pallor that had come over the Marquis. He did, though, observe with interest his shaking hand.

'Write and tell him I will give his proposition some thought.'

'And what, pray, will you do if the situation in Paris worsens and there is a revolution?'

For a moment the Marquis said nothing, just stared fixedly at the candle. 'That is inconceivable,' he said at last. 'The King will put down any such revolt.'

For the first time he was experiencing the odd sensation of doubt. The letter that wretched little man had brought him had upset him more than he cared to admit. It wounded him to think the Count should turn on him like this.

'The King has already lost his power,' the lawyer went on. 'His army will not fight against its own people. The sovereignty of France now rests with the National Assembly.'

'Rubbish,' shouted the Marquis.

There was a sudden din outside in the corridor. The Marquis ordered Jacques, the butler, to go and investigate. He returned with the Marquis's valet, who could hardly contain his excitement.

'What is going on?' said the Marquis, standing up. 'Can the servants not be controlled?'

'Sir,' said Luc, 'we have just received extraordinary news from Paris. The Bastille has fallen.'

'Fallen?' repeated the Marquis. 'What do you mean, fallen?'

'The citizens have stormed it. They fired cannons at the wall and brought it tumbling down.'

'The Bastille is no more!' said Jacques. 'The Governor and the Provost have both been killed. Their heads are being carried through the city on pikes!' He was carried away by his enthusiasm. 'Vive la Nation!' he cried.

The Marquis collapsed on his chair.

The day the Bastille fell was the day Sido was released.

Chapter Fifteen

I t was the Comte du Verrier who had brought the extraordinary news of the fall of the Bastille, on his way to Versailles. The poor man had taken fright and fled Paris, certain that they would all be killed in their beds if he stayed. Little did he know that three years later, crying like an infant, his head would be guillotined from his body.

The Comte du Verrier's valet, Baptiste, found himself that warm July night in the kitchen of the Marquis's château in an unusual position of authority, for he alone there had borne witness to the making of history.

The Marquis's staff gathered around, dumb-struck, as he related what he had seen.

'Did you take part, then?' asked a young groom called Philippe.

'Not exactly,' said Baptiste. 'I wish I could have done.

For my sins, I was stuck with my master. I can tell you this, though, he was trembling when he looked out of the window and saw the crowds.'

'What was he doing in Paris when he should have been at court?' asked Luc.

'What are all men doing when they are where they shouldn't be? Seeing their mistresses, that's what. No doubt he had his breeches down about his stockinged ankles while the Bastille fell.' He laughed. 'When he's old and he is asked where he was on this great day, how will he account for himself, I wonder?'

'If he's lucky enough to live that long,' muttered Jean Rollet, the chef.

'I heard cannon fire,' said Baptiste, not wanting to lose this moment in fame's fickle flame. 'I saw men and women, fearless citizens of Paris, take to the streets. I was told that they tore at the Bastille with their bare hands. They stopped the clocks and started them again to show that the world had begun afresh. You could see smoke for miles around and the sky went white with papers. I ran out and caught one, I did.' He brought a singed piece of paper out of his pocket and held it up for them all to see. 'I'm going to keep this and show it to my children as proof that I was there.' He began to put it back in his pocket.

'Wait, wait!' said Luc, grabbing it from him. 'Not so hasty. What does it say?' He looked uncertainly at the paper, disappointed that he was unable to read it.

His fiancée Lucille came forward.

'My mistress can read. Why don't I show it to her?' she

145

said, taking the paper and folding it up before putting it in her apron.

'Did they release hundreds of prisoners?' asked Jean.

'Seven.'

Everyone started talking at once. 'Only seven!' 'That's all?' 'That can't be right.'

'The rumour on the streets was that the prison was emptied ahead of time,' said Baptiste. 'They'd been tipped off about what might happen.'

'It doesn't matter how many,' said Luc, getting to his feet. 'What matters is what the Bastille stands for and the fact that the King's army didn't shoot at the crowd. This is the end of the old regime. Today, ladies and gentlemen, is the dawning of a new age.'

Jacques also got up from the table. 'This demands champagne, for today we are all equal, we are all kings.'

The wine soon loosened everyone's tongues and their pent-up grievances against their master.

'The truth is,' said Jacques, 'that if the Marquis had been half as much liked as his father—'

'Or his half-brother,' interrupted Madame Gournay, the seamstress. 'Now *there* was a nobleman who knew how to look after his servants and land.'

'Hear, hear!' They raised their glasses to the memory of Armand de Villeduval.

'I tell you this,' said Alain Grimod, the gamekeeper, 'I always thought there was something not quite right about that business.'

'Now, now,' said Bernard, 'no good will come of raking up the past.'

'As I was saying,' said Jacques, 'if the Marquis hadn't been a tyrant and a bully, he might have won our loyalty.'

'What did he call us?' said one of the footmen. ' "Less important than the furniture and definitely less valuable." '

'I'll tell you this for nothing. I hate my master. He's just a painted peacock,' said Jacques. 'I say if the people can bring down such men as he, then long live the Revolution!'

'I'll drink to that,' said Jean Rollet. 'Here's to the fall of the Bastille.'

'Well said!'

There was another loud cheer and Baptiste stood up. 'Do you know what they called out on the streets? They were shouting for liberty, for all men to be equal!'

'Equality! Do you think in the future we might all be equal, men and women, servants and masters?' asked Luc.

'For all our sakes, let us hope so,' said Jean.

———◆———

U pstairs, the moon shone brightly into another chamber, that of the Marquis. Behind his walls with their gilded panels he could not hear the celebration below. He was not concerned one jot with the political turmoil in Paris. His thoughts were taken up by the Count's letter, which taxed him greatly.

He could not for the life of him work out what had overcome his friend, whose generosity up to that point had been faultless. Why should he so unreasonably demand his money back now? He wondered for a brief moment quite how much Sido stood to inherit. He remembered once being told the figure and had noted it only in that it could be called on at a later date. It must be a fair sum if it would cover all his debts.

On further reflection, he decided that such a proposal had a lot to recommend itself. After all, had not the Queen herself been married at fourteen? And the Duchesse de Lamantes had been fifteen at the time of her wedding to that old libertine, the Duke. Tomorrow he would tell Maître Tardieu that he would agree to the marriage. It might not have been his first choice, but nevertheless it got rid of two unpleasant things that niggled at him – his debt and his daughter.

Lucille had come rushing into Sido's chamber at midnight, through the secret panelled door, to rouse her mistress.

'Look, mademoiselle!' She held before her the key to the main door.

Sido, half-awake, propped herself up on her elbow as Lucille lit a candle. 'What are you doing?'

'Watch,' said Lucille, opening the door as if she herself were freeing a prisoner from the Bastille. 'I'm sure you needn't be confined to your chamber any longer. You're at liberty! Isn't that a wonderful word – liberty?'

'I don't understand.'

'Oh, mademoiselle, the most exciting thing has happened! The Bastille has fallen!'

Sido was now sitting up, fully awake. For a moment she had no idea what Lucille was saying. It seemed unthinkable. The Bastille, that huge blackened fortress that sat like a rotten tooth in the mouth of Paris, gone! Impossible.

'Are you sure?'

Lucille came over to the bed and took her mistress's hands.

'Oh yes, mademoiselle, certain. It's the start of the Revolution.' She was now talking so fast that the words fair skipped over themselves as she related all that she had been told.

'Here,' she said, gasping for breath, 'see what Baptiste brought.' She handed Sido the piece of paper. 'He said the sky went white with letters like these, thousands of them, there were. What does it say, mademoiselle?'

Sido read aloud, '"Give me a sign you are still alive and I may breathe again." It's part of a love letter,' she said, looking at its burnt edges.

After Lucille had gone, Sido sat by the light of the candle for a long time, thinking about all that she had been told and wondering how it would change the future. And suddenly the image came to her of all the love letters from the Bastille, raining down over Paris like tears from the sky.

The next morning the Marquis took his time dressing for an audience with the King at Versailles, making sure that he was properly wigged and powdered.

He had decided to wear his finest dusty pink silk brocade coat, embroidered with small diamonds. The silver buckles on his soft leather shoes were decorated with diamonds and pearls. Finally, dressed and perfumed and meeting with his own personal approval, he called for the lawyer.

He was an imposing sight as he looked down his curved aristocratic nose at Maître Tardieu.

'I have decided to agree to the Count's request,' he announced. 'I see much that is agreeable in this marriage, and leave it to you to discuss terms.'

'Sir,' said Maître Tardieu, 'forgive me, but last night I thought—'

'Count Kalliovski is a very presentable choice, and there's an end to it,' interrupted the Marquis.

Maître Tardieu followed him out through the main entrance. His hip was hurting. He hadn't slept from worry.

The Marquis said to his valet, 'My daughter is to be brought down from her chamber.' Then, waving a dismissive hand at Maître Tardieu, he said, 'I leave it to you to inform her of my decision.'

He walked out to his waiting carriage, passing the footmen who stood lined up like toy soldiers, and was helped up inside, his coat rearranged with much fuss so that he would not arrive creased. 'I think I should wear the King's cockade,' he said, leaning out of the carriage door.

Luc clicked his fingers and a footman went rushing back indoors to fetch it.

Maître Tardieu stood on the gravel, silent and watching. He wondered if foolish men ever became wise. If the Marquis was anything to go by, the sad answer had to be no.

The Marquis, only half looking at him, said peevishly, 'You have not noticed the buckles on my shoes. What say you to their elegance?'

The lawyer stared down at them, baffled. The Bastille might have fallen, France might be standing on the brink of civil war, but all the Marquis could think of was buckles. Maybe, in the end, all that would be left of his great fortune would be buckles.

'I thought of wearing the ruby ones, but I felt they might clash with the brocade.'

'Quite,' said Maître Tardieu. 'Quite.'

The footman came back and handed the white cockade to Luc, who pinned it on to the Marquis's coat. As he did so, his master stuck his chinless head forward like a turtle coming out of its shell.

'The Queen's black cockade,' said the Marquis, 'would of course have complemented my coat better than the King's white one. But I am not about to support the insupportable.'

With this, the carriage door was finally closed. Maître Tardieu and the servants stood and watched the coach disappear into the distance.

Lucille had brought Sido a message to say that Maître Tardieu wanted to see her. Madame Gournay, the seamstress, came in carrying a white muslin gown run through with blue stripes, and a red sash.

'What do you think?' she asked.

Sido clapped her hands with delight. 'It's lovely! It must have taken hours to make.'

Madame Gournay, who was employed solely to look after the Marquis's wardrobe, had found his daughter to be an altogether more delightful model. The Marquis was forever changing his mind, ordering bolts of silks and satins that were immediately discarded, demanding alterations which, when made, were never satisfactory. She found in Sido an appreciation that her master never gave.

'Making clothes for you feels as if I am playing my part in the Revolution. There,' said Madame Gournay, standing back. 'You look beautiful.'

Sido stared at herself in the mirror. Beauty she did not see, only that her leg appeared stiffer from lack of exercise.

'Perhaps,' said Sido, turning and smiling at the seamstress, 'if I were to be pulled along on a child's cart I might be passable. The moment I walk I am afraid all is lost.'

'No,' said Madame Gournay firmly, 'you make too much of it. A little hesitation in a lady adds to her charm.'

Maître Tardieu saw before him an anxious-looking young girl with large blue eyes, dark hair, and pale porcelain skin. It made the Count's letter and what he had to impart all the more distasteful.

'I wish I had happier news for you, mademoiselle,' he said, 'but I have not. I think it is best that you read this yourself.' And he handed her the black letter.

Sido, unlike her father, needed no explanation. Her response was immediate.

'I can't marry him.'

Maître Tardieu sighed. This young girl was not to be duped as her mother had been. He had known at the time that Isabelle Gautier did not love the Marquis: she had been blinded by his wealth and the promise of luxury, the seduction of jewellery.

Maître Tardieu cleared his throat. 'I greatly regret it, but your father has instructed me to agree to the marriage. You have no choice in the matter when his debts can be so easily solved by this union.'

Sido looked at the letter again, taking in the three words written in red ink at the bottom.

'Do you know what he means by "remember your wife"?'

'No, alas, I do not.'

Sido bit her lip and said, 'Why have I no family to advise my father against this ill-judged marriage?' She looked up at the old lawyer, fighting back tears.

He suddenly took pity on her and said something that

had been locked away for many years, something he had been forbidden to pass on.

'You have family in London,' he said quickly.

Sido stared at him, uncertain if she had heard the lawyer right.

'Family in London?' she repeated.

Poor Maître Tardieu looked appalled by what, without due legal consideration, had just tripped off his tongue.

'Oh dear. I have always been under strict instructions to say nothing on the matter. What is to be done now?'

'Where in London are they?' asked Sido, hardly able to contain her excitement. 'How can I find them?'

'I have no idea. I know your mother had a sister there at the time of the accident. She married an Englishman, a Mr Laxton. Whether she is still alive, I cannot say.'

'What is her name?'

'Please, mademoiselle, do not press me. Truly, I shouldn't have said a word. And do not put too much store by this news. She is surely dead by now.'

'Why?' asked Sido.

'Because,' said the lawyer floundering, 'because the English have a very poor diet. They live a shorter time than the French.'

Sido looked at Maître Tardieu and felt sorry for him. He looked quite exhausted and his face was grey. She could see that he was not a well man.

'I must leave. I am too old to be doing this, too old and powerless to know how to help you. I wish it were not so.'

She knew it was no good questioning him further. He

looked half-terrified by what he had already said.

'Are you going back to Paris now?' she asked.

'I am. Immediately. I am worried about my wife. She is not in the best of health and with the state of things in the city ...'

She followed him out to his waiting carriage.

'Before you go, may I ask you one last thing? Do you think the Revolution might save me? Or is it already too late?'

'I think the world we knew has gone,' said Maître Tardieu. 'What that means only time will tell.'

———— ◆ ————

An early morning mist hung like a veil over the garden. Sido, still reeling from all she had been told and the joyful knowledge, for what it was worth, that she wasn't alone in the world, lifted her skirts and for the first time in seven months ran down the grassy paths. Nearly falling, she steadied herself on the statue of Pan. At last, finding her balance, she took the walk at a slower pace, pleased to feel her leg becoming less stiff. She wandered down paths where statues of goddesses watched over her. She saw a vista of fountains, and the lake beyond. The groves were full of birdsong.

It did not take her long to discover the metal cages. Pushing back the leaves, she saw aviaries full of wild birds, thrushes, blackbirds, nightingales, wrens, chaffinches, hidden amongst the foliage. She walked back up the path and discovered that the aviaries ran along every one of the groves. What cruelty, she thought, to do this to birds that own the sky.

She was trying to find out how the aviaries might be opened when a group of people appeared ghostlike out of the mist. They were armed with pitchforks, swords and guns. She stood still with her back to the aviaries, recognising some of the servants.

'Where are you going?'

'To Paris,' said Jacques. 'We have come to free the birds.' He pulled out a key and said almost shyly, 'Would you like to do it, mademoiselle?'

One by one, Sido unlocked the cages. They stood there, all of them silently watching the birds thrill to find the wind once more beneath their wings. Only when every one stood empty did they part, the servants taking one path and Sido another.

Chapter Sixteen

U nder the shade of the oak tree Sido could see in the flickering patterns of the leaves her life already mapped out, her future decided, her husband chosen. It was to be Count Kalliovski.

To Sido he seemed soulless, with his impossibly smooth skin, his face stripped of lines and wrinkles, his features wiped clean of life's tempests. She wondered what pact he had made with the devil, that time itself should not wish to embrace him.

She thought back to that evening of the party some seven months earlier when he and his great black hound had sat in her chamber watching her. It had felt as if the very air was being sucked out of the room, his presence as heavy as mercury.

It was after the fireworks, when she was alone again, that Sido had her dream. She was walking along snowy treetops. The road up ahead was a silvery ribbon in the starlight; it appeared to be far off, yet it wound its way towards her. There on the highway she could make out a coach standing diagonally across the road, as if it had just avoided some terrible catastrophe. The coachman was mopping his brow, looking shaken. By the side of the horses stood Yann. He was holding the bridles and she could clearly hear him talking to them in his curious language. She reached out to touch him, and in that moment he turned towards her and smiled.

Then with a jolt she was back in her room. That was when she knew, as if she had always known, that Yann Margoza would be in her life for ever.

At the convent there was a nun called Sister Ignatius, whom Sido liked very much. She was kind and wholesome, her feet firmly planted in the soil. She surprised Sido by telling her that when she was nine years old she had seen a vision of the Virgin Mary standing on ripe ears of barley, holding a baby made of light. In the gentle breeze she seemed to be walking on a golden sea. Sister Ignatius had known from that day forth that she would be a nun. Maybe, Sido thought now, you could have the same certainty about a living person. Maybe her dream too was a vision, a premonition.

In the days that followed, Sido told herself her premonition was just wishful thinking. As the days and weeks slowly tied themselves into months she gave in to her fantasy, for loneliness threatened to overwhelm her, to destroy her spirit.

Sometimes she wondered if dreaming about someone you hardly knew was sinful. Then she decided she didn't much care if it was, for thinking about Yann made the isolation bearable. She told herself the same story over and over again, and every time it comforted her like thick hot chocolate on a cold winter's day.

This dream of Yann had idled away many desperate months, until at last he seemed so real to her that she could almost believe he was sitting on the chair by her bed watching her.

Today, though, the dream stopped abruptly, for in her mind's eye the smooth, soulless face of Count Kalliovski smothered her vision like a black velvet curtain, snuffing out her hope of freedom.

<hr />

The Marquis de Villeduval returned home that same afternoon and called for Sido. She entered the room to find him with his back turned towards her, looking out over the garden. He did not turn round, but started to describe the building of the wall and the landscaping of the terraces as if his daughter hadn't been there while all this activity was taking place. She stood staring at him, wondering what she should say; but every word felt like dust on her tongue, so she said nothing.

Her silence had an immediate effect. For the first time in Sido's life, it seemed that her father was prepared to show a grudging interest in her. He took her to the locked antechamber where he kept his collection of shoe buckles, as if to see them was her reward for months of solitude.

It was like the inside of an ornate jewellery box, and glimmered with diamonds, rubies, emeralds, sapphires and pearls.

The Marquis said with pride, 'What do you think of this? My collection is priceless. Not even the King can boast of such fine buckles as these.'

Sido didn't answer. She had discovered a treasure all of her own: the golden power of silence.

It was the beginning of a strange time in her father's house. The Marquis spent most of his time at Versailles and Sido was left alone to explore the château and read the unread books. On his return her father would talk of the parties he had attended and how well he had been received, of Madame this and the Duchess of that. He never discussed Sido's forthcoming marriage, just as he never discussed politics or the Revolution. The closest he came to acknowledging that anything untoward was happening was when he bemoaned how many of his friends had seen fit to leave for long vacations abroad. Of Paris all he had to say was that it had become 'dull, very dull indeed'. Of Versailles he talked more favourably, of balls, parties and the card tables, though here too he had his complaints.

'I observe,' he said, 'that standards of dress are slipping. It is a tragedy, the loss of whalebone in corsets. Whalebone gives women such excellent stature. Now the fashion is all for ladies to look like milkmaids in their white muslin gowns, without proper support or lacing. As a result,' he announced, as if it were the most shocking piece of news ever, 'women are slouching! *So* inelegant.'

Sido listened quietly, relieved that there was no need for her to comment, for what could she say to such a kaleidoscope of folly? She found that she had become a silent witness to her father's idiocy. She realised that, like the King himself, the Marquis was out of touch with what was happening all around him. The decadence, the waste continued, and still the poor stayed poor while her father and his acquaintances determinedly danced, dined, gambled, gossiped and spent their way to disaster.

It was only after the murder of his friend Madame Perrien that the fact that something terrible was happening dawned upon him. By then, it was all too late.

Chapter Seventeen

I t had started with one of the Marquis's extravagances, a grand fête, given for all his friends that late summer after the fall of the Bastille, and designed to take their minds off the tedium of the Revolution.

It was held on an overcast day full of clouds that whirled menacingly, windmill-like, across the sky. The skeleton staff of gardeners who had not yet left for Paris had been obliged to work around the clock, for the Marquis refused to acknowledge any change. His only concession to economy had been to hold no parties for the past eight months.

Now that the National Assembly had collectively lost its mind and agreed to pass this ridiculous declaration of the rights of man, he felt it his duty to throw one of his spectacular parties, a reminder, if one was needed, of how preposterous this Revolution was. For the idea that all men were equal was laughable; no one in his right mind could believe it. In his opinion, the sooner the populace was crushed the better.

For the time being the Marquis was more concerned about deciding on a theme for his fête, and he called for the painter Etienne Bouchot to design the setting and the winged chariot in which he was to make his entrance.

After days of deliberation he settled on the idea that everyone would come dressed as a character from the Commedia dell'arte: Zannis, or clowns, with interesting costumes and witty masks, were much in fashion. An informal picnic would be held in his Arcadian garden. The guests would be transported across the lake to an Italian piazza, where they would dine and be entertained by jugglers, fire-eaters and tightrope artists.

The Marquis fussed and threw tantrums over every detail of this fête. His fury at finding that the cages had been emptied of birds knew no bounds until one of the gardeners suggested a novel idea which the Marquis immediately claimed as his own, and set all his poor tenant farmers to work with butterfly nets.

On the opposite side of the lake a stage was built, while in front of the temple itself a wooden floor was laid and painted to look like a marble piazza. Scores of scene painters, carpenters and metalworkers were needed to make such an ambitious vision reality.

The invitations had been sent out, with one notable and fatal exception. The Marquis had not asked Count Kalliovski. His reason for leaving the Count off the guest list was childish, with, alas, no thought to the consequences. The Marquis was bitterly jealous of Count Kalliovski's new acquaintance with Robespierre, a bourgeois lawyer from Arras, one of the leaders of the Revolution. It was beyond his comprehension as to why the Count would want to keep the company of such a humourless, dull man, of little or no consequence. Misguidedly, he believed that once the Count discovered he had not been invited to this party, he would come back full of remorse: for how could he ever have risen so high in court circles without the Marquis's help and guidance? You could say the Marquis had a talent for rearranging unpalatable truths to suit his narrow point of view.

What concerned him the most at the present time, and had almost turned the pink clouds of his mind grey with worry, was what to wear so as to outshine all his guests. Finally he concluded that none of the characters from the Commedia dell'arte reflected his noble nature or did justice to the ancient name of Villeduval, so he decided upon a costume that would truly enhance the glories of his personality. He would be the Sun itself. To create the desired effect, tailors, shoemakers, glovers and perfumiers, fan- and mask-makers and suppliers of gold and silver stuffs were called for.

All this fevered activity shook the château awake as if it were emerging from a long afternoon's sleep. The Marquis felt alive again, with a total disregard for any form of self-restraint. It was as if the Revolution had only been a glint in a starving man's eye.

Sido, on hearing that the Count was not coming, had

felt a huge sense of relief. Now she could enjoy the fête without any worries about her forthcoming betrothal. Yet in all the preparations her father never once asked to see her, and as the day drew nearer she realised that she had once again been forgotten.

On the eve of the party the Marquis, as if at last remembering her, called for Sido to be brought to his chamber.

He was sitting in his dressing-robe, his feet in a bowl of rosewater while his fingernails were attended to, a tall glass of champagne in the other hand, and beside him on the table a small pyramid of confectionery.

As the last rays of sunshine broke forth through the shutters, he looked at Sido and said irritably, 'Don't stand there. The light is most unbecoming.' He dusted the corners of his mouth with a napkin and addressed Luc, his valet. 'She may observe the party from the side room in the temple, but that is all. I don't want her wandering about tomorrow. Everything must be charming.' With that he lifted his pampered hand and waved her away.

Not for the first time did Sido wonder why it was that her father disliked his only child so very much.

———◆———

On the day of the fête, the servants were up at dawn, bringing down long tables and laying them with fine damask, porcelain and silver. An ice sculpture in the shape of a harlequin was placed in the centre and cut-glass chandeliers were hung from a series of ropes.

They looked like strange, elaborate beehives floating in the sky above the tables. All around were urns filled with huge displays of flowers.

Boats shaped like swans and peacocks, their painted wooden feathers splayed out, were brought down to the lake on carts, and sackfuls of pink rose petals were floated gently on the metallic surface of the water.

Before the party started, Sido was taken down to the temple where a concealed door in the wall was opened to reveal a cubbyhole with a good-sized window to look out of, and a spyhole to see into the temple itself. Gazing out of the window, she was reminded of the toy theatre she had had as a small child. The scene before her had the same magical quality.

The orchestra struck up, and the guests began to arrive.

They came as Punchinellos, Scarpinos, Scaramouches, Harlequins, Pantaloons, Pierrots, Columbines. Tumblers and jugglers from the Paris circus performed amongst them, while a tightrope walker in a harlequin costume crossed back and forth above their heads.

At last the Marquis made his entrance to the sound of trumpets, his winged chariot pulled by four men dressed in tunics with headdresses in the shape of the sun, their bodies oiled and shining. The Marquis was helped out, an apparition in gold silk brocade. He wore a breastplate with the face of the sun on it. His wig was gold, studded with gems. His mask was made of thin gold leaf, and looked as if it had been blown across his face. The effect

166

was dazzling: so much so that the sun might well have decided not to shine, out of envy.

From Sido's vantage point, not only did she have a perfect view of the proceedings but she could hear equally well all that was being said, for many of the guests came to gossip under the round dome of the temple where their voices echoed.

By late afternoon the sky had turned the colour of iron. Sido watched as the guests floated off in their swan and peacock boats and the footmen surrounding the lake opened baskets, letting out hundreds and hundreds of butterflies that in the eerie light of the oncoming storm looked like jewels taking flight.

The highlight of the afternoon's entertainment was the arrival of an Italian singer who was enjoying a great success at the Paris Opera House. Her voice soared through the gathering clouds, calling to Zeus himself who answered in his deep bass voice with a mighty rumble of thunder as lightning forked its way towards the lake, followed by a sudden downpour of torrential rain.

The guests hastily abandoned their tables, spilling wine and knocking over chairs as they ran for cover, tall wigs flopping in the rain. Servants rushed here and there with umbrellas while the guests, like hissing geese, took flight back towards the château. They were followed by the musicians and the opera singer who waddled behind like a flat-footed duck, her dress trailing in the mud.

Sido watched as the rain washed away the cakes, their

pink icing running down damask tablecloths, the weight of the water half sinking the wooden boats that were illuminated, electric white, against the inky darkness of the waters. The scene, so wonderful, so magical at the beginning of the day, lay in ruins.

She was just opening the door of the temple to leave when, to her surprise, she heard her father's voice above the sound of the rain. He was deep in conversation with a lady. They were taking shelter in the temple – she could see them all too clearly through the crack in the door. Sure that at any moment she would be discovered, she decided that it was best to stay where she was.

'I have no money to repay the Count,' said the lady.

'Surely Monsieur Perrien can help you out of your little difficulty,' replied the Marquis.

'My husband's château was destroyed last week by a fire. He has lost everything, and after all he has been through I dare not tell him about my gambling debts. I am terrified of what the Count will do. He wrote me a letter on black paper with white ink. You know what that means.'

'There has been a little misunderstanding,' said the Marquis. 'It signifies nothing.'

'It is no misunderstanding,' said Madame Perrien. 'I implore you to lend me the money. You are my last hope. If you do not, I am as good as dead. I promise to repay you.' She reached out to take his hand but the Marquis quickly pulled it away, disgusted.

'Madame, this is no way for a lady of your rank to behave,' he said curtly.

She laughed a hard laugh. 'I tell you this, Monsieur le Marquis, not inviting the Count was a grave mistake. Do you really think it will be that easy to have nothing more to do with him? I think you will come to regret this oversight bitterly.'

'I have no idea what you are talking about, madame. I advise you to pull yourself together.'

'This is no child's game we are playing.'

'It is, alas, one of the faults of the weaker sex to take matters of little consequence far too seriously. Madame, my advice to you is that this will resolve itself. Let us go back to the château for a glass of champagne. I find that champagne always lifts the spirits when one is feeling a little flat.'

Madame Perrien was not listening. 'The Count could destroy all of us if he wanted to!'

'Madame,' said the Marquis stiffly, 'this has gone far enough.' He tried to step away but was stopped by Madame Perrien, who grabbed hold of his gold costume and collapsed to her knees.

The look of revulsion on the Marquis's face would have been comical if it were not for the seriousness of what Madame Perrien was saying.

'At the beginning I thought, like you, that it was just a silly game. I had to give him something precious in return for the loan. When I explained that I could not give him jewellery as security, he said he wanted no such trinkets, he was after just a few little secrets. I gave him letters; letters which I now fear incriminate me. When I asked for them back he laughed and said he had them under lock and key and would use them to his own advantage if I did not repay him.'

Madame Perrien now had the Marquis's full attention. He took off his gold mask as a flash of lightning skimmed the lake. She let go of his coat and pulled herself up, leaning on the pillar.

'What secrets did *you* give the Count, I wonder, in return for his generosity? They must have been worth a king's ransom that he should have lent you so much. I dread to think what he will want in return.'

The Marquis pursed his lips. 'This does not apply to me. He did it purely out of friendship.'

Madame Perrien made a mirthless sound. 'What folly! Tell me this, then. If he did so much for you as a friend, what do you think he would do if you were to become his enemy? He once told me what his private motto was. Shall I tell you it? "Show no mercy, have no mercy."'

The Marquis, who had swum all his life in the shallow waters of polite society, avoiding at all costs any meaningful conversation, suddenly realised that the largest pike in the river was after him. He straightened his back and looked at Madame Perrien coldly.

'I cannot speak for you, madame, though I would say that your dealings with the Count have been unwise. Now, if you would excuse me, I must join my other guests.'

Sido watched her father turn his back on Madame Perrien to walk down the steps, where two footmen were waiting with umbrellas to escort him towards the château.

'We made a pact with the devil,' she called after him, 'and the devil is coming to get us!' The Marquis did not turn round. Madame Perrien called louder this time, not caring who heard her. 'Count Kalliovski has bought our souls!'

Sido stood frozen to the spot, not daring to move. She could see Madame Perrien holding on to the pillar with her white hand, watching as the Marquis walked away. A low rumble of thunder seemed to shake the earth, followed by a flash of lightning that snapped a rope that was holding up one of the glass chandeliers. It crashed down on to the table below, knocking the ice sculpture into the lake. Unforgiving raindrops of glass showered on to the painted marble floor.

Oblivious to everything, Madame Perrien started to walk slowly down the steps, her Pierrot costume soaked through, her white make-up running, her skirt of watered silk trailing in the mud through the broken glass, the wasted food, the spilt wine.

Sido had heard every word Madame Perrien had said. She had sounded flat, stripped of all hope, as if she had seen into the eternity of darkness and knew it to be waiting for her.

She had said, 'I am done for, I am dead.'

Chapter Eighteen

At the beginning of October the Marquis received a letter from Madame Claumont, who wrote to inform him that after the dreadful business with poor Madame Perrien she had decided to cross the Channel and and go to visit her friends in London. She advised the Marquis to do the same.

What dreadful business? The Marquis had no idea and immediately sent a servant to Paris to enquire after Madame Perrien's health. The man returned with a letter from Monsieur Perrien. It made shocking reading. Madame Perrien had been murdered. It was, wrote her husband, unimaginable to think who could have done such a terrible deed. She had been found wearing a necklace of red garnets. Her maid said that she had never seen it before. The matter was now in the hands of the police, although, since the country was on the brink of ruin, he doubted that much would come of their enquiries.

The Marquis was shaken to the very centre of his being by this news. He remembered with terrifying clarity what she had said that day of the fête: 'We have made a pact with the devil!' No, he wouldn't think about it, he would put this unpleasant subject out of his mind. It had nothing to do with him. What could he possibly have done? He was in no way responsible for her death.

Still, he felt ill, plagued by some malady that had upset his nerves, making him jump every time wheels were heard crunching on the gravel outside. He even started to see the ghost of his dead wife wandering silently around the house.

Finally, he took to his bed, complaining of a headache. A doctor was called for and he was bled. Despite all the treatments he was given, he still found little rest from the uncomfortable thoughts that kept tormenting him.

The Marquis's health recovered somewhat when he received an invitation to a banquet in the Opera House at the Palace of Versailles. The guest list included the officers of the Flanders Regiment, the Montmorency Dragoons, the Swiss Guards and other officers and noblemen. It convinced the Marquis that at last the counter-revolution had begun. He dressed in his finest suit, his tallest wig, and shoes with red heels and diamond buckles, and set off for Versailles in his gold-painted carriage. To Sido he looked like a canary in a gilded cage.

In the early hours of the next morning the Marquis

arrived home shouting '*Vive le Roi!*' at the top of his voice, waking up the whole household. Sido got sleepily out of bed to see what the commotion was about and looked over the banisters to see her father in the hall, swaying from side to side and bellowing.

'The counter-Revolution has started! The monarchy is to be restored to its former glory!' He lurched towards Jacques, the butler. 'Then you peasants will know your place once and for all.'

He stood in the hall, swaying like a full-rigged galleon on a sozzled sea of red wine.

'You should have heard how we drank to the King, and how we cried out with one voice, "Long may you reign! *Vive le Roi! Vive la Reine!*" You should have seen the Queen holding up the little Dauphin, a symbol of the continuation of kings, as the tears rolled down her cheeks! I tell you, we will deal with the rabble! We will bring down their Revolution! *Vive le Roi!*'

He spat the words in Jacques's face.

'No one toasted the nation – the royal bodyguard would have none of it ...' His voice was carried away in a wave of passion.

For a moment Sido thought the Marquis was about to capsize. Two footmen rushed to steady him, and he pushed them aside angrily, holding on to the banister as he slowly righted himself, though his wig, like the rigging of a ship, was starboard bent.

Sido watched as Jacques and the footmen did their best to help her father up the stairs. As he passed Sido on the landing he stopped and said, 'Who are you?'

'Ssh,' said Agathe, the scullery maid, 'not so loud. What if the Marquis were to hear you?'

'I wouldn't worry about it,' said Michel. 'What did he call the footmen? Furniture? He thinks we don't even exist when he's not around, let alone have a thought in our heads.'

'I tell you, the King had better watch out,' said Jean, 'otherwise he'll find himself abolished.'

'And the Marquis too,' added Bernard.

Just then the door to the kitchen opened and four of Count Kalliovski's grooms came in, their coats trailing water on the floor. No one in the kitchen said anything, for the Count's men looked as mean and as brutal as their master. Jean snapped his fingers, and Agathe went to get wine, bread and cheese for them.

'It took us an age to get here. The road to Versailles is blocked,' said one of the grooms.

'What do you mean, blocked?' asked Jean. 'Blocked by what?'

'Women. Women, heaven help us! Maybe ten, twenty, thirty thousand of them.'

'Why? What are they doing?'

'Gone to get bread, and to kill the Queen while they're about it.'

Agathe was so startled by this that she dropped the lid of an iron pan on the flagstones with a deafening crash.

'Where do all these women come from?' asked Bernard.

'Women from the market in Paris started it, outside the Hôtel de Ville. Then other women joined them, thousands of them, all armed with pitchforks, swords, guns; they're even dragging a cannon.'

Jean looked round at the kitchen staff. 'We'd best be on the lookout. I've heard stories of lootings, burnings and suchlike. We don't want them taking a fancy to this château as they march past.'

Michel started to chuckle.

'What's so funny about that?' asked Jean.

'Nothing,' said Michel. 'It's just that he went and made that there wall with too much sand, didn't he?'

'What do you mean?' asked Agathe.

'I mean,' said Michel importantly, seeing that he had everyone's attention, 'that the thing will fall down when it's pushed, like children's building bricks, and serve him right.'

'Well, whatever you do, don't tell the master,' said Jean.

One of the Count's men helped himself to another glass of wine and sat back in his chair. 'Don't worry. I overheard him say he didn't think they'd bother with you today.'

'Is that a threat or a promise?' asked Jean.

———◆———

Upstairs in the library, the Marquis, like a startled stag caught in a forest of books, was taken completely off guard by Kalliovski's unannounced arrival. It took him a moment or two to take in the Count's appearance. His hair, instead of being powdered white, was black: the Marquis would never have supposed the man to have such dark hair, and so much of it. Instead of his usual finery he was wearing a plain black woollen jacket and woollen breeches with black riding boots that did not even have a red heel. As he placed his hat on a table the Marquis saw that pinned to it was the revolutionary cockade. He stared at it in disbelief. Could all that he had heard about the Count be true?

'What foolish things you all did at your party this week, citizen,' said the Count, helping himself to a glass of cognac. 'Drinking to the health of the royal family, in short forgetting your loyalties to the nation. Really, citizen, was this wise?'

'Citizen, citizen,' repeated the Marquis. 'What nonsense is this?'

Kalliovski clicked his heels. 'I am Citizen Kalliovski, a friend of the Revolution, at your service.'

'Impossible!' said the Marquis. Then he laughed out loud. 'Very good! It is so long since I've seen you that I'd forgotten what a wit you are; you've come in disguise! Oh, very clever indeed.'

'I am in deadly earnest,' replied Citizen Kalliovski. 'I am here on business. As soon as the papers are signed, I will be gone.'

'What papers?'

'Have you already forgotten my very generous offer to you?'

The Marquis said nothing. He was still trying to take in Kalliovski's new appearance.

Kalliovski rang a bell and a footman entered. 'Fetch Mademoiselle Sido,' he ordered. He turned his attention back to the Marquis. 'You have heard of the death of Madame Perrien, I imagine?'

The Marquis had not encountered this bluntness in Kalliovski before, and it worried him.

'Why, yes. Dreadful.'

Kalliovski smiled.

'She asked you for your help, I believe.'

'I don't know what you're talking about,' said the Marquis hurriedly, his colour changing. Even under the make-up his cheeks glowed red.

'Then let me enlighten you. Madame Perrien asked for your help with her gambling debt. The foolish woman asked the wrong person, of course, for you possess nothing but unpaid bills.' He smiled again, the corners of his lips curling mockingly. 'There are angry craftsmen in Paris still waiting for their money for your ridiculous fête.'

'They will be paid in due course.'

'Not by me,' said Kalliovski, and he took from his pocket a necklace of red stones that he played with in his hand like a rosary.

The sight of it made beads of sweat appear on the Marquis's forehead.

'Madame Perrien paid the price for disloyalty,' said Kalliovski. 'Madame Claumont believes that by emigrating she will escape me. If she thinks she can get rid of me that easily she is very much mistaken.'

The Marquis bit his lip. The full impact of what had happened to Madame Perrien hit him like a blow to the stomach. He put out a hand to steady himself. With as much dignity as he could muster, he sat down heavily on a chair.

'Do you remember what we agreed when you last borrowed from me?'

The Marquis said nothing.

'Then let me remind you. You have a choice, albeit a limited one, but a choice nevertheless. I could let certain papers find their way into the right hands. I am sure there are people who would be most interested to know how your wife died.'

'No,' said the Marquis. His lips were white. 'You wouldn't do that, would you?'

'Without a moment's regret,' said Kalliovski.

'You were as much involved as I, if not more so,' said the Marquis, grasping at straws.

'That is where you are so very wrong. Nothing leads back to me. Your mark, your signature, is on everything. I made sure of it.'

The Marquis's mouth felt very dry.

'How can it be stopped?'

'By agreeing to this marriage. You see, citizen, the Revolution needs funds. The time has come for me to call in my debts.' Relishing the worried look on the Marquis's face, Kalliovski laughed. 'Unlike you I have familiarised myself with the terms of your late father's will. He did not much care for you, did he? But oh, how dearly he loved his pretty little granddaughter. On her wedding day she inherits a fortune, and it will all be mine.'

'I cannot let that happen! That cannot be the price I

have to pay!' cried the Marquis. 'After all I have done for you, all the introductions I have given you! Your rise in society would never have taken place if I had not facilitated it.'

'Believe me, I can do this. I will do this. Oh, how I have waited for you to fall so low! I have no mercy. I will show no mercy.'

The Marquis wiped his dripping forehead and regretted ever having had the fire lit.

'The body of Isabelle Gautier, now do correct me if I am wrong, was found in a field. Oh dear, I have forgotten. Was she found with a necklace similar to this? Do you remember?'

He held up the necklace with its bright red garnets that looked like drops of congealed blood.

The Marquis swallowed hard, his mouth ash-dry. He trembled as a tidal wave of sound came crashing into the room from outside, engulfing the house with drumming, screaming, screeching, a wailing of women.

'We will have bread!'

The Marquis got up to stare, bewildered, out of the window, at what appeared to be a never-ending stream of women passing close by his gates.

'What are they doing?'

'Going to fetch the King and Queen, that's if they don't kill them first. They plan to take them back to Paris, where the National Guard can keep an eye on them, make sure that they don't get carried away by any more such extravagant banquets. I tell you, citizen, soon the streets will run with blood and no one will care. Now, back to business.'

Above the noise the Marquis let out a thin cry. It was the sound of his fragile mind breaking, like fine porcelain.

———◆———

S ido knew the minute she entered the library exactly the reason for Kalliovski's visit. Her father, his face funereally grim, walked towards her just as a stone was thrown into the room, breaking the window and spraying glass on to the Persian rug. The Marquis stopped and stared transfixed as if the stone were a fragment from a comet.

'You've brought this on yourself,' said Kalliovski. 'Fortunately for you, today they're out for bigger fish. But never fear, your time will come, you can rest assured of that.' He walked slowly around Sido. 'Do you now agree to the marriage?'

'I can't think. My head hurts,' was all the Marquis could say. 'Later, leave it till later,' and he turned to look once more out of the window.

Citizen Kalliovski touched Sido's face. She recoiled from him, stifling the words that were about to erupt from her. Yet again, she knew that silence was her only means of survival.

'Such soft skin, velvety like rose petals. Still too thin,' he said.

Sido stood stock still, hardly daring to breathe, Kalliovski's hand now resting on her neck.

'There is no later,' he said, 'just an urgent now. So I take it that you agree to this marriage?'

'Have I any choice?' asked the Marquis.

'No,' said Kalliovski. 'It was, and it always will be, checkmate.'

Outside the women shouted:

'We want liberty!

We want bread!

Give us what we want

If you value your head!'

Chapter Nineteen

At fifteen, Yann looked older than his years. The gossip of where he had come from had long since ceased. It was generally agreed that he was a distant cousin of Juliette's whom the Laxtons had adopted.

Mr Trippen had turned out to be an excellent tutor. By now Yann could read and write, was accomplished with sword and pistol, was a graceful dancer, and proved to have an uncanny way with even the wildest of horses. His great love, though, remained the theatre. It was here that he felt the closest to Têtu and home. He would spend many an evening with Mr Trippen watching famous actors performing Shakespeare and Sheridan; but the shows he loved best always touched on magic.

He had seen the great illusionist Katterfelto lecture on natural philosophy, and had paid close attention while Katterfelto performed tricks with dice, cards, moneyboxes, medals and glasses, claiming that he knew the secrets of the occult.

Mr Laxton had been most impressed by the show, and Mr Trippen saw it as one of the wonders of the world. Only Yann stayed silent. He had not found in anything he had seen or heard what he was looking for.

The magic that he wanted to understand, Têtu alone had performed. He had read with interest about gold threads that the magicians used to achieve their illusions. Gold was lost to the human eye in the subdued light of the oil lamps, yet Yann knew for certain that Têtu had used no such devices. It made his magic all the more mysterious and tantalising.

He felt sure that such magic came from deep within. It must be a force as powerful as anger, grief, or love – you had somehow to connect with it to make it work. It did not rely on sleight of hand, or baggy trousers from which a never-ending stream of handkerchiefs appeared.

Today, as he walked through Covent Garden, the sun was shining watery bright. The city looked as if it had put on its best clothes for the occasion. London in all her finery thrilled Yann. The Piazza was, as always, full of people. There were street-criers selling bread and buns, shouting out their wares. Porters rushed here and there with parcels. Apprentices stood outside their masters' shops, begging passers-by to go in and peruse the goods, each one shouting a little louder than his neighbour.

He had finished his fencing lesson, and had a tingling

of tiredness and a good hunger. He was on his way to his favourite coffee-house to pick up the latest news when he saw a young couple, brightly dressed, with shiny rings in their ears and silver buttons on their clothes. The girl had dark eyes and jet-black hair, and she caught Yann's attention, not only because she was pretty but because she was speaking a language he understood. He stopped to listen, and the girl smiled at him.

'Would you like me to read your fortune, sir?' she said. 'Cross my palm with silver . . .'

Yann laughed and answered in Romany, 'Not now.'

The girl and the young man looked surprised. Taking in Yann's fine clothes, they asked uncertainly, '*San tu Rom?* Are you a gypsy?'

For a moment Yann hesitated. Then he said, '*Da, pralo.* Yes, brother,' accepting at long last the truth of what he was saying.

'Glad to meet you, brother. I am Talo Cooper and this is my wife Orlenda.'

They shook hands and the girl, smiling sweetly, asked, 'Are you from the royal city?'

'No, I am not from London. I am from Paris, the city across the water.'

After a while Yann walked away, looking back over his shoulder as Talo started to play his violin, the sound of his music filling the Piazza with its sweet, aching melody.

Yann sat in the coffee-house and ate his meal in silence, thinking back to the night of the Marquis's party when Topolain had died. Deep down he had never quite got over the idea that he was responsible for what had happened, that if he had kept silent that evening when he was asked what the Pierrot saw, everything might have been all right. The memory of it made him bring his fist down hard on the table.

'Steady on, sir!' said the gentleman opposite.

Yann looked up, almost surprised to find himself in the middle of this busy eating house. In his head he was floating in a soundless sea of unanswered questions, driftwood for the mind. He stood up, his plate unfinished, paid for his meal, and left.

As Yann walked away he thought about Têtu, as he often did, and he wondered if the magic and the answers he was hungry for lay not in the theatre but with the gypsies themselves. There was also another reason for seeking them out. This one was less simple, a tangle of feelings that try as he might he couldn't untie.

For all the Laxtons' kindness and generosity towards him and their genuine concern to make him feel at home, Yann had known ever since he had first arrived in Queen Square that it was Sido who should have been there, not him. He understood all too well the longing Mrs Laxton had to see her niece again, and when she told him about her sister and the accident, the girl with the sapphire-blue eyes whom he hardly knew had become a presence in his life. When he heard the news of her forthcoming marriage, his rage against Kalliovski surfaced once again.

The one comfort Yann took was the idea of how he would revenge himself on the man he held responsible for the murders of Topolain and Têtu. Magic would be his weapon of choice, though how he was to achieve the powers he needed he did not know.

It was getting dark as he neared Seven Dials, where he knew the gypsies camped in winter, and fog had begun to descend. The camp, a small city of tents, rolled out before him as far as the eye could see. It was not a place to go walking in unless you had business there. Groups of young men eyed up his fine clothes and wondered which gypsy girl had bewitched him enough for such a gentleman to come calling.

At last Talo Cooper appeared out of the fog.

'Orlenda knew you would come,' said Talo. 'She's never wrong in these matters. I will take you to my grandfather, Tobias Cooper. He is waiting for you.'

A very old man sat at the entrance of his tent, smoking his clay pipe. Yann sat down beside him and stared out at the thickening fog that hung down over the camp like the muslin petticoat of some monstrous giantess.

'What is it you want to know?' said the old man, looking at Yann as if he could see right into his heart.

'I want to know how to move objects without touching them.'

Tobias laughed. 'What makes you think I would know such things?'

Yann shrugged his shoulders. 'A feeling. I was brought up by a dwarf called Têtu, who was of the Romany blood. He worked a wooden Pierrot in a theatre in Paris. He did it all from the wings; he never once touched it, still, he could make it dance.'

'Then he knew the ways of the ancient magic. What

makes you think you have any right to such knowledge?'

'My mother could do the same, and my grandmother. I never knew them. My mother died when I was a few weeks old. I worked in the theatre with Têtu and the wooden doll. I made it talk, I read minds and sometimes I even foresaw the future. Then one day I saw and said too much, and my gifts left me. Shortly after that Têtu was shot and I was brought to the royal city. All that is left to me now is that I can still throw my voice; but it is a cheap circus trick, nothing more.'

'Show me.'

Out of the fog came the noise of a man wheezing, gasping for breath, asking Tobias for a pipe of tobacco.

Tobias smiled and said, 'Very good indeed. Choose an object.'

Yann picked the first thing that caught his eye, the old man's hat lying inside the tent.

Without touching it Tobias appeared to lift it off the ground where it hovered, as if listening to what was being said, before vanishing. In its place, suspended in mid-air, was a red rose.

'Yes!' said Yann excitedly. 'That is what I want to be able to do, that kind of magic.'

'You need, then, to be able to see into the spaces in between things,' said the old man. 'Can you do that?'

Yann squinted. 'I see nothing. There is nothing to see.'

'Then you are blind.'

'I'm not!'

'The eye plays tricks, fills in the gaps, so that we see

what we want to see. Objects are only solid because of our desire that they be so.'

This did not make sense to Yann. He said, 'A hat is a hat, a cup is a cup. I would prefer to trust in solid objects.'

'Well, then, don't come knocking on my door,' said Tobias with a shrug. 'Go on believing in the flat lands of your mind. I tell you no magic lies there. If you see the world that way, that is all you will ever see of the world.'

'I don't understand what you're talking about,' said Yann furiously. Had he come all this way just to be told he was blind?

'If you will let her, Orlenda will read your palm. That might help me to know what it is you are fighting,' said the old man.

He called for her and she came out of the tent with Talo. The firelight caught her pretty face, and she smiled at Yann, taking his almond-shaped hand in hers, looking carefully at his palm, moving it towards the light.

After a while she straightened up and said, 'I am sorry, grandfather. The gift has left me for tonight.'

'Are you afraid of what your hand might reveal, boy?' Tobias asked.

Yann felt annoyed, as if somehow he had been cheated of what he needed to know. He wasn't going to be so easily put off having his palm read.

'You don't frighten me, old man,' he said. 'I am not afraid.'

Orlenda stared deep into his eyes.

'You are a true gypsy, and you could be a great shaman.

You have a rare gift.' She stopped, letting go of his hand.

'Go on,' said the old man. 'Tell him. Isn't that why you came here, boy? To know what the future holds?'

'Yes,' said Yann through gritted teeth.

Orlenda took a deep breath as if going under water.

There were three things she told Yann that foggy afternoon, and it was the third one that shocked Yann to the core, as she had known it would. It made him feel as if he were standing on the edge of a ravine, looking down into nothingness. It was an abyss that he had seen before.

'You have survived one bullet, but another is waiting for you in the city over the water.'

Yann had got up without saying a word and started to walk away.

Tobias called after him. 'I will be here when you come back.'

By then he was running, feeling as if he were suffocating.

In Covent Garden Piazza, totally out of breath, he had bent over to take in huge gulps of soupy air. What a fool he had been. Did he truly believe in all that hocus pocus? He laughed out loud, a hard, bitter sound. This much he knew: he was done with trying to find out Têtu's secret. Magic belonged to a world he wanted nothing more to do with. If he was ever to take revenge on Kalliovski he would use a pistol, as any rational man would.

This was the moment when Yann decided to turn his back on notions of sorcery. He would concentrate on the opportunities given to him, and live like a gentleman. No one would ever take him for a gypsy again; no one would ever know where he had come from.

———◆———

Two years had passed since that momentous day. It was the summer of 1792, and Yann was now seventeen years old.

He had never told a soul what had happened at the gypsy camp, and he had long given up the idea of revenge. The burning flame of grief had lost its urgency: there was so much more he wanted to do. He had worked hard at his studies, acquitted himself well and was a credit to the Laxtons and to Mr Trippen. A future he couldn't have envisaged a few years ago was his for the taking – a place at Cambridge University this autumn, the possibility of becoming a lawyer. London suddenly seemed to be filled with pretty, flirtatious girls whom he met at private balls and public dances. He had made the pleasing discovery that young ladies liked his company, would giggle, flounce their curls, pout and generally look charming to get his attention.

'It's because you dance so well, Mr Margoza,' Sophie Padden had whispered to him.

The Laxtons' house in Queen Square had become a meeting point for many of the émigrés who now found themselves in London, under what they felt to be grey skies and diminishing circumstances.

Mr and Mrs Laxton's parties were renowned for excellent food and talk. The conversation was often heated, and the ideas expressed both radical and conservative.

The distant drum of Revolution could be heard loud and clear across the water here in London. It had started out as a glimmer of hope for a new generation, when slavery would be no more, when men and women would be equal, and people would be judged, not by their birth, but by whom they were, not divided by race, class, or creed. Yann believed passionately in these ideas.

At one supper party he had met Charles Cordell for the first time. Madame Claumont, a lady from Paris, had also been amongst the guests, along with her friend, Sir John Randall.

Yann, as he often did, listened intently rather than join in. But then Sir John Randall said, 'We have heard everyone else's views round this table except yours, sir. Speak up – they say Revolution is a young man's sport. What have you to say for yourself?'

It was not from a lack of opinions that Yann had kept silent. 'I thought when the Bastille fell that all men might truly be free,' he said. 'It struck me as a good enough reason for stopping time and starting the clocks anew: a fresh beginning when all men would be equal. But what I hear and read is that the people of France are no freer than before. A whole lot of wigs, hats and crowns will have changed heads, but it looks as if the new masters will be as bad as the old.'

'Wise words, young man,' said Sir John Randall.

'Alas,' sighed Mr Laxton, 'what bonfires we make of Utopian dreams.'

'I'm sure the poor will forever help the rich become

richer,' continued Yann. 'Whatever flag you fly, whatever song you sing, whatever church you worship in, it will always be the same. What's the point of playing at politics? All that matters is people.'

'Steady on, sir, that is going too far!' said Sir John.

Charles Cordell looked with interest at this young man who spoke with such passion, and he asked, 'So if you have no alliance to king or country, what does interest you?'

'What it is to be human,' said Yann.

'Go on,' said Cordell. 'I'm listening.'

'Well, sir, as far as I see it, we're all housed in the same skin, be it black, white or brown. The same blood pulses through all our veins, the same heart beats. Yet some men believe that through birth and privilege they stand above everyone else. I don't believe that. I think that kings have had their day, and the future should be in the hands of the people.'

'These are revolutionary views indeed,' said Sir John Randall, taken aback by Yann's zeal.

'And views I violently disagree with!' interrupted Madame Claumont. 'There must be order, otherwise society will collapse. People only thrive when they know their place. Absolute monarchy is the only possible way to ensure this.'

'Too late, my dear madam,' said Cordell. 'Your good king didn't seize his chance to put down the Revolution. Now it is too late. With Marat as leader, the Revolution has given birth to a reign of terror that is growing in power day by day. I believe that in the end it will rule everything, destroy everything.'

⸻ ◆ ⸻

It was shortly after this that Madame Claumont disappeared. Her body was retrieved at low tide, half buried in the Thames mud near Cheyne Walk, her little dog whining beside her.

Henry Laxton accompanied Sir John Randall to identify the body. Madame Claumont was wearing a necklace that was caked in mud, like the rest of her. A red garnet caught Mr Laxton's eye. He took the necklace away with him, washed it until its colour was restored, and studied it carefully. It was, as he had suspected, a red necklace like those Charles Cordell had described to him, and the sight of it made him feel sick to the stomach. Madame Claumont had been a good client of the bank. What part, he wondered, had Kalliovski played in her murder?

A terrible, undeniable truth struck him. This was the man Sido was to marry. How could he possibly stand by, knowing what he did, and let her be sacrificed to this monster? Something must be done before it was too late.

Chapter Twenty

These days Yann was feeling that the past was well behind him. Then, with three simple words, the world that he thought was his to inherit slipped through his fingers like sand. It was what Orlenda had predicted, and what Yann had chosen to bury somewhere deep in his unconscious mind: that his destiny and his fate lay across the water.

On a hot summer's evening, with the study door open on to the garden, Mr Laxton had read him a letter he had just received from Cordell. The three words that stood out, illuminated diamond bright, were: 'Têtu is alive.'

It seemed that Têtu, after three years working in provincial theatres where he knew Kalliovski would not find him, had returned to Paris, confident that with all his other activities the Count's interest in him had waned.

He had been to see Cordell, and was proud and delighted to hear how well Yann had acquitted himself.

Cordell had asked Têtu if he knew anyone who could be trusted to get Sido de Villeduval safely to England, and Têtu had suggested Yann. If Sido refused to abandon her father, then the last resort would be to try to get them both out. For that they would need papers and passports.

As Yann listened, he knew that his future lay not here, but in France; and he remembered with a shudder Orlenda's three predictions and realised that one, if not two, had already come true. Orlenda had told him that he was to take comfort that Têtu was still alive. The next thing she had predicted puzzled him greatly and made him sure that she must be wrong about the dwarf. She told him he had already met the only person he would ever love.

'What is her name?' Yann had asked.

'It begins with S.'

All he could think to ask was, 'Will we be happy?'

'This love could be the death of both of you,' said Orlenda.

Only now could he acknowledge that she had meant Sido – not Sophie Padden. Perhaps, if he was honest with himself, he had always known it, even from the very first moment he had seen her.

The last of Orlenda's three predictions had been the one that had terrified him the most and made him run away. It had been the reason he had wanted no more to do with magic. Finally he realised that there was no more running to be done; he would have to go back and face the bullet. Perhaps, like the magician, this time he would be able to catch it.

Mr Laxton put down the letter and said firmly, 'These are very dangerous times. You don't have to do this.'

'But I do,' said Yann. 'I can't explain why. All I can tell you is that I have known this day was coming. I have been waiting a long time for that letter to arrive.'

His determination to give up all that he had earned took Henry Laxton completely by surprise.

'What about university?'

'It can wait. But Sido can't.'

Mr Laxton paused. 'Yann, as I said, this is not going to be easy. Kalliovski will not take kindly to anyone trying to take away what belongs to him. You are dealing with a very dangerous man.'

'That makes it all the more important that we succeed.'

'In that case I will need a couple of weeks to get all the papers in order; then you can go.'

Mr Trippen sat back at the table after a good Sunday lunch and listened to all Yann had to say about his decision.

'Well,' he said, 'if the fates are calling you, then go you must. "There is a tide in the affairs of men" ...'

'Do you think,' interrupted Yann, well-versed in his tutor's love of Shakespearean quotes, 'we're simply puppets in the hands of destiny, or do we have the power to change our fate?'

Mr Trippen contemplated the question, while the youngest of the Trippens played on the floor with a ball Yann had bought him. His sisters sat listening, looking adoringly at the young man in his fashionable coat, each one wishing that his black eyes would rest on her and twinkle, if only for a moment.

'It is a question,' replied Mr Trippen, 'that philosophers, playwrights, poets and artists will go on asking until the world stops spinning and the sun is snuffed out like a candle. A question, my dear sir, that your Mr Trippen has struggled with and has no answer for. Though I did once know a man in the Queen Anne Tavern who claimed he had the solution, if not the answer.'

'What was it?' asked Yann.

'Aha!' laughed Mr Trippen. 'It lay, according to him, at the bottom of a good tankard of port wine. In other words, my young sir, the question is king, and the answers are different for all men.'

'Why don't you do magic tricks any more, Yann?' said the eldest girl impatiently. 'You used to be able to make apples appear from nowhere and do card tricks. Now all you do is talk like Papa and use long words.'

'My pudding blossom,' said her father, 'you have a very good point. Well, young sir, we are all ears.'

'I stopped believing in magic,' said Yann softly.

Mrs Trippen came into the room, gathering up the children to take them to visit her mother.

'Don't be long,' called Mr Trippen, 'oh flower of my life, apple of my eye, the reason my heart keeps on beating!'

Mrs Trippen smiled cheerfully. She enjoyed owning furniture weighted down with the gravity of a healthy income. Life was good.

The front door closed and the babbling-brook voices of the children disappeared, leaving only the muted sounds of horses' hooves outside, and inside, the ticking of a clock and the chirping of the two canaries whose cages hung in the window. Mr Trippen brought out his snuffbox.

'Many men,' said Mr Trippen, taking a large pinch of snuff, which immediately brought on a bout of sneezing, 'spend their lives living in the wrong corner of their souls, mainly out of fear of what they might find on the other side.'

He took out his handkerchief and blew his nose.

'When I first met you, I would say that you were the most mysterious, magical young man I had ever had the privilege to run into. In the last couple of years it has struck me that you have been merrily trying to board up that side of yourself, close the shop, put up the shutters, so to speak, and old Trippen has noticed the effect it has had on his young Hamlet's countenance. The "To be or not to be" question has brought about a lopsided quality to your gait. Instead of standing up straight, your right shoulder slopes as if one part of you is in constant disagreement with the other half.'

'Yes,' said Yann, 'I recognise that. What should I do?'

'Whether 'tis nobler in the mind to suffer being ordinary or take arms against a sea of troubles, and by opposing them . . . except that you are *extraordinary*. Celebrate the magic that you have at your fingertips. Stand up straight, put your head above the parapet.'

'Aren't you disappointed that I won't go to Cambridge?'

'No,' said Mr Trippen. 'I never thought you would. Doesn't mean I didn't think you could. My advice, for what it is worth, is this: face your demons.'

Yann knew what Mr Trippen meant. While there was still time, he must go back and find the gypsies.

Early the next day he took his black horse and rode out to Hainault Forest, to the Fairlop Fair. Here, each year, gypsies from all over the country gathered under a huge oak tree, making the most of the chance to gossip and trade in the horses and ponies penned in a hastily erected corral. Beneath its canopy of leaves they set up stalls selling trinkets, food and drink, and the local farmers and their families crowded the little booths to see the puppet shows, to watch the boxing matches, bear-dancing, and sword-throwing, to bob for apples, and have their fortunes told.

Yann arrived in the morning, but it was evening by the time he found out where Tobias Cooper was. He had to ride some three miles before he smelt the woodsmoke and saw the camp nestled at the edge of the forest.

Tobias walked down the green grassy path to meet him as the sun, round and red, was going down behind the trees in a burst of colour. He embraced Yann.

'I knew you would return,' he said, 'and I know we have not much time, because you are going back across the water.'

He took Yann to his tent and they sat down together in front of the fire where the kettle bubbled away.

'Now let us try again,' said Tobias, as if no time had passed. A cup rose into the air and the kettle tipped and poured tea into it, without the help of a human hand. Yann had seen Têtu do this many times.

'What do you see?' asked Tobias.

'A cup having tea poured into it by an invisible hand.'

'I did not ask you to look,' said Tobias. 'Looking is what all fools do. I asked you to *see*. That is the difference. Now try again. Look at the spaces in between the objects, then tell me what you see.'

This time a burning stick was lifted from the fire and stood on end like a torch.

'A burning stick,' said Yann, completely at a loss. 'What else is there to see?'

'Everything. You see with your eyes. I am asking you to see from here.'

He pressed his thumb hard in the middle of Yann's forehead. 'This is how you must learn to see. Not with your eyes. They will only deceive you, as I told you before. They are so easily tricked. Now drink.'

Yann held the cup tight. He needed the warmth of the tea for comfort. He said, 'I stopped believing.'

'That goes without saying,' said Tobias.

It was not until the moon had taken sovereignty over the night sky that Tobias and Yann left the camp and started to walk through the forest, where the trees stood like sentinels watching for intruders.

Yann kept tripping up; he had lost the basic skills that he once took for granted. Tobias, on the other hand, walked on as if it were broad daylight. At last they came to a clearing, an eerie place surrounded by oak trees on top of which the moon seemed to be balancing. It was a circular clearing, off which led seven paths. Yann had the sensation of walking not on the mossy ground but on a membrane that divided two worlds.

Tobias sat down in the middle of the clearing, Yann beside him, and started to play a penny whistle. It made no sound, or at least none that Yann could hear. After a while, lights began to appear down each path. Phantom-like figures came into focus from nowhere. They seemed no more substantial than mist. Yann watched, hypnotised, as on the path directly in front of him stood a wizened woman.

'Who called for me?' she asked.

Tobias stood up and gave a deep bow. 'I did. I have brought the young man as I promised I would.'

Yann watched as she seemed to fade and then become whole again.

'Come here,' she called out to him.

Then the strangest thing happened. Without moving, without taking a step, he left his body. He could see himself still standing next to Tobias. The old woman held her hands out and he took them. He was being lifted off his feet, up into the night sky, whirling round and round, higher and higher until he was above the treetops, almost touching the moon.

Then, without a word, the old woman let go of his hands and he fell back down to earth. He felt the two parts of himself collide, become one again. So great was the blow that he remembered nothing more.

He woke the next day to find Tobias Cooper sitting at the opening of his tent, filling his clay pipe, talking to Orlenda and Talo. They greeted Yann with warm smiles, Orlenda showing him her little baby before they set off to the fair.

Had last night been a dream? Yann wondered.

'I have been thinking. Have you a talisman?' asked Tobias.

'No,' said Yann, feeling strangely different, as if some great burden had been lifted from him.

'Every tawny boy needs a talisman. You need one more than most,' said Tobias, and he took from his pocket a small bag and brought out a perfect seashell.

'*Baro seroeske sharkuni*, the very shell of the shells,' he said, handing it to Yann. Yann examined it closely. He had never seen one like it.

'It is the shell of a sea snail, and holds great magic. I have been waiting a long time to hand on this talisman. It is meant for you.'

'No,' said Yann firmly. 'It is too precious. I cannot take it.'

'You must, for you are alone. But you have a friend,

Têtu, and I believe he meant you to find us. He wouldn't have wanted you to return until you had learned to accept your powers without fear, until you stopped hiding from what Orlenda saw in your hand.'

Yann knew then how foolish he had been. 'I had hoped that the S might have stood for Sophie Padden.'

'And it didn't, did it?' chuckled Tobias.

'No. No, indeed, it did not. Nor did it stand for Sarah Hinds.'

'Though both, no doubt, taught you a lot.'

'Maybe,' said Yann with a mischievous smile.

'You are a king amongst the gypsies, Yann Margoza. Take the talisman, wear it with pride and it will keep you safe.'

That night they returned to the heart of the forest. This time the old woman was seated in the middle of the clearing. A fire was now burning away with a kettle above it. In amongst the trees hovered the ghost-like figures Yann had seen earlier.

'Go to her,' said Tobias, standing on the edge of the clearing.

The old woman patted the ground next to her and Yann sat down.

Close up, her face looked as wise as the earth is broad. In her eyes he could see all that was known and all that was still to be learned. It felt as though she was looking straight through him. A pain struck him in the middle of his forehead as if she was pressing a finger through his skull.

'Give me your hand,' said the old woman. Yann felt

her papery skin. Her fingers looked like twigs, all twisted and gnarled, her nails like seashells. He flinched, for there was such power in her grip, and suddenly everything disappeared and he was walking across a field, towards a road lined with tall poplars. He could see the wheels of an upturned carriage spinning round and round in a ditch, and started to run towards it. The wind rustled in the trees. A young woman was lying by the roadside, all broken like a china doll. A man was holding her, his horse grazing a little way off; a flurry of autumn leaves swept across the field and there, in a furrow, he could see an infant, her leg broken, her little face contorted with pain. He knelt down beside her, wondering if she too were dead.

With a jolt he was aware of being back in the clearing. The fire and the old woman had disappeared. Yann looked around and for the first time he saw spider-threads of light streaming from all the ghostly figures, over-arching him like a huge cat's cradle, until with the sound of a violin string snapping they were gone.

Yann turned to look at Tobias. He too had threads of light coming from his fingers. And he watched, astounded, as the old man flicked them as a fisherman might cast his line to catch a fish.

'I can see,' shouted Yann, 'I can see!'

'At last,' said Tobias. 'Now we can start.'

It was a week later, early on a bright and sunny morning, that Yann, having made his farewells to the Laxtons and the Trippens, caught the Paris-bound coach from the Strand, the perfect picture of a young English gentleman misguidedly off to visit Paris for the first time. On him were papers and passports and enough money to get out the Marquis de Villeduval and his daughter Sido.

Chapter Twenty-two

On the eleventh of August, the Duchesse de Lamantes, worried for the Marquis de Villeduval's safety, sent a messenger to inform the Marquis of the serious situation in Paris, and to tell him that the throne of France had been demolished, the Swiss Guards massacred and the royal family arrested. It was the Duchesse de Lamantes' opinion that they were no longer safe. She also thought the Marquis should know that Count Kalliovski was calling for the execution of the King.

In the light of all these developments, the Duchesse de Lamantes was sure that her friend could not now countenance his daughter marrying such a man, and she advised him to leave France at the first possible opportunity.

The Marquis de Villeduval refused to receive the Duchess's messenger. He no longer trusted the written word, for he saw it as the sword of Damocles hanging over him. The trouble was that since Kalliovski's last visit, reality had become a stranger to him. While the frayed edges of his sanity daily unwound, he chose to remain locked away in his suite of rooms, studying his collection of shoe buckles and remembering which balls, banquets and fêtes they had been worn at. Nightly, now, he walked through the château's empty salons while ghosts danced before him, dressed in all their finery and tall powdered wigs.

It was left to Sido to read the letter, and after that she knew that it was all too late for herself and her father. France, like a pan of milk left too long on a hot stove, was about to boil over.

She slipped downstairs to join the servants in the kitchen, where they crowded round the Duchess's messenger.

'I've never seen anything like it. Why, the very air in the city is electric! At midnight the church bells rang out from steeple to steeple – that's the tocsin that alerts you to danger – followed by a thousand drums and the boom of guns. I'll wager not one person slept, for the terror those bells awoke in them.'

'Oh dear lord, what will become of us?' said Agathe.

'Quiet,' said Jean. 'Go on. What happened then?'

'Yesterday morning, at dawn, the citizens rose up and

marched to the Tuileries Gardens. They were shouting "Down with the veto, down with the tyrant." The troops from the south sang the Marseillaise. They were armed to the teeth – guns, knives, bayonets, swords, you name it. They hacked the Swiss Guards to death. They didn't stand a chance – the King just abandoned them. Only interested in his own skin.'

'Oh, lordy lord!' wept Agathe.

Jean sighed. 'A bonfire of hate has been ignited. God alone knows what earthly force can put it out now.'

'Did you see anything else?' asked Luc, putting his arm round Lucille's waist.

'Did I see anything else? What these eyes didn't see! All the waters of France won't wash these images away. They're burned into me with a red-hot branding iron.'

'Tell us, then.'

'Well, when I arrived at the Tuileries by the Palais Royal entrance, the walls were pock-marked with gun- and cannon-fire. I could hear the sound of crashing plates and dishes coming from the royal kitchens – pots and pans thrown all over the place, everybody snatching what they could, either to break or more likely to keep as souvenirs. In the wine cellars I saw a sea of outstretched hands, all fumbling in the sand to pull out bottles of the King's fine wine. They broke the bottles open in their haste to drink and the wine spilt on the floor, mingling with the blood of the corpses. What a shambles! In the chapel, oh Lord, what I saw! All that blood, all them bodies, all them flies, and the smell! The sound of the rabble as it trampled on thousands of fragments of price-less porcelain.'

Sido listened silently. Lucille began to weep.

'And the rest of Paris?' asked Bernard.

'There are fires burning all over the city. The citizens are breaking into the aristocrats' houses, looting, killing their servants, smashing their furniture and burning and destroying anything of value.'

'Will they do the same here?' asked Lucille. She was almost beside herself with fear.

'Who knows? When I left they were calling for the blood of the nobility to wash the streets of Paris clean, and they'd started to tear down buildings where aristocrats had taken refuge.'

'Enough,' interrupted Jean. 'You're frightening everyone.'

'Well, you asked. I'm only telling you how things stand.'

By the time the messenger had left, Sido could see what would happen next.

'I have a wife and children,' said Michel Floret, the gardener. 'I'm afraid to be found here.'

This seemed to go for all the servants, who sorrowfully and apologetically made their excuses and filed out of the kitchen: even Lucille, who, clasping Sido's hands and with tears rolling down her face, said, 'I'm so sorry to leave you, I really am sorry, but I can't stay. I don't want to die. I'm too young.'

'I know,' said Sido. 'Don't worry. You go home with Luc.'

Only two stayed sitting at the kitchen table, Jean and Bernard.

'*Eh bien,*' said Jean, getting out a bottle of wine. 'There is nothing more for it. We'll just have to sit it out and make plans for our escape if the château is attacked.'

'I agree,' said Bernard.

'No,' said Sido, 'you must go too. I shall stay with my father.'

'But mademoiselle, it's not safe for you here. You must get him to understand.'

Sido tried to look calm. 'As you know, the Marquis has put all his hope for our survival in the wall. He will not leave.'

Bernard raised his hands to the air and let out a whistle. 'That wall is a farce,' he said.

'What do you mean?' asked Sido.

'His labourers hated him for putting the rents so high and taking them away from the land. Their revenge was to use more sand in the mix than they should have.'

'I don't understand,' said Sido.

'It means the wall will collapse if it's attacked,' said Bernard. 'It will fall as easily as a child's castle of bricks.'

Sido felt weak and sat down. 'Even more reason for you to go, then.'

'No,' said Jean firmly, 'we're not leaving you. Someone has to stay and help.' He poured her a glass of wine. 'Though I think I speak for both of us when I say that we are staying out of respect for the late and great Marquis, your uncle Armand de Villeduval, and your beloved mother.'

Bernard lifted his glass. 'Tell you this much – if your uncle were still here, his servants would have fought to the bitter end to protect you all.'

'I thank you,' said Sido.

———◆———

That evening the Marquis, unaware that anything was wrong, sat down as usual to supper. Annoyed to find that it was late, he rang the bell angrily.

With a heavy heart, Sido opened the door to the dining chamber.

'It is quite intolerable to be kept waiting at my own table,' he snapped. 'I have guests.'

'Papa, all but two of your servants left this morning.'

'Did I give you permission to speak?' asked the Marquis.

'No, papa, but I think it might be wise to make plans just—'

'You think,' he interrupted sarcastically. 'You think? And of what significance are your miserable thoughts? You are just about bearable when silent. When you speak I find your presence quite insupportable.'

Sido could take it no longer. She felt overwhelmed by all that she had been told, and with the knowledge that the wall, like her father's mind, appeared to be crumbling. Tears welled up, and the colour rushed to her face.

'What have I done that you should hate me so much?' she cried.

The Marquis looked up at an invisible point just above

her head and rang the bell again with force.

'Please tell me,' said Sido.

He still refused to look at her. 'Been born, and once born, been a mere girl.'

'Is that my only crime?'

'How dare you ask such impertinent questions in front of such distinguished company? Leave the room. I wish to see no more of you.'

'Why?' said Sido. 'Why, when we should stand together, do you treat me so?'

'Be quiet. I will not be spoken to in this way. You moan and groan like some peasant.'

The Marquis got up and walked towards the door. 'Tell my valet that I shall be dining in my apartment.'

'He has left, like the rest of the servants,' said Sido.

'Out of my way,' said the Marquis as he pushed past her, his head held high. 'My guests are waiting.'

After he had gone Sido slid miserably down on to the floor. Who could save them now? Kalliovski?

She went back down to the kitchen to find Jean still sitting at the table.

'I take it he didn't like what he was told?'

'He wouldn't listen. He loathes me. He said it would have been better if I'd never been born. I should have died along with my mother, then he would have been rid of me.'

'Don't say that, mademoiselle. It would have been a terrible waste.'

'If I had been a son, would he have loved me? And if I didn't limp? Everything I do is wrong.'

Jean looked at Sido. 'If it is of any comfort, mademoiselle, I don't think the Marquis cares for anyone or anything, apart from his possessions. He is like an actor who needs the whole stage to himself. There is no room for anyone else, not even his daughter.'

'But what can I do?' said Sido.

'Nothing. No matter how much you try to please him, even if, God forbid, you lay down your life for him, he will never love you. It would be best just to accept this, and let acceptance make you stronger. I am sorry to speak out of turn, mademoiselle, but that's how I see it. Is there no other family you can turn to?'

'There's my mother's sister in London. She is married to an Englishman, a Mr Laxton.'

'Well, then,' said Jean, 'what's the sad face for? At least you know there's someone who will be pleased to see you.'

'Yes, but how would I ever get to England?' said Sido.

'Goodness knows, but if things carry on as they are, you may be glad to have relatives there. If it is of any comfort, Bernard and I have worked out an escape route from the château in case the mob should come. Shall I show you?'

He took a lantern from the dresser and guided her out of the kitchen and down the steps that led to the wine cellar. 'Follow me,' he said, pushing back a small wooden door and lifting the lantern high to show her a long tunnel.

'Where does that go?' asked Sido with surprise.

'To the stables. It was built so that your father would not have to see any tradesmen unloading wagons. You never know, his vanity may yet save us.'

Sido smiled.

'That's better. Bernard is going to keep a carriage ready night and day. Does that make you feel a little less fearful?'

———◆———

For the next two nights Sido hardly slept. Certain that they would be attacked at any moment, she watched from her window, looking for lights and figures amongst the dark shadows. Only as dawn broke did she allow herself to lie down.

A week later, what Sido had been dreading finally happened. At two o'clock in the morning there was a sudden terrible sound that broke the stillness of the night. She looked into the garden and saw a small army of people advancing on the château, carrying torches and singing loudly, emboldened by wine.

Quickly she dressed and ran to the Marquis's bed-chamber, just as Jean burst through the door. The Marquis was standing by the window in his robe, looking in disbelief at the crowd down below.

'Who let them in?'

'No one did, papa. They stormed the wall.'

'Impossible.'

At that moment the window broke. A burning torch landed on the floor and rolled towards the four-poster bed, setting the drapery alight. Sido grabbed a jug and threw water on the flames, while Jean seized the hangings and tried to smother them. It was no use. No sooner had he done so than another torch was thrown in. Downstairs they could hear the sound of breaking glass and hammering on the front door.

'We must leave,' said Jean. 'They'll be in the house at any moment.'

'Not without my buckles,' said the Marquis. 'I won't leave without them.'

He pushed open the door to the antechamber. The room was ablaze and he staggered back from the billowing smoke.

'Hurry!' shouted Jean as the Marquis desperately tried to beat out the flames to get to his beloved buckles. 'If you don't come now, we're leaving you.'

The front door gave way and a sound like a wave came crashing into the hall.

In desperation, the Marquis grabbed a red-hot buckle and let out a piercing scream as the burning silver branded his hand. Like a wounded child he allowed Jean to lead him down the secret passages, while all around them they could hear the sounds of furniture being broken, ornaments destroyed, and the roar of the fire about to engulf the château.

They rushed down to the cellar, closing the door behind them and stacking baskets of bottles against it in the hope of delaying the mob. Jean went ahead as they groped their way along the dark musty corridor that led to the stables.

Bernard was waiting, trying to calm the two terrified

horses that he had harnessed to a carriage. The other horses he had let run wild.

The Marquis, on seeing that it was not his finest carriage, demanded that the horses be unharnessed immediately and his gilded coach used instead.

'Get in!' shouted Bernard, losing his patience.

'Surely you don't expect me to travel in a carriage intended for the use of servants?'

'Please, papa,' implored Sido, who was already inside. She looked back and saw the château lit red against the sky as the mob began to move toward the stables.

With great presence of mind, Bernard and Jean pushed the Marquis into the carriage and set off at great speed. The mob ran after them, throwing stones that ricocheted off the coach, one breaking the back window and hitting the Marquis on the head. They were all thrown across the carriage as it swayed dangerously from side to side, bumping over stones from the fallen wall.

There was no choice as to direction. An angry crowd of peasants was waiting, blocking the road leading to Versailles and Normandy.

The Marquis, stunned, sat in the corner of the carriage. Blood trickled down his forehead as he looked back at his beloved château, now consumed by flames.

They reached Paris just as the gates were opening. The turnkey, who was more used to seeing people trying to leave than entering, opened the carriage door and sniffed at the all too familiar smell of burnt clothes and hair.

He smiled at the Marquis, who was sitting in his dressing robe, without his wig, and said with relish, 'Now you're one of us. No more the great man, eh, citizen?'

The Marquis, who had appeared to be in a trance for most of the journey, looked at the turnkey, astonished.

'You are without doubt the ugliest man I have ever had the misfortune to encounter,' he said in a dismissive tone.

'What's that?' said the turnkey, leaping inside the carriage and grabbing hold of him. 'You say that again if you dare.'

'Please,' begged Sido, 'my father is not himself. He has lost his mind. Surely you can see that?'

The turnkey looked at her and then threw the Marquis back on to the seat of the carriage like a sack of flour.

'Are you here by appointment, my man?' asked the Marquis.

'Am I what, citizen?'

'You see,' said Sido, 'he is not well.'

The turnkey brushed himself down and looked at Jean. 'And who are you, citizen?'

'This is a friend of the family,' said Sido quickly. 'He

is helping me take my father to the nuns at the Hôtel-Dieu. They will care for him there.'

Jean took the basket that he had had the presence of mind to bring with him and handed it to the turnkey. 'It must be hungry work, checking all these coaches for traitors to the Revolution. I admire your dedication, citizen.'

The turnkey's mouth began to water as he pulled back the cloth and looked hungrily at the pâté, bread and cheese. His face was so thin that his cheekbones made a bridge across the flat planes of his features. He took the basket. 'Away with you, and don't let me see him come this way again. Is that understood?'

———◆———

Early as it was, the heat of the city wrapped itself round them as they made their way through the eerie, deserted streets.

Sido had asked Bernard to drive to the Duchesse de Lamantes' townhouse on the Place Royale, which was the only address she knew. They arrived to find it full of packing cases and the Duchess preparing to leave. The Marquis sat down on a crate, staring before him like a statue, while the Duchess, in dismay, addressed herself to Sido.

'My dear child, why on earth did you come to Paris? It's not safe here. I am leaving, going abroad. Did your father not read my letter?'

'No,' said Sido.

'Oh dear.' Almost in a whisper, she asked, 'And have you seen Kalliovski?'

'No.'

The Duchess looked around, terrified, as if she expected him to be standing nearby listening, like a cat waiting for a mouse to move.

'I have found someone who will help me to escape. I advise you to do the same. You won't be able to leave without a passport, though, and they are like gold dust. Have you any money?'

'No,' said Sido, 'we have nothing.'

'Oh dear, oh dear, did the Marquis not make any arrangements?'

'No.'

The Marquis, his hand held out before him, muttered, 'My collection of buckles was even more valuable than the King's.'

'I do advise you,' said the Duchess, ignoring him, 'to leave here as soon as you can. They are arresting all aristocrats as traitors. The prisons are full. It will end in a bloodbath.' She went over to her desk and scribbled something on a piece of paper. 'By all means stay, but I beg of you, if Kalliovski does come looking for you, not to tell him where I've gone. This is the person you should use to get you out of Paris. I will tell him you need help.' She glanced at the Marquis. 'I will pay him to get you both out.'

'Thank you,' said Sido, 'oh, thank you for your kindness.'

'In these troubled times we must support each other,'

said the Duchess, kissing Sido. 'Goodbye. I hope we will all meet again in London.'

The Marquis looked very grave and replied, 'I knew, of course, the minute whalebone corsets went out of fashion that things were coming to a pretty pass.'

Sido watched as the Duchess left and then looked at the piece of paper she had been given. On it was written the name of a Mr Tull.

The gates to Paris were now barricaded, for there was a tangible fear that the enemies of France were poised to take the city. Everyone coming or going was a potential spy, or a counter-Revolutionary trying to escape, every coach suspected of carrying an aristocrat or a member of the clergy. Papers were lingered over and bribes given.

Yann and his fellow passengers stood in a line. A lady from their party became quite alarmed to see her portmanteau opened and her garments sniggered over by the National Guard.

Lefort the gatekeeper, whose domain this was, looked on like a small king of his castle. He had a squint, and dark bushy eyebrows that dominated his face and made up for the lack of expression in his eyes. He was proud of his work, showed no mercy to man or priest, let no one slip through his iron grip. He walked to and fro in his own bilious cloud of tobacco smoke, occasionally spitting out large yellowish gobbets of saliva.

They all heard the mob before they saw what had brought it tearing on to the street. A large coach painted yellow, not unlike the one the King and Queen had used for their failed flight to Varennes, was waiting to leave the city. Its grandeur was causing quite a lot of commotion.

'It's the King trying to escape again,' jeered one of the onlookers.

Lefort quickly lost interest in the passengers from London and was walking over to the yellow coach when out of nowhere came a group of angry men and women, all wearing the red bonnet of liberty, armed with pitch-forks, their sleeves rolled up ready for action. Yann had never seen such hatred as he saw now, etched upon their faces.

The coachman looked terrified as one of the men leapt at the yellow door, forcing it open with animal ferocity so that it fell off its hinges.

'Shame on you,' he shouted at the occupants, 'trying to smuggle out the wealth that belongs to France! You're traitors to the Revolution! The enemy within, that's what you be. Well, you'll soon see how we deal with the likes of you.'

The husband and wife and their two terrified children were unceremoniously dragged out, screaming. Yann, who had a sudden urge to help them, moved forwards. He was stopped immediately by the hand of a fellow passenger who whispered urgently to him, 'It isn't worth it, sir. They'll have you thrown in prison for your efforts. Believe me, there's nothing we can do. Just thank the Lord you're not a Frenchman.'

Lefort waved away the cloud of tobacco smoke. Seeing that he had caught himself a mighty catch, he had no interest whatsoever in the London stagecoach. Without so much as a second glance, he let it go.

Yann sat back in his seat. From the window he caught a last glimpse of a child's frightened face. What had happened to this city, to its citizens, that they should have so much hatred for their fellow men?

The gentleman whose hand had restrained Yann said, 'This is a godless city. I get my business done as fast I can and get out again. Wouldn't catch me staying here any longer than necessary. It's a tinderbox that will self-ignite and go up in flames.'

'What will happen to those poor people?' asked the woman whose clothes the National Guard had found so amusing.

'They'll be arrested and sent to prison as cattle fodder for the masses.'

The coach rumbled on over the Pont Neuf where the statue of Louis the Sun King had been torn down. In the distance Yann could see bonfires still burning.

'So this is Paris,' thought Yann. He felt a thrill of excitement. For better or worse he was back home at long last.

Monsieur Aulard had been well served by the Revolution. For the time being at least, all theatres were free to put on whatever plays they chose as long as they supported the Revolution, made fun of the clergy and mocked the greed of the aristocrats.

Wisely, seeing which way the wind was blowing, Monsieur Aulard had renamed his small theatre the Theatre of Liberty. In so doing, he had won the approval of no less a figure than Citizen Danton, one of the most influential men in the National Assembly. With such patronage the theatre manager no longer needed to hire magicians to perform cheap fairground tricks to a half-empty auditorium. He now put on productions full of spectacular effects, filled with revolutionary zeal. There was never an empty seat or a dry eye in the house. The only other time the takings had been this good was in the old days of Topolain.

Success had brought sobriety. He treated wine like medicine, doctoring himself with a certain amount each day and not one drop more. In times like these, a man needed his wits about him if he were to survive, for politicians, like audiences, are a fickle lot. What worked well today could be the end of him tomorrow.

This self-imposed regime suited him. He looked younger. He had thrown out his ill-fitting wig and now, in the fashion of the moment, had the air of a man who didn't spend too long worrying at the mirror. His clothes were new, but not flashy. Like an actor, he had reinvented himself for his role as a man of the people. A cockade was securely fastened to every one of his many jackets lest he should absentmindedly forget and find himself mistaken for an aristocrat.

It was well over three years since Jacques Topolain's body had been left sitting in his office chair, holding the sawn-off head of the wooden Pierrot. It was a memory that continued to haunt Monsieur Aulard. So terrified was he of Kalliovski paying him another visit that he had taken the precaution of promoting Didier from caretaker to bodyguard. It was Didier's job to follow Monsieur Aulard wherever he went and to check that nothing and no one was waiting for him in his office.

This morning Monsieur Aulard was more jumpy than he had been in a long while. Last night amongst the audience he could have sworn that he saw Kalliovski; but then again, he seemed to see the man waiting for him on every street corner.

Yann stood in the rue du Temple and wondered if this could possibly be the building he remembered, for it had undergone a huge change. It no longer looked as if it was about to topple into the street but stood upright and proud, with *Théâtre de la Liberté* painted large and bold across its front. A revolutionary flag was draped across its façade like a badge of honour.

He walked round to the stage door and stepped inside, reassured to find that here at least little had changed. It smelt, as it always had done, of stale tobacco, wine and slapstick make-up. Madame Manou was sitting as usual in her sentry box, lit by a single candle.

Yann's eyes took a moment to adjust to the dark. He smiled when he recognised Madame Manou.

'May I see Monsieur Aulard?' he asked.

'Not another,' sighed Madame Manou. 'What are you? A writer? An actor? A musician?' She peered out at him. 'You must be an actor, by the looks of you.'

Yann was about to contradict her, but she went on, 'I don't know what this city is coming to, theatres popping up everywhere, actors on every street corner, musicians in every basement, writers in every attic. And you know what? They all want to work here.' She lifted her shoulders in disgust. 'Have you any idea how many stairs there are up to Monsieur Aulard's office?'

'Eighty-two,' said Yann.

'*Hein?* How do you know that?' said Madame Manou, quite taken aback.

'I used to work here. You probably don't remember me. My name is Yann Margoza ...'

Madame Manou leant out of the box for a closer look. 'No, never! Get away with you! You? That street urchin? The Revolution is working miracles.' She peered round the side, looking for Didier, and then remembered that the old bear had gone out for a loaf of bread. She had not the slightest intention of walking up all those stairs herself, no matter what that fool Aulard had to say about it.

'Don't need me to show you the way, then, dear, do you?'

Yann went up the wooden spiral staircase two steps at a time, smiling at the memory of a younger version of himself running up. He stopped at the door and knocked.

'Come in,' said a familiar voice.

Yann entered to see Monsieur Aulard sitting at a desk piled high with manuscripts. Pieces of paper littered the floor like autumn leaves.

Monsieur Aulard looked shocked. 'How the hell were you allowed up?' he said angrily. 'Where's that fool Didier? What do I employ him for—'

'Don't you remember me?' interrupted Yann.

'I'm sorry, I don't. Are you an actor?'

'No.'

The theatre manager pushed his chair back. 'Then you *want* to be an actor,' he said. 'You and the rest of Paris, my friend.'

'I was Têtu's assistant. I worked with the magician Topolain. I have been away in England and have just returned.'

Monsieur Aulard stood up. 'You're Yann Margoza! Is it possible? My word, yes, I can see it now. It *is* you.' He laughed. 'Your eyes should have told me. You always had the most extraordinary eyes.' He seized Yann's hand. 'Who'd have thought you'd turn out such a handsome fellow!'

Yann smiled. 'Who'd have thought to see you so sober and successful, Monsieur Aulard!'

'The cure, my son, is the Revolution,' said Monsieur Aulard proudly. 'Never in all my life have I done so well.'

'I've come to see Têtu.'

'Hush,' said the theatre manager nervously, looking around him as if he half expected the door to be flung open and Kalliovski to be standing there, pistol in hand. 'Walls have ears,' he said. Taking Yann by the arm he whispered, 'Come with me.'

Yann followed him down the stairs towards the stage door, where Didier was just coming in with his bread.

'Do you need me?' asked Didier.

'No, no, just be outside my apartment in an hour's time.'

'Wait!' called Didier as they left. 'Aren't you Yann?'

'Not now!' said Monsier Aulard firmly, as if he were directing the scene.

'But – but—' said Didier.

Yann turned and mouthed, 'Good to see you, too.'

Monsieur Aulard set off up the boulevard and led Yann into the maze of streets that he knew so well. He walked at a brisk pace, checking behind and in front of him at every corner to be sure that they were not being followed.

'How is Têtu?' asked Yann.

'He's all right. It's good to see him again, after all this time. He turned up the other day, just like that, as if nothing had happened.'

'What *did* happen?' asked Yann. 'I've only just heard that he's still alive.'

'Didier found him bleeding to death in the courtyard of the Hôtel d'Angleterre, and carried him back to the theatre. You know, he never said a word. I wasn't even

231

aware that Didier was living in the theatre, right up in the attic. He carried Têtu up there, removed the bullet and nursed him back to health. There was Têtu, right under my nose, and I knew nothing!'

'When did you find out?'

'Like you, only recently. He left the theatre as soon as he was better, and went to work in the provinces. More than that, I can't tell you.'

They stopped next to a battered wooden door. Monsieur Aulard produced a key and opened it, holding on to the iron handle and leaning out slightly to see if they were being watched.

'He's staying with me now. I still feel very worried about the whole thing.'

'I can see that,' said Yann, smiling.

The street was all but deserted. Satisfied that they were not observed, Monsieur Aulard hurried Yann into a wide courtyard. They walked up the stone stairs to the first floor and entered a much larger apartment than the one Yann remembered. Iago the parrot still sat on his perch, looking, like his owner, in better health.

Monsieur Aulard went over and opened the shutters, peering out to check that there was no one down below. Sunlight flooded the room. Yann could tell by the state of the apartment that Têtu was around. He couldn't imagine the theatre manager keeping it this neat and tidy. As if to prove the point, Monsieur Aulard threw down his hat and disappeared into the next room.

Yann stood looking down through the windows on to the cobbled courtyard. It was overgrown and unkempt, plant pots lay neglected and a cat, long and lazy, had spread itself, asleep, across the step, warming its belly in the sun.

'Yannick, is that really you?' It was the high-pitched voice he knew so well.

Yann rushed towards Têtu, lifting him off his feet and hugging him tight as tears rolled down Têtu's cheeks. 'Oh, it is so, so good to see you!'

'Put me down and let me get a proper look at you,' said Têtu, wiping his eyes and walking round Yann, studying him carefully. 'Well, what a fine gentleman you've turned out to be. Look at your clothes! Can you speak English? Oh my word, what your mother would have given to see her handsome son all grown up. Tell me, can you read and write?'

'I can,' laughed Yann, 'and I speak English like a gentleman, without even a trace of an accent.'

Têtu clapped his hands and danced with joy. 'Well, well, who would have thought it!' He paused, his face suddenly solemn. 'Do you forgive me, Yannick, for letting you believe I was dead?'

'There's nothing to forgive. I have so much to thank you for, Têtu. Never once have I felt unloved or unwanted. Without you, I would have been left to die. You have been both mother and father to me.'

'No, no, Yann, stop it, there's no need to say all that. Love needs no justification. You were always wanted, right from the very beginning. Whatever happens, don't forget that.'

'You've been incredibly brave,' said Yann.

'Rubbish. You know, it was never my intention to get shot. Finding myself in that strange predicament, I felt fate had intervened. I tell you this, Yannick, it was the hardest thing I have ever done, not to let you know I was all right.'

By now Têtu had brought out some bread and cheese and put them on the table. He sat down and looked at Yann, who was still standing, the sunlight illuminating his face.

'Those things I used to be able to do – read minds, read the future,' said Yann, 'those gifts left me the night Topolain was killed, the night the Pierrot said "I see you all drowning in a sea of blood." I still have no idea why I said it.' He stopped and sighed. 'For a long time I felt responsible for what had happened. If I had kept quiet . . .'

'Yann, it had nothing to do with that. It would have happened whatever you said. Remember the red necklace that you found?'

'And you took.'

'Yes, but that's not important. I've been making a few enquires. Did you know that a red necklace just like it was found round the neck of a Madame Perrien, a friend of Kalliovski's?'

'And a similar one was found in London, round the neck of a Madame Claumont,' said Yann. 'Mr Laxton believed it had something to do with Kalliovski.' He thought back to his vision of the woman lying in a field. Try as he might, he couldn't remember if she too was wearing a red necklace.

Têtu interrupted his thoughts. 'Cordell told me about Sido de Villeduval and her forthcoming marriage. A terrible business. There is no question we must try and rescue her. I would do it myself but my size is against me; once I've been seen, once I've been heard, I'm hard to forget. I didn't want you to come back to Paris and put yourself in danger, but when Cordell told me how you'd turned out, it seemed to me you would be the person to rescue the girl. Cordell thinks you're very clever. I know you're very clever, but I also know you're better suited to adventure than to studying.'

'You're right.'

'A pity, though, your gifts leaving you like that. You were quite remarkable when you were younger. So, what can you do now?'

Yann sat down at the table and cut a thick slice of bread.

'Throw my voice, ride, fence, read, write ... oh, and ...'

Over on the shelf opposite he saw a bottle of brandy and two glasses. He pulled at the threads of light.

Monsieur Aulard entered the room and stood there dumbstruck to see a bottle suspended in mid-air. The cork was removed and the bottle tipped up, filling two glasses, before all four objects landed on the table without a drop being spilt.

Têtu's face broke into the widest grin. 'Why didn't you tell me you could see?' He leapt up and flung his arms round Yann.

'How fortunate that you have returned to us with such

magic in your fingers,' said Monsieur Aulard, putting on his hat. 'If they ever tire of revolutionary zeal I am going to give them magic the like of which Paris has never seen.'

'No,' said Têtu firmly, 'you are going to do no such thing, is that understood?'

Monsieur Aulard shrugged his shoulders. 'Understood,' he said sadly, opening the front door. 'Maybe when the Revolution is over ...'

'If we live that long,' said Têtu.

After Monsieur Aulard had gone Têtu began to talk about the situation in Paris.

'Things are very bad indeed, and getting worse each day. The National Guard have started doing nightly raids to smoke out aristocrats, or priests who haven't sworn allegiance to the Revolution, breaking down doors, pulling up floorboards. The jails are full to bursting.'

Yann and Têtu sat talking till late. Yann told Têtu about Tobias Cooper, and about his life in London with the Laxtons, and Têtu told him a little about his three years living and working in the provinces.

At last Yann said, 'I've told you everything, and as usual, Têtu, you've told me nothing about yourself. I'm glad to see you haven't changed one bit. You're still the same mysterious person you've always been.'

'Now,' said Têtu, changing the subject, 'let's talk about how we're going to get Sido de Villeduval out. This is going to be difficult and dangerous, Yann. We'll have to plan very carefully. We just might be able to save the girl on her own, but I can't see how we'll ever get the Marquis out undetected.'

'But I've brought papers for both of them,' said Yann.

'It makes no difference,' said Têtu. 'We have Kalliovski to reckon with, and he has a razor-sharp mind. He has spies. Nothing escapes his attention.'

Yann got up and went over to the window. The cat, now awake, one leg pointed skywards, was balancing precariously on the narrow window sill, busy cleaning its sleek fur.

'I had a letter this morning from the Marquis's lawyer, Maître Tardicu,' Têtu went on. 'It's addressed to Cordell, but as he is away he had it forwarded to me.' He handed a sheet of paper to Yann.

'There's nothing on it. It's blank.'

'In times such as these, when wise men fear even their shadows, it is prudent to take precautions. It has been written with sympathetic ink.'

He lit a candle, and as he held the letter up to the flame the words began to appear.

Yann read it carefully. 'What do you think Maître Tardieu is so desperate to tell us?'

'I don't know. I'll arrange for us to see him tomorrow.'

Outside there was the sound of a pot breaking on the ground. Red geraniums lay scattered; the cat had vanished.

'If only,' thought Yann, 'I could do the same for Sido.'

Chapter Twenty-four

It was a stifling hot morning when Yann left the lodgings he had taken in the Marais to go and meet Têtu. He was now dressed in the French mode, wearing a long sky-blue coat with the revolutionary cockade pinned to the lapel, over a red-striped calico waistcoat, under which he wore a shirt of fine cotton, his cravat tied high round his neck. To finish his dashing outfit he wore breeches and riding boots, so that no one seeing him would think him any different from any other fashionable young man of this city, filled no doubt with the same fashionable revolutionary zeal as all other patriotic young men of his time.

Têtu was seated in his usual place at the Café Godet, a corner table facing the street, from which he had a perfect view of all the comings and goings.

'Good!' he said, seeing Yann. 'Maître Tardieu will see us at three o'clock this afternoon.'

He turned and tried to catch the waiter's eye. The man steadfastly ignored him.

'Never can get served here,' said Têtu tetchily. 'Listen, I sent Didier out to do some snooping for us yesterday, instead of sitting cooped up in the theatre. He's perfect for the task. No one will think he's up to anything, other than occupying vacant space.'

'I thought he only worked for Monsieur Aulard.'

Têtu huffed and raised his hands. 'His talents are wasted there. Didier's no fool. He might well possess the face of a mooncalf but, as I've told him, in times like these his looks could be his fortune; for this is soon to be a city of idiots, where clever men will need to hold tight to their heads if they wish to keep them.'

Yann looked round the café. It was as busy as it had always been. At the next table, an argument broke out as to what should be done with the royal family.

'Kill them! They're traitors, the lot of them,' said a burly man with a red face. 'That's what I'd do with them. Know what he said the day we dethroned him, when he was taken through the Tuileries Gardens to the National Assembly? He said, "There are a great many leaves: they fall early this year."'

His companions burst out laughing.

'Good Frenchmen being slaughtered, and all the idiot

can talk about is leaves!' said the burly man. 'Would you credit it?'

Didier pushed his way into the café. He was still wearing the tiny red liberty cap, which looked ridiculous on his huge head, and sweat was pouring down his face. He pulled out a chair next to Têtu. 'It's too hot, too hot by half, and it ain't even midday.'

Têtu stretched up and pulled the cap from his head. 'Take care, my friend. With a cap that ill-fitting, you might be seen to be mocking the cause.'

'It's the biggest I could find,' said Didier, offended.

Yann laughed. 'Better get someone at the theatre to make you one that fits, in that case.'

'Have you any news?' asked Têtu.

Didier turned round and looked longingly at the counter, where waiters were busy pouring wine into pitchers.

'At least let me have a drink, will you? It's thirsty work finding out what people are doing in this weather, I can tell you.'

'*Garçon*, a jug of coffee and some bread,' shouted Têtu.

'I've only got one pair of hands,' the man snapped.

'Anyone would think he was doing us a favour, instead of serving up stale bread and watered-down coffee,' said Têtu.

Yann got up and elbowed his way through to the counter where the proprietor's wife sat knitting and keeping a beady eye on the customers. She looked up from her stitches, about to say, 'Wait your turn like everyone else,' but seeing Yann said instead, 'What can I do for you, my lovely?'

'How do you do it?' asked Didier as the woman brought over their order, smiling at Yann.

'By being a proper gentleman, with manners,' said the woman with emphasis. 'They're rare in this dog kennel of a city, I can tell you.' She ruffled Yann's hair and walked away, swinging her hips.

Têtu stared at him through narrowed eyes.

Yann laughed.

Didier didn't wait to be asked. He tucked straight into the bread and then started to speak with his mouth full, spitting out food in the process. He wiped his mouth on his cap.

'I've been making enquiries about the Marquis.'

'Yes, and what have you discovered?'

'His château was torched three days ago. There's nothing left of the place.'

'Was anyone hurt?' asked Yann quickly.

'No. From what I gather, all the servants had already scarpered, except two, who helped get the Marquis and his daughter out. They're now staying near you in the Duchesse de Lamantes' old residence in the Place Royale. She's left for Jersey.'

'What about the Marquis and his daughter?' asked Yann.

'Give us a chance,' said Didier, mopping his face. 'You're getting me all flustered. Where was I? Oh yes, I've seen a girl with a limp. The servants – a chef and a coachman – don't get out much because the master

241

can't be left alone, so the girl goes to the market, that's what I was told. I followed her down the rue des Francs-Bourgeois. She don't spend much.'

'Was anyone else watching the place?' asked Têtu. 'Any of Kalliovski's men?'

'Not that I could see,' said Didier. He was about to cram another huge chunk of bread into his mouth when Yann snatched it away.

'What do you think you're doing?' growled Didier.

'Finish your story and I'll buy you a jug of wine,' said Yann.

'Oh, so that's it. You want to know about the young lady, what she looks like. I got your ticket. Well, she's pretty. Looks like a ripe cherry waiting to be plucked from the tree, if you get my meaning.'

'We do, and most of your crumbs too,' said Têtu sharply.

'I'm impressed that you managed to find out so much,' said Yann.

'I have my sources,' said Didier.

'Which house is it?' demanded Yann. He got up. 'I'll go and see if I can talk to her.'

'Good,' said Têtu. 'Try and get her to agree to leave her father.'

Yann went up to the counter and ordered wine and more bread for Didier.

'I'll see you at three o'clock at the theatre,' he said over the heads of the customers, and slipped out of the door and headed down the Boulevard du Temple.

It did not take him long to walk to the Place Royale. Its arcade gave welcome shelter from the blistering sun. On the corner was a café, and along the inner wall stalls had been set up by women selling an odd variety of wares. Yann took his time to work out the best place to stand so that he had a clear view of the main door to the Duchess's residence.

He waited, leaning against the cool stone.

From his vantage point at the corner of the square he was able to observe Sido before she saw him. Her mass of dark hair was tied up with a crimson ribbon, her face porcelain pale. She was dressed in a white muslin gown and carrying a basket, limping slightly as she walked towards him. Only when he said her name did she stop.

'Mademoiselle Sido. Do you remember me?'

She looked at him, her head to one side, wondering for a moment if hunger had made her hallucinate or whether it was just an incredible longing to see him again that had conjured up this apparition that stood before her.

'Yann Margoza,' she said softly, as if the words were stepping-stones across an unknown river. She wanted to touch him, just to reassure herself that he was made of flesh and blood rather than dreams and desires.

'Yes.'

Her face lit up.

'Oh, yes,' thought Yann, 'I always knew you were going to be lovely.'

'What are you doing in Paris?' she asked.

'What is anyone doing in Paris? Trying to survive,' he answered. 'Would you like to eat?'

'I have to go and get food for my father.'

'We can do that later. Why don't we eat first? I would like to talk to you.'

They walked together to the Café des Bains Chinois on the rue des Rosiers. Yann asked for a table at the back, where he hoped they would not be observed.

The smell of food was like an intoxicating perfume that made Sido feel faint.

'Can this be happening?' she thought. 'He looks even more handsome than I ever dreamed he would.'

Yann turned to look at her, startled.

'What an unguarded thing to say,' he thought.

'I am very flattered that you ...' He stopped abruptly, realising with a shock that Sido was not talking, yet he could hear what she was thinking. Had his gift come back? Could he once more read people's minds? He turned to look at the other customers in the café, wondering if he could hear what they where saying. Nothing. Not a word, only the chitter-chatter of voices, the clinking of glasses, the clicking of cutlery. Only Sido's thoughts rushed in upon him.

'You look well,' she managed to say. 'When I last saw you ...' and here she stopped herself, suddenly aware of his dark eyes on her. It was as if he had walked inside her head and could see for himself just how much and how often she had thought of him since they last met.

The meal arrived. Yann was glad of the interruption.

It gave him time to try to think straight, as her thoughts flooded his mind.

'Eat it slowly,' said Yann kindly. 'If you eat too fast you'll be sick. Take some bread and then eat.'

'How do you know I haven't eaten?'

'Because I do.'

She was quiet, savouring the food in her mouth as if she was eating life itself. She remembered how she had felt when she had first seen him three years ago at her father's château. The sense of being in church, that her soul was visible, that there was nowhere to hide from him.

'I've been staying with some people called Laxton,' said Yann, pleased to be talking aloud.

Sido stopped eating and looked up at him, shocked. 'Did you say Laxton?'

'Yes,' he said, studying her. She had sapphire-blue eyes, and a long elegant neck down which an endearing curl of dark hair had fallen. 'Lovely' was the wrong word to describe her. 'Lovely' didn't do her justice. No, Sido was beautiful.

'You know my aunt? Can this be true? Tell me ...' Once again she checked herself. She felt her emotions were about to spill over, like water in a glass. She feared she would say too much. Best to keep these thoughts to herself, so she asked, 'But how?'

'Têtu. Do you remember the dwarf?' and he told her as much of the story as he dared, leaving out the bullet.

'They want you to come to London. That's why I'm here.'

'I must be dreaming,' said Sido. 'You have come back to take me to London?' The idea seemed, in this terrifying city, nothing more than a chariot of clouds.

She was quiet for a moment. 'I fear it's too late,' she said at last. 'I can't leave. Earlier this year I was formally betrothed to Count Kalliovski. He came down from Paris with my father's lawyer, Maître Tardieu, and papers were signed.'

What she didn't say, and what Yann could hear loud and clear, was that she had felt like a piece of unwanted furniture, to be sold for the right price.

'How is the Marquis's health?' asked Yann.

'He's not well. He burned his hand badly in the fire.' She paused. 'It's not just that. It is in his mind that he is most disturbed. My father has become obsessed with Count Kalliovski, convinced that he ordered the burning of the château. He believes him to be the devil, come to tempt virtuous men to tread the path to hell.'

'And this is the man you are betrothed to?' Yann interrupted, almost shaking with rage.

'I am uncertain now. My father has written to Maître Tardieu instructing him to inform Count Kalliovski that the marriage is off.'

'When did he do that?'

'He wrote the letter the day after the fire. There are fleeting moments when his mind becomes clear.'

'Do you have anyone to help you?'

'Jean Rollet, my father's chef, has stayed with us; Bernard the coachman, too, but he has family in the city. His wife is worried that he will be sent to prison if he is seen to be still working for an aristocrat.' She stopped talking and bit her lip, trying her best not to cry.

It was what she was not saying, more than what she said, that struck Yann powerfully: the Marquis was haunted by visions of his dead wife, who stood before him; the present was only a fleeting stranger, the past took up most of his quarrelsome days.

Sido didn't want to cry, but still she could not prevent tears welling up in her eyes as she said quietly, 'Such is the state of my father's mind that I can now hardly be in the same room with him before he takes to shouting and demanding of invisible footmen that I be removed. In truth, he frightens me.'

Yann then reached out and touched her hand. Her skin was rose-petal soft.

Sido wiped her eyes. 'What will people think of us?'

'That we are lovers having a quarrel.'

Sido's face turned deep crimson.

'Leave your father, let me get you out. I can do it, I have the papers and the money,' said Yann. 'There is a new life waiting for you in London.'

For all his passionate words he could hear her thoughts and could see all the knots, the longing to be loved by a father who would never love her. He said in desperation, 'He has never cared for you. What do you owe him?'

Sido looked bewildered. Had she said these things out loud?

'Come away with me today,' begged Yann.

'I cannot. I couldn't live with myself if I did.'

He sighed, and pushed back his chair. 'I knew you would say that. Is your father willing to go to England?'

'Yes. The Duchesse de Lamantes, who took us in, has recommended a man who will help us escape, once my father is well enough to travel.'

'How are you going to pay him?'

'The Duchess very kindly said she would loan us the money, and that she would pay this Mr Tull for us.'

'Mr Tull, did you say?'

Sido nodded. 'Do you know of him?'

Yann remembered Mr Tull only too well. How was it, he wondered, that he was in Paris helping émigrés escape?

'Have you met him yet?'

'No, but we've had a message telling us to contact him when we're ready.'

Yann said earnestly, 'Please don't. Let me get you out instead of Mr Tull. After all, that's what I'm here for.'

'I don't think my father would consider it. The Duchess suggested Mr Tull, and so Mr Tull it has to be.'

In spite of the clamour in the café, they could hear the church bell chiming the hour.

Sido wished, as they shopped together for food, that she had the power to slow down time, even to stop it altogether, or at least never to forget each passing moment. They walked back slowly towards the Place Royale. With every step that took them nearer to her front door she wondered if she would ever see Yann again.

As they parted Yann said, 'I will be here at the same time tomorrow.'

He walked back to the theatre floating on air. The colours all round him looked brighter than they had done two hours ago. Never could he remember feeling so alive. Why should that be? he wondered. He smiled at himself. As if he didn't know! It was because she had been thinking about him all this time.

He jumped up in the air, hit the sky with his fist, and laughed out loud. She loved him. It was so simple. At that moment he realised something that he hadn't dared whisper even to himself, something that Orlenda had seen so clearly in the palm of his hand: there was only one person for him, and that was, and always would be, Sido de Villeduval.

The gravity of this realisation made him once more aware of his feet upon the street, Didier's words a pebble in his happy thoughts, 'Like a ripe cherry waiting to be plucked from the tree'. A sudden and terrible dread overcame him. He was now certain that the involvement of Mr Tull did not bode well.

Chapter Twenty-five

T êtu was waiting impatiently in the wings of the theatre, watching a couple of tumblers practise their moves and a juggler throw his unlit torches up into the air.

'Where is Yann? Curse the boy,' he said under his breath.

On stage Monsieur Aulard was shouting loudly and without much effect at a singer whose voice was flat and whose rendition of the Marseillaise left a lot to be desired.

'No, no, mademoiselle,' Monsieur Aulard bellowed. 'We want to stir the audience to a patriotic fervour, not send them screaming from the theatre.'

Têtu turned round to see Yann slip through the shadows.

'At last!' he hissed. 'I thought you'd forgotten our appointment with the lawyer.'

'Quiet!' shouted Monsieur Aulard. 'How's one

expected to work when there's bedlam going on back-stage?'

'I saw her,' said Yann.

Têtu took his arm. 'Come on, you can tell me about it on the way there.'

Once out of the theatre they set off towards the Left Bank.

'Well,' said Têtu as they walked along, 'did you tell her our plan?'

'Yes.'

'Good. And did she agree?'

'No. She told me that they had made a previous arrangement. The Duchesse de Lamantes had recom-mended that they use Mr Tull.'

'Mr Tull,' said Têtu. 'Why Mr Tull?'

'He was the one the Duchess had employed to take her to London. She left disguised as a governess.'

'Now that's interesting. I'd heard that Mr Tull was working in Paris. By all accounts he's doing good busi-ness.'

'He speaks terrible French, and he's not very bright. I have a feeling he must be working with someone here.'

'Maybe,' said Têtu. 'But he has done this many times before.'

Yann kicked at a stone. 'I don't like the idea of Mr Tull being involved.'

'If it is of any comfort, it was Mr Tull who took you safely to London: why should he not do the same for Mademoiselle Sido and her father?'

'I don't know.'

'He must have got the necessary papers. Anyway, I can tell you this much, we would never have been able to get both of them out. The girl, maybe; the Marquis, impossible.'

'I still feel uneasy.'

'Tell you what we'll do. The minute we're finished here I'll get Didier to make enquires for us as to Tull's credentials, so that when you see Mademoiselle Sido tomorrow you can advise her what to do for the best.' He stopped walking and looked at Yann. 'You will be seeing her tomorrow, I take it?'

'Yes.'

'Good, very good. You never know, by then she may have changed her mind and decided to go with you by herself.'

'I doubt it,' said Yann.

The lawyer's house was near the Sorbonne, down a dingy covered passage off the rue St-Jacques. It was so dark that the lanterns hanging in the niches were all lit. Yann and Têtu stood there waiting in the gloom for the door to open, sensing eyes peeping out of all the buildings, spying on them. In the window of the shop opposite a solitary candle dimly illuminated its macabre contents, waxwork heads stuck on pikes. One was of Louis XVI, another was of Marie Antoinette. Yann felt a shiver go down his spine.

'My word,' said Têtu. 'A glimpse of what is to come.'

'Yes?' said the maid, opening the door.

'We have an appointment to see Maître Tardieu.'

The girl took them up a narrow, dark staircase that

led to a room of miserable proportions. Lit only with a few candles, so used was this room to the perpetual gloom of twilight that the outside world seemed almost divorced from it.

The lawyer reminded Yann of a mole. He was dressed in a worn-out black velvet coat, his face gravestone grey, worry etched into every feature, thick heavy spectacles stuck firmly on the bridge of his nose. He did not look a well man. He was sitting at a table piled high with papers. Next to him stood an inkstand and a stone jar of quills, beside which were the remains of an unfinished meal. He seemed lost for words as they entered the room, not knowing what to make of this pair, while the maid fussed with the plate and straightened a forlorn-looking chair.

'That's all, thank you,' said Maître Tardieu firmly, and the door clicked shut behind her. Never for a moment had he imagined Cordell sending him a mere youth and a dwarf, apparently from the circus. He had been expecting two serious and well-connected gentlemen to help him. Had Cordell no idea of the urgency of the situation?

'We live in strange times indeed, sir,' said Têtu, reading the lawyer's thoughts.

'No, we live in terrible times,' said Maître Tardieu. 'Who would think that I would live so long as to be rewarded in my old age with such times as these.' He took off his glasses and nervously wiped them on his sleeve, with the effect of evenly coating the already smeared lenses with more grime. 'I take it you've heard about the Marquis's château?'

'About the fire?'

'Yes. What a dreadful business. The last of the Marquis's great fortune gone up in flames.' The lawyer sighed. 'He wrote to me a few days ago instructing me to break off Mademoiselle Sido's betrothal, said she wouldn't be marrying the devil.'

'Have you informed Kalliovski?'

Tardieu mopped his forehead. 'I have, sir.'

'Have you had a reply?'

'None,' he said, absent-mindedly moving papers from one pile to another for want of something to do.

'I am aware, sir,' said Têtu kindly, 'that we are not what you had in mind when you asked Monsieur Cordell for help.'

'Quite,' said Maître Tardieu. 'Quite.'

'But whatever else you may think of us, we are to be trusted, of that I can give you my word.'

'Yes, Cordell wrote and told me as much ...' He stopped, then started again. 'But sir,' said the lawyer, standing up, 'I didn't expect ...'

'A dwarf,' interrupted Têtu.

'Quite, quite.'

'My size, sir, is of no importance to me, though I see it more often than not reflected badly back at me in the eyes of my fellow man.'

'This, sir, is a most sensitive matter. I am afraid it is for Monsieur Cordell alone.'

'That is not possible,' said Yann. 'He is away in Coblenz.'

For a while the silence in the room felt almost tangible. Then Maître Tardieu said, 'This goes against my better judgment, but I see there is nothing else to be done.' He put his hand under his chin as if to prop up the weight of his head, and lowered his voice. 'Something very distressing has come to light. Oh dear me, yes, very distressing indeed. I have received a packet from a Monsieur Giraud, a lawyer of my acquaintance who lives in Normandy. He was called in to help identify the remains of a body found on the Marquis's estate, near where Mademoiselle Sido's mother was killed. Monsieur Giraud concludes that this ring, found amongst the bones, was the property of the Marquis's half-brother, Armand de Villeduval, who disappeared about the time of the accident, and that the remains were his.'

He tipped the contents of the packet on to the table. Out fell a ring and seven blood-red garnets.

'The ring,' continued Maître Tardieu, 'bears, as you can see, the coat of arms of the Villeduval family. I remember that Armand de Villeduval used to wear it on his left hand. The garnets . . .' He paused. 'Will you wait here? There is something else I must show you.'

When he left the room, Têtu picked up one of the garnets and studied it.

'Does it remind you of anything?'

'Yes. The red necklace I found in Kalliovski's room.'

Upstairs they could hear the lawyer shuffle across the

255

floorboards as the ceiling creaked above them.

'How can anyone live in this place?' said Yann.

'Moles like the dark.'

The lawyer came back carrying a velvet drawstring bag.

'This,' he said, 'belonged to Mademoiselle Sido's mother. She instructed her maid that if anything happened to her she was to give the purse to me.'

He emptied it on to the table. The brightness of the jewels that fell out shone even in the darkness of the gloomy room. In amongst them lay a red ribbon studded with seven garnets.

Maître Tardieu brought out his handkerchief and mopped his brow again, the heat a sticky, unwelcome visitor.

Têtu picked up the red necklace. 'How did this get in amongst such valuable jewels?' he asked.

'The maid told me that she had taken the necklace off her dead mistress, along with her rings. She had no idea if it was valuable or not, and just added them to the other jewels. Does it signify anything?'

'The seven garnets found with Armand de Villeduval's ring were once attached to a red ribbon identical to this,' said Têtu. 'It is the signature that is left on every one of his victims.'

'Sir,' said Maître Tardieu, 'you are alarming me greatly. Please, in heaven's name, explain yourself. Whose victims?'

'Kalliovski's. I think it proves that Armand de Villeduval and Madame Isabelle de Villeduval were murdered, but the question – and one you might have the answer to – is why?'

'We must call for the police,' said the lawyer.

'That would be unwise,' said Yann. 'It would be as good as signing your own death warrant.'

'Oh dear, oh dear, what is to be done?'

'What we want to do is get Mademoiselle Sido to London where she has family and will be out of Kalliovski's reach.'

'I agree that would be best. If Kalliovski were to marry Mademoiselle Sido, he would be in control of her inheritance. Can I ask – how do you plan to get her out?'

'We have been told that Mr Tull is to take her and the Marquis to England,' said Têtu.

'Not the Marquis. The man, you know, is quite mad. If anything will scupper the plan, he will. Do you really believe this Mr Tull is up to the job?'

'That's what we're going to find out,' said Yann.

'But, young man, I don't want anyone but yourself taking these jewels back to London, is that understood?'

'Yes,' said Yann. 'I will make sure that Mademoiselle Sido receives them safely.'

'I can't tell you how delighted I shall be to see them with their rightful owner at last. I am an old man: I don't like keeping such valuables in my house, not in times like these.'

'Then, sir,' said Têtu, 'we will make the necessary arrangements to relieve you of the jewels.'

They left the lawyer's house with two vital questions still unanswered. If Kalliovski had murdered both Sido's

mother and Armand de Villeduval, what was his motive?
And what part had the Marquis played? The questions
hovered there angrily, like stormclouds in search of
thunder.

The next morning Yann was back at the Place Royale,
eager to tell Sido of her unexpected good fortune.
He took up his position as before, not wanting to draw
attention to himself. There were spies all over Paris,
looking out for potential émigrés.

By half-past one, Yann had to acknowledge that something was wrong, and the unpleasant image of Mr Tull
came back to haunt him.

Yann moved nearer to the door, wondering if he could
have missed her, hoping beyond hope that she would
still come down. As he leaned against the wall, he could
hear the women nearby gossiping.

'That poor girl! There she was, trying to stop him
from shouting, and he kicked her in front of everybody.'
The woman folded her arms and huffed. 'Most probably
that's how she got that limp in the first place.'

'Well, he's not right in the head, is he?' said her friend.
'You could see that. Mad, like the lot of them. Too much
inbreeding, I say. That's what's wrong with all these
stinking aristocrats.'

At that all three women chuckled.

'He was a sight for sore eyes, wasn't he? Did you notice
that one side of his powdered hair was stuck to his head,
as if he'd been sleeping on it?'

'Telling us all to keep away because he was a Marquis and shouting out at the top of his voice that the devil was coming to get them! I thought the National Guard would come and arrest him, the noise he was making.'

'It took two strong men to get him into that carriage, didn't it?'

'You had to feel sorry for the girl, though. She was in tears by the time they took off.'

Yann had heard enough. A wave of panic flooded through him as he walked past the women and towards the door. He knocked hard, but he knew it was hopeless. He should have got her out when he had the chance. Now he hated to think of the danger she was in.

———◆———

By the time Yann returned to the Theatre of Liberty it was early evening. The curtain was due to go up shortly, and crowds were queueing outside, eager to see the show, and being entertained by musicians and tumblers. Yann went through the stage door and up the stairs to Monsieur Aulard's office.

Têtu was in the middle of a terrible argument with the theatre manager. Didier, his great arms folded across his chest, stood watching his boss and the dwarf bellow at each other. Têtu had his sleeves rolled up as if ready to start fighting.

'He is here to protect me, not to run errands for you,' Monsieur Aulard was shouting.

'You don't need protection. You're not in any danger. We, on the other hand, need vital information, and that old mooncalf of yours is the one for the job.'

'Don't keep calling me a mooncalf!' snapped Didier. 'You're always doing that. It's irritating me.'

'Stop it!' shouted Yann. They turned to look at him. 'Stop it! Sido's gone. Tull came last night. She's left with the Marquis.'

'Well, that was fast,' said Têtu, out of breath. 'With luck she'll be well on her way to England by now.'

'No, something's wrong. When the carriage came last night the Marquis kept screaming and wouldn't get in. A crowd gathered and he kicked Sido in front of them and insulted them all.'

'He is deranged,' said Monsieur Aulard. 'What do you expect?'

'If he was making that much of a din then their attempt to escape must have been obvious,' said Têtu. 'Why wasn't he arrested?'

'They probably thought he was being taken to the asylum,' said Monsieur Aulard helpfully.

The implication of Têtu's question suddenly hit them all like a hammer blow. Têtu rolled down his shirtsleeves and pulled at his jacket, all notion of fighting gone.

'That scoundrel,' he said. 'We need to make immediate enquiries about Tull. I take it you don't mind if I use Didier?'

'Of course not. Did I ever say I did?' said Monsieur Aulard.

'Don't worry,' said Didier, shoving his red cap on to his head. 'I'll be back in time to take you home after the show.'

'Thank you,' said Monsieur Aulard, taking hold of Didier's hand. 'You are a good man.' He went back to his desk. 'But Didier, for pity's sake go down to wardrobe and get a hat that fits.'

Têtu and Didier set off towards the cafés on the rue du Temple. Yann decided to take the maze of small streets that led off the rue des Francs-Bourgeois in search of anyone who had information about the coach or its driver that might lead him to Tull.

It was well past midnight when he gave up. By then the streets were deserted. Occasionally he would come across groups of Sans Culottes swaying as if the city were at sea, singing patriotic songs.

'Goodnight to you, citizen,' they would call drunkenly.

Suddenly an idea came to him. He remembered how partial Mr Tull was to his beer. Where in the city, he wondered, was a café that sold beer to tempt an Englishman? Of course, the café in the Palais-Royal!

By the time he arrived, most of the clientele was emptying lazily out on to the street. The few customers remaining looked as though they were glued to their chairs. The place smelled of stale wine and beer, and was filled with the smoke from too many pipes. The barman looked up when he saw Yann enter.

'We're closed, citizen.'

'I haven't come for a drink. I'm looking for an Englishman by the name of Tull. Does he come in here?'

'What's that to you?' said the barman, putting down the glass he was rubbing with a dirty cloth.

'I need to speak to him,' said Yann. 'It's urgent.'

The barman grabbed him by the lapels of his sky-blue coat.

'Beat it. As I said, we're closed. Now, you wouldn't want me spoiling those good looks of yours, would you?'

He let him go. Yann felt a surge of ice-cold fury rush in upon him. He lifted his head slowly to see threads of light coming from everything and everyone in the café. Yann stood there like a puppet-master, feeling in complete control. Instinctively he put out his hand, pulling at the threads, so that first one glass and then another fell, smashing all around the startled barman, who stood petrified as he watched the young man orchestrating objects to move at his will.

The last customers ran from the café as chairs went flying across the room. Yann slammed the door behind them. He laughed. He was enjoying himself. He turned back to the barman.

'Let me ask you again. Does a Mr Tull drink here?'

'Yes, yes,' said the barman anxiously.

'And do you know who he works for?'

The barman beckoned him closer and whispered into his ear.

'You promise you won't say anything?' he said. 'I'm a dead man if you do.'

Exhausted, Yann walked back to his lodgings. The performance in the café had taken all his strength. Now, more than anything, he needed to sleep. Suddenly he understood why Têtu had always looked so ashen after working the Pierrot.

He dragged his way up to his room to find Têtu sitting on the stairs waiting for him.

'Where have you been?' he asked.

'Trying to find out who Mr Tull works for,' said Yann, opening his door. Even though it was nearly dawn, it was still stifling hot inside. The air hadn't cooled down. There was no wind, not even a breeze, just insufferable heat. He sat down heavily on the bed.

'The Duchesse de Lamantes was brought back to Paris two nights ago under the arrest of the National Guard,' said Têtu. 'Apparently Tull has a lucrative trade in double-dealing his customers.'

Yann lay down on the bed. 'Tull,' he said, looking up at the skylight, 'works for Kalliovski. I'm sorry, Têtu, I need to sleep.'

Têtu got up to leave. 'There is one last thing you should know. Two more prisoners were delivered to the Abbaye last night. The Marquis de Villeduval and his daughter.'

Chapter Twenty-six

Mr Tull felt that he had earned his money good and proper. The night before last had been hard work indeed. It had taken him longer than he had expected to get that lunatic of a Marquis into the coach. The noise the man had made was enough to wake the dead, blast his blue blood! He attracted unwelcome attention. Mr Tull had had to bang loudly on the roof of the coach.

'Bloody well shut up! If you don't, I'll come and deal with you.'

The sound of Mr Tull's large fist and rasping voice reverberated round the inside of the coach. It made Sido jump, but it had the desired effect. The Marquis stopped banging on the windows. He looked at Sido, aghast.

'Hear that? The devil is up there and he's coming to get you. As far as I'm concerned he can have you, wretched cripple that you are.'

Sido sat huddled in the corner. She felt vulnerable. Her leg hurt from where her father had kicked her, and there was no Jean Rollet to protect her if he decided to attack again. She just hoped that Jean would be all right. He had told her he had relatives he could stay with for a while, that she was not to worry. Seeing him disappear had been hard indeed, as if the last brick in the ruins of this life had come tumbling down. She didn't like Mr Tull, and she didn't trust him.

Since Sido spoke hardly any English, and Mr Tull's French was so bad that she had trouble working out what he was saying, there was no way of discovering whether she had reason to be concerned. All she knew was that they were leaving behind everything that was familiar.

'Well,' said the Marquis, as the coach made its way through the darkened streets, 'what is it you want from me?'

'For you to calm down,' replied Sido.

'And if I do, will you and the devil disappear?'

Sido turned away from him and looked longingly out of the grimy window. She thought of Yann and wondered what he was doing. This Revolution should have been so glorious, she thought. It should have been her salvation, yet here she was, tied by birth to one of the pillars of the old regime. Everything her father stood for she loathed, yet she felt that the word liberty, a word that was used so often and with such passion, would never apply to her.

At St-Germain the carriage slowed down and then came to a sudden stop. She could hear people speaking outside, and dimly through the grubby windows she saw that Mr Tull was not alone.

Suddenly she realised what was happening. A feeling of suffocating panic overtook her. She tried desperately to open the carriage doors and gave up, defeated. They had been tricked. They were not going to England. They were being taken to prison.

'Sit down,' said her father sharply. 'It is not your place to open the door. Leave that to the footman.'

Mr Tull unlocked the carriage and stood aside as one prison guard took charge of Sido and two others dragged the Marquis out, taking the precaution of tying his hands behind his back. Mr Tull stood there looking unconcerned. He couldn't care less. They were just another pair of lost sheep rounded up for the slaughter. He would get a good purse for the Marquis and his daughter, more than enough to settle his bills and allow him to forget his cares in this stinking sewer of a city. It was another night's work successfully done, though it hadn't been as much fun as duping the old Duchess. He chuckled at the memory of seeing her dressed up as a governess. He had heartily enjoyed her humiliation. Still, the girl stuck in his gullet a little. She didn't deserve her fate, but orders were orders and who was he to judge the right and the wrong of it.

'Anyway, money's money,' he said under his breath as he climbed back up on to the coach. 'They've brought it on themselves, all these lords and ladies. Let *them* eat cake.'

The Marquis entered the prison of L'Abbaye as if going to stay at a grand château. He did not notice the dirtiness of his surroundings, nor did he hear the growls of the jailers' dogs. He stood there tall and proud, a man to be reckoned with.

'What is your name?' the clerk at the desk asked.

'I am the Marquis de Villeduval of the Château de Rochefort des Champs.'

The clerk smiled. 'You don't say, citizen.'

The turnkey, an ugly, bad-tempered man with a paper-cut for a mouth and an all too generous helping of teeth, stood swaying back and forth and smelling strongly of liquor. At his side were two ferocious hounds that looked more than a little peckish and saw all new prisoners as potential dog meat.

'And your name, citizeness?'

'Sido,' she said quietly. She did not give her surname. It seemed pointless. What did any of it matter any more?

'Which would you prefer, citizen, a cell with two beds or one?'

'I need an apartment to myself,' said the Marquis imperiously, 'and I shall need a room for my valet.'

'And what about the young lady, citizen?'

The Marquis looked round the room and, appearing to see no one, lowered his voice. 'She hasn't followed me, has she? Been trying to shake her off, you know. If

267

you see her, don't let her in. Demand to see her papers. She's in the employment of the devil and I know for certain that she's dead.'

The clerk looked at him, puzzled. 'You're a strange one, you are. Well, I take it you want two single cells? That will be thirty livres a month, not counting your meals which are extra, as is water and a glass. We aim to provide the highest service here.'

The Marquis appeared not to have heard a word; he stood with his eyes fixed at some invisible point before him.

'Show me to my apartment,' he demanded.

'Not so fast, citizen, payment up front. Nothing on the slate. We don't know how long your stay is likely to be.'

The guard standing behind him started to laugh.

'Do I know you, sir?' asked the Marquis.

The guard directed a great gobbet of spit on to the stone floor.

'I don't think I've had the pleasure,' he smirked.

'We have no money,' said Sido quickly. 'We have nothing.'

'No money!' snarled the turnkey. He laughed disdainfully.

'Then you will both be living in the banqueting hall,' said the clerk. He called to another guard to take the Marquis to the men's quarters.

'Which cell for her?' asked the turnkey.

'The one for non-paying guests.'

'My pleasure,' said the turnkey. 'This way.'

'Papa!' cried Sido as the Marquis was led away. He did not turn round.

'Friendly kind of man, ain't he?' said the turnkey. 'This way, citizeness.'

The dogs were now pulling so hard that Sido thought at any moment the turnkey would topple over. He yanked the dogs back, holding on tight to a rail with his other hand.

'These are the women's quarters.' He held up the lantern to reveal a row of doors, each with a small barred window. In one of them the face of the Duchess appeared. Sido could hardly believe that it was only a week since she had seen her, so altered was her appearance.

'Oh no,' she called out, seeing Sido, 'not you as well. I am so sorry, I didn't ...' Her voice trailed off, lost as the turnkey prodded Sido down the long dark corridor.

If there is a hell, thought Sido, this must be how it would look, how it would smell. How she wished she had had a drink of water before she'd got into the coach. She felt so unbearably hot and thirsty.

'This,' said the turnkey, opening a door, 'is for lady customers who can't pay for their board and lodging.' He pushed Sido inside. 'Sweet dreams, citizeness.'

Sido stood with her back against the heavy door, in a soup of thick darkness, unable to see a thing. The key turned noisily in the lock.

It took a while for her eyes to adjust. She was in a long dormitory with two rows of beds, one to each side. There was a narrow table down the centre. It was stifling hot, the air heavy with the smell of unwashed flesh and urine.

'There's one free at the end.'

Sido jumped, not sure where the voice had come from.

With her hands out before her she made her way slowly down the dormitory, at last finding the free bed. It was no more than a wooden board. Never in all her life had she felt more wretched than she did now. She started as something brushed past her ankles, and quickly pulled her feet up on to the plank. She could just make out the shape of a large rat sitting up and twitching its whiskers before scurrying away. She put her shawl into her mouth to stifle a sob. Was it really only yesterday that she had seen Yann, sat in a café with him? Had he truly said that he would take her to London? Here in the stinking darkness it seemed as if it must all have happened in a dream, in another life, a long time ago.

***

In the morning, Sido's rowdy companions were all curious to know what such a sweet innocent was doing sharing their dormitory.

'This 'ere, *chérie*, is for those who ain't got a sou to their name.'

Sido said nothing. The women looked to her like brightly coloured parrots, their haggard faces painted with rouge, their hair tangled and matted with grime.

'Look what the dog brought in last night,' said one of them, laughing. 'She would have made you a bit in your house of sin, eh, Madeleine?'

'Ain't she sweet, soft to the touch like fresh baked bread. What d'you bet she's never lain with a man?'

Sido put her hands over her ears and tried to block out the comments and catcalls.

'Leave her alone,' came a voice she recognised from the previous night. An Amazon of a woman came forward. 'Go on, shut up the lot of you. She don't need to hear your vulgar tongues.'

At once all the women fell away.

Sido said quietly, 'Thank you, madame.'

'They call me La Veuve Joyeuse, the merry widow, on account of my late husband. They accused me of murder. Self-defence, more like it. Does that shock you, my pretty?'

'No,' said Sido, 'nothing seems to do that any more.'

The woman laughed. 'Stay close by me and I'll make sure those hyenas leave you be.'

'Who are they?'

'Riffraff, my dear. Not to be trusted. They'll sell their lousy bodies for whatever they can get.'

The cell door opened and the turnkey stood aside as a guard brought in a pail and a basket of bread which was put on the table.

'Well,' said the guard, grinning at Sido. 'How do you find our citizens of the night? Sweet and innocent just like you? I think not!'

The food was handed out, beans and hard, stale black bread. Tepid water, brown in colour, was all there was to drink.

'It's the Café Royal,' said one of the young women, grinning at Sido through broken teeth. 'Eat up, citizeness, and welcome to hell.'

271

Sido felt so desperate for a drink that she gulped down the water. It tasted revolting.

'Easy now,' said her new friend.

She bit into the stale bread. It was so hard that it was impossible to chew. The beans made her gag.

'If you don't eat, my pretty, you'll get ill and die,' said the widow.

Sido tried again. Her stomach registered its protest and she was violently sick. She lay on her plank, longing to be able to wash, not to be this filthy, to smell this rotten. When the turnkey came back she still felt so unwell that she could hardly get off her bed.

'Didn't the maggots agree with you, then?' sneered the turnkey.

His dogs growled at her, showing off their fangs, and Sido, without being able to help herself, was sick on the turnkey's shoes. 'You little hussy, you did that on purpose!' He lifted his hand to slap her.

La Veuve Joyeuse stepped forward.

'She's not well. Can't you see that?' And so tight was her grip on the turnkey's arm that he started to whine and call out for help.

'Anyway,' said the widow, 'your dogs have cleaned it up for you, so there's no cause for complaint, is there?'

———◆———

That night Sido lay on her wooden board, her stomach still heaving, feeling that death would be preferable to this. She finally fell asleep, but at around three in the morning she was roughly woken by a guard.

He grabbed hold of her arm and dragged her through the dormitory.

The women, woken by the noise, sat up. 'Where are you taking her?' shouted the widow.

'None of your bleeding business.'

Sido felt giddy from having been woken so abruptly, and she couldn't help stumbling. Her leg hurt. Her head ached.

The guard locked the door behind him.

'So you've been royally looked after, I see.'

Sido said nothing.

'Do you know how she got her name, that friend of yours, La Veuve Joyeuse? Shall I tell you?'

Still Sido said nothing.

'She tore her husband limb from limb, because he betrayed her, turned her in as the leader of a gang of brigands. Now there's one to tell your children – if you live that long.'

Sido was taken back the same way she had been brought the previous night, then up some stone stairs to another smaller door.

The guard knocked and pushed her inside, closing the door behind her.

It was dark in the room but she knew instantly that she was not alone. There was a smell of expensive cologne that she recognised.

'We meet again.'

The voice seemed so close to her that it made her jump, as in the darkness a light was struck and a candle lit. There before her stood Citizen Kalliovski.

S ido looked completely broken, her face pale, her dress filthy. On seeing her, Kalliovski was in no doubt that she would be his, regardless of the Marquis's objections. The game was all but won.

Only two women in his life had ever had the wit to resist him. One would have nothing to do with him, and the other . . . the other . . . had revealed in him a weakness that no true gambler can afford. Weakness was what he looked for in others; to detect it in himself was unforgivable. His strength was to know that every man had a flaw, every soul its price. Just once had he been powerless against passion, defeated by the Queen of Hearts. Never again.

He dusted down his tailored coat. 'How do you find your new home?' he asked, as a thin smile curled across his lips. Sido averted her eyes. He repulsed her, his face waxwork-smooth, a mask that hid the beast within.

Through waves of nausea she now saw him as a large black cat, playing with its prey, waiting to pounce.

'You wouldn't be in this situation if your papa had been wiser. Such an ill-advised escape. Leaving France in its hour of need is, mademoiselle, in case you didn't know, a criminal offence.'

Sido said nothing. All she had to protect herself against him was silence, the one skill in which she had become an expert. It comforted her to see a flicker of irritation cross his emotionless face.

'I have seen your father. He is not himself. He believes me to be Lucifer, the all-powerful. In the circumstances, I have to take it as a compliment.'

He stopped, observing beads of sweat on her forehead. How pale she looked.

'You will be glad to know that when your father wrote to me saying he wished to end the betrothal, I saw it as no more than a symptom of the madness that now afflicts him. I am a generous man and my offer of marriage still stands. If you agree I will make sure that the charges against you are dropped and that you are both freed. I see no reason why your father should not live out his days at the château in Normandy.'

Sido began to feel icy cold, even though the room was hot and stuffy. She could hardly breathe for lack of air. Still she remained silent.

Kalliovski let out a mirthless laugh as he remembered the way her mother had stood before him all those years ago when she had refused to become his mistress. She had paid a high price for that mistake.

'I need a reply,' he said.

Sido felt as if the walls were slowly moving in on her as he came closer.

'Don't flinch,' she told herself desperately. 'Stand tall, think of Yann.' She suddenly had a vision of him waiting for her in the Place Royale. Tomorrow, or was it today? She had lost all sense of time. She held her breath as Kalliovski stroked the side of her face, then her neck, pressing his thumb and forefinger into her soft flesh, feeling for her pulse. She knew from the power of his grip that he could strangle her with ease. Still she stood silent, shivering as his hand moved slowly down towards her breast, her heart beating like a caged bird's. She looked at the floor, feeling she was going to vomit as once again a wave of nausea overtook her.

Her quiet resistance was beginning to fascinate him. It seemed that he might have been wrong about her; maybe after all she would turn out to be a worthy opponent. If she had fallen on her knees and begged for mercy he would have despised her. That was the usual way with women, whining and weeping, saying they would do anything as long as they weren't ruined. How bored he was by charms so easily won.

Could it be that this docile girl was a more serious-minded version of her mother? That would be something to savour, and the thought thrilled him. Oh yes, she was proving herself to be a prize worth waiting for.

Instinctively Sido turned her face away and tried to free herself. He took hold of her arms, pinning them behind her back so that she could not move.

He said in a whisper, his lips brushing against her neck, 'There may be a way out of this prison, but there is no escape from me. I will be the first man to kiss you, to bed you. Whether you come willingly or not, you will be mine and mine alone. Do you understand?'

Sido could hardly hear the words above the whirling sound in her head, the throbbing of the blood in her veins, which was drumming to a frantic beat. A wave of heaviness swept over her.

She hoped that she had said, 'I would rather die than marry you.' She could not be sure, for all there was turned black.

———◆———

Sido woke to find herself not back in the dormitory on her wooden board but in a proper bed in a small room with the luxury of sheets. There was a window, high and barred, and a chair on which was placed a vase of bright red, blood-red roses, their petals lush and out of keeping with their grey surroundings. She sat up as the door opened, expecting to see Kalliovski. Much to her relief a plainly dressed woman with a bunch of keys at her waist entered, carrying a tray.

Citizeness Villon was a buxom woman, the wife of the prison governor. Carefully she set the tray with its bowl of soup and freshly cut bread on the bed.

'You gave us quite a scare,' she said, handing Sido a spoon. The soup, chicken broth with herbs and potatoes, tasted delicious. She sipped it, savouring its rich flavour.

'It's good to see you looking better. Citizen Kalliovski

has undertaken to pay for all the little extras too. What a charming, thoughtful man! You're lucky to be under his protection, if I may say so. Why, he's even gone to the trouble of ordering you a new dress.'

'How long have I been here?'

'Several days. Prison fever. Now, eat up. Have a little more soup and bread.'

'Do you know where my father is?'

'He's been moved to a cell of his own. Citizen Kalliovski has been good enough to have a bed brought in for him to make his stay comfortable.'

Later that morning Citizeness Villon returned with two warders who brought in a tub of water. Sido bathed herself and washed her hair, beginning slowly to feel more human. Cleanliness, she thought, stands for hope, dirt for despair. She dried herself and dressed in her new gown. It smelled of lavender, reminding her of the château garden where she used to walk on sunny afternoons.

Citizeness Villon inspected her charge.

'You must go back to the main prison now,' she said, handing her over to the turnkey. 'But don't you worry. I'll bring all your meals as well as your clean laundry.'

'I see you've been promoted to your own cell,' said the turnkey as he walked her back along the corridor. He leered at her. His breath stank of stale tobacco and rotten teeth. 'You smell nice. I like it when young ladies smell nice.'

He unlocked a door. 'Well, here it is. Versailles itself

278

can't compare.' He chuckled as he bolted and locked the door behind him.

The cell had nothing in it apart from a bed, a bucket, and high up in the wall, a small window. At least, Sido thought, I don't have to share it.

She slept badly that night, disturbed by screams and sobs from down the corridor. She lay looking up at the window, watching the moon as its large round face peeped in through the darkness, asking her what she was going to do.

She had no answer to that question. It seemed there was nothing she could do, other than accept Kalliovski. There was, as he had said, really no choice. It was a *fait accompli*. The thought of him touching her again made her shiver and tears rolled down her face on to the lumpy mattress.

Next morning Sido woke to the sound of the bolts to her door being pulled back.

'You're a popular couple of high-ups, ain't you?' said the turnkey. 'Get up, your lawyer wants to see you. Look lively.'

He led her to a whitewashed room with a table and four chairs, and closed the door behind him. Next to enter was her father, followed by Maître Tardieu and a clerk.

Her father appeared quite altered. His hair had turned completely white and his skin seemed to have fallen from him like the tide pulling away from a pebbled beach. All that remained was the haunted, frightened look in his eyes.

He turned upon Maître Tardieu. 'I won't read the will. I refuse. You shouldn't have let him change a word. I hold you responsible for this outrage, sir.'

'Please, Papa, Maître Tardieu is here to help us.'

The Marquis's voice rose, as did the state of his agitation. 'Be silent, madame. Where are my servants? Take me back to my room this instant.'

'Please calm yourself.'

Her father lashed out at her, hitting her hard across the face. She stumbled, to be caught by Maître Tardieu's clerk.

'Are you all right?' he asked softly.

For a moment Sido thought she was dreaming, for it was Yann who had caught her.

Putting his finger to his lips, he helped her to a chair. 'Don't say anything,' he whispered.

'It's the only way to deal with ghosts, thrash them!' shouted the Marquis at the top of his voice.

The turnkey, hearing the commotion, came rushing back into the room.

'What's going on here?'

'That man,' said the Marquis, pointing at the lawyer, 'is no more than dog muck on my shoe. I will not speak to him.'

'Then hold your tongue,' said the turnkey. 'You've ten minutes here and then I'll be back for the pair of you.'

'No,' shouted the Marquis. 'Take me away now. Keep her from me. I've had enough of that dead woman. I say again, you can both rot in hell.'

'Better take him then. I'll be as quick as I can,' said Maître Tardieu, looking despairingly at the turnkey and rubbing his aching temples. The heat and the smell were overpowering. He sat down at the table.

The door closed with a loud thud. Maître Tardieu looked around nervously and put a finger to his lips. He spoke almost in a whisper.

'Mademoiselle Sido, I tried to get to see you earlier this week, but it was impossible because you were ill. I think you should know that Kalliovski is applying to have you released as long as you agree to marry him. Is that what you want?'

'No, no. I honestly thought—'

'That Mr Tull would get you to England,' interrupted Yann. 'He was working for Kalliovski. You didn't stand a chance.'

Maître Tardieu coughed. 'May I continue? Time is of the essence. Your case comes up before the tribunal in less than two days. You and your father are accused of being counter-Revolutionaries and of trying to escape from France, taking with you a vast fortune.'

'But that's nonsense. We have nothing. You know we have nothing.'

'It matters not.' He let out a heavy sigh. 'I am an old man, and there is much still on my mind and much that is unresolved. I want to rest easy in my grave.'

'I am sure you will,' said Sido kindly. 'You have been very good to our family.'

'No, I feel that I have failed you and your grandfather, to whom I was devoted.'

'No, sir, you are too hard on yourself . . .'

'Please, mademoiselle,' Maître Tardieu broke in. He leant towards Sido and whispered, 'Put your trust in Yann Margoza. It is your only chance of escape.'

'But sir, I can't leave my father here.'

Yann was concentrating so hard on Sido that he didn't notice the look of anguish that crossed the lawyer's face at these words.

'Sir,' said Sido, rising, 'are you ill?'

'It is nothing.' He clasped his chest. 'My heart is not as strong as it used to be.' Yann helped him to a chair. 'Lord forgive me, please, mademoiselle, think of yourself. Unlike others, you have family in England waiting for you . . .'

Yann, now almost desperate, interrupted. 'Danton is stirring people into a fever of hatred against all those held in the prisons. It will explode and you will be caught in it unless we do something.'

Along the corridor they could hear the sound of boots and the click-clack of dogs' claws against stone.

'I am going to come for you,' said Yann. 'When I do, you must be ready.'

The turnkey opened the door. 'Well, old lawyer, is she going to plead innocence? That the horse had a mind of its own and took off to see an old mare in England?' He laughed heartily at his own joke.

Outside the prison, Maître Tardieu gulped desperately at the fresh air, his hand holding the railing tight. Overcome by the heat, he felt unsteady on his feet. Yann led him into a nearby café and ordered him a drink.

'What can we do?' asked Yann, looking at the grey face of the lawyer. 'She's not going to leave him and I can't see any way of getting that madman out.'

'I can assure you he isn't worth it. Mademoiselle Sido, though, is a different matter; she has courage and dignity, she is a true de Villeduval, takes after her uncle and grandfather. The late Marquis's first wife, you know, was just like her son, a weak-minded woman who ended her days in an asylum.'

He picked up his glass and drank. 'Oh dear, oh dear,' he continued. 'I wanted to say something in the prison, but I couldn't bring myself to voice it. After all, it is only rumour and hearsay. I deal in proof, in evidence: that is the *raison d'être* of a lawyer. Gossip is not to be trusted – it could not be upheld in any court of law. All the same, there is Mademoiselle Sido left to rot in hell's waiting room. How did it come to this?'

Yann was barely listening. He pushed his hand through his hair. 'There must be a way of getting her out.'

'I debated with myself about telling her,' said Maître Tardieu. 'Maybe I should have. It might have helped.'

'What might have helped?' said Yann, turning to look at the lawyer.

'It was rumoured that Armand de Villeduval and Mademoiselle Sido's mother were lovers, and that they were planning to flee to England, taking the child with them. My late master told me on his deathbed that in the portmanteau that had gone missing were letters that led him to believe ...'

Yann sat bolt upright. He finished what the lawyer was about to say. 'That Armand de Villeduval was Sido's father?'

'Precisely. Find the letters and you may well have enough evidence to make her change her mind about leaving the Marquis, for I believe there is blood on those pampered pink hands of his.'

'Where do you think those letters are, sir?' asked Yann.

'The first place I would look is in Kalliovski's apartment.'

On the wall opposite the café, scribbled in dripping red paint, were the words 'Kill the enemy within'.

Yann knew there was hardly any time. The only way to get her out was to be bold – and bolder.

T he letter that Monsieur Aulard had just signed sat worryingly on his desk. Never had a piece of paper frightened him so much. He knew it held the power to snuff out life itself. More to the point, *his* life.

What was that children's game, he thought bitterly to himself, the one with paper, stone and scissors? Which one was it that won over paper? With a shudder, the answer came to him. Scissors – the guillotine! Yes, his neck was on the block. He was about to send two tickets to Citizen Kalliovski inviting him to bring one of his famed automata to the theatre that very night. The letter said that an old friend of Topolain's wanted to talk to him about the threads of light, and it was signed, 'From a well-wisher.'

This hadn't been Monsieur Aulard's idea; far from it. He could not imagine what the threads of light were. It was part of Têtu's master plan to get Kalliovski away from his apartment so that Yann could break in and search for Armand's letters.

'Do you really think Kalliovski will take the bait?' he asked.

'He won't be able to resist,' replied Têtu.

Monsieur Aulard stared transfixed at the letter, remembering only too clearly the Pierrot's head sitting in the lap of the dead Topolain.

'I still don't understand why Kalliovski killed Topolain,' he said.

'It was because Topolain let slip that they'd met before in St Petersburg. Topolain used to do card tricks to entertain the gamblers. The man who was later to take the name Kalliovski was there.'

'Why didn't Topolain just keep quiet?'

'Why indeed? He wasn't thinking straight. He was trying to impress and said the first foolish thing that came into his head. Kalliovski didn't want his cover blown. He couldn't be sure that one day Topolain wouldn't remember the exact circumstances of their meeting. He could not allow anyone to have that power over him.'

'Why? What would it matter?'

Têtu sighed. 'Is your knowledge box not working? Has your brain shut up shop?'

'I just want to be clear,' said Aulard, offended.

'It was in the gambling dens of St Petersburg that the self-styled Count Kalliovski started his meteoric rise to fame and fortune.'

Yann heard with a start the word that Têtu was thinking but not saying. Usually Têtu's mind was shut to him, but one word had slipped under the barricades. A word that sparkled like a diamond in the mud, too bright to be missed. Gypsy.

What Têtu was really saying was: 'He was a gypsy we used to know.'

'A gypsy,' said Yann out loud.

Têtu spun round. 'I never said that.'

'You thought it.'

'It's a figure of speech, that's all.'

'Not one that you would ever use.'

'Yann, forget it, I didn't mean anything by it.'

'What does it matter?' said Monsieur Aulard. 'What's wrong with you both, that we're now arguing over a word that Têtu never said?' He threw his hands in the air. '*Mort bleu*, my life is on the line and you … are beyond belief!'

Têtu looked closely at Yann. 'That is the first time you've been able to do that. You're getting good.'

'When you've both finished talking gobbledygook, could we get back to the matter in hand? I have invited Kalliovski to the theatre. Why would he come here?'

'For the same reason he wanted us to perform at the Marquis's château. He wanted to see if we could work the threads of light.'

'I'm lost. Threads of light? What are they? No, on second thoughts, I don't want to know. In case you haven't noticed, Paris is nearly under siege, the enemy is only miles away, men are going off to fight and we will have an empty house tonight. No one will come, especially not Kalliovski.' Monsieur Aulard was struggling to keep his composure.

'In that you are very wrong,' said Têtu. 'Your theatre will be full and Kalliovski, I can assure you, wouldn't miss it for the world.'

Perspiration now dripped down Monsieur Aulard's forehead and his hands were shaking. He was trying to stop himself from crumpling up the paper before him. He wanted to refuse to have anything more to do with this foolhardy plan.

'Are these letters really so important?' he said pathetically. 'Why don't you just get the girl out? Leave Kalliovski alone.'

'I could, if she would leave her father, but she won't,' said Yann flatly. 'I need to be able to show her some evidence that her father was involved in the death of her mother, and maybe prove who her real father is.'

'Wait, wait, not so fast. Didier, my medicine!'

'No,' said Têtu firmly. 'You need your wits about you.'

'*Mort bleu!* Are you telling me you don't believe the Marquis is her father?'

'Yes,' said Têtu. 'We think it was his half-brother, Armand. And we are sure that the Marquis, with Kalliovski's help, had something to do with their murder.'

'Murder? This gets worse with every word! We should report it to the authorities and let them deal with it. For goodness sake, you are magicians! I run a theatre! This is out of our field.'

'We are the only people who can save Sido,' said Yann, 'and if we can do this well, then maybe we can get other

288

people out and save them from the guillotine.'

'Tell me I'm not hearing this. Have you lost your mind? That's a criminal offence! We could be accused of counter-Revolutionary activities, of being spies. I can see it now, your heads not on the poster outside my theatre but on pikes with pretty ribbons of blue, white and red.'

'So we just do nothing?' said Yann. 'We sit back and let the slaughter begin? Should we be glad to be part of it? I love France, but I'm not going to join those who think that slaughtering French citizens will do any good. All I want to do is to try and stop this insanity.'

Monsieur Aulard swallowed. 'Spoken like a true hero! But do we have to stick our heads above the parapet?'

'Spoken like a true coward,' said Têtu.

'Listen,' said Yann, 'none of us can afford to turn our backs on what's going on. There are spies everywhere in Paris. The press has been shut down. Free speech does not exist – speak out of line and see where you end up. So much for liberty! Look how many people have been rounded up in midnight raids, and not just aristocrats and priests. The prisons are full to bursting. Don't you want to help us?'

'It's still better than the old regime,' said Monsieur Aulard weakly.

'It won't be if the leaders of the Revolution have their way. They're calling for all the prisoners to be killed, talking about tearing them limb from limb, ruling by terror and terror alone.'

'They don't mean it literally, I'm sure,' said Monsieur Aulard.

Yann threw his head back and burst out laughing. 'Oh, I see, so we're expected to be able to tell the difference. A man will stand there reading the poster and saying to his friends, "Good old Marat, the people's friend, uses such fine and descriptive words. What he meant to say was …"'

Monsieur Aulard sat back in his chair, defeated. He had no idea how he had managed to let himself be hoodwinked into this mess. If he was caught, dear Lord … Couldn't he just go back to the good old days? To yesterday, even, when all he'd had to concentrate on was giving the public what they wanted, a show full of patriotic drivel and heads on pikes, a pantomime of folly.

He was so busy making up his own epitaph that he hardly heard what was being said. He looked up wearily as Didier started talking. That was another thing. Didier, yes, Didier, whom he employed to protect him, now seemed to be working full time for Têtu. Oh, he thought miserably, for what I am about to receive, may someone help me.

'Well, Didier, did you find out how we could get into Kalliovski's apartment?' asked Yann.

'Yes, yes, I did,' said Didier. 'Citizen Kalliovski has one servant whom he leaves to guard his apartment. His sole task is to make sure that no one enters while his master is away.'

'How do you know?' asked Monsieur Aulard. Despite

his anxieties, he was impressed with Didier's skill. Who would have thought the old mooncalf had so much going for him in the upstairs department?

'I've become friendly with the concierge of the building where he lives, on the rue Payenne.' Didier blushed. 'She's called Jeanne.'

'How long has this fellow been with Kalliovski?' asked Yann.

'She says he's been with him the longest of all his servants. Got a funny eye.'

'Milkeye,' said Yann.

'Do you think she'd let Yann deliver a basket to Kalliovski?' asked Têtu.

'If we went in by the side entrance, I don't think she'd mind.'

'Tomorrow,' interrupted a mournful Monsieur Aulard, 'is the second of September, my birthday, if any of you are interested. My last birthday, no doubt, for as sure as there is a sun in the day and a moon in the night, I shall be murdered by Kalliovski. When I am dead, and if you haven't been guillotined, Didier, would you be so kind as to put lilies on my grave?'

Têtu jumped up from his seat and turned on him furiously.

'This is not about you! This is about an innocent girl who will be killed if we don't act. This is about saving lives. This is about Yann. He is the one you should be worrying about. If you don't wish to be involved, go home and put your head under a pillow. But if you want to try and find some semblance of bravery, you could

291

pull yourself together and stop being a big girl's bonnet.'

Monsieur Aulard looked crushed by the impact of the dwarf's words. It was true he was a mouse of a man when it came to bravery; still, he was doing his best.

'Take this and put it on,' said Têtu, pulling out a black cap from his jacket pocket.

Monsieur Aulard looked at it. All the questions he wanted to ask and dare not sat heavily on his bushy eyebrows.

'Well?' said Têtu. His voice hadn't softened at all. 'What are you waiting for? Just put it on. Don't make such a drama out of everything.'

Timidly, as if it were a candle-snuffer, Monsieur Aulard put the cap on his head. 'It doesn't fit!' he complained.

'Where has he gone? What've you done with him? He's disappeared!' shouted Didier. 'What a good trick!'

Such was his relief that Monsieur Aulard suddenly felt liberated from his worries. He was surprised not to find himself floating up to the ceiling with relief.

'This is wonderful, Têtu,' he said, putting his two very visible hands on either side of the dwarf's face and kissing him loudly. Forgetting his fear of Citizen Kalliovski, he said with the excitement of a child, 'I'm going to find out if anyone else can see me. Wait here.'

'If you see your reflection, don't worry. No one else will,' Didier called after him.

They waited until he had gone.

'I told everyone at the theatre to pretend he was invisible if they saw him wearing the black cap,' said Didier seriously.

Yann chuckled.

'Yann, it's not funny,' snapped Têtu. 'If this fails he'll be a gibbering wreck and useless to us. If it works, he might find the courage he needs.'

'How did you get everybody to agree to it, Didier?' asked Yann.

'Simple,' said Didier. 'I told them they wouldn't get paid if they let the cat out of the bag.'

'Brilliant. Masterly,' said Têtu with a sudden laugh.

'It works!' said Monsieur Aulard, rushing back into the room. 'We could make our fortune with this.'

'No,' said Têtu, bringing him down to earth with a bang. 'If we manage to stay alive, that will be fortune enough.'

———◆———

Before he left that night for Kalliovski's, Yann went down and stood in the centre of the empty stage. There was no one around. The wings were dark, as was the auditorium. A workman's lamp hung down from the fly tower, casting a faint light upon him in the gloom all around. He looked out over the shadowy shoreline of empty seats. It seemed to him there was no lonelier place to stand than here on the empty stage, the home of illusion with its haunting dread of failure.

In the silence, in the darkness of the wings, he could almost see Topolain and the wooden Pierrot walk on to the stage, hear the magician call out to the audience, 'No bullet can harm me! I am invincible, I have drunk from the cup of everlasting life!'

Yann knew then that he had come back to Paris to face the pistol, to catch the bullet. If he survived, Sido too would be free.

As he stood there he heard a voice he recognised from a long time ago. It came from the stalls. He didn't call out, or ask who was there; he knew enough now not to question what the spirit said.

The voice was gentle.

'There is nothing to fear except the power you give to your own demons.'

Chapter Twenty-nine

I t was a warm evening as Didier and Yann made their way towards the rue Payenne. The news on the street was not good. The Duke of Brunswick's army was advancing steadily towards the capital. There was a crackle to the atmosphere, like the fore-warning of a terrible storm.

Still, for tonight at least the sky was clear, with a tinge of watercolour rose spilling into the darkening clouds. By dawn those with an appetite for violence would take over the city and change the course of the Revolution for ever. For the time being, liberty still wore its bridal gown, a bright promise in the hearts of its citizens. Tomorrow it would lose its innocence, be drowned in blood.

The mansion where Citizen Kalliovski lived was home to members of the Revolutionary council, just as once it had been home to the great and the good of Parisian society. Its new clientele enjoyed exactly the same privileges as the previous residents; only the banner which flew from the ornate balcony was different.

Yann and Didier were watching as, on the dot of seven, Kalliovski's beetle-black carriage pulled up outside the building. Two servants came out, supporting a woman between them, and lifted her into the carriage. The only hint that she was not human was that her feet never touched the ground. Shortly afterwards, Kalliovski and his hound Balthazar climbed into the carriage, and it set off in the direction of the theatre.

Yann smiled to himself. The man had taken the bait.

At the side entrance, Didier knocked three times. The door was opened and the beaming rosy face of Jeanne appeared. She stood on tiptoe and threw her arms round Didier's neck, planting kisses on his face.

'What kept you, my old bear?' She stopped, seeing Yann. 'Who's this?'

'He's a friend. He has to deliver something to Citizen Kalliovski and, well, as I was seeing you I thought I would bring him with me.' Didier leant forward and kissed her. 'You don't mind if he goes up the back way, do you?'

'His apartment's on the first floor,' whispered Jeanne, looking around anxiously.

'Is there anyone else who might demand your attention this evening, apart from me?' asked Didier.

She giggled, and he squeezed her tight.

'No, they've all gone off to a meeting somewhere. They tell me it's going to be a long night, and I need protection. I'm all alone, my old bear, with only your strong arms to keep the enemy from charging in on your sweet little Jeanne.'

Yann left them to it and quickly moved up the stairs that led to the main part of the house. Here all was quiet. The silence had a strange, eerie quality to it, as if the house had become detached from the rest of the world.

On the first floor was the apartment he was looking for. Taking a deep breath, he knocked on the door. It was opened by Milkeye.

'This is for Citizen Kalliovski,' said Yann.

'He's not in,' said Milkeye hoarsely, moving as if to close the door.

'Will you at least take the basket?'

Yann pulled back the cloth to reveal a round cheese, a loaf of bread, and a bottle of red wine. The smell was pungent and tempting. Milkeye grabbed the basket.

'My master doesn't like cheese,' he said.

Yann shrugged his shoulders and reached to take back the gift. With his outstretched palm Milkeye pushed him so hard that he landed with a thud on the opposite wall, with the door slammed firmly in his face.

Ten minutes was what Têtu had reckoned before the wine and cheese worked their magic and Milkeye would

297

be fast asleep. Yann gave it fifteen to make sure before gently trying the door. To his relief, it opened easily and he found himself in the dark empty hall.

There was just enough light for him to make his way cautiously into the salon. It was an enormous room and furnished on a grand scale. He looked around, half expecting to see Milkeye felled like a tree on the floor.

There was no sign of him, just the basket on the side table. The bottle of wine was missing but the cheese was untouched. This was not a good sign. It would take both to knock him out completely. Yann wondered why he could hear the beating of a drum; then he realised it was his own heart. He spun round, fearing to see Milkeye in the long shadows. But the room was empty.

Guardedly he went through the interconnecting doors to the next salon. Surely he must be here some-where – behind this door maybe? Every sound echoed cannon-ball loud in his head. Something was very wrong. Yann felt his mind whirling. He walked through to the third salon. The door was ajar and he pushed it open, to be greeted by a blast of cold air.

Yann stopped, hearing voices. Jeanne had told Didier that no one was allowed into the apartment while Kalliovski was out. He listened intently.

'Velvet and violence.

Brocade and blood.

Damask and death.'

There were several voices, none of them Milkeye's. The words came in a high moan, sharp and urgent to his ear, as if some bizarre game was being played. But by whom? Didier must have been wrongly informed.

'Fur and fury.

Calico and corpses,'
came the whispered words. Yann felt every sense in him alert as he pushed the door further open. The room was in total darkness, the shutters closed tight against the light. He felt his breath coming fast, as if he had been running to get here.

'Calm down, calm down,' he said to himself, waiting for his eyes to get used to the darkness. He lit a candle, and immediately the voices stopped and everything went deathly still.

The room had been made into a workshop with a bench and a long table; in the half-light he could see shelves filled with glass jars. What was inside them he couldn't make out. Books were piled high, charts and maps of the heavens were scattered about, and there were burners, jars and surgical instruments on the workbench.

He heard something rustle and spun round, expecting to see Milkeye behind him. There was nobody there. He was slowly moving the candle to look more closely at what was in the glass jars when he heard the whispering voices say, 'Calico and corpses.'

Yann stopped, transfixed to the spot. The sight in front of him nearly caused him to drop the candle, for ranged along the back wall of the chamber stood six automata, their eyes shut, only their ruby wax mouths moving.

The thing Yann despised in others he now saw clearly

in himself. Fear had wrapped itself around his heart. If he were to let it get the better of him he would be dead; that much his reason knew. The other part of him just wanted to get the hell out of there. The battle inside him was won when he saw the dull threads of light coming from the automata and he realised with a shudder that someone had already pulled them tight as violin strings. Tight enough to keep the six automata whispering all night long.

Yann set to work to loosen the threads of light and as he did so, he heard the automata calling to him with their songs of sorrow that seemed to come from a dark place indeed and to have little to do with the living. He watched almost hypnotised as six pairs of glass eyes opened and stared at him. Now he noticed that they all wore identical red necklaces. The hairs on the back of his neck tingled, and in that moment everything slowed down as if time itself were yawning.

'You think I'd fall for such a cheap trick?' said a voice from behind him. Milkeye was standing in the doorway, a pistol in his hand. 'I've waited a long time for this.'

All Yann could think was, 'I should run,' but he couldn't. He was paralysed by the knowledge of what was coming next, the inevitability of it. He had the insane desire to burst out laughing, for this moment was what he had been dreading. Here it was in all its glory, and it seemed almost nothing, compared to the long endless terror of waiting.

The pistol went off, the noise surprisingly shocking. He saw the flame from the gunpowder, the bullet graceful in its slow arc across the room towards him, trailing smoke as it went.

It had taken years for this bullet to find him. He reached out for it with his mind, tried to catch it in his hand. It scorched his flesh before piercing through his skin and lodging in his shoulder. Pain flooded him like water from a dam; the impact of it knocked him off his feet. He slumped down by the workbench. Milkeye was now coming towards him, the pistol reloaded, his finger on the trigger.

Yann fought not to lose consciousness. He pushed himself back towards the automata and felt the folds of a taffeta skirt fall round him as one of them bent over to take the bullet in her back. Yann couldn't see where Milkeye was, for her stiff and dusty hair had fallen in his face. Her blazing eyes looked straight at him.

'We,' she said, 'are the Seven Sisters Macabre. One of our party is missing. What is your name?'

'Yann Margoza,' he managed to say, as blood-black curtains threatened to close in front of him.

'Calico and corpses,' she said, and her graveyard breath brought him to his senses.

Once more he experienced the feeling of leaving his body, as he had done before in the forest. Now he stood in the middle of the room, a puppet-master of the threads of light.

At his command, the Sisters Macabre began to walk towards Milkeye, the dusty taffeta of their skirts trailing behind them like waves upon a shore. Milkeye loaded his pistol for the third time and fired at the oncoming automata. It did not stop them.

Yann felt the two parts of himself collide once again. The pain brought with it crystal vision. He dragged himself up by the workbench, feeling that he was ten feet tall and invincible. He pulled at the threads of light, lifted a chair and brought it down on Milkeye's head, then picked up another chair and another, until Milkeye let out a grunt and collapsed on the floor.

The room and its occupants began to spin round and round. For a moment Yann couldn't remember why he was there. Then he felt a cold wax hand touch his face, and with a start became conscious of one of the Sisters Macabre standing next to him.

'We are his experiments. He believes that in us he can find the secret of perpetual youth. He believes he can hold time back for himself. We have been robbed of our lives. We have been robbed of our rest. What is it you want of us?'

'Letters, love letters written by Armand . . .' The name, what was the name? Why couldn't he remember . . . de . . .

'Villeduval,' said all the sisters together. 'All you had to do was ask.'

Yann leaned lopsidedly on the workbench, trying to find his balance.

'Velvet and violence.

Taffeta and terror,' said the Sisters Macabre as Milkeye writhed on the floor, his legs twitching.

'If only the pain would stop,' thought Yann, 'I could

think straight. I would know what to do.' All his thoughts now were consumed by this burning ache in his shoulder. There, he could hear it again, that sound of the distant drum fading away as his strength ebbed from him.

'Is this what you came for?' asked a Sister.

He heard a ripping sound as the fabric of her dress rent apart, and where the womb should have been two doors sprang open to reveal a blood-red empty chamber. She reached in with her white wax hands and handed Yann a bundle of letters.

A second Sister pulled out a blood-red drawer from where her stomach should have been, and handed him a black book.

'This is for you. It is the Book of Tears. It is bound with our flesh.'

'He stole our lives.

He stole our hearts.

He stole our deaths,'

whispered the Sisters Macabre together as they gathered round Yann, making sure that the letters and the book were safely in his coat pocket before they lined up once more against the back wall, their eyes closing, their mouths whispering.

'Velvet and violence.

Brocade and blood.

Damask and death.'

Yann was still clinging on to the bench when he became aware of the grisly contents of the jars. They were filled with parts of bodies: in one, a head, in another, limbs, in another a stack of hearts.

'Calico and corpses.

Satin and suffering,' whispered the Sisters Macabre.

Yann's shirt was wet and he wondered why it was red.

The room was spinning again and into this unsettling scene came Milkeye. Like some monster he had grown more arms and legs, all trying to get him. Yann kicked out desperately, but still those hands kept coming.

He staggered and sank to his knees. Someone should warn Têtu that Kalliovski can work the threads of light, he thought, as the curtains of his mind, blood-black, treacle-thick, came down for good: the show well and truly over, the end of the performance.

Chapter Thirty

'*Nom de dieu!*' said Monsieur Aulard, entering his apartment with Têtu to see Yann stretched out on his kitchen table and Didier, his shirtsleeves rolled up, washing blood from his hands in a basin. 'Is he dead?'

'No,' said Didier. 'Luckily the bullet didn't go into the bone and the wound is clean. He should be all right.'

Têtu climbed up on a chair to take a closer look at Yann.

'What happened?' he asked, cautiously inspecting Didier's work.

'To tell the truth, I'm not sure. I didn't hear the gun go off, but I was worried because he'd been so long. I rushed into the apartment to see Milkeye with his hands round Yann's legs. He'd been shot. I thought he was dead. There was blood all over the floor.'

Têtu felt Yann's forehead. 'At least he has no fever. That's something.' Seeing the bullet sitting in the basin, he picked it up and examined it. 'As always, you've done well, Didier.'

Didier gently lifted Yann up and took him through to the next room. 'I'll put him in your bed,' he told Monsieur Aulard.

'Can't he sleep somewhere else?' asked Monsieur Aulard.

Didier looked disgusted. 'No,' he said, 'not after I've cleaned up that tip of a room of yours and put fresh linen on the bed. He needs to rest.'

'Clean linen too,' thought Monsieur Aulard. 'Do they think I'm made of money? Have I nothing left to call my own?'

Didier came back into the room with a fresh basin of water and scrubbed the table clean. Then he went over to the cupboard, brought out a bottle of Monsieur Aulard's best brandy and three glasses, and rolled down his sleeves.

'I don't know about you two, but I need a drink and no mistake. How did your evening go?'

'Tricky. Tiring,' answered Têtu.

'And nothing to show for it but a bullet,' said Monsieur Aulard.

Didier said nothing.

———◆———

Kalliovski had arrived at the Theatre of Liberty, causing quite a sensation with his automaton, which looked as though it was modelled on that poor woman Madame Perrien. Monsieur Aulard had once seen her at the theatre and remembered her as being

306

pretty, with an infectious laugh. The automaton was a hideous mockery of what she had once looked like.

Though the audience had clapped when she walked unaided to her seat, her movements were jerkier than Kalliovski would have liked. To a perfectionist such as he was, it was one of the many flaws that needed ironing out. After tonight, with Têtu working for him, everything would be different.

He sat himself down in the front row next to his automaton, with Balthazar at his feet, and stretched out his legs. He all but had Têtu within his grasp, for he was certain that it was the dwarf who had sent the invitation. With the coming of the Terror, Têtu would need protection. Together, what couldn't they do! Yes, it was worth coming for that alone.

He took out his watch. It was a beautiful piece of craftsmanship, the face showing an image of the Grim Reaper. If he left at the interval he would get to the meeting on time. He smiled to himself.

From the prompt desk, Monsieur Aulard dared himself to look into the face of his daemon, for the man sitting in the front row had haunted him ever since that terrible day when Topolain's body had been found in his office, and here he was, not three metres from him. He held on tight to the black cap in his pocket. The feel of it comforted him and calmed his shredded nerves.

'Are we ready?' he asked Têtu nervously.

'Oh yes, my friend, and I think you are going to enjoy seeing a true master at work.' Têtu flexed his fingers as if about to play a piano. 'Bring up the curtain.'

Kalliovski appeared to take little pleasure in what was happening on stage. The show itself was an affront to his intellect. It was just a cacophony of patriotic songs, drivel for the masses that fed into the fever of the moment.

Têtu was interested to see how tightly Kalliovski controlled his automaton. No wonder she had moved so stiffly. He started gently to play with her threads of light, expecting at any moment that Kalliovski would become aware of what he was doing, for a true shaman would know instinctively when someone else was interfering. It didn't take him long to discover that Kalliovski was a mere amateur, with no natural gift.

Têtu stood the automaton up. Standing next to Kalliovski, she started to sing the Marseilleise. In the flicker of the oil lamps, the audience and the actors on stage whose performance had nothing to do with magic were taken aback by this creature and her ethereal voice.

A shout went up from the audience. 'Bring up the lights! Let's have a proper look.'

As if on cue, the automaton turned to bow at them. Try as he might, Kalliovski could not regain control of the threads of light; his mind did not have the strength. He could do nothing but sit there and envy the brilliance of such sorcery.

The audience were soon out of their seats and singing along with the automaton, tears rolling down their faces.

Kalliovski was caught, and he knew it. He was forced

to take unwarranted credit for his patriotic creation. By the time the curtain came down, the applause was deafening. He was unable to leave his seat as members of the audience came to stare at the automaton and ask him questions about it.

He hissed to one of his henchmen, 'Fetch me the theatre manager.'

At this point Monsieur Aulard broke into Têtu's story of the evening's events.

'Go on, tell Didier what I did.'

And Têtu, who generally declined on principle to give credit to anyone, softened slightly and said, 'There is no doubt that without our friend's bravery, Kalliovski would have left the theatre long before the final curtain call.'

***

Monsieur Aulard had refused to be hurried down the gangway, no matter how many times Kalliovski's henchman prodded him in the back. He insisted on stopping and talking to the odd patron who would jokingly ask whether he was going to offer Kalliovski's automaton a job in his theatre. He walked towards Kalliovski as if towards the guillotine itself. With every measured step, he felt a little braver. At last he reached the front row. Kalliovski had a look that said: 'You will be dead unless you can explain this'. He nodded at one of his men, who handed him the invitation.

'Are you responsible for sending me two tickets to your wretched fleapit of a theatre to see this travesty of a show?'

Monsieur Aulard held tight to the black cap in his pocket; just to know it was there gave him courage. He leant towards Kalliovski, a smile stuck fast to his face. 'I don't think the rest of the audience think it a travesty.'

Kalliovski stood up. He towered above Monsieur Aulard, who instinctively took a step backwards as his stomach lurched forwards. He had forgotten quite how frightening the man was. It was something about his face and those eyes that burned straight through you like drops of acid.

Monsieur Aulard kept talking. 'Why, citizen, I thought by the reaction to your remarkable automaton that you were enjoying the performance.'

'The dwarf is in the theatre, I know it,' hissed Kalliovski.

'You mean Têtu?'

'You know I do,' spat Kalliovski.

'I don't know if he is here tonight or not. I will make enquires, but first I must congratulate you, citizen, and ask you how such magic is accomplished.'

He knew he had him. Kalliovski's pride was such that he was not going to admit that the automaton's performance had little or nothing to do with him.

'If he's here, shall I say you would like to see him after the show?'

'No, I will see him now.' Kalliovski nodded towards his two henchmen as each took an arm of the automaton.

Monsieur Aulard handed back the invitation. 'Forgive me, but won't you stay to see the end of the show ...'

He never finished what he was saying, for the automaton said loudly, 'I don't want to go home. Don't take me home. I want to stay.'

The audience started to clap. 'That's it, citizen, you tell him!' shouted someone. 'Sing us some more songs!'

'If you wish,' said the automaton.

'We do!' shouted the audience.

Kalliovski shot a murderous look at the theatre manager.

The bell rang for the second half to begin, and the little band started to play. Monsieur Aulard bowed and took his leave, saying he hoped Citizen Kalliovski would enjoy the rest of the show. He returned backstage, still stroking the black cap in his pocket as the curtain came up.

Just after the first song was over, one of Kalliovski's men came in to give him a message. Once again it looked as if he were about to leave. Têtu acted quickly. He made the automaton rise into the air so that she hung there, hovering above the seats. The audience gasped in amazement. 'She's floating!' cried someone.

It was then that Têtu became aware that he had an invisible helper. Often when he played with the threads of light he had found that spirits would interfere. He had been concentrating so hard that he hadn't realised there was someone else out there. As the automaton floated above the audience, out of it emerged a phantom in the shape of a beautiful woman, a spirit made of light that illuminated the auditorium.

Balthazar hid under the seat, his ears pinned back,

whining miserably. A stunned silence broke over the audience.

'Who are you?' someone called out at last.

The spirit said nothing.

'Are you alive?'shouted another.

'I was alive once. I was murdered.'

At these words Kalliovski leapt up from his seat and backed away towards the wall of the auditorium where his two henchmen stood, terrified.

The apparition hovered above the seats, her dress flowing behind her, moving ever closer to him. Then, with a sudden wild laugh, she vanished. The audience, silent for a moment, started clapping and cheering, shouting for more.

Kalliovski, recovering himself, stared piercingly into the wings, wishing now that he could pull the theatre down brick by brick until he found what he was looking for – the dwarf. What he would give to have that power! And he *would* have it; he would become master of the dark arts; nothing was going to stop him.

The final curtain came down. He clicked open his watch. He was late. He got up and started for the door, leaving his automaton behind, nodding to his henchmen to bring her. But before they could reach her she called out, 'Sweetie, wait for me,' and Kalliovski turned to see his waxwork lady gliding up behind him, all stiffness gone. As she reached the doors to the auditorium Têtu let go of the threads of light, and she collapsed lifeless on the floor, leaving Kalliovski's men to pick her up.

The dwarf was exhausted. Sleep, he knew of old, was the only cure for his state. Still he waited until the last of the audience had left, for he was curious to know the identity of the spirit that had come to his aid. Once more the darkened, empty stage was filled with light, and he saw her standing before him. There was no mistaking who she was. No wonder Kalliovski had been so frightened. She was even more beautiful than he remembered: the only woman he had ever loved.

'Anis,' he said softly, 'so it was you. I should have known you would have been here for him.' He held out his hand towards her and felt something brush softly against his cheek, smelled for a moment her intoxicating perfume.

'Be careful,' she whispered as she faded away, 'you are not out of danger yet.'

'Anis, Anis,' said Têtu longingly into the impenetrable darkness, but she was gone.

He wiped his eyes. Was he becoming a sentimental old fool? He told himself it was just tiredness as, tears running down his face, he walked back into the wings. Grief once more had made the world seem unbearable.

'You should have lived,' he said quietly. 'You should have raised your own son. You would have been so proud of Yann.'

———◆———

Monsieur Aulard caught up with Kalliovski at the main door of the theatre.

'Têtu would be delighted to see you,' he said, still

313

holding tightly on to his black cap. 'He is backstage. He was most impressed by your abilities with the automaton, and so was I. I hope that if you ever need employment, you will remember my humble theatre.'

Kalliovski grabbed hold of Monsieur Aulard by the lapels of his coat.

'Tell him I will see him later, and as for you – the guillotine is a hungry lady. Be careful.' He let the theatre manager go, and Monsieur Aulard stood there mopping his brow as he watched the driver flick the horses' flanks with his whip, reassured to see that Kalliovski was not heading towards his mansion. Finishing his story, he told Didier and Têtu with pride, 'I wasn't scared, because I had my black cap.'

Têtu stayed quiet. He had said nothing about knowing who the spirit was. 'Some things,' he thought, 'do not belong here. They live in the hinterland between this world and another.'

'Still, for all our grand gestures and daring deeds, this is a disaster. We have failed dismally in our task,' said Monsieur Aulard dramatically.

'Don't be so hasty,' said Didier, bringing out Yann's coat and taking from it the packet of letters and the leather-bound black book. Têtu grabbed them, and nearly dropped the book when he realised what the binding was made of.

'Why didn't you tell me you'd got the letters?' he cried.

'But Yann was shot! How did you get hold of these?' asked Monsieur Aulard.

'You shouldn't have taken it for granted that because he was shot, he failed,' said Didier. 'There's more to that boy than meets the eye.'

'You're brilliant,' said Têtu.

'I didn't do it. It was Yann.'

The two men stopped as Yann came shakily into the room. Didier rushed forward to help him to a chair.

'What are you doing up?' asked Monsieur Aulard.

'I'm feeling better,' said Yann. He looked as white as snow.

'You've done very well to have got all this,' said Têtu.

Yann smiled. 'The letters were hidden inside one of the Sisters Macabre.'

'Sisters Macabre?'

'They are automata. One had a red chamber in her stomach, containing the letters. Another gave me this. She called it the Book of Tears.'

'Wonderful!' said Monsieur Aulard.

Têtu rummaged about until he found a little bag of herbs. He put it in a jug with some boiling water, strained it into a bowl and handed it to Yann.

'Here, drink this.'

It smelt and tasted so revolting that Yann spat it out immediately.

'What are you trying to do, Têtu? Poison me? Give me some water. That is the most disgusting thing I've ever tasted.'

'It will do you good, make you heal quickly. Come on now, drink it up.'

Yann did as he was told, and shortly afterwards his

315

eyelids began to close and Didier carried him back to bed.

That night only Didier and Yann slept. Monsieur Aulard and Têtu sat up reading the love letters of Armand de Villeduval and Isabelle Gautier.

'It breaks your heart to read of such great love. And that poor little daughter of theirs, lost and neglected! To think that she's to be given to that monster Kalliovski! We have to save her!' said Monsieur Aulard passionately.

'We must get back to the prison,' said Têtu. He picked up the Book of Tears and started to look through it. 'What's this?'

'Just blank paper,' said Monsieur Aulard.

'I think not,' said Têtu. As he held it up to the heat of the candle flame, page after page of writing appeared. 'You see? It's sympathetic ink that can only be seen when it is heated.'

On the title page were the words 'The Red Necklace', and the following pages listed the names of all those who had borrowed money from Kalliovski, how much they owed, and what secrets they had given up for the loan.

'So much blackmail! Is there anyone he hasn't bought?' mused Monsieur Aulard.

'There may be a few who were not blinded by his wealth and connections, but only a few, I'd say,' replied Têtu.

The dawn chorus had started when Monsieur Aulard at last put the book down. As he did so, a sheet of thin folded paper fell out, covered in elaborate flowery handwriting. He pored over it.

'Têtu, this is what we've been looking for!' he exclaimed. 'If Sido is in any doubt about leaving her father, this will not fail to convince her.'

It was a letter from the present Marquis de Villeduval, addressed to Count Kalliovski, asking him to arrange the deaths of his wife and his half-brother and of their daughter Sido.

C itizen Kalliovski's carriage made its way slowly through the busy streets towards the Tuileries Palace. It was a warm night, the buildings still retaining the heat of the hot summer. Nothing had cooled down, not the temperature, not the citizens, not the Revolution, not the war. The gated city felt like a vast witch's cauldron, the flotsam and jetsam of its population slowly rising to the top, ready to boil over with frustration, hatred and murder.

Kalliovski had not yet been home. There had been no time. The note that had been delivered to him at the theatre was from Citizen Danton, telling him of a meeting that he should attend if he wanted Sido de Villeduval's release papers signed. He sat cursing the fact that he was already late, angry with himself for having stayed so long at the theatre, and wondering why Têtu had brought back Anis's ghost. He raised his gloved hand and brought it down hard on the side of the carriage. Damn it, tonight of all nights. He didn't need to think of her. He had sworn he would never think of her again.

He took out his pocket watch. He was now over an hour late. The carriage edged along, slower than a funeral march. He banged loudly on the ceiling with its painted cherubs.

'Can't you go any faster?'

'No, sir,' the coachman called down. 'Too many people.'

Kalliovski thought angrily that Danton would not have the manners to wait for him. No, they would all have conveniently forgotten just how much he had helped by supplying the money to buy extra pikes and arms. It was all well and good, wanting the citizens of Paris to put an end to the traitors in their midst, but bare hands and fine words weren't enough. They needed weapons to be successful.

Tonight's meeting was unofficial, by invitation only. It would be the last chance for Danton, Marat and their cronies to trawl through the prison registers and to make quite sure that no one important had been rounded up by mistake, for tomorrow the killing would begin. Justice, for what little it was worth, would then be in the hands of the people: sheep, the lot of them, led by Marat, a leader of sheep who had ignited their

319

imaginations with his clever words. What use was it, Marat argued, for a man to go off to fight for his country when the prisons were full of counter-Revolutionaries? They would break out at the first opportunity and kill the innocents at home while the men of Paris were away fighting.

Kalliovski gave a thin smile as he thought, 'Oh world, beware of clever sheep. They are the truly dangerous ones, for they understand the stupidity of the flock, know just how easy it is to lead the people to slaughter.'

At last the carriage stopped at the Palace and Kalliovski made his way through the ill-lit entrance hall and down the forsaken corridors. Portraits of solemn, stiff-looking men in powdered wigs still hung on the walls in their gilt frames. How horrified they would be if they knew what was being discussed behind closed doors tonight! Not long ago the place had bristled with footmen and attendants, with dukes and princesses, with gossip and rumour and tittle-tattle. How many times had he been called upon to help some distressed viscount or embarrassed prince out of a difficulty? He had made a great deal of money from their follies. Now he saw no one, heard no one, just the click-clack of his own boots, and the scratching of Balthazar's sharp claws, upon the marbled floors.

Whom did he prefer? This bunch, with their bull-like orators and clever sheep, rich in words but not much else? Or the King and the aristocracy, foolish, narcissistic people who could hardly babble out a sentence without tripping over their own protocol, but whose pockets were lined with gold, ready for the taking?

The question remained unanswered as Kalliovski entered the large antechamber adjoining the room where the meeting was being held. The imposing double doors were firmly closed. He was surprised to find so many people waiting, a motley group who must all, like him, have paid handsomely for release papers to be stamped.

Kalliovski walked past all of them and knocked loudly at the main door. It was opened by a lizard of a man with hooded eyes.

'I have a note from Citizen Danton summoning me here,' said Kalliovski. He was about to walk straight past, but the man put out a firm hand to stop him.

'Not so fast, citizen.'

'Do you know who I am?'

The lizard-man studied him carefully, from his immaculate black coat and high necktie right down to his shiny black boots.

'Well-heeled,' he said, closing the door hard, like a full stop.

Kalliovski did not take kindly to such treatment. His blood boiled at the injustice of it. After all he had done for this miserable crew, he had no intention of waiting. Carefully brushing off any trace of the hand on his coat, he knocked again loudly. The same man opened the door.

'I have come for the release papers for Sidonie de Villeduval. I was told that they would be ready by now.'

'Then you have been misinformed, citizen. Look around you. You're going to have to wait like everyone else. You're no bleeding different. Equality, remember? That's what it's all about.' And once again the door was slammed shut.

Kalliovski was outraged. Such rudeness would not have been tolerated under the old regime. The man would have found himself in the Bastille for his impertinence. He went to knock on the door a third time. No one dismissed him like that.

'Sir, I wouldn't do that if I were you,' said a thin, anxious-looking man, getting up from his chair. 'They've already arrested one person for being impatient. I am hoping to get my son out of prison. They took him in the middle of the night – for what, we haven't been told. My wife . . .'

He stopped, seeing the look of indifference on Kalliovski's face, and quickly returned to the safety of his chair.

Once more Kalliovski took out his pocket watch to check the time. His well-constructed plan must not fail at this last important stage. As soon as he had Sido's release papers, he would go straight to the prison and have her freed, and then without further delay they would be married. He had even found himself a Catholic priest, one of the very few who was not languishing in prison, to carry out the deed. He wasn't going to risk having a Revolutionary wedding, not with the Duke of Brunswick so close to victory. He wanted the certificate to be above board, to hold Papal weight, for then and

322

only then would the considerable fortune finally be his. He might not have had the mother, but fate would give him the daughter and her inheritance. Revenge becomes all the sweeter, he thought, when it has been ripened by misfortune and then served cold, icy cold.

He smiled to himself. If the Duke of Brunswick were to invade Paris, he would have no hesitation in changing sides again. He was well aware that to have allegiances, to make a stand, to hold a firm political view, was the recipe for a short life. When the winds are liable to change quickly, it is best to be a reed and know how to bend. He had one motto, and it had not failed him yet. Have no mercy, show no mercy.

He walked back and forth, Balthazar by his side. Still the door remained closed. He had not bargained on this delay. He had planned to have Sido out of prison by now.

Time was dragging its feet, refusing to go any faster, as if it were hoping to keep night pinned to the stars. At last it let go and the inky dark sky gave way to the blood-red dawn.

The door of the antechamber opened. Everyone turned to see who the new visitor was. One of Kalliovski's henchmen entered the room.

'What is it?' Kalliovski asked brusquely.

'I'm sorry to report, sir, that there's been a break-in at your apartment.'

'You must be mistaken. Milkeye wouldn't have let anyone get past him.'

'I am afraid I'm not, sir.'

'Where is Milkeye?'

'Out cold, sir. We can't wake him.'

'Anything taken?' Kalliovski's voice was like the hiss of a viper.

'No, sir. Milkeye must have shot the intruder. There's blood all over the place.'

'Any sign of a body?'

'No.'

'Anything else?'

'Not that we can see.'

Kalliovski felt a warm rush of relief. Now, if the Book of Tears were to have gone, that would be a different matter. At least the Sisters Macabre wouldn't give up their secret so easily.

'There is one other thing, sir, but it's not important.'

'What?'

'It's the automata, sir.'

'What about it? Speak, man.'

'Two of them have been opened.'

'Did you look inside?' asked Kalliovski in a menacing whisper.

The man trembled. 'Yes, sir. They were empty.'

Kalliovski brought his fist down hard into his gloved hand. He paced back and forth, his eyes wild. He knew that only someone who could work the threads of light would have been able to open the secret chambers, but Têtu had been at the theatre and there was no one else capable of doing such a thing.

'Are you sure?' His hands automatically went towards

the man's throat and he began to strangle the life out of him.

The people in the room, shaken from fitful sleep, now did their best to separate the pair. Kalliovski shook himself free and looked down at the man on the floor, who was crimson in the face and gasping for air. Terrified, he pulled away from his master.

Kalliovski's eyes sparked with flashes of pure rage. He kicked hard at the wall.

'Go and wake Milkeye. I want to know who did this, and I want them found and brought to me alive. Everything must be returned to me. Do I make myself clear?'

At that moment the door to the meeting-room was opened. 'Wait!' said Kalliovski. White with anger, he pushed his way to the front of the queue to ask for his document.

'There's no one by the name of Sidonie de Villeduval on the list,' said the lizard-man, with some relish.

Kalliovski ignored him, scribbled a note and handed it to him.

'This is for Citizen Danton, and if you value your life you will give it to him.'

'Are you threatening me?'

'Yes,' said Kalliovski, 'and if you don't do as I ask, I will kill you and take pleasure in it.'

'A good joke, citizen,' said the man, blowing smoke through his nose like a dragon. For all that, a shiver went down his spine, and he took the note and closed the door behind him.

All those waiting shifted uneasily on their feet. Only a few had left with the documents they needed.

Church bells rang the tocsin and in the distance, cannons boomed.

<hr />

Kalliovski was left wondering if it was possible that Têtu had tricked him. Had he set up that charade at the theatre in order to keep him there while someone broke in? But who? No, that couldn't be . . . they would never have known where to look unless . . . he stopped. Unless . . . whoever it was had been able to make the Sisters Macabre talk, and only a powerful shaman could do that.

He supposed Têtu might have broken in earlier. No, on second thoughts that was unlikely.

Then it came to him, a moment of realisation just as the day was dawning. 'Damn!' he shouted out. 'Of course, the boy!'

Why hadn't he put the pieces together before? The boy, the one who got away, was back in Paris. Why had he been so slow?

Anis had had a child!

That night, all those years ago, after she had run away from him, when he had found her working with Têtu and Topolain in the circus: that night, he had begged her to be his wife, promised he would change. She had refused . . . stood there, her dark hair, her eyes blazing, so mysterious in all her beauty . . . if he couldn't have her, then he was determined no one else would . . .

He remembered the delicious softness of her neck, how he had put his hand round her throat and she had smiled at him, showing no fear. Her eyes, flecked with gold, had stared into his soul and saw who he was, what he would be capable of. He hadn't meant to harm her; he just wanted her to close her eyes, not to look at him like that. He had pressed his hands tighter and tighter round her neck. The sense of power tingled within him; he was walking on the edge. He had shaken her like a doll, felt the flutter of her heart as it ceased beating beneath his hand.

In the silence that followed, before regret threatened to break him in two, in the last moment he had ever allowed himself to feel anything for anyone, he had heard the soft sound of a baby crying.

Only much later – too late – had he found out that she had had a child. What had happened to it he never knew. He had put it from his mind.

Now he realised, of course, of course, Têtu had taken the child, brought him up. The boy at the château on the night of the Marquis's party – that was him!

He could still hear Anis laughing from beyond the grave.

Chapter Thirty-two

S ido had been awake most of the night. She had lain there trying to remember how long she had been in prison, and failing. Time had become a blank, possessing no marked features. Each day was the same, played out to the background noise of weeping, clanging doors, and barking dogs. She felt that she had always been in jail, and that life outside was no more than a passing interlude.

She had seen her father only once since Yann and Maître Tardieu had come. She had gone to sit with him in the large hall that had once been a chapel. The minute she had spoken, he had exploded with rage.

'Dying was the only good thing you ever did, you wretched woman!' He was shouting so loudly that the guards had come running, and had to restrain him from attacking Sido. 'Away with you and your bastard!' he yelled. 'I will have no more to do with you.'

Sido had stood transfixed, watching the guards wrestling to control him. She said under her breath, 'I have a right to my life. It was given to me. It is mine to cherish. It is mine to claim. To throw it away is a sin.'

She said it aloud to cut out all the vile things he was shouting. Once back in her cell it finally struck her that there was no point in trying to help a man who had always hated her. Sane or insane, his sentiments had never altered. Only when she was silent had he shown the slightest regard for her. Why? Because then she could be anything he wanted.

She let out a sigh as the moon made a welcome appearance at the bars of her window, its sad face frowning.

'What do you want?' it seemed to ask.

'Why, what everyone wants,' she replied. 'To be loved for being myself rather than what someone wants me to be.'

Was that such a bad thing? With Yann she had simply been Sido and she had felt so free, as if she had feathers as white and wide as swans' wings, ready for the wind to lift her up, to fly, to float, weightless, between the clouds.

She sat up knowing that she had arrived at a decision. If Yann came for her, she would go.

'I have a right to my life, it was given to me, and it is mine to cherish. It is mine to claim. To throw it away is a sin.' Saying it made her feel stronger. She wanted nothing more to do with the name de Villeduval. If ever she was free again, she would call herself by her mother's name. She at least had loved her.

Just before dawn, the church bells started to ring all over the city. This was no pleasant Sunday sound, the gentle call to prayer. In the frenzy of their chimes, loud enough to wake the dead, the bells sounded a warning of oncoming danger, their clamour heightened by the barking of the prison dogs.

The bells were still ringing and the dogs still barking by the time the sun was up. This was unusual, for the dogs were normally released by this time, to do the rounds with the guards.

Normal, she thought, was such an ordinary little word. It was only when normality was gone that you realised how much you missed its presence. What would she give to see the turnkey this morning, arriving as he usually did, his voice as rough as gravel, fighting a hangover and leering into the cells, hoping to catch a glimpse of a woman in a state of undress. But this morning the corridor remained empty. And that was not the only thing that was unusual about this day.

Normally, Citizeness Villon brought breakfast to her. Like the guards, she had not turned up. The plate from last night's supper sat on the chair, its gravy stains hardened to its surface like glue.

She watched the shadows cast by the sun and thought it must be well past midday, but still no one appeared.

The atmosphere in the prison was electric. Sido could feel frenzied waves of terror rushing through the cells, a sense that something terrible was looming. This nameless fear began to spread like an uncontrollable fever as the prisoners started to bang on the doors of their cells, the sound swiftly reaching a crescendo that in itself would normally have guaranteed the arrival of a guard, furious to have been dragged away from the guardhouse and his card game.

Today, it seemed, nothing was normal. She sat on her bed trying her best to keep calm, staring at the stone wall of her cell in whose uneven surface she could make out a face that reminded her of Yann. It was the memory of that one glorious hour in the café that had kept her from dwelling too much on what was happening in the present. Escaping to this imaginary place had been the only way to block out the atrocities of prison life.

For the past four days, more and more people had been brought here. Some were dragged, others walked with their heads held high. Mothers carried their children, who looked scared and bewildered, their young voices pitiful with their questions of 'Why are we here? Where are we going? What have we done wrong?'

Sido's daydream was shattered by the chilling cry that came over from the male prison: 'They are going to slaughter us all!'

Now panic was given full reign, with screaming, shouting, pleading, and desperate cries for the guard to come. These were silenced by other, more dreadful noises from outside and the groans and screams of the dying at the hands of the bloodthirsty crowd. What the prisoners had feared the most had started. At about four o'clock the iron door at the end of the corridor in the women's section was clanked open to admit three persons: two Sans Culottes, their sleeves rolled up and the red cap of liberty on their heads, and a jailer who carried a torch to show them the way. They peered in at all the prisoners, their eyes wild, their voices so brutal and their accents so thick that it was hard to tell whose name they were shouting.

At last it became clear that they were calling for the Duchesse de Lamantes.

Sido heard a key turn in the lock, heard the Duchess beg to be left in peace, and then a commotion as a chair was knocked over. The men dragged her out into the corridor, calling her every name under the sun, while the Duchess wept noisily and screamed, 'Where are you taking me?'

'To the jailer's office, citizeness, to be tried before the People's Tribunal as the traitor you are,' came the cold reply.

The Duchess was dragged down the corridor, making one last desperate grab at the iron bars of Sido's cell as she passed. Her eyes were wide with fright.

'Don't let them do this to me!' she cried as a wooden truncheon hit her hard on the knuckles. Shrieking with pain she let go, to be hauled unceremoniously past the row of cells. The iron door closed with a deadly thud. For a moment all was silence, broken only by the quiet sobbing of the other terrified inmates.

'We are like sheep,' thought Sido, 'waiting to be taken to the slaughterhouse.'

She slid down the corner of the stone wall, buried her

head in her arms and tried to take herself back to that magical place where there was just Yann. Only too soon she heard the sound of boots on stone again, advancing down the long corridor and stopping before her cell. She watched as the key turned in the lock.

So this was it. This was her end and she knew it. She didn't even look up to see who had come for her. She felt their strong arms, smelt their unwashed flesh, their sweat. She was not going to let herself be dragged like the Duchess. She stood up straight and shook herself free from their clutches. What did any of it matter? She was as good as dead.

'We are all equal, but I, unlike you, am not armed,' she said calmly. 'Please take your hands off me.' The two brutal-looking men, astonished to be spoken to in such a manner, let go of her. Sido took a deep breath and walked down the corridor, trying her best not to limp. She didn't want anyone's pity.

'To La Force,' she heard as the Duchess came out of another room. Seeing Sido standing on the stairs waiting her turn, she shrugged her shoulders as if to say that it wasn't too bad. Then the street door was thrown open. For a moment Sido was blinded by the light; then she saw all too clearly a sea of swords and pikes. The Duchess, realising what fate held in store for her, tried to pull away from the guards, only to be caught screaming by three men carrying bloodstained sabres. She raised her hands above her head.

Sido saw them lift their swords. She closed her eyes and tried to shut out the nightmare cries and the loud grunts of the men as they wielded their weapons. Then the street door was slammed, leaving the stone-paved floor splattered with the Duchess's blood.

Sido's legs were trembling as she was taken into the jailer's office.

The room was lit by torches, and in the shadowy light she could see that it was full of men. Behind the table sat a man called Stanislas Maillard. He was dressed in black, his long lank hair pulled back into a queue at the neck: he had a gaunt face and deepset eyes. That made Sido think that if death ever had a face to call its own, it would look like his.

Maillard had been elected to carry out the duties of the President of the People's Tribunal, a task he took no pleasure in, yet nevertheless performed meticulously. On the table before him were the prison register, a stack of paper, a bottle of wine and a glass. Sido could tell from the men's voices that they were from Marseilles and other parts of France, all eager onlookers of the spectacle.

'Name, age, and place of birth?' said Maillard, drawing his bony index finger slowly down the list.

Sido answered the questions clearly.

Having found her name in the register, he glanced over the charges and consulted his grim colleagues. Then he informed her that she was being held for high treason against the nation.

'How do you answer?'

'I support the Revolution and wish its success with all

my heart,' said Sido. She knew that any other answer would mean death.

'Then why did you try to leave our glorious country?'

'I was born into a family where my wishes and views held no weight.' It sounded to her as feeble as it was. She knew it wouldn't save her.

At that moment the door to the makeshift courtroom burst open and another prisoner was dragged in before the President. His guards pulled back his head.

'Another priest we found hiding in the chapel.'

Maillard sighed and methodically checked the prison register to find him. His menacing eyes flickered round the room.

'Did you take the oath?' he asked.

'I am not afraid to die,' the man said bravely.

'Away with him!' came an angry roar from the men in the room. Death hovered there above the priest's head as Maillard waved him away.

Sido shivered. His shrieks filled the room.

The president refilled his glass and looked again at the papers.

'Put some gunpowder in your wine, citizen,' said one of the guards. 'That's what we do. It'll put fire in your belly and rage in your heart.'

The president shook his head and looked again at the papers. This one was definitely prettier than any of the others he had got rid of this morning, and she had a lovely voice.

'So you say you had no way of stopping your father being a traitor to his country?'

'That is right, sir.'

'Enough. How do we find the prisoner?'

'To La Force,' came the shout from round the room.

In other words, thought Sido, guilty as charged. The president brought down his hammer and cried, 'To La Force! Take her away.'

Sido was determined to keep her head up high, to look him straight in the eyes so that he would not forget her. Two guards seized her roughly by the arm as the judge brought down his wooden hammer and shouted, 'Next!'

At that moment the door to the office was pushed open and a dreadful apparition charged into the room. The guard, if guard he was, was drenched in blood. He looked exhausted. Furious, he stood in front of Maillard and slammed his bloodied fist on to the table.

'What do you think we are?' he shouted. 'We've been hacking and killing all day without a stop. We ain't machines, you know. A man needs his rest. A man needs something to eat.'

Maillard looked up at the clock and spoke to the two men who were about to take Sido out. 'Leave her!'

Sido was shoved forcibly down on a bench.

'What shall we do with her?' said one of the two guards. 'We need a break too, you know.'

Maillard looked at Sido. There was no getting away from it; she was a problem he didn't want. A pretty problem, and she had nice eyes. He tapped his fingers rhythmically on the table, looking for a way out of his predicament.

Bringing up his hammer, he bashed it upon the table again and proclaimed, 'Innocent!'

For a moment Sido wasn't sure if she had heard him right or whether this was a coded message for them to kill her later, but then a shout went up in the jailer's office. '*Vive la Nation!*'

Her guards rushed forward to congratulate her, lifted her up and carried her out of the street door towards the gate, shouting, 'We have one who is innocent.'

From her position high up on their shoulders Sido could see every detail of the scene before her. A huge fire had been lit in the prison courtyard which added an eerie light to the pile of bodies heaped together, many with their limbs hacked off, while around the railings to the prison the faces of the citizens pressed closer, eager to have a look at the new butchers of Paris. The dogs, freed at last, were licking the ground as the men sat by the heaped corpses, eating their lunch and laughing heartily, holding up wine bottles and dipping their bread in the blood.

Sido, still held up high, floated through this unreal world. She fixed her eyes on the gate, sure that if she were to look away for a moment all chance of freedom would vanish. She was set down outside to join the press of onlookers.

'Life is mine,' she said to herself and with those words she felt the thrill of freedom.

Suddenly, an arm locked itself tightly round her waist and a hand, a black-gloved hand, covered her face. Her freedom had lasted for less than a minute. She was pushed into Kalliovski's carriage and fell back heavily against the velvet cushions. The feel of the luxurious fabric went through her body like an electric shock. She let out a scream as the automaton slumped forward across her lap. She pushed it back, gasping at the ghostly apparition of Madame Perrien.

'I owe you an apology,' said Citizen Kalliovski. 'I had hoped to get your release papers signed before this bloodbath began.'

She looked at him in horror. Then, remembering the agreement, she asked, 'My father, did you get his release papers?'

Kalliovski took a letter from his pocket. He dangled it in front of her.

'I said to you that if you came willingly, your father would be released. Do you come willingly?'

She sat as far away from him as she could, pushing herself into the seat.

'Do you?'

Sido nodded.

'Kiss me then, show me that you mean it.'

Sido sat trembling, battling with herself. Finally, taking a deep breath, she bent forward to kiss him on the cheek. He grabbed her and pressing his thumb and forefinger into her jaw forced her to look at him. His lips, like a blood-filled wound, came closer and without thinking she spat at him.

Kalliovski hit her hard across her cheek, making her eyes smart with pain, and threw her back into the seat.

Bringing out a pure white handkerchief he opened it up carefully and wiped his face.

'Who would have thought you had such a wild spirit. It will be a pleasure to break it.' He laughed. 'And break it I will. Shall I comfort you a little after your ordeal by saying that even if you had come willingly, I would not have had your father freed? I don't like what is happening but there is something inevitable about it, a certain poetry. Your father and all his spoilt and silly kind have brought this upon themselves.'

He knocked on the ceiling of the carriage and it started to move slowly away through the crowd.

'Would you like to know what today is?'

Sido turned away and looked out of the darkened windows.

'The day the box of demons was opened,' she said quietly, more to herself than to him.

'No, *ma chérie*,' he said, smiling, 'today is our wedding day.'

Chapter Thirty-three

O ver on rue Barbette, Didier had been
woken at noon by the frenzied clang
of church bells accompanied by shouts and
the sound of boots on cobbles. Wasting no
time, he had hurried down to find out what
was happening. The clamour of the mob
reverberated round the rabbit-warren of
shops and apartment buildings as it surged
along the street.

Didier rushed to the baker's shop in rue des Rosiers
and knocked so hard on the door that the glass panes
rattled. The terrified face of the baker, dough-white with
fear, peeped out from behind the blind. Seeing it was
an old friend, he quickly let him in and double-locked
the door behind him. Talking non-stop, he took Didier
through to the back room where his family was sitting

round the table eating. They looked as startled as rabbits caught by the sound of the gun.

'What's going on?' asked Didier.

'Haven't you heard? They say Verdun has fallen and that the Prussians are marching this way. They're just a few miles outside the city gates. Notices have been put up on all the street corners, saying that if we don't kill the enemies in our prisons they'll break out and slaughter us all.'

'Rubbish,' interrupted Didier. 'Priests, nuns, children, prostitutes, an assortment of aristocrats and forgers – can you really believe people would kill them?'

'I don't know. I'm only telling you what I've heard. There are calls for all the traitors to be torn limb from limb.' He stopped, steadying himself against his oven as if for the first time the true meaning of his words had dawned on him. 'It's a terrible day,' he said sadly. 'Makes you wonder if we're any better than the beasts of the forest.'

He handed Didier a loaf of bread. The smell was comforting in a world that suddenly appeared to be made up of jagged ends.

'Thank you,' said Didier, thrusting it inside his coat.

'If you don't want to be caught up in a bloodbath,' said the baker, 'I'd advise you to stay inside.' He put an arm round his wife and patted his children's heads. 'Call me a coward if you like, but that's what I'm going to do.'

He saw Didier to the door. 'They say it's going to be a good day for the gravedigger. Take care, my friend,' he whispered after him.

Didier pushed his way along the street to Monsieur Aulard's apartment to find Têtu up and making coffee and Monsieur Aulard, barely awake, sitting slumped in a chair with his stockings down around his ankles.

'Where's Yann?' asked Didier. 'There's not a moment to be lost. I think the massacres are about to start.'

'I know,' said Têtu. He did not finish what he was saying, for Yann appeared in the doorway.

'What's happening?' asked Yann. 'Why have all the bells gone crazy?'

'Something's going on at the prisons,' said Didier, taking the warm loaf from his coat and putting it on the table. 'It seems that we're about to be invaded.'

'Then why did you let me sleep?'

'Because you've been wounded,' replied Têtu, bringing a pot of coffee to the table. 'I've managed to get a carriage to meet us at the St Denis gate at seven o'clock, which should give you time to get your strength up for the journey. I've had word from Cordell that he will be in Dieppe, staying at the Hôtel de Paris, so that is where you are to take Kalliovski's Book of Tears.'

'I'm going to get Sido out before I go anywhere.'

'It may well be too late to save her.'

'No, don't say that – it can't be!'

'Yann, I am sorry, the world has gone mad. You would never make it to the prison in time, even without the wound.'

'No, no!' shouted Yann angrily. 'I haven't come this far to give up now, just like that.' He turned away in disgust. 'What do I do? Tell the Laxtons that I was slightly wounded and didn't feel strong enough even to try to get Sido out? Still, never mind, they should be pleased I got the Book of Tears! Têtu, I would rather die trying to get her out than do nothing.'

He went back into the bedchamber and came out a few moments later already dressed and pulling on his sky-blue coat, wincing as a sharp stab of pain went through his shoulder.

'I was told by a fortune-teller that there was a bullet waiting for me in Paris,' he said. 'The fear of it nearly stopped me from coming back. Last night the thing I dreaded the most found me, and I survived it. Têtu, I am still alive, more alive than I have ever been. I know I can save Sido, I *know* it.'

'Then if you don't want an infection, your wound will need to be re-bandaged.'

Reluctantly Yann gave in and sat down, fidgeting impatiently while Didier attended to the wound.

'You're not fit to go anywhere, not even Dieppe, rattling about in a bone-shaker of a carriage.' Didier bandaged him up again. 'Also, you have a slight fever.'

'Stop fussing.'

'Before you go,' said Têtu, 'I should tell you that I found out last night that Kalliovski went to get Sido's release papers signed. I don't know if he managed it or not. Your only hope of finding her is to find Kalliovski. If I were you I wouldn't bother with the prison.'

'Thank you,' said Yann. He leant down towards Têtu and spoke to him in Romany. 'One last thing. Did you know Kalliovski can use the threads of light?'

'Yes, like a feeble child with a puppet. He is an amateur, for the time being at least. Unless ...'

'Unless what?' asked Yann.

'Unless the devil goes walking.'

Yann kissed Têtu on both cheeks. 'Don't worry,' he said in French. 'Today I feel invincible. Today I am ten feet tall and as strong as Hercules.'

'Today you have a fever,' said Têtu.

'I will be there in time for the coach. You bring the Book of Tears, Sido's papers and the letters.' At the door he turned back. 'Wait – the jewels! You must get them from the old lawyer.'

'I know,' said Têtu. 'Now go.'

'Oh, *mort bleu!*' said Monsieur Aulard, leaping to his feet in desperation. 'No, no, Yann. Can't you see that once Kalliovski finds out what has been stolen, all hell will break loose?'

'Just get the jewels,' said Yann, and he left, taking the stairs two at a time.

Têtu looked at Didier, who was clutching a thick slice of bread, knowing full well what was about to be asked of him.

'Get after him and try to stop him being killed.'

'I'll do my best,' said Didier, picking up his cap and taking a quick swig of coffee.

After he had gone, Têtu grabbed his coat and hat. 'What are you doing just sitting there?' he said to Monsieur Aulard. 'Come on, get dressed. We have a lot to do. We've a lawyer to see, jewels to collect, and a carriage to meet.'

'*Mort bleu!*' said Monsieur Aulard. 'We'll never do it! Will this never end?'

Just as if he knew exactly what Monsieur Aulard was thinking, Têtu said soothingly, 'You are doing well, my old friend. You are braver than I ever thought you could be. Now, my size is against me. I need you to help me get through the crowds.'

Monsieur Aulard, holding tightly to his black cap, squared his shoulders and sighed, 'Then we'd best get going. I will protect you.'

***

It took Didier some time to catch up with Yann, who had managed to weave and duck his way through the back alleys and down less crowded streets. At nearly every turn his way was barred by the sheer volume of people armed with spades, pitchforks, kitchen knives and rusty swords. It was as if they were welded together like one determined, monstrous body made up of flesh, sinew, teeth and hair. With one purpose, with one mind, with murder beating in their hearts, they moved inexorably forward. They had no past, no future; they were caught in the great unthinking moment, their hearts and minds driven wild by the frenzied ringing of the tocsin, the firing of the cannons. It was as if Paris itself had a voice and howled its terror for all to hear.

It had taken Yann hours to get anywhere. He had made it as far as Kalliovski's apartment, to be told he had not returned. He went back to the Pont Neuf, but here, just as earlier, the press of people made progress almost impossible. Yann felt time slipping through his fingers like sand. Every now and then news would reach his ears of what was happening in the prisons, each report more horrific than the last.

They say the butchers of Paris had to show the Sans Culottes how to kill a man.

They say the blood is running down to the Seine.

It's harder to kill a man than you think. Some of them were running around squawking like chickens, with bits missing.

These snippets of conversation made Yann more and more desperate. He climbed up on to the parapet of the bridge to get a better view of how far the masses stretched. On the opposite bank he could see the crowd divided. One half was setting off towards the Champ de Mars, the other making its way towards St Germain and L'Abbaye.

Yann stood looking over the crowd, his mind whirling, the pain in his shoulder sharp and jagged. He cursed the fact that he had failed to persuade Sido to leave while there was still a chance.

Didier was now able to see Yann standing there in his sky-blue coat like a sailor looking out over an awesome sea of people. What was he searching for? Why was he drawing attention to himself? Didier wanted him to get down before he was pushed into the river.

'We'd best get off this bridge and make for the bridge of Notre Dame,' he shouted above the noise.

'Wait,' said Yann.

It wasn't the first carriage he had seen that day but the others had been abandoned, turned over, splintered, many set alight, making the movement of the masses even harder.

As it got closer Yann recognised it as Kalliovski's beetle-black coach with six fine white horses, the one in which he and Têtu and Topolain had travelled when they were taken to the Marquis de Villeduval's château. He smiled to himself, for this meant only one thing: Kalliovski had had no time to return home after the meeting. Otherwise he would have chosen to travel in a humbler coach, for this one stood out like a beacon of wealth and privilege as it fought its way against the oncoming tide of people. He must already have been to the prison.

In that moment Yann was certain that Kalliovski had Sido in the coach with him.

'Didier,' he shouted, 'look!'

Didier too had seen the coach, but unlike Yann the sight of it gave him no cause for joy. It was proof that they needed to get the hell out of there.

'Get down, Yann. If he sees us, he'll kill us. Let's aim for the Palais Royal.'

'No,' said Yann. 'Come on, follow me.'

Didier knew he had no choice. Yann was now walking along the parapet, making his way ever closer to the coach. Didier followed, ploughing through the crowds until at last he had his hand firmly on the door and his huge face pressed up hard against the darkened glass of the window. He could see Kalliovski, with Balthazar snarling at his feet. An automaton was sitting in the middle, and Sido was hunched in the corner, her hands to her face.

Didier looked to Yann and shouted, 'They're in there all right.'

'Get those horses,' came a cry from the crowd. 'They should be pulling cannons, not carriages.'

A man leapt up and the coach driver did his best to push him off, shouting, 'I have a member of the Revolutionary Council in here.'

For a fleeting moment sanity prevailed. The mob parted as the coach started to lurch forward again.

'Stop them!' shouted Yann, as the terrified horses snorted, rearing up and showing the whites of their eyes. The coachman tried to calm them down and made one last frantic attempt to get free of the crowd.

'It's an aristocrat trying to escape, a traitor to the cause!' yelled Didier at the top of his voice.

The crowd needed to hear no more. That one seed of doubt worked its magic, and they swarmed upon the carriage and cut free the horses. Again the crowds parted, this time to make way for the horses to be taken like trophies won on the field of battle. The coachman slumped over on his seat, clutching a dagger that stuck out of his belly.

From where Yann was standing, he could see people pulling wildly at the doors, rocking them violently from side to side. The coach looked like a huge black beetle being swarmed over by ants. He could hear Kalliovski shouting that he was a friend of the people. Some men had now climbed on top of the roof and were about to put their axes through it, waiting to make firewood of the coach and its passengers.

He could see the automaton being flung out, ripped limb from waxen limb, as Balthazar snarled, savage and futile. Then he became aware that Sido had been dragged out, her arms pinned behind her and a knife at her throat. Didier was battling to get to her, but Yann knew that he wouldn't be able to make it in time and for a moment he could hardly think straight. Then he realised he could see threads of light surrounding her. He felt his fingers tingle with excitement.

Yann pulled hard at the threads of light. The knife flew free of Sido's throat and stabbed a man some way away. The victim screamed with pain and collapsed, while Sido's captor looked on amazed. In that moment Yann lifted him off his feet and threw him so that he fell backwards into a startled and unwelcoming mob.

Those who witnessed these events were convinced that there was an invisible force at play amongst them. They prayed it was on their side.

Sido felt as if she was in a nightmare. She hadn't seen Yann, let alone heard him call out, 'Run!'

It was too late. Another man came forward to grab hold of her. Sweat was beginning to roll down Yann's forehead as he pulled once more at the threads of light. The man holding Sido, terrified by this invisible foe, let go of her and started to wield his axe round and round his head. There was a scream of anguish as it flew out of his grasp and landed in the red bonnet of one his comrades. Before he could do anything, Yann lifted him as high as he could and dropped him on to the crowd below.

Didier now took his chance. He charged towards Sido like a bull and hauled her up on his shoulders.

'It's all right,' he said urgently as she tried to resist him, 'look,' and he pointed at Yann, standing on the parapet of the bridge. To her eyes he looked as an avenging angel might.

By now the crowd was in a fever of rage, like some grotesque creature that had started to feed upon its own flesh. Fighting had broken out, panic had set in. Yann leapt down, and following Didier they wove their way through the mob.

Yann caught a glimpse of Kalliovski: then he was engulfed by the crowd. His gravel-deep voice rose in one last cry.

'You will never get away from me! I will find you!' Then his words were drowned by the shouts of 'Kill the traitors to the Revolution!'

When at last they were off the bridge Didier put Sido down. Yann took her hand and they pushed their way through the crowds.

'Where're you taking her? She's an aristo like him,' a voice screamed. The woman was an apparition of ghastliness, her teeth black, her hair wild, with the smell of the fish market. She screamed it out again.

'No,' shouted Yann, 'no, you're wrong. That bastard had snatched her from me. She's my sweetheart.'

He didn't wait for a reply. He didn't even turn round to see if they were being followed, and at last they broke free of the mob. Now they were running until all three were completely out of breath. Sido, gasping for air, pulled at Yann's hand.

'I can't go any further.'

There were just forty-five minutes left to get to the meeting point.

They stopped and Didier, leaning his back against a wall, turned his head this way and that. In the distance they could just hear the faint sound of the crowds and of cannons being fired.

Yann, his heart pounding with excitement, could hardly believe what they had done. He laughed out loud and looked at Sido.

'Life is life,' he shouted.

Sido needed no one to tell her what that meant, she who only a few hours ago had narrowly missed death and had now escaped marriage to a man she detested. Instead, by some strange magic she could not understand, she was alive and free and with the person she had dreamed of in those dark hours in her prison cell. Oh yes, life was life and may it never stop being so.

Chapter Thirty-four

I t was now five minutes past four o'clock.
Têtu was sitting in a deserted café near
the gate of St Denis, while the coachman
across the road held fast to the horses, frightened more of losing them than of losing the
carriage. Horses in a city at war, he knew well,
were more valuable than gold.

Monsieur Aulard chewed nervously at his fingers, as
he had not done since childhood, wondering what on
earth could have happened to Didier and Yann. The
street was eerily quiet. Occasionally shutters would be
gingerly opened and he would see a frightened face
peering out. No doubt the residents were wondering
whom the carriage was waiting for and how long it would
be before the enemy came marching in through the
gates.

Never had the theatre manager wished more that

horses didn't snort quite so loudly or that their bridles and harnesses didn't sound like alarm bells going off. They were attracting unwanted attention, of that he was certain.

'Where are they?' he said desperately, taking out his pocket watch and opening and closing it for the umpteenth time.

Têtu, despite his earlier concerns, seemed unperturbed by the fact that they hadn't arrived. He had his eyes shut and his feet up on a chair in front of him.

They had both come from Maître Tardieu. The old lawyer looked as if his heart wouldn't hold out much longer.

'This will be the death of me,' he had said miserably as he had scurried away to dig out the jewels, terrified that his every movement was being watched by some invisible eye that could see straight into the heart of his molehill house. He had virtually thrown the bag of gems at Têtu, begging him to take them and be gone, relieved that at long last he could be free of this incriminating evidence.

'Think,' said Têtu cheerfully to Monsieur Aulard, 'you could be sitting in your theatre, bored rigid by the patriotic rubbish you have to put on. Instead you're here, centre stage in a real life drama for a change.'

'*Mort bleu, mort bleu!* Are you trying to be funny?' said poor Monsieur Aulard, pausing from chewing his nails to wipe the beads of sweat from his face.

'They'll be here any minute,' said Têtu reassuringly.

He stood up and went to pay at the café bar. 'Patience, my friend, patience.'

Monsieur Aulard followed Têtu as far as the middle of the road where he stopped, hoping upon hope that Yann and Didier might turn up. But the street remained empty.

Têtu walked past him towards the coachman, who was as jittery as a carpet full of fleas.

'Better get ready. They will be here shortly.'

'Where? But where?' said Monsieur Aulard, waving his arms wildly. 'There is no sign of them.'

Without even turning around Têtu said, 'Look again.'

Monsieur Aulard was a man who had spent his whole life working in the theatre. A man who could boast of having been born in the dressing-room between the acts of a Voltaire play, a man who after recent events most sincerely believed that nothing could ever surprise him again, but who was completely taken aback by the sight of Yann, Sido and Didier suddenly appearing in the road before him like a mirage. So much so that he was stripped of the tools of his trade. Words simply failed him.

'I'm sorry we're late,' said Yann. 'We had a hell of a time getting here.'

'I can imagine,' said Têtu, bowing graciously. 'My dear young lady, we meet again and it is with great pleasure.'

'It is so good to see you too, sir,' said Sido.

The driver, relieved at last to have his passengers, climbed down and opened the carriage door.

'Your documents are all in order,' said Têtu. 'You

should have no trouble travelling. You're going as brother and sister, Sarah and Robert Laxton. You are meeting Charles Cordell in Dieppe, at the Hôtel de Paris. He has chartered a boat. I have already sent a messenger to say that you will be there in the early hours of the morning.'

Monsieur Aulard interrupted him, anxious to speak to Sido.

'Since your papers state that you are both English, it might be best to let Yann do all the talking. Now, the reason for your stay is that you have been at school here learning French and due to the political unrest your brother has come to take you home. I've packed some clothes from the theatre for you – you can't travel in your prison clothes – and enough food for the journey. You will be stopping just outside Paris so that you can change.'

While Monsieur Aulard talked away, Têtu took Yann aside and spoke to him in Romany so that they would not be overheard.

'You've done well. I knew you would. What of Kalliovski?'

'The last I saw of him he had been overpowered by the crowd and they were in a murderous mood,' said Yann. 'I don't see how he can have survived.'

Têtu looked relieved. Now Yann would never need to know the truth of who his father was.

'Yann, I'm proud of you. Now hurry, get Sido to Dieppe and come back as soon as you can. There is so much still to do. You promise?'

'I promise.'

E arlier that morning, happy was not a word Sido imagined she would ever use again, but despite all that had happened, happy was what she felt, unbelievably so, as the carriage made its way through the St Denis gate and Paris disappeared from sight as the windmills of Montmartre came into view.

Yann, sitting opposite her, smiled, and they both burst out laughing, at what they didn't know. At the fact that they had done the impossible? At how fate and luck had been with them? What did it matter? They were on the road to Dieppe. They talked of everything and nothing, with the ease of long-lost friends. All Sido's shyness was gone.

The coach stopped at the inn at Pontoise, a low, timbered building that bustled with people and coaches, none heading in the direction of Paris, all relieved to be away from the city and all hoping to reach the coast. Inside, the rooms were packed with customers waiting to be served, elated that they were, so they believed, as good as free. Some spoke loudly and carelessly, their voices betraying their aristocratic roots.

Yann instinctively disliked the place. The innkeeper, a hard-looking man, appeared to be encouraging these unwise fools while others, more timid, stayed quiet, pressing themselves against the walls. All the comings and goings were overseen by the innkeeper's wire-thin wife, whose tiny button-like eyes saw everything and missed nothing. The main room had tables and gnarled wooden beams that loomed oppressively over the diners as if they too were keen to hear what secrets were being told.

While Sido went to change her clothes, Yann found a table in the corner by the fireplace, where he could keep an eye on the door.

He looked around him, seeing frightened people who hoped that their passports would be good enough to take them through to London. Some, he was sure, were without even the money for food, having spent all they had just to get out of the city.

At the next table sat a group of men who had drunk more wine than was good for them, all talking loudly. Every time their glasses were empty the innkeeper kindly refilled them. Where was their driver? Yann wondered. He had a strong feeling that the man had taken their money and scarpered.

One of the men stood up, swaying slightly, and bowed when Sido came back into the room.

'Get up, you libertines,' he shouted to his friends. 'Can't you tell when a lady of breeding has entered the room?' With a clatter of chairs, all the men rose and bowed, so that those at the other tables looked curiously at her.

Yann whispered urgently to her as she sat down, 'Don't speak. We're leaving. Just follow me.'

It was too late. At that moment the door to the inn was thrown open and three soldiers in National Guard uniform entered. Yann knew that escape was now impossible. He watched, certain that the innkeeper and his wife were well acquainted with these men. The customers all shifted in their seats like a shoal of fish that knows sharks are near.

The man in charge, an officer of sorts, had a face that looked as if it had been chiselled from granite. His nose had a gobbet of snot hanging from it, which he wiped on his sleeve. He looked around the room, inspecting the customers.

'I see before me, if my eyes don't deceive me, which they don't, men who should be doing their duty for France and the Motherland instead of sneaking off to England like the aristocratic rats they are. Your papers, vermin!'

The other two soldiers started to go through the room, pushing and shoving the customers. One of the group at the next table, winking to his companions, held up a bag of coins and whispered something to one of the soldiers, who spat on the floor and slipped the purse into his pocket.

'Another charitable contribution to the war fund!' he shouted out, lifting the man's arm up high above his head. 'Thought he could bribe his way out of being a traitor.'

No doubt, thought Yann, this and everything else they gathered would be divided between the innkeeper, his wife and the three soldiers.

The same soldier made a great show of examining the men's passports.

'Look at this,' he guffawed. 'Forgeries, every one of them.' He handed the passports to the officer.

The travellers started to protest. The officer ignored them. 'Take them,' he ordered. 'They'll enjoy a night trip to Paris.'

More and more of the customers were dragged out. At last only the regulars and Yann and Sido were left.

Now all eyes turned to watch the last bit of sport until more coaches arrived from Paris and the whole show began over again.

'What have we got here?' said the officer, leering at Sido. 'A pretty little aristo if ever I saw one.'

'Excuse me, sir,' said Yann in broken French. 'Where arc your manners? This is my sister you are speaking to. We are English.'

'English?' said the officer, snatching their passports. 'You English? You're too dark to be an Englishman.' He sniffed and wiped his nose.

Yann could feel Sido shaking beside him and he put his arm firmly round her.

'Pretty, pretty little bird, what have you to say about your brother?'

Sido said nothing.

'Here to learn French, eh? Bet you can speak it like a native.'

The officer studied their papers again, holding them up to the light. He handed them back. 'Well, you can go.'

Yann felt Sido move but he held her fast, knowing that to do so would give the game away.

'Go then! Don't you understand any French?' bellowed the officer. It wasn't until he had gestured towards the door that Yann and Sido walked out. The sight of all those wretched men and women rounded up, standing roped together on tumbrels, made Sido feel weak-kneed. She knew exactly where they were being taken. Back to the prisons and certain death.

'Stop!' shouted the officer, coming to the door after them and spitting on to the ground. 'What did you say your names were?'

Yann carried on walking towards the carriage.

'Hey, you lad,' shouted the officer. Yann turned and made a gesture with his hand as if to say 'Is it me you want?'

The officer waved them away and relit his pipe. Ten out of ten stupid fools fall for that one, he thought, saying their names out loud and clear in French, titles and all. Either that young man was honest or he was one of the best actors he'd come across for a long time.

Sido sat back in the carriage, her heart racing.

'All those people, and like us they thought they had escaped,' she said. The enormity of what had just happened made her shiver. Then, looking at Yann, she asked, 'Do you think my father's been killed?'

Yann nodded.

'I just hope he kept his arms behind him. I could see that those who tried to protect themselves had the slowest of deaths. What am I saying? I'm talking about killing people! Why? What has happened to us?' A tear rolled down her face. 'It's madness. I left my father without a second thought because I'd grown tired of his hatred of me. Does that make me as bad as them?'

'No, Sido, it doesn't.'

'And Kalliovski?'

'I can't see how he could have survived that mob,' said Yann. 'And it isn't wrong to hope that today, when so many innocent people have been slaughtered, they

361

might have found one guilty person who deserved it.'

'Is anyone truly innocent, I wonder? I thought I was, but look how I abandoned my father. I just left him to his fate.'

'Sido,' said Yann, 'there was nothing you could have done. Today wasn't about choice, it was about luck. You were one of the lucky ones.' He brought out a blanket and wrapped it around her. 'You need to sleep, and then you'll feel better.'

She curled up on the seat beside him with her head in his lap.

Yann sat staring out of the window. The sky was black and starless as they made their way with all haste towards Dieppe.

In the rocking motion of the carriage Sido fell fast asleep. Yann leaned back in the seat, lost in thought. He knew now what he was going to do. All those travellers tonight had needed help to escape. There must be better ways of getting people out of Paris than leaving them to the mercy of two-timing crooks like Mr Tull and the innkeeper and his wife. The great hope of Liberty, Equality, Fraternity, he thought sadly, that should have meant a better world for all, appeared to have been massacred by man's own worst enemies: Stupidity, Greed and Terror.

Looking back over the day's events he realised that every time he had worked the threads of light he had become stronger at it, the pain in his head a little more bearable. What was he going to be capable of with practice? There was still so much to learn, so much Têtu had to teach him and tell him. He looked down at Sido and gently brushed a strand of hair from her face, remembering how she had looked when he had first seen her asleep on that huge four-poster bed.

If things were different, if there were no revolution, no war, no threads of light, if he were rich, would he go back to London with her and ask for her hand in marriage? He smiled, for the answer was simple. Yes, yes, he would.

It was just the times they lived in that complicated the matter. 'One day I will make my fortune,' he said out loud to a silent carriage, 'and then . . .'

He stroked Sido's cheek and bent down to kiss her, whispering what his heart had always known, what he had never said before to anyone, 'I love you. I always will.'

Sido didn't stir. For the first time in days she had felt safe enough to fall into a deep, dreamless sleep.

She woke just as they were coming into Dieppe and sat up dazed for a moment, not knowing where she was: then, remembering, she smiled and straightened herself out.

'You've slept through all the changes of horses and a lot of shouting, and you didn't once stir,' said Yann. 'Do you feel better?'

'I think so.'

Yann handed her a flask and she took a drink. Then he took from his knapsack a small package of letters tied with ribbon, and the letter the Marquis had written to Kalliovski.

'What are these?' asked Sido.

'They are for you to read when we get to Dieppe, and then you will understand, and realise that you were very much loved by your mother and your father.'

'No,' said Sido. 'You're wrong, very wrong. My father hated me. He said he would have preferred me dead.'

'Why do you think he hated you?'

'How can you say one minute that he loved me and then the next ask me why he hated me? It was because of my limp. He liked things to be perfect.'

'It wasn't because of your limp. What if the Marquis were not your father?'

Sido sat there thinking. It was an idea that had never occurred to her, yet it made more sense than anything else had. It explained her father's hatred of her. It explained why he never mentioned her mother, and why she was not buried in the family tomb.

'Oh dear,' she said at last. 'I thought it was just to do with his insanity, but I see now why he was bellowing at me. He thought I was my mother. No wonder he told me to take my bastard and be gone.'

She was quiet for some time.

'I have a strange memory of him, the only happy one I have,' she said at last. 'It doesn't fit with anything else. Maybe I dreamt it. I remember we were at the château, and he was with my mother.' She stopped. 'Do you know who my real father is?'

'Yes. It was the Marquis's younger brother, Armand de Villeduval. He was your father.'

Sido gasped. 'Are you sure?'

'Certain. When you've read the letters you'll understand. The Marquis wrote to Kalliovski, asking him to have you all murdered. Kalliovski obliged – but you survived. Your grandfather suspected foul play. He had his will changed and left you a large proportion of his estate, which will go to your husband on your wedding day. The Marquis must have thought he would have control over your money if he chose a suitably stupid husband for you, someone he could manage. What he hadn't bargained for was Kalliovski.'

———◆———

It was very late when they finally arrived, exhausted. They were pleased to find that Charles Cordell had waited up for them.

'You made good time,' he said. 'I got them to leave some food out.'

They sat over their supper talking about what had happened in Paris.

'The messenger from Têtu told me that they hadn't stopped the killing, though they ran out of prisoners at L'Abbaye and made their way to the Conciergerie, among other places,' said Cordell.

'There would be no hope for the Marquis,' said Sido. It was the first time she had not referred to him as her father. It was a great release, a heavy cloud lifted.

'No. I gather his mind had gone. I should think it would have been quick; he wouldn't have been aware of what was happening. I am most terribly sorry that you have been through such a dreadful ordeal. Tomorrow, if the tide is right, we should be away from France by mid-morning.'

Sido said goodnight. On the stairs she turned and looked back at Yann. 'Will you be here tomorrow?'

He said nothing, just smiled.

'Well,' said Cordell, 'I suppose you too are wanting your bed. Shall we talk in the morning?'

'No, sir, I shall be leaving early for Paris. Could we talk tonight?'

'How is your shoulder?'

'It throbs, but it is healing.'

'I have called for a surgeon to examine it.'

'There was no need.'

'You might think not, but I can assure you that Têtu would kill me if I didn't ask someone to look at it.'

'It won't stop me from going back.'

'You are still young and I thought that maybe . . .'

Yann took out Kalliovski's Book of Tears. Cordell looked at it, stunned.

'What is this?

'Open it and see.'

Tentatively Cordell opened it at the first page and read the words 'The Red Necklace'.

He sat down, and burst out laughing. 'Yann, you are good and no mistake. Where did you find it?'

'Inside one of the automata. Kalliovski has a collection of them, the Sisters Macabre. One of them was the keeper of this book. She called it the Book of Tears.'

Cordell flicked through the pages of names. He looked up, and taking off his glasses, rubbed his temples.

'This is beyond anything I thought possible. All these people and the terrible sums they owe him! Many, I may say, the bank's clients. You have indeed turned over a stone and found a deadly viper there. Tell me, has Kalliovski created a near-human machine, as he claimed?'

'No, he was not even halfway there. What knowledge he has he can't use properly. Did you know that Mr Tull works for him?'

'No, I didn't, but I am afraid it doesn't surprise me.'

'There are people out there making money by double-selling their clients. I should think they will make a tidy sum from such unscrupulous work.'

'You are right, Yann. After today there will, I believe, be a flood of desperate people who will risk everything to escape from France. I'm not just talking of nobles. I mean anyone who supplied goods to the aristocracy, anyone who looks intelligent enough to ask the unanswerable question: what happened to this great and glorious idea?'

'That's what I think. Têtu and I can help these people. We have the perfect set-up in the theatre. No one would suspect what we're up to.'

'Mr Laxton and I have been discussing this very matter,' said Cordell. 'You have already proved that you can get people out of Paris. You and Têtu between you could save a lot of souls. You have unique talents, Yann, which I believe will be much needed in the months to come. Tell me, before we part, are you sure Kalliovski is dead?'

'The last time I saw him he was in the hands of the mob. I am sure they will have murdered him.'

'Good,' said Cordell. 'For all our sakes, I hope so.'

The two of them shook hands.

'Have a safe journey back. I will be in touch,' said Cordell.

That night in the city of the slaughtered, while the massacres still continued, the devil went walking. He could never resist the call of fresh blood, and now there was a rich harvest amid the blighted victims of the carnage. He was searching as always for one cursed soul into which to breathe his fiery life. He was not to be disappointed, for lying amongst the broken and the near-dead was one Citizen Kalliovski with his dog, Balthazar.

Kalliovski was raging at his own demise: that he, a gambler, should have been cheated by the Queen of Hearts and her bastard, the Jack of Diamonds. For Anis had had his child, and it was Yann Margoza.

T he next morning Yann woke early. He had told Cordell he intended to leave before anyone was awake, by which he meant before Sido was up, for he had decided in the carriage that he would not trust himself if he were to see her again. His mind, so fixed on returning to Paris, did not need a moment of doubt.

He washed and got dressed. The fever he had had yesterday was gone. Picking up his knapsack, he made his way down to the hotel lobby.

Sido stood waiting for him.

'You were going to leave without saying goodbye,' she said.

'I just didn't want to upset you.'

'You see, I sometimes know what you are thinking,

too. If you had done that I would never have had a chance to thank you. I read the letters.'

'Now you know how much you meant to them.'

'Yes, they were going to England to start a new life. I wish . . . I wish . . .'

What she wanted to say she couldn't. Instead she said, 'I wish you didn't have to go back.'

He took her arm and they walked out into the garden.

An early morning mist hung over the lawn. The air smelled of sea salt and leaves. Once the sun was up it would be a bright day. They walked on in silence, both lost in their own thoughts.

'The truth is,' said Yann after a while, 'that if I were to come to London with you, I would find it impossible to say goodbye and return here. But there is so much more that needs to be done, so many people to be saved. And I could do it, Sido, I could do it.' He took the shell from around his neck. 'This was given to me by a gypsy called Tobias Cooper. It is a talisman, a lucky charm. It will keep you safe, and one day I will come back to collect it. I promise.'

She looked at it carefully. It came from a land she would never know, and yet she understood. Holding it tight, she said, 'You must go.'

Lifting her face up to his, he kissed her. If a promise had a taste, Sido's sweet mouth would be it. It was a kiss that sealed both their fates, interweaving the threads of light that had bound them together since they had first met.

'Live your life, Sido, whatever happens. Live in the

moment, don't live with regret,' and he took his last kiss.

She stood there for a long time after he was gone, and thinking that he could not hear her, not now, she held the shell to her lips and whispered all that she had felt too shy to tell him. Her words were caught on the breeze and though she did not know it, they would find him, would travel with him, they would haunt him and become the magic charm that one day would call him home to her.

Our story is over, though in its end lies its beginning.

Some Historical Background

The Red Necklace is a work of fiction. I am a storyteller, not a historian; though I have immersed myself in the period, I am aware that some details may not pass the scrutiny of a specialist historian. A vast number of excellent books have been written on the Revolution, and I have consulted a great many of them, as well as eyewitness accounts and letters of the time. Any historical inaccuracies are my own responsibility as storyteller.

While the Revolution is well documented, the history of the gypsies, whose story is woven into my book, is less so. Their suffering and persecution has continued throughout time and in all countries.

Paris in the eighteenth century was the epicentre of intellectual thinking, of fashion, of taste. While in the countryside feudal lords held sway, the city was the birthplace of the Age of Enlightenment. Meanwhile, the King still ruled by absolute power.

On the world stage France's great enemy was England. Humiliated in 1763 by the English conquest of Canada, the French in the 1770s saw rebellion in America as a chance for revenge. King Louis XVI raised huge loans and sent a fleet out to help the fledgling nation. In 1781 the British surrendered at Yorktown, a victory for the Americans that secured their independence. The French hoped to profit by driving the English out of trade with their new–found friends, but the Americans preferred to do business with their old partners. As the king's loans fell due, the country was plunged into crisis.

France's territories at this time were divided into hostile provinces and its population into rival classes. The nobles and the clergy had all the privileges and paid no taxes. The people possessed no rights and were taxed heavily. The country was now facing bankruptcy. The King, in hope of finding a solution to the worsening crisis, called a meeting of the Estates General. The First Estate was the church, the Second was the nobility and the Third Estate the peasants and the middle class. It was the Third Estate that paid all the taxes. If anything, it did little but illustrate the injustice of the situation.

As France looked towards the Estates General, in the summer of 1788, there was a terrible hailstorm that flattened the wheat and spoilt the olive and the grape harvest. It was followed in November by one of the worst winters on record. Everything froze; people began to starve. When the people stated their grievances for the Estates General, they looked for sweeping change, but the King and the nobility resisted. The result was the forming of a National Assembly by the members of the Third Estate, determined to have power for the people.

Louis XVI, fearing he was losing his grip, gave orders that the hall where the National Assembly met should be closed. The Assembly moved themselves to a nearby tennis court and swore an oath that they would not be separated until France had a constitution.

The King and his court plotted to defeat the National Assembly, beginning by firing Necker, the Swiss banker appointed as Minister of Finance. Necker was wildly popular, and had blocked other attempts to halt the National Assembly's work. The people of Paris, seeing their last hope of salvation gone, took matters into their own hands and stormed the Bastille. Three days later the King visited the city, surrendering to the Revolution.

In August 1789 the feudal system was abolished, as were the many privileges given to the nobility and the clergy.

In April of 1791 Louis XVI's true feelings were revealed when the royal family attempted to escape and were brought back to Paris in disgrace.

The following year war was declared on Austria and her allies, who were sheltering noble counter-revolutionaries and plotters.

The monarchy was finally abolished in August 1792, and on 2 September the massacres began. Around 1,500 people were slaughtered, but at the time many believed that tens of thousands had perished.

The guillotine, the symbol of the Terror, was modelled on two earlier devices, the Halifax Gibbet and the Scottish Maiden. What made the version that bears the name of Doctor Joseph-Ignace Guillotin unique was the efficiency of his modifications, with the angling of the blade and the head brace.

My story covers the beginning of the French Revolution. It was fired by noble ideals of equality and freedom, from men such as Robespierre, Danton and Marat who were frustrated by the injustices of society. Once the Terror started, these fine ideas were lost and no one was any longer safe from the insatiable appetite of the guillotine. It was to become a horror story that today still makes us shudder at the cruelty and stupidity of mankind.

As Danton said: 'You have seen nothing yet but roses.'

Acknowledgments

I would like to start by thanking Jane Fior for all her support and help in getting out a polished first draft; Judith Elliott for her tireless editorial work and support and her husband Donald Davis for doing without her through the last very intense months; and Jacky Bateman for having done all the spelling corrections, and understanding my terrible grammar.

I also want to thank Diana and Bruno Costes Brook at La Puisaye, Auve, Normandy, for feeding and looking after me in great style, arranging for me to see chateaux and places of interest and making my time in France a complete pleasure; Mary Stewart for taking me around eighteenth-century Paris; Lauri Hornik for all her astute and helpful notes; my agent and dear friend Rosemary Sandberg; Dr David Andress, Reader in Modern European History at the University of Portsmouth for taking the time and trouble to read the manuscript and correct historical inaccuracies; Thomas Acton, Professor of Romani Studies at the University of Greenwich for sharing his extensive knowledge with me.

Finally and not least I would like to thank Fiona Kennedy and all her team at Orion, as well as the sales and marketing departments, for all their hard work, with a special mention to Lucie Stericker for making the cover look sumptuous.

It seems to be a fashion among authors these days to thank absolutely everybody and everything; but I am truly grateful to all those mentioned. All have had an enormous input and impact on the writing of this book.

Please allow me one indulgence. Oscar, my dog, deserves a mention for all the hours he has sat beside me while I ticker-tacked away at my laptop, for his patience while I read the book aloud to him, for sacrificing walks when things were going well, and putting up with me when they were not. I am still waiting to hear what he thinks of *The Red Necklace*.

THE SILVER BLADE

For Judith.

I am the writer I am today because of you and for that I am eternally grateful. With your help and love I found my voice.

SG

Prologue

T here is no more terrifying a sight in all Paris than that of the guillotine. Never before has it been so easy to exterminate so many so quickly. Come rain or shine, come fog or snow, this indomitable killing machine is heedless of the weather or the passing seasons. It has no opinion of its victims or the number of times its blade is made to rise and fall in a single day. It is as blind to the innocent as it is to the guilty; both receive the same dreadful, swift punishment. Never before has Death walked with such an assured step as it does in these dark days of the Reign of Terror.

The guillotine stands in the Place de la Révolution between the Garde-Meuble and the pedestal on which the Statue of Liberty has been erected. At night it is protected against the elements by a large canvas cloth tied fast with ropes. Even covered in its bloodstained winding sheet, it is a sight that inspires fear, and it is fear itself that like a contagious fever has taken hold of the city. It takes away all rational thought, bringing with it a delirium in which even your own shadow cannot be trusted. It spares neither the wise man nor the fool, the brave man nor the coward. Fear feeds on fear and, in March of 1794, it never goes hungry, for it is the devil's own supper.

Midnight in Paris and the bells ring out the hour, each peal skimming like a pebble over the surface of the city. Not a peaceful lullaby to the end of the day, but a troubled warning: 'Lock your doors, shut your shutters and hide.'

You can almost hear the universal prayer on every citizen's lips: that the morning light might find them still asleep in their bed; you can never tell which door the National Guards will come knock-knock-knocking on next, whose name will be written in that little black book.

'What's that noise?'

'There on the step.'

'Who's coming in at the gate at such an hour?'

'Shh, listen, isn't that the sound of boots upon the cobbles?'

'Who's next to be arrested?'

'Did you hear that the seamstress was taken on the death cart only yesterday? Four children she leaves behind, orphaned.'

'As long as it is not us.'

'Quiet! What was that?'

'Pull your sheets about your ears, go to sleep, my dear.'

Out there in this gated, barred and locked city, a foggy

mist rolls up the Seine from Rouen, clinging like a lady's veil just above the water line. It spreads into the narrow streets of the Place du Carrousel with its wretched hovels. Here lives Remon Quint. Once keymaker to the King, he sits in his tiny apartment regretting he hadn't left Paris when he had the chance. Now, blowing out the candle on his way to bed, to lie tossing and turning in a dreamless sleep, he wonders if it is all too late.

The mist rolls on to spy into cracks and crevices as it makes its way up the pickle of streets, by the ruins of a church, past the riding-school, hanging like ghostly leaves on the rows of bare lime trees. In sight of the Tuileries Gardens, it lingers in the gutters, moving through the overcrowded slums where live the bird-sellers, the brokers, jugglers and dentists, quacks and dog gelders. Gathering strength round Loup's butcher's shop, with its sign of a black iron pig that wheezes on rusty hinges, it sneaks up to look in through the chink in the shutters. Madame Loup, the butcher's wife, is all alone tonight. The two people she dreads most in the world, her husband and her son Anselm, are away from home. Where they are she doesn't know, she doesn't care. Lying in her wooden bed she dreams of her child-hood, when she skipped barefoot through fields of sweet purple lavender, when the world was young and there still was hope.

In the Place de la Révolution, the moon has drawn back the heavy clouds which have been shading its mournful gaze to see, emerging from the shadow of the guillotine, Count Kalliovski. He is tall, meticulously dressed, but his clothes offer little protection against such an inhospitable night as this. And though a wind is beginning to chase the mist away, making a threadbare thing of the vapours, it blows not one item of his clothing.

If you were a mouse, and a brave one at that, you might have the courage to creep closer, for those are expensive riding boots he wears, that have to them a red heel. Whoever this man is – whatever this man is – he is reckless indeed to wear so openly such decadent symbols of aristocracy as red heels, black silk breeches and a silver buttoned waistcoat embroidered with tiny silver skulls. He has red kid gloves, the colour of poppies, his cravat is white as white can be, studded with a huge ruby pin like a single drop of blood. His coat collar rises to meet his hairline so that it looks as if his head is perched on, rather than connected to, his body. He appears to be a man of disjointed parts. But it is his face beneath the hat that makes all the rest quite forgettable. Those black eyes do not look human, so dark and dead, eyes from which no light shines. His skin is like tallow wax, his hair, swept back, is black, his lips a red wound. This is a face of nightmares.

———◆———

Kalliovski goes walking here every night, the smell of blood drawing him time and time again to the guillotine. It is like a fine wine to his nose, a perfume to savour. He takes a last deep breath, inhaling the scent of death before setting off towards the Pont Neuf. He walks without a shadow to mark his passing.

On the shoreline of the Seine, near the Louvre, he stops and whistles. He hears the wolfhound before he sees him. Balthazar is no longer the loyal dog he once was. He looks larger, his fangs longer and sharper, his claws have the sound of iron in them. His coat is mangy, grown odd in patches, he lacks the grace that once was so natural to him. He lacks the devotion to his master that once marked him out.

On the south side of the river they make their way up to the rue St-Jacques. Here in a passageway lives Maître Tardieu in his mole-like house. One miserable lantern lights his door. Kalliovski looks up at the shuttered window and wonders if the old lawyer knows where she is, and if he does, would he tell? It matters little. He will find Sido de Villeduval with the lawyer's help or without it. Nothing will stop him.

His motto is and always will be the same: have no mercy, show no mercy.

Balthazar, restless to be gone, is at his master's side as they set off together down the deserted streets of the rue Jacob. They alone inhabit the night, spectres of terror made visible, and Kalliovski revels in it. It has taken him time to accept that his power comes within the limitation of darkness. At the Place de Manon, Balthazar breaks away, howling, a sound which sends shivers down the spine of the living, a sound loud enough to wake the dead.

Kalliovksi calls him back, but the dog has vanished. Turning on his heel, he curses as he walks up the rue des Couteaux until at last he reaches a shop with three dimly lit red lanterns glowing in the window.

Inside the shelves are bare. But from behind the velvet curtain at the back a man appears, dressed from head to toe in black. Seeing his master he bows.

'Has it arrived, Serreto?' asks Kalliovski.

'Yes, master.' He stands back to let Kalliovski pass, notices that once again Balthazar is not with him.

At the back of the shop Kalliovski starts his descent, down the spiral stone stairs into the bowels of the earth where the air has a familiar smell of home, for twenty-one metres beneath the city is where the Count now resides, in the catacombs. For years he planned his new abode, as if he had forseen his own terrible destiny.

This is a palace as detached from reality as a ship from the shore. It is a world where Kalliovski makes the rules, he is its king. Now he sits in a wing-back chair studying the table before him.

In a frosted-glass dome, like a cake in a pastry shop, sits the waxwork head of the needy, greedy Marquis de Villeduval. It has been copied by Madame Tussaud from his death mask, for Kalliovski had only one request when he ordered the murder of the Marquis on the eve of the September Massacre: that his face should remain unmarked.

'My mad Marquis, what say you to your fate?' Kalliovski asks.

The wax head is silent, its watery blue eyes lost.

'Nothing to say, my dear foolish friend? Why, has the cat got your tongue?'

Kalliovski stretches his long legs, puts his poppy-red gloved hands in front of him, dark threads spinning from his finger tips towards the wax head. His thoughts are a smouldering cauldron of revenge. He will have Sido. This time there will be no escape. He will play his high card and the game will be his.

The thin waxen lips of the late Marquis de Villeduval begin to move.

'The devil take you,' he says.

Kalliovski throws back his head and laughs.

'He already has.'

Chapter One

Yann Margoza was dressed as a vagabond in an old greatcoat that had seen better days, with a muffler wrapped round his neck and a hat that had equally lived life to the full. Only if you saw his dark eyes with their unmistakable intensity would you ever have recognised him. His companion, Didier, was a huge bear-like figure of a man. Both had one thing in common: they possessed the ability to merge almost unseen with their surroundings.

They had been on the road now for three days and, although it was late March, they could still feel winter's bitter breath in the wind. By late afternoon, an eerie yellow light flooded the woodland path before pitch-blackness descended as if the sun had been snuffed out.

Thunder trumpeted in the approaching storm, a furious call to arms. Lightning tore at the fabric of the sky. Finally the heavens opened.

Didier once more had the feeling that had troubled him ever since they left Paris three days previously: they were being followed.

'Listen,' he said.

'It's the wind,' replied Yann.

'It sounded more like the howl of a wolf to me.'

Yann kept on walking, not listening, not looking, thinking only of Sido. The thought of her weighed heavily so that he barely noticed how cold, footsore and hungry he was. Or that Didier was right.

'Sido, Sido.' In his mind's eye he could see her oval face, her blue eyes, her mass of wavy dark hair. He knew there was no other road his heart would travel but the road that led to her.

His thoughts had been thus engaged ever since leaving Paris; a tangled knot of desires. His mind drifted back to when he'd first seen her, all those years ago, at the Marquis de Villeduval's château. A fateful night that had changed the course of both their lives. His employer, Topolain the magician, had been shot dead by Count Kalliovski, and in the space of a few hours he had not only met his greatest adversary, but a young girl destined to be his greatest love, the keeper of his soul.

Kalliovski was long dead and Sido free, safe in England. No harm could come to her there. Why then did he have this feeling of foreboding?

Balthazar had followed Yann. Keeping his distance he

was looking for telltale signs that he was on the right track. Mere mortals can't see in the dark without the light of a full moon or a lantern to guide them, especially not on such a stormy night as this, but the young man in the vagabond coat was different. Like his master he walked with an almost supernatural confidence, as if it were broad daylight. Balthazar watched his every move, could smell his blood, hear his heart beat, almost taste his flesh.

He longed to find his old voice. He had been robbed of it; the only sounds left to him were those of a wild beast. He gave a mournful howl, as hunger for the young man overcame him.

'I'm right, aren't I?' said Didier, water dripping miserably off the brim of his hat. 'There is something out there.'

'Let's just keep walking,' Yann shouted above the scream of the wind.

Didier, still feeling uneasy, reassured himself with the sound of his footsteps. One-two, one-two, the rhythm comforted him. He thought back to the time when Yann, spiriting a prisoner out of La Force, had left a silver blade from a street pedlar's toy guillotine suspended over the sleeping head of a corrupt corporal. The weasel-faced man, instead of keeping his foul mouth shut, had boasted to one and all that the next time the Silver Blade, as he called him, came into his prison he would have his guts for garters, so he would. Didier, even in this bitter wind and with a stomach like an empty larder, felt comforted thinking of it. The corporal's boasting had backfired. He was sent to fight and was never heard of again, while the Silver Blade became a legend, a name whispered on the lips of despairing men, a name that brought hope to a city where hope had been banished.

———◆———

No one who had been lucky enough to see Yann Margoza perform as the Harlequin in Paris at the Circus of Follies would ever in a thousand years of Sundays have suspected that the star of Monsieur Aulard's pantomime led a double life. But that is exactly what he did. The theatre was a smokescreen for an altogether more subversive operation, that of helping citizens escape from the guillotine. Every member of the theatre company played his or her part in this dangerous venture, all knowing that their lives depended on Yann's talent. Their backers were two English bankers: Charles Cordell, who lived in Paris, and Henry Laxton, with whom Yann had spent three years in London when younger. It was due to Laxton that he had received the education of an English gentleman. Both men had immediately seen the potential in Yann, demonstrated by the near-impossible feat of snatching Sido de Villeduval from the carriage of Count Kalliovski. Neither doubted that Yann could save many more lives, for he possessed courage and an ability to hold his nerve, no matter what situation he found himself in. That on its own would not have been enough, but Yann was of gypsy blood, and had unusual skills. He was able to read people's thoughts, and had a gift for making clients forget quite how they ever came to be rescued in the first place, so his identity had remained something of a mystery. Without Yann's talents, the whole enterprise would have amounted to nothing more than a barrelful of good intentions, but with him it had proved to be one of the most efficient operations in Paris.

Têtu, the dwarf, and Citizen Aulard, the theatre manager, worked together behind the scenes. It was their job these days to make sure that Yann and Didier had everything they needed to make each assignment a success, and recently, with the rumours of impending massacres once more circulating in Paris, their workload had doubled if not tripled.

———————◆———————

Their business, this time in Normandy, was to arrange the escape of the Duc de Bourcy and his family.

It had been Têtu's decision that Yann and Didier should not travel from Paris by coach or on horseback, for such things would be remembered and such memories could prove fatal. Instead he had insisted for their own safety that they take a boat up the Seine into the heartland of Normandy and go the rest of the way on foot.

What Têtu hadn't reckoned on was the weather. Originally they were only meant to be gone for five days, three of which had already passed and they were yet to arrive. The delay put their whole operation at risk, leaving poor Monsieur Aulard and the rest of the company to cover for the Harlequin's absence.

'Did you hear it? Did you?' asked Didier, desperate not to be the only one to hear the low, menacing growl. 'Wasn't it you who told me that a wolf at the beginning of a journey is bad luck?'

'No,' said Yann. 'Russian gypsies believe it is a good omen.'

'I hope to God they're right,' said Didier.

Lightning flashed, illuminating everything with looking-glass sharpness. They were in an abandoned graveyard, filled with silver birch trees which stood guardian over the crumbling tombstones and broken, wingless angels. In the middle were the skeletal remains of a church, its roof long gone, only three walls preventing it from total collapse.

Yann moved towards it, quickly followed by Didier, both glad at last to have some protection, feeble as it was, from the spiteful wind which hissed and wheezed round the masonry.

Looking into the bleakness of that devil-dark night, Yann heard no wolf howl, he heard nothing but his own gallow's-bird thoughts.

Why hasn't Sido replied to my letter? Three weeks and not a word. Perhaps I misunderstood her. What did she write?

> Oh Yann, I long for thee.
> Come back to me.

No, I didn't misunderstand her. We have hidden nothing from each other. Nothing. Except I have never told her I'm a gypsy. I will when the time is right. Now I have told her what I should have told her ages ago, that I love her.

In the dark of the forest, in the light of his imagination, he pictured Sido as they had stood alone in the garden two years before, the smell of sea and autumn in the air, that moment when he had kissed her and held her. Why hadn't he had the courage to tell her then he loved her? Instead he had given her his precious talisman to wear, an amulet, the *baro seroeske sharkuni*, the shell of the shells. She had held it in her hands and brought it to her lips as he turned and walked away. She had whispered into it and he heard her words, soft as the waves kissing the sea shore. Even then he could have changed everything. Why hadn't he? It was simple: he wanted to earn her love, to prove, despite his gypsy blood, he was worthy of her.

That was when he started writing to her, frightened he might have lost her altogether. Soon their letters, dangerous as they were, became their lifeline, each more poignant, yet still skimming over what they longed to say.

Why do I torment myself? I am a tightrope walker over the Valley of Death. If I lose my balance I am lost. Sido's feet are on the ground, she owns all her tomorrows, has all her years to be arranged. A suitable husband, children. She lives in another country, her time is measured by another clock, her life has longitude and latitude, mine has only now. If I live to see the end of the Terror, I will be a fortunate man.

He hit his hand hard against the side of the building. Didier looked at him.

'Are you all right?'

'Yes,' mumbled Yann.

I love her. What is wrong with that? Everything, and I know it. It will take more than a revolution before society smiles on a gypsy marrying a marquis's daughter.

'Can you hear it now?' said Didier.

Hell, why haven't I been paying better attention? Didier is right. And a wolf at the beginning of a journey is not a good omen to French gypsies.

'Yes,' said Yann.

Didier had started shivering. 'I don't like this place. It may sound daft, but my feet don't feel as though they're standing on solid ground.'

Yann had the same feeling.

'Is it man or beast?' asked Didier, blowing into his mittened hands.

'I'm not sure.'

Didier looked about nervously.

'That's not like you,' he whispered. 'Can't you see none of those threads of light thingumajigs you always see?'

The threads of light, thought Yann. Why are there no threads of light? Even tables, chairs, have straight ones. Everything has threads of light ... except the dead.

'Shh!' said Yann.

A twig snapped.

Didier stood stock-still, feeling the hairs prickle on the back of his neck. All around him was an endless, wet, smothering, velvety blackness.

'It's something evil, I feel it,' he whispered to Yann.

'It belongs to the darkness, not the light, that's all I know.'

They walked through the graveyard, Didier clinging to Yann's coat, fearful of losing him. They passed the broken remains of a large dovecote and emerged in the formal gardens of a château. The rain turned to icy sleet as they made their way up the stone steps. On either side of the front door stood statues of roaring lions, their mouths open, water dripping off their chiselled teeth.

Yann looked back the way they'd come. It was then he heard her voice, caught on the wind's breath.

'*Run. The devil's own is on your trail.*'

He knew that voice, a ghost calling to him on a soulless night.

At that moment he saw it on the gravel drive – a liquid black shape of a great dog or wolfhound. It stayed watching him before moving into the shadow of the gardens. Balthazar, thought Yann, Kalliovski's dog. But that was impossible for he, like his master, was dead, killed by the mob on the Pont Neuf.

He shuddered as he remembered what Têtu had told him. That was the day the devil had gone walking, searching for one irredeemable soul to blow his fiery life into. There could be no man more deserving of the devil's attention than Count Kalliovski. If he was alive then no one was safe.

Sido was not safe.

Chapter Two

The Duc de Bourcy was a tall, thin man whose face had been etched grey by worry and fever. He was standing in a chamber of elegant proportions that was awash with furniture, as if a great tide had rushed through, gathering all in its wake. Sofas, chairs, tables, cabinets, screens and writing desks stood forlornly, and scattered in-between them was a collection of clocks, ticking loudly, hoping to keep time from running out, for the hour was fast approaching when all this would be swept away. The Duke hoped – no, his fervent prayer was – that he and his family would be saved before the National Guard arrived to arrest him.

He'd been waiting over a week for Cordell's man to turn up, but no one had come, and every day the situation seemed more hopeless. Like a drowning man he held fast to the belief that Charles Cordell would not abandon him, that he would, as promised, send his very best man.

———◆———

His beloved château, unlike those of many of his acquaintance, had so far been spared the ravages of the Revolution. Not that attempts hadn't been made. The worst had happened shortly after the storming of the Bastille.

On a summer's day the villagers, fired with revolutionary zeal, and armed with pitchforks, swords, old kitchen knives and axes, had marched up the long, slow, steep hill ready to storm the château. The Duke, on being told they were coming to destroy his property, had instructed that his cellars be emptied and wine, cheese and bread left in baskets outside the gates.

When the villagers arrived hot and thirsty after their long, slow, steep march, they were delighted to see that their needs had been so well catered for. Having eaten and drunk their fill, they began to forget why they had come in the first place. One of the tenant farmers even started praising the Duke. As the sun went down, they drank the last of the wine and rolled back down to the village, singing songs as if they had spent the day at a country fête.

<hr>

After that the Duke had believed himself safe. It seemed a cruel twist of fate to find that a letter he had written to a friend abroad had been intercepted and found its way into Robespierre's hands. A warrant for his arrest was issued and he'd wasted no time in asking for urgent help from his banker and good friend Charles Cordell.

Now, pacing back and forth, his movements were constricted by the clutter of furniture. He looked up relieved when Didier and Yann entered the room, and went to greet Didier.

'Monsieur, I cannot tell you how pleased I am to see you. There is no time to be lost.'

Didier said politely but firmly, 'This is the gentleman you are after.'

The Duke turned to look at Yann and an expression of incredulity spread over his face.

'You?' he said, making it sound like an accusation. 'You! *Mon dieu*, Lord above preserve us! Has Cordell lost his mind, sending me a young lad?'

'My age shouldn't concern—'

'This is ridiculous,' interrupted the Duke. 'I have wasted precious time waiting for – what? For you two?' His hands were shaking. He stopped in mid-stride and by the light of the fire they could see that he was not a well man.

'Have you brought the papers?'

'Yes.'

'Then we must leave without delay.' He moved to ring a bell.

Yann reached it before him.

'No.'

'What the—?' The Duke turned on him. 'I have given an order!'

'No,' repeated Yann calmly, 'you are not in a position to give me orders. You will do what you are told; otherwise I will not be taking any of you. Do you understand me?'

'I don't want your help! I didn't pay Cordell all that money to be insulted. Oh, *mon dieu, mon dieu!*' He stopped, throwing his hands up in despair. 'Time is of the essence. Give me the papers, sir.'

Yann stayed where he was.

'You are dismissed. I shall not require your assistance.'

'It's tempting,' said Didier, 'very tempting indeed.'

'I will not be spoken to like this,' said the Duke, sweat glimmering on his forehead. 'You will respect what I say, do you hear me?'

Yann laughed. 'Do you think the Bluecoats will respect you when they come to arrest you? That they will bow three times and call you by your full title? No, you'll be treated worse than a farm animal. Without our help, I can promise you, you will not make it to England.'

'Are you threatening me?'

'No,' said Yann.

'Cordell gave me his word that he would send only his best man to help us, a gentleman. You, sir, are no gentleman.' The Duke stopped, overcome by a fit of coughing.

The door of the antechamber opened and the Duchess came in with her two children. She was still a young woman, elegant in bearing and solemn in appearance. Once, no doubt, she possessed beauty; the remnants of it remained in her steady grey eyes. Cool in her troubled face, they shone with an iron will.

Both the children had the same solemn expression as their mother. The younger, Louis, had just turned five. He had a mop of blond curls and large brown eyes, while his brother, Hugo, looked like a miniature version of the Duke.

'I beg you, Raoul, calm yourself. This is going to make you ill again,' said the Duchess, leading her husband to a sofa. Defeated, he sat next to his wife. She took his hand gently in hers. Hugo sat beside his mother while Louis leaned back on his papa's legs, sucking his thumb.

To break the awkward silence, Didier said, 'If you don't mind me saying, there's a lot of furniture in this room.'

'There are looters who steal treasures and have them smuggled to England, so we have taken the precaution of keeping our valuables up here with us,' replied the Duchess.

'We've been informed that the Bluecoats are in on it. There's a certain Sergeant Berigot who runs the operation with the help of an Englishman. Anyway, what does any of it matter? It's too late. We'll never escape, not now,' said the Duke miserably.

'Please, young man,' said the Duchess, turning towards Yann, 'don't be offended or think us ungracious. My husband has been very ill. So many terrible things have happened. Friends of ours have been arrested, their homes destroyed. Some have been executed.'

'I can assure you that Monsieur Cordell knew what he was doing when he sent us. We will leave in the morning once the storm has subsided. I advise you, sir, get some rest. You are all going to need it.'

'I think I should inform you that I shall not be travelling with you,' said the Duchess.

'That's madness!' said Didier. 'Monsieur Cordell told us the whole family would be leaving.'

'I know that's what we said,' replied the Duke. 'But after a great deal of anguish we have made a decision. My wife is going to stay here and divorce me. It's the only way we have of saving the estate.'

Yann stood dumbfounded. Didier was right to call this madness.

'There's a loophole in the law,' the Duke went on. 'If she divorces me on the grounds of my being an émigré, all my property goes to her and we hope, when this is over, we can be reunited.'

'*Maman*, please come,' said Louis, throwing his arms round his mother's neck. 'I don't want to leave you alone.'

'My darling,' said his mother, 'we are doing this so that one day we can all be together again.'

The Duke interrupted. 'I'm damned if I'll let this land be given to the Convention to be wasted and squandered. It has been in our family for generations.'

'Still, it's lunatic—'

'Quiet, Didier,' said Yann, seeing tears roll down the faces of the little boys. 'Perhaps the children should go to bed.'

The Duchess rang a bell. It was answered by a maid whose wooden clogs sounded loudly on the parquet floor.

Louis and Hugo clung to their mother. Yann knelt beside them and from behind Louis's ear he conjured a spinning top.

Louis's eyes lit up. 'Do it again!'

'Now, watch carefully and you might learn something,' said Yann. And from behind Hugo's ear he brought out a wooden soldier.

'More, more!' shouted Louis and Hugo, clapping their hands.

'In the morning,' said Yann softly.

The Duchess kissed the two boys. 'Be good and go to bed.'

After they had gone, the Duke stood up unsteadily. He looked like a bowed willow, bent by the strong winds of troubled times.

'My wife,' he said, taking the Duchess's hand and kissing it, 'is determined to stay here, and all I will add to that is "God bless her". We will leave in the morning with you, sir. I see that we have no choice but to put our trust in you. Until then, *adieu.*'

He left the room, leaning on his wife's arm.

Didier stood, bewildcred, while the clocks started to strike the half hour.

'She can't possibly mean it,' he said, finally, as the last chime died. 'Lord knows why I should care one way or the other. What angers me is that we risked everything to get here, to be insulted, and now we'll be late getting back, leaving Têtu and Citizen Aulard in a predicament, for the sake of a couple of numbskulls, with whom I have no sympathy. For that matter, I've no sympathy with any aristocrat foolish enough to put more store in property than people.'

'Be careful, Didier, it's not that simple. The word "aristocrat" has been redefined; it includes merchants, bankers, tradesmen, clerks, lawyers. I tell you this much: soon the *sans-culottes* will have you arrested for addressing someone as "monsieur".'

'For a slip of the tongue?' said Didier.

'You think not? Use the word "monsieur" in public and I assure you that you'll be arrested for hankering after the old regime. "Citizen" is after all the most honourable of titles; the definition of a virtuous man.'

'Look, it's simple. This is a battle between the haves and the have-nots.'

Yann laughed. 'I think it's much more complicated than that, and the green-eyed monster plays a larger part in this drama than you give him credit for.'

'What green-eyed monster?' asked Didier.

'Mr Trippen, an actor and my tutor in London, loved quoting Shakespeare. One of his favourites was *Othello*: "Beware, my lord, of jealousy; it is the green-eyed monster which doth mock the meat it feeds on." Most men, if they're honest, would like to live in this house, to have servants, to own land.'

'Not you, not me.'

'We, my friend, might well be the exceptions,' said Yann, going over to the window and opening one of the shutters.

Outside the storm raged and the rain slashing at the windowpane made it impossible for Yann to see anything but his own reflection.

Didier shrugged. 'I would choose life over property any time,' he said, unbuttoning his coat and hanging it over one of the many chairs in front of the fire. He took off his boots and rested them on the grate to dry.

'You should do the same,' he said, looking at Yann still wrapped in his sodden greatcoat. 'I'll go and find something to eat.'

Yann stood by the fire. Steam rose from his soaking clothes.

How many times have I arrived at a château just like this one, he thought to himself, to be greeted in the same dismissive manner? I suppose everyone's idea of a saviour is different. I am never what anyone expects. The Duke spoke the truth.

My mother was a gypsy, she told fortunes, had the gift of working the threads of light. She danced for fine gentlemen. What was the rhyme Têtu used to tell me?

406

O, I am not of the gentle clan,
I'm sprung from the Gypsy tree,
And I will be no gentleman,
But a Romany free.

It matters not. No, it matters. It always has mattered.

Yann leaned forward, his forehead cooled by the marble mantelpiece. Looking down into the burning city of coals, he knew his airs and graces had been hard won.

'He is a good man,' came the soft voice of the Duchess. She was standing behind him. 'It's just that we had been expecting the Silver Blade. Foolish, I know. It's only a name, but his reputation had led us to believe that once he arrived we would be safe.'

Yann didn't move. He kept his eyes fixed on the burning coals.

'The Silver Blade is just a name on the street. He doesn't exist.'

'I believe he does. For all our sakes, I pray he does,' replied the Duchess. 'I am told that when someone escapes or disappears from under the eyes of the police, they look frantically for the small silver blade, suspended as if by a spider's thread.'

'A fairy tale, nothing more,' said Yann.

'We need fairy tales, to have some belief in magic. Without that, aren't we all lost?'

'Perhaps,' replied Yann.

'Monsieur Cordell told us you helped Sidonie de Villeduval escape.'

At the sound of her name, Yann turned to the Duchess. His dark eyes studied her face intently before he asked, 'You know the Marquis's daughter?'

'No, we knew her uncle, Armand. He was one of my husband's best friends and instrumental in forming his philosophy towards his tenants. A kinder and more considerate man would be hard to imagine. His was a terrible loss. Tell me, was it you who rescued Sidonie?'

Yann nodded.

She went up to him and kissed his hand. 'God bless you,' she said. 'I, unlike you, monsieur, believe in fairy stories.' She turned to leave. Pausing at the door she asked, 'Have you seen the guillotine?'

'Yes.'

'I am told that the blade falls so fast the mob feels cheated of the spectacle. Is that so?'

'It is indeed very swift.'

'How absurd is life when it is valued so cheaply,' she said, closing the door behind her.

———◆———

D idier returned with a plate piled high with bread and meat, and carrying a jug of wine and two glasses.

'A feast, and the good thing is there's more where that comes from,' he said. Pulling a chair up near the fire, he started to eat. 'What are you waiting for, Yann? You must be famished. Come on.'

From outside, a howl like a wolf's penetrated the room. Didier stopped eating.

'Did you hear that?'

Yann nodded.

'It gives me the shudders. Sounds like it comes from the graveyard.'

Just then all the clocks in the room began to chime. Father Time, who knows the hour of each man's death, was beating out the last minutes of the day and still above the cacophony of noise that dreadful howl could be heard.

Whatever it was that lurked out there in the dead of midnight, Yann felt certain of one thing. It was waiting for him.

Tick-tock, tick-tock.

Chapter Three

Mr Tull sat in the corner of L'Auberge des Pêcheurs not far from the village of Greville. Outside, the sign creaked in the wind and the round bottle-glass windows rattled. Such was the battering the storm was giving this humble dwelling that, had it not been for the solidity of the floor, he might have believed himself to be at sea and likely to hit the rocks at any moment.

Mr Tull, who was seated at a table beside the fire, was much changed of late. Gone was the stocky figure with the bulldog manner; in its place sat a haunted-looking man whose bulbous eyes constantly darted to the door as if whomever he was expecting might have already slipped past him unseen.

'Another cognac,' he shouted, as the spiteful wind

hissed its way in through the many cracks, causing the tallow candles to flicker and falter.

The innkeeper, placing a bucket on the floor to catch the raindrops from the leaking ceiling, glanced at his one and only customer.

'Be with you in a moment, citizen,' he said, nodding towards his daughter to go and serve him.

Mr Tull, half-watching from the corner of his eye, could tell she had refused. He shifted uneasily into the shadows, realising that she was frightened of him.

'Maybe I have the mark of the devil on me, and she can see its stain,' he thought wretchedly. 'My life would be good – I would be good – if only I could rid myself of my master.'

He shuddered at the thought of the man and set his mind on more cheerful subjects, such as the cottage he had just purchased by the sea in Kent, where he planned to retire and grow cabbages, a morsel of consolation for all his hard work.

The innkeeper, apologising for the delay, came over with the cognac. Mr Tull snatched the bottle.

'Are you expecting anyone else, citizen?'

'Two more, and we shall want dinner.'

The innkeeper was without doubt wondering what in God's name had brought him out on such a night. What had brought him was furniture, the stealing and shipping of stolen goods, and a very profitable business it had turned out to be. Furniture, unlike would-be émigrés, didn't fuss or suffer from seasickness, furniture wasn't prone to weeping and wailing, furniture always

411

kept its price and could be satisfactorily explained away. He had had a tip-off from Sergeant Berigot that the Duc de Bourcy was going to be arrested tomorrow. If he wanted to break into the château, he had been told, best to do it before the Bluecoats decided to make kindling out of the Duke's possessions.

His partners in crime these days were the butcher, Citizen Loup, and his unexpectedly beautiful seventeen-year-old son, Anselm. They had first met by chance at a café in the Palais-Royal. Citizen Loup was at the time feeling much aggrieved, for he had been reprimanded for taking a chair from a château that was to be burned to the ground.

'Surely there must be some perks for tearing down the symbols of oppression? I only took what rightfully belonged to me.'

Mr Tull had bought him a drink, and by the end of the evening the three had agreed to go into partnership.

Tomorrow, thought Mr Tull, stretching his legs, he would be on his way to England, accompanying the Duke's possessions to an auction house. He wouldn't be returning, not for a while. His master had business for him in London. He wanted him to locate a certain young lady, one with whom Mr Tull had had dealings before – Sido de Villeduval. And locating people was what Mr Tull was good at.

He sat there, waiting, watching, drinking as another leak in the ceiling appeared. Drip-drop, drip-drop, water inside, water outside, everywhere there was water.

At that moment the wind took hold of the door and

threw it wide open, blowing the sawdust off the floor.

The innkeeper rushed forward, cursing; then, seeing the imposing figure of Citizen Loup and his son in the doorway, backed away.

'What kept you so long?' said Mr Tull, getting up to greet them. The butcher, a beast of a man with pig eyes in a ruddy face, entered, followed by Anselm, whose beauty shone like a beacon in this dimly lit inn, making him appear as if he had come from another world entirely.

'*Merde alors*, have you noticed the weather, *rosbif*? We've had the devil of a job getting here,' said the butcher, shaking the water from his coat like a dog. 'I hope it's going to be worth it.'

He sat down and ordered a bottle of wine, while Anselm went over to the innkeeper's flustered daughter, who couldn't believe her good fortune that the wind should have blown in one so handsome.

Mr Tull watched the lad walk away. There was something about that young man that made his flesh creep. On the whole, he thought to himself, he liked his fellow thieves and villains to look as devious as the trade they performed. Like Citizen Loup: what you saw was what you got. Angels made him uneasy.

Anselm had grown up looking more beautiful than many a young girl. His skin had not one blemish to spoil its perfection; his cheeks possessed the blush of a fine autumn apple.

He had learned at an early age the power his beauty had over people. Even when he was naughty he was rarely scolded. No one could quite bring themselves to believe a child with such angelic looks could do anything wrong. The only person he had failed to impress had been the downtrodden Madame Loup. She knew the truth of his birth. He was not of her flesh and blood. He had been abandoned in a basket of putrid animal entrails at the back of the shop. The butcher had wanted to slaughter the infant, but she had pleaded to be allowed to take it to the nuns. Then something had happened. The butcher saw in the baby's yellow eyes another wolf, and wolves don't kill their own kind. The butcher had threatened to slit Madame Loup's throat if she ever told the boy the truth. He soon forgot he was not his son; she never could. All her babies had been stillborn; their eyes never opened, their hunger for life a whisper in a candle flame, snuffed out. This baby had been ravenous for life and clung to it with a tyrannical grip that repulsed her.

As a child Anselm had become fascinated by his father's trade, saw him as a giant, an ogre who possessed an almost mythical power over life and death. The butcher saw in Anselm a kindred spirit, someone worthy to inherit the business.

Few people can claim they are born into the right period of history. Most of us have to make do with the times we find ourselves in. This could not be said of Anselm, nor for that matter his father, for never had a revolution come at a better time. It liberated them completely from any morals they might have had. In any other age both would have been called murderers.

Instead, the September Massacre had raised father and son, the beast and the beauty, to the status of heroes. They had been called the Spirit of the Revolution.

'How long have we got before the château's raided?' asked the butcher.

'My sources tell me tomorrow, about nine o'clock in the morning,' said Mr Tull, relighting his clay pipe.

Anselm returned and sat down, while the innkeeper's daughter, having lost her fear of Mr Tull and blushing bright red, served them their supper.

The rain battered at the windows and the wind listened through the cracks to what the three crooks had to say. They agreed there would be no point leaving the warmth of the inn until the worst of the storm had abated.

The plates were finally cleared and another bottle of cognac placed on the table. Anselm stoked the fire so it roared and hissed while his father settled back in his chair, tired after their journey, annoyed that the pain in his chest had come back. He closed his eyes and fell fast asleep, snoring loudly.

Mr Tull on the other hand was wide awake. He poured himself another glass. With no one to steady his hand he'd drunk more than enough.

'Pa tells me that you also work for a very mysterious gentleman indeed. Is that true?'

Mr Tull couldn't remember ever having had a conversation with Anselm before. Usually the boy looked bored rigid by everything he had to say.

'I do indeed have another job,' he said, taking from his pocket a rather fine watch.

Anselm still had his bewitching eyes fixed on Mr Tull, who felt somewhat uneasy at the intense look of innocence that this young lad's face possessed. He snapped the watch shut. Even though he had never learned how to tell the time, he hoped it gave him a look of authority.

'Come on, have a drink with me. Or can't you take your liquor?'

'It's not that, Mr Tull,' said Anselm, smiling, 'I don't want any more.' To himself he said, 'but I would buy you a vat of cognac if it would loosen your tongue.'

'Come on, pour us another,' said Mr Tull and he started to sing,

'Old Nick is ailing
He's complaining tonight.'

'So tell me about your master, then,' said Anselm.

'Old Nick is ailing,' sniggered Mr Tull. 'I wish he was. Many men would pay high to know about my master.' He leaned towards Anselm. 'It's as dark as Hades down there. Hell don't burn bright with flames, no, it damn well don't. It's dark, it smells of dead men's bones. I should know. I work for a man who lives under the city of Paris, in the catacombs.'

Anselm knew of the catacombs all right, a grim network of tunnels where many bodies from the September Massacre had been dumped, twenty metres

416

below the city. He couldn't imagine who would choose to live down there.

'He sounds like a strange one, he does.'

'I suppose, if you can't stand the light,' said Mr Tull, letting out a laugh, 'it's the best place for you.'

'What? He lives in one of them dark tunnels like a rat?'

'I'll tell you something that will shock you,' said Mr Tull. 'There is nothing dark about the apartment my master lives in.'

'What do you mean, apartment? There are only tunnels and dripping water down there. It's where the dead go to rot.'

'That's what you think. My master is one of the richest men in Paris—' He stopped for a moment. His words were beginning to slur. 'He's had the most stupendous set of chambers built for himself. Lined, they are, all in human bones covered in gold leaf. The chambers are lit by thousands of candles. He has a lake and a ballroom down there! What do you say to that?'

Anselm wasn't sure whether to believe Mr Tull, but he didn't think the old rogue had the imagination to make up such a thing.

'Why does he live down there then, if he's so rich?'

'I told you, didn't I, he doesn't like the light.' Mr Tull finished his glass. 'What – you still not drinking?'

'Want to keep a clear head for the work, don't I, Mr Tull,' Anselm said, smiling. 'You, on the other hand, don't have to worry.'

'You're right, lad. Now, what was I saying?'

'You were telling me the reason for your master living down in the catacombs, remember?'

'Yes, that's right, he got hurt, didn't he. Him and that dog of his got taken down there. Has to stay out of the light ... shall I tell you a secret, boy?'

Anselm nodded.

Mr Tull's vision had lost focus now. Anselm appeared more angelic than ever, a halo of light shining around his head. Yes, he was an angel come to save him.

'Will you forgive me my trespasses?' said Mr Tull, his frog-like eyes beginning to close.

'I will if you tell me your secret,' said Anselm.

Mr Tull shook himself awake. Secret? What secret? What had he let slip to the boy? Sitting bolt upright, he said, 'You forget about the Seven Sisters Macabre, you just forget about them, all right? I never said a word!' He had a feeling he was saying things that in the sober light of day he would come to regret.

Anselm, longing to know more and fearing that Mr Tull might fall asleep at any moment, asked, 'What sisters?'

'They're half-alive and always dead.'

Anselm was beginning to feel like throttling the old drunk. He must have made up the sisters, he thought, to stop me asking about his master.

'Is he a young man?'

'Who?' said Mr Tull.

'Your master.'

'No, he claims to be as old as Charlemagne.'

'Is he the Silver Blade?'

Mr Tull was beginning to feel too tired to be bothered with any more questions. He yawned and said, 'Let's talk about something different. Have you a sweetheart?'

'Lots,' said Anselm quickly. 'No, really, Mr Tull, I am interested in what you have to say, honest I am.'

'Sure you are. I'm just going to close my eyes. You should do the same,' Mr Tull muttered. His French was never good at the best of times.

'Who is your master? What's his name?' asked Anselm.

Mr Tull's lids closed over his eyes and his head lolled forward as a drunken sleep began to overtake him.

Anselm, desperate now to know, asked again.

'Your master, what name did you say?'

Gently, Mr Tull began to snore.

Anselm was having none of it. He shook him and asked the question again.

More asleep than awake, Mr Tull said, 'My master is the devil.'

Chapter Four

I f you were an owl that evening, swooping over the wind-tossed trees, you would see with your round wise eyes the château of the Duc de Bourcy and the surrounding woods spread out beneath you. And there, where the trees are thickest, you might catch the glimmer of a light bouncing from one bare branch to another. And if, from curiosity, you were to fly closer still, you would not be surprised to see Mr Tull driving his hired cart and horse, with the butcher sitting hunched beside him while Anselm, feet dangling, sat at the back. They were making their way unobserved, or so they hoped, towards the château.

The success of these robberies lay in Mr Tull's ability to plan for all emergencies. In this alone he was neat and methodical. The cart carried blankets, a saddle, some rope, pistols, an axe and his house-breaking tools wrapped in a leather pouch. Never did he undertake a job without an accurate layout of the château he was going to raid. This one had proved easy. A servant who had once been in the Duke's employment had furnished him with detailed plans.

Mr Tull and his two accomplices saw the work they did as a necessity, not so much breaking the law, more supporting the Revolution. After all, Citizen Loup and his son were thought of as heroes in their community. If tonight they were to stumble upon anyone who was pig-headed enough to stand in their way, they would kill him without a moment's regret.

The three were soaked through and none of them was in a particularly good humour, each for very different reasons. Mr Tull had drunk more than he should have and his head was throbbing badly. Anselm was fed up at having to leave the innkeeper's daughter, who had so willingly given of her kisses. As for the butcher, the pain in his chest was even worse.

'You got everything you need?' asked Mr Tull as the cart came to a halt. 'The clocks, remember the clocks. Tall ones, small ones as long as they're ornate. And don't forget the paintings, of course.'

'Shut up, you fat gutted dog,' said the butcher. 'We've been over this more times than I care to say. What, you don't trust me? Think yourself better than me, do you?

Think I wouldn't recognise the hen painter?'

'No, no. And the painter's *name* is Poussin,' said Mr Tull.

'I don't care what the scum was called. Be careful how you talk to me, citizen. Remember, *rosbif*, we're all equal.'

'And I'm an Englishman.'

'You'll be a dead one if you don't shut that potato trap of yours.'

Mr Tull felt rattled. Never had the butcher been quite as touchy as he was tonight. The horse snorted and stamped its hooves.

'Keep that animal quiet, *rosbif*, if that's not too taxing a job for you.'

The butcher pulled up the collar of his coat and stuck his favourite pig-killing knife into his belt, muttering to himself as he walked towards the château.

'All this wealth in the hands of the stinking rich, who've done nothing for it but feed off the carcasses of the poor.'

Anselm laughed.

'What's so funny?' said the butcher, turning on him.

'Nothing, nothing, pa. I just agree with you, that's all.'

The butcher's rage was more with himself than anyone else. The pain in his chest was worse than ever. He waited outside by the window, keeping a lookout, while Anselm went round to the main door.

Locks had never been a problem. Anselm enjoyed breaking them and had found ways to make even the strongest yield. With the use of a few good tools he managed to open the ornate carved door. Once inside, he stood in the hall, listening to see if anyone was awake. Calmly he lit his lantern and stared at the plans.

The large double doors at the end of the hall creaked loudly as he slipped through them. For a moment he wasn't sure he was in the right room. Lifting up his lantern he could see quite clearly that it was empty. There was not a clock, not a painting or a stick of furniture to be seen.

Outside, the butcher was impatient to get started. Seeing a light through a crack in the shutters, he tapped on them.

'Hurry up, what are you waiting for? I'm half frozen out here.'

Anselm forced the window open. The butcher, unlike his son, was not light on his feet and the din he made heaving his ample frame over the windowsill was the noise that gave them away.

Yann had been standing by an upstairs window. He saw a light flicker in the trees, then disappear.

'Come here, Didier,' Yann said. 'What do you see?'

Didier stared into the darkness. 'Nothing. But I don't have a good feeling about this business. Never have had, not since I first heard that creature howl.'

'Shh!' said Yann. 'Did you hear that?'

'What?' said Didier. 'This place makes more noises than a creaking galleon. Which one of the many in particular caught your attention?'

They both stood stock-still, listening.

Now Didier heard it as well. 'Maybe it's a servant who couldn't sleep, just—'

He stopped. This time the sound was unmistakable. A window had been forced open and the noise was coming from downstairs. Yann moved quickly towards the door.

Didier went over to his knapsack and brought out his pistol. 'I tell you this much: I'll be mighty pleased to see dawn.'

'So will I,' replied Yann, opening the door. 'You stay here, I'll go and see what's going on.'

The butcher took the lantern and looked round the room.

'Where're the clocks, then?'

'That's what I wondered,' said Anselm. 'Do you think we're too late and the Bluecoats have been already?'

'No,' said the butcher. 'Mark my words, the tyrant of oppression has taken his furniture upstairs. I'll go and investigate, and you go back and get that thick-skulled rascal Tull here now. We're going to need all hands on deck.' Anselm climbed out of the window and had started to make his way towards the cart when he heard a muffled shout. Turning, he saw the room ablaze with light, more light than ever one lantern could make. Silently he moved closer, pistol in hand, the trigger pulled back. Peering round the side of the window he saw a young man standing by the door. Anselm quickly pressed himself against the cold brick wall before daring to take another look. He had a strange feeling that he had seen this person before. He didn't stand a chance against his pa, whoever he was.

The young man was unarmed and the butcher charged towards him, wielding his pig-killing knife, ready to split his head open like a watermelon. Anselm felt a thrill of delight at his father's power and the inevitability of it all.

Then something happened, something that Anselm couldn't fathom, that went against all logic. For a start, the young man didn't move. He didn't duck or dive as the butcher came for him. Far from it. He had a smile on his face and his hands raised before him like a conjuror. In that instant the butcher's knife was snatched from his grasp and, instead of landing with an enormous clang on the floor, it hung suspended in midair.

Anselm felt something he had hardly ever experienced. Fear. It crippled him and fascinated him. He watched in awe as his father's feet left the ground, lifted up as if by some invisible threads.

And then the memory, diamond bright, came to him: on the parapet of the Pont Neuf on the first day of the September Massacre he had seen this very same young man, in a sky-blue coat. Like an avenging angel he had unleashed an invisible force causing knives and axes to fly from their owners' hands; a man had been lifted high in the air and thrown into the mob. In the mayhem of that moment he had childishly believed in the impossible, before the grimness of the bloody day crushed all such infantile thoughts. Now, witnessing this magic close up, he knew he would give his soul to possess such power.

Never had Anselm been so aware of his own mortality as he was in those few seconds before his father's diseased and swollen heart burst. The butcher's lifeless body was left hanging, a worthless lump of meat.

Didier, pistol drawn, rushed down the stairs the minute he heard the commotion, followed by the Duke. They entered the chamber ready to do battle and froze when they saw the butcher, his head lolling and his eyes glassy with fright. Blood trickled down his chin and dripped on to the polished parquet floor.

'He's dead,' said Didier, looking up at him.

'All I did was suspend him,' said Yann.

'He must have had a heart attack,' said Didier, closing the window and pulling to the shutters.

The Duke stared at Yann as if seeing him for the first time. He bowed deeply. 'I hope you will accept my sincere apologies for my rudeness to you earlier. I would never have imagined that one so young could wield such power. I see now that Cordell did indeed send me his best man.'

<hr>

Anselm, wet and trembling, crept away until he reached the nearest copse.

The wind blew and the rain fell. Shadows loomed and Anselm's heart was in his mouth. Too terrified to move, he pushed his nails deep into the bark of a tree trunk.

A howl pierced the night as a crack of light broke

through and the hope of a new day could be seen. Anselm, frightened out of his wits, stood rigid as he saw on the ground the shadow of a mighty hound, black as coal, liquid as molten iron, before it vanished among the trees, chasing the tail of darkness. With rain and sweat rolling down his face and in a blind funk of panic, he finally saw the light on the cart.

Mr Tull was feeling very uneasy waiting there. He took a swig from his flask to steady his nerves. What the hell was keeping them?

'My pa's dead,' said Anselm.

Mr Tull nearly jumped out of his skin. 'I didn't see you coming. What did you say?'

'My pa's dead.'

'Think you can make a fool of me, you double-crossing rogues?' He jumped down, grabbed Anselm by his muffler, and pushed him against the cart. 'You think I buy your meddlesome mischief?'

Anselm gasped for air. Mr Tull had a strong grip.

'No, no, honest, I tell you he … Pa was … it was like he was hanging on an invisible rope! I ain't making it up, honest I ain't, and I tried to get here sooner, but I think there's a wolf out there.'

At the word 'wolf', Mr Tull let go. Anselm pulled the muffler from round his neck so that he might breathe better and seeing Mr Tull untying the horse from the cart cried, 'Wait! Don't leave me all alone, please!'

Mr Tull, now stone-cold sober, put the saddle on the horse, grateful that he had had the foresight to bring it with him.

427

'What're you doing?' said Anselm. 'We can't leave my pa like that.'

Mr Tull, ghost white, said, 'You sure it was a wolf?'

'Yes . . . no . . . I don't know. It was a shadow . . . but my pa is inside there, dead.'

'A shadow,' Mr Tull repeated to himself as he mounted.

'Please, Mr Tull, what are you doing?'

'What does it look like? Getting out of here while I still can. If you value your life I advise you to do the same.'

'But what about—'

Mr Tull wasn't listening. He had already started off at a gallop.

The storm was dying, the sky striped ruby red. Anselm, his nerves torn to shreds, walked, baffled, towards the breaking day.

Chapter Five

From the colour of dawn next morning one might have suspected the gods of fighting a gargantuan battle, wounding the sun itself, for the sky ran blood red, saturating the earth in scarlet. In this raw new day, Didier carried the body of the butcher like a slab of meat on his massive shoulders.

They buried the butcher under the rotten floorboards in the derelict dovecote, among white discarded feathers and dried-up bird droppings. Only the wind heard them, only the crows saw the butcher's final resting place.

'May the Lord have mercy on him,' said the Duke.

'And may the worms be spared the blackguard's foul flesh,' added Didier, brushing the mud from his coat.

Yann said nothing. He knew there were no words to save the butcher, for he could see, standing among the pink of the beech trees, the ghosts of his many victims. Like the dawn itself, each was stained blood red. They stood watching, waiting, ready to greet their murderer. Yann doubted the butcher would find peace eternal beyond the grave.

The household was already awake by the time they got back, muddy and wet. The fires had been lit and hot chocolate, bread and butter waited for them on the table.

Yann took no notice of these niceties. He didn't even take off his coat. Instead, he asked for three of the Duke's fastest horses to be made ready, so they could leave without delay.

'Surely you will eat something?' asked the Duchess.

'There is no time,' said Yann. 'We should have left over an hour ago. If we fail to make the tide, the boatman won't wait for us and all hope of escape will be lost.'

The Duchess understood the need for urgency. She embraced her husband, both gathering courage, as their sons were brought down the stairs by their nurse, Marie.

The Duke stepped forward and without a word led the little boys towards the front door. At that moment, Louis, realising something was wrong, broke free. He hadn't said goodbye to his mama. He ran to her, sobbing. Hugo too, anchored himself to his mother's waist.

'I want to stay, Papa, please let me stay,' said Hugo. 'I will look after *Maman*.'

The Duchess, her eyes filled with tears, did her best to reassure the boys that all was well. Still they clung to her, knowing it wasn't.

Didier shrugged his shoulders and looked at Yann as if to say, 'Now what?'

Yann knelt in front of little Louis and turned the small tear-streaked face to his.

'You know you must be quiet,' he said gently. Louis nodded and, fixated by those deep dark eyes, stopped his crying. A sleepy calmness overcame him.

'You know you must be brave,' continued Yann.

Louis nodded and put his thumb in his mouth, letting go of the folds of his mother's pale-blue, watered-silk dress, his small handprint like a treasure shadowed there. He leaned his head on Yann's shoulder. Yann lifted him and handed him to Didier.

Then he knelt again and, cradling Hugo's face in his hand, stopped his crying. Didier carried them both out of the hall and down the stone steps to the waiting horses.

The Duchess watched, tears running down her face. She handed Yann a long thin rag of patchwork.

'Louis is fond of it,' she said. 'Thank you.'

Yann went down the steps two at a time, mounted his horse, took hold of the reins, and checked that all was as it should be. Didier had Hugo in front of him, just as the Duke had little Louis.

They set off at a gallop. Only at the gates did the Duke glance back at the château and say, 'How did it come to this?'

Last night's storm had brought down branches, filling the roads with debris, so for safety's sake they went by untrodden paths beside furrowed fields and stagnant streams, through empty forests, the horses' hooves sounding like a drumbeat as they galloped over the moor where the sky was vaster than the land.

Yann stood in his stirrups and breathed in, feeling at one with his horse, relishing life.

I have seen too much of death. I have seen too many good men defeated at the guillotine. And what has been gained by such senseless waste? If the tree of liberty grows out of bloodshed what rotten fruit will it bear?

Sido is like me, he thought. Why have I doubted her? She is my strength, not my weakness. She is my desire. We are bound by the golden threads of light.

Ahead lay a dense wall of fog. It rolled in off the sea, taking with it all the surrounding scenery, swallowing up the horizon. Hidden somewhere in its folds was the faint sound of waves rushing in on the pebbled shore. 'This is as far as we go,' said Yann.

The Duke looked worried as he dismounted. Holding Louis tight, he shouted, 'There's no way down the cliff here. It's an almost sheer rock face.'

Yann took no notice of him. He gathered the reins and walked the horses a little way off.

'I tell you ...' The Duke stopped what he was saying. He was watching Yann whispering to the horses before letting them go. 'I thought gypsies were the only

432

people on God's earth who could talk to their animals like that.'

'So I've been told,' said Yann.

He went over to Didier. 'I think we might find a reception party waiting for us down there.'

Didier took out his pistol. Yann nodded. 'We'd better hope the boatman hasn't left.' He looked back at the Duke. 'Are you ready?'

Yann went first, edging his way along a narrow path at the top of the cliff, and then dropping into a crevice. There, hacked out of the rock, well hidden from view, was a flight of precarious stone steps leading to the pebble beach.

'It was a smugglers' cove, I believe,' said Didier. 'Still is, more than likely.'

They could hear the roar of the sea close by. Out of sight, hidden in the pocket of fog, the tide had begun to turn. It wouldn't be long before the cove was under water and all hope of rescue gone.

Suddenly they heard voices.

'Soldiers?' whispered Didier.

'Yes,' replied Yann. 'Half a dozen, I think. No doubt waiting for the butcher, to make sure they're not swindled out of their money.'

'Where do you think they are?' asked Didier.

'Hard to tell, but we must find the boatman before he's forced to leave.'

They set off along the beach. Even the sound of the foaming waves failed to mask the noise of their feet ringing loud like bells on a Sunday.

'Halt! Who goes there?' shouted a disembodied voice. 'It's Sergeant Berigot. Is that you, Citizen Loup?'

'That's right,' growled Yann, as Didier continued down to the sea, relieved to see their boatman rowing with difficulty towards the beach. He waded into the sea to greet the sailor. Holding the prow of the boat, like Gulliver he hauled it towards the shore, as if it were a child's plaything, then carefully put Hugo in it. The boy sat quietly. He seemed in a trance.

'Have you got Tull with you?' shouted the sergeant from the beach.

Tull, thought Yann, shocked. That old rogue is in on this. He called out, 'Yes. Where are you?'

'Over here. Where are the goods? Have you got them down on the beach? My men are waiting to help.'

The Duke, certain he was about to be arrested, pushed past Yann and began wading towards Didier and the boat.

'Tull, where are you?' Out of the white fog a blue-coated soldier appeared, pistol at the ready. He stared at Yann, amazed. 'Who the blazes are you?'

Yann's answer was to rush at him. The pistol went off. The Duke, turning to see who was firing, lost his footing, and he and Louis disappeared beneath the waves. As Didier let go of the boat to try to save them, the Duke emerged from the water.

'Louis has gone! I had him in my arms and then—'

By now Yann had another Bluecoat down on the pebbles. Sitting astride him he knocked him unconscious. In the distance came the sound of more feet crunching along the beach towards them. He stood up, tore off his coat, and ran into the sea.

'Get out of the water, Didier! You can't swim; the weight of your coat will pull you under. Just keep these soldiers off me.'

Didier did as he was told and waded towards the shore, pulling a knife.

'Get into the boat!' Yann shouted to the Duke.

Hugo had woken from his trance and was standing in the boat crying, while the sailor tried his best to stop it from capsizing.

Yann dived. Instantly the freezing water blinded him. He could feel his skin shrink on his head, the coldness of the water snatching his breath. He came up, then went down again, everything so dark, time running out. His mind was whirling.

'Don't use your eyes. Your eyes can't be trusted.' The words of Tobias the gypsy came to him in the misery of the icy water.

He could sense the child being buffeted one way and another by the strong current that slowly but surely was sucking him out to sea. Yann grabbed the threads of light. They were losing their living zigzag quality. He knew the child's life was ebbing, and pulled as hard as he could, coming up for air again as he did so.

Didier was still battling with the soldiers when the fog cleared sufficiently for them to be distracted by the sight of a child emerging from the sea as if being reeled in on a giant's fishing line. It was the last image the soldiers saw, for in that moment Didier delivered his final knock-out punches.

Yann climbed into the boat, lifting Louis up and instinctively breathing into him.

'Oh Lord,' wept the Duke, 'is he dead?'

Gradually Yann felt life coming back to the child as Louis began choking and spluttering.

'Quick, a blanket!' he ordered the sailor, and wrapping Louis up tight gave him to the Duke. He climbed out of the boat into the sea.

'When you arrive in Brighton, ask for Mr Laxton.'

'I owe you my life, sir,' said the Duke, 'and that of my son. God bless you.'

Yann waded back to shore and, picking up his coat, draped it over his soaking clothes; he watched the boat disappear into the fog.

Didier looked at the prostrate bodies of the sergeant and his men, all knocked out cold, sprawled on the shingle like flotsam and jetsam.

'I wish we could leave silver blades pinned like medals to their coats.'

'Come on, Didier.'

'Don't you think they deserve them?'

'I think I should never have done such a foolish thing in the first place.'

'Why not?'

'Because it could easily have given us away. Anyway, Têtu has forbidden it.'

Didier sighed. 'That's another story.'

Yann didn't reply. He walked wearily towards the cliff

steps. Both of them were soaking wet and shivering, water squelching in their shoes. Up on the cliff top Yann whistled for the horses.

Didier mounted and rode off, imagining Sergeant Berigot's face when he came to.

Yann sat for a moment in his saddle looking over the Channel toward the English coast and asked the wind how long it would be until he saw Sido again.

A notice had been posted at the front of the theatre of the Circus of Follies. It read:

BY ORDER OF THE COMMITTEE OF PUBLIC SAFETY
the show *The Harlequinade* will reopen tonight.

The whole company knew exactly what that meant and how much danger they were all in, for Yann and Didier had not returned from Normandy, and without Mr Margoza there was no Harlequin.

Basco, the Italian fencing teacher, was at his wits' end and he had good reason to be. Since the success of *The Harlequinade*, Citizen Aulard had let it be known that the star of the show was Aldo Basco, the great Italian clown from Naples.

'But I am a fencing master from Sicily,' Basco protested.

'It doesn't matter,' said Citizen Aulard firmly, 'that's our little secrct.'

'What if I have to act?'

Heaven help us if that day arrives, Citizen Aulard thought, but said, 'Don't worry; as long as we keep Yann's true identity from the authorities all will be well.'

These were the days of conscription when young Frenchmen like Yann were expected to fight for their country. The trouble was that although Basco looked the part, he had been completely honest when he said he could not act his way out of a paper hat. Now, with less than an hour before the curtain was due to rise, the poor man was feeling sick to his stomach. Clutching his rosary, he prayed with all his might that the Virgin Mary and any other saint of wayward and lost travellers would hear his prayer and bring Yann back in time, bcfore they were all sent to the Tribunal and the death carts.

Upstairs in his office, Citizen Aulard was pacing back and forth, his nails chewed to the quick, while Têtu sat on the edge of a chair with Iago the parrot perched on the back.

'I suppose Basco could come in on crutches and limp through his part. After all the theatre has been closed for five days on account of his supposed sprained ankle. *Mort bleu*, I wish now I'd said he'd broken a leg.'

'It would have made little difference,' said Têtu, looking sadly at his friend. 'We would still have been ordered to put on a show.'

'Five days I've been rehearsing Basco,' said Citizen Aulard, who looked tired, 'and there has been no improvement, none. He's a wooden doll, a puppet. What are we going to do?'

'I'll work the magic,' said Têtu, 'and make it look as if he's performing Yann's tricks.' He got out of his chair. 'I'm teaching Yann a new one.'

'What's that?'

Têtu handed Citizen Aulard a piece of paper.

'Where did you get this from?' asked the theatre manager.

'Get what, my friend?'

'Why, this bill! Who spent this money?'

'Look again.'

Citizen Aulard stared in amazement. Nothing. Just a plain piece of paper.

'Why, that's marvellous, quite extraordinary!'

'Then I will do the magic tonight.'

'It's not the magic that worries me,' said Citizen Aulard. 'He'll give the game away the minute he appears on stage.' He threw up his arms and exclaimed, 'We are lost. What will become of Iago?'

———◆———

Much had changed since the days when Citizen Aulard had managed the Theatre of Liberty in the rue du Temple, and one of the main transformations started with the theatre manager himself. He had become passionate about the real-life drama that was happening outside his proscenium arch; the appalling tragedies played out daily, seasoned as always with the pepper of pathos, in the court rooms of the Tribunal.

The injustice of it all had struck Citizen Aulard like a bolt of lightning, for what is liberty, what does liberty stand for if it is not the right to free will, the right to free speech? The right to come and go as one pleases? More important still, what did it say about the leaders of the Revolution if they cared so little for their fellow men that they argued there was virtue in terror? Surely that way lies the end of the world?

Têtu agreed wholeheartedly with his sentiments.

'Fine words are what all actors want,' he replied, 'but only the few and the brave are called upon to act.'

To Têtu's astonishment Citizen Aulard had acted, and Têtu had been genuinely moved by this newly courageous man, a sheep in borrowed lion's clothes, who was determined to play his part helping citizens escape, even if it cost him his life.

Yann, Têtu and Citizen Aulard had set about gathering a small company of trusted actors, an eccentric menagerie of misfits. Every one of them had his or her reasons for joining such a dangerous venture; all of them knew their lives were at stake if it failed.

The decision to move to new premises had arisen due to Citizen Aulard's realisation that the theatre on the rue du Temple was too open to prying eyes. After all, this was the age of spies, of busybodies and nosy neighbours, of flapping ears and loose tongues. There was no choice but to find another venue with easier access to the road to the coast.

The Circus of Follies, as it was known, was on the south bank of the Seine situated in a muddle of streets

441

off the rue Jacob, hidden in an undistinguished square. There, squashed in between the crowded tenement blocks with a few wretched shops and one grubby café to keep it company, it looked ill at ease with its surroundings, desperately waiting to be found.

And Yann had found it, not from above but from below in the catacombs, while he was trying to find a way out of Paris that bypassed the barricades and gates. Down in those ancient Roman limestone quarries, long since abandoned, was a honeycomb of tunnels and caves and passages. This is where Yann began his search.

In between shows, he would disappear for days, carrying with him enough supplies to last up to a week. On these journeys he started mapping the routes, helped by work carried out before the Revolution, when the catacombs had been reinforced to stop Paris from subsiding into the abyss. The workers, afraid, Yann supposed – as he was himself – of getting lost, had written on the walls the names of the corresponding streets above.

To begin with Yann was disorientated by the darkness, a sensation he wasn't used to, for the dark had never bothered him. Yet here, where no sunlight had ever been, the darkness had an altogether unfamiliar texture. No dawn would break through these shadowy corridors. This darkness would never remember the light of a lantern; it would be nothing more than a pinprick in the liquid heart of eternal night. So powerful was this absence of light that for the first time Yann experienced the sensation of being blind.

After a while, he began to find in this strange subterranean world a place of peace where he could think, without the lights and noise of Paris to distract him.

Over the weeks he refined what he needed to take with him. A hammock was essential, so when exhaustion played havoc with his sense of direction he could restore it by sleeping.

The beauty – the underground streams, the cavernous chambers, the mysterious writing on the walls – began to work a magic on him. The discovery of an abandoned shoe touched him deeply. A memento weighted with all the desire for life, made more poignant still by the bones brought from Paris graveyards and arranged along the walls.

It was one day, one night – he didn't know – after many hours of exploring when Yann finally stopped, knocked some nails into the walls and climbed into his hammock. He was drifting off to sleep in a twilight between dreams and reality when he thought he heard whispering.

'Damask and death,

Velvet and violence.'

The Sisters Macabre were singing to him.

He was out of his hammock in a flash. Lighting his lantern, he lifted it high and looked behind and in front. Nothing, just a long passage that disappeared into blackness. Was it a dream? They had appeared to him before in nightmares, the Seven Sisters Macabre, the tragic automata Kalliovski had created from the corpses of his most beautiful victims.

'Calico and corpses,
Taffeta and torture.'

By the light of his lantern Yann saw a passage hewn out halfway up the wall. He knew now that he was awake. He crawled into the dank space, pushing his knapsack ahead of him. He emerged in a high-ceilinged room. It was empty. Shining the lantern he looked up and realised he was staring into a shaft: an escape route. Yann took out his map. He had found many such escape routes, but for various reasons none were usable. They were too exposed or just plain unsafe. He needed one that came up into the city out of sight. Carefully he clambered to the top of the shaft where an old, rickety spiral staircase protruded into the void, and cautiously started to climb, uncertain if it would collapse under his weight. It was sturdier than he had thought and he found himself in a cellar. At one end was a narrow wooden door which needed all his strength to open. It led into a derelict building that was home to hundreds of startled pigeons. As far as he could make out it was a small playhouse that looked as if it were about to come tumbling down.

Next day Citizen Aulard made enquiries into who owned the building and with the financial backing of Charles Cordell and Henry Laxton he bought the rundown theatre.

Citizen Aulard oversaw its restoration, organising carpenters and scene painters to repair the stage and

444

generally make the place more appealing. On the opening night the show, a pantomime, went well. Magic was what nearly all the citizens of Paris hungered for, anything to escape what was happening day by day. Those faithful few in the audience who could remember Topolain and his talking Pierrot were in agreement that Basco's Harlequin outshone even the great magician.

With a stage full of actors, and many changes of scenery, there was so much to distract the eye that one hardly noticed there were extra players on some nights: a portly clown, or Colombine's charming maid, or two butcher boys, who were in reality a merchant and his family in disguise, waiting to be taken to the catacombs and then out of Paris and to the coast.

Now there were fewer than twenty minutes to the moment when the drums would begin to roll and the curtain would rise on a terrified Basco.

———◆———

Citizeness Manou, who guarded the stage door, entered the theatre manager's office. She was an unprepossessing sight, with the pipe she had taken to smoking attached to her bottom lip, wrapping her in a fog of wispy smoke in which she wheezed and puffed continuously.

'Are they back?' said Têtu, spinning around.

'No,' she puffed. 'Here, this came for Yann.' She handed Têtu a letter. 'Thought it might be important.'

'No sign of him? Nothing, nothing at all?' asked Citizen Aulard.

445

'No, unless he has become invisible. Nothing would get past me. Just the letter.' She left, her shoes echoing loudly on the wooden stairs.

'That's another thing,' said Citizen Aulard. 'These letters. If they fell into the wrong hands, you know what that would mean.'

'Death,' said Têtu helpfully.

'*Mort bleu*, as if we didn't have enough to worry about. I thought you'd spoken to Yann. No good will come of this infatuation. The world may have gone insane, but it still clings tightly to its prejudices.'

They were interrupted again, this time by Harlequin's leading lady, Colombine, dressed in full costume and holding her mask.

'Are we going on stage or not? The cast are downstairs and they don't know what's happening. Is there any news of Yann?'

Colombine was a pretty girl with a sharp, foxy face. She could have been a fine actress if she had not been so in love with herself, and with making sure that everyone in the company felt the same way about her. Only one person had not succumbed to her charms, and that was Yann. And nothing attracted her more than a man who refused to see what she had to offer.

'I mean I can't do this show single-handed, and I can't act with a lump of wood.'

Basco entered dressed as Harlequin, looking as if he were about to go to the guillotine.

Colombine sighed, 'Give me strength.' Putting her hands on her hips, she said, 'Well, it looks like we'll all

446

be laying down our lives if Yann don't show up.'

The tears had started to fall down Harlequin's cheeks. Citizen Aulard handed him his handkerchief as once more the door opened.

'What?' shouted Citizen Aulard. 'Does no one knock in this building? Is my room just a thoroughfare?'

'Sorry, chief,' said Pantalon, one of the oldest members of the company, an actor who would have retired if it were not for the fact that most young men were in the army.

'It's a full house, chief, I'm pretty sure I saw Robespierre in the audience. I mean, this isn't going well, is it?'

'No!' shouted Citizen Aulard.

'That's what we were thinking. I was wondering if running away and hiding might be the answer.'

'No,' said Têtu.

'Thought as much,' said Pantalon.

He looked at Basco. 'Oh, no, chief, you ain't really going to put him on stage?'

'*Vive la Révolution!*'

Everyone jumped to attention. Everyone except Têtu.

'Iago, not now,' said Citizen Aulard, looking angrily at the parrot. 'I'd like to know whose little joke it was to teach my parrot that.'

There was silence.

'Well, that's that then,' said Pantalon. 'I mean, we are in for it.'

'Oh, get out the lot of you,' said Citizen Aulard, 'and Basco, pull yourself together. Curtain up in ten minutes.'

Once the actors had gone Citizen Aulard sat down with a bump in his chair.

'*Vive la Révolution!*'

'*Mort bleu! Mort bleu!*' said Citizen Aulard, leaping to his feet again. 'Will you stop saying that!' He threw a book at the parrot, who flew to sit on Têtu's head in indignation.

'My friend,' said Têtu, 'Best we keep our nerve. All is not lost.'

'Not quite. In ten minutes, yes.'

———◆———

The musicians started to play, the actors took their places. The curtain rose, the drums rolled, cueing Harlequin's entrance.

'Remember,' said Têtu to Basco, 'stay where I can see you.'

Basco had sweat pouring off him and was looking wobbly.

'No, no, no, you don't faint in my theatre,' said Citizen Aulard, snapping his fingers in Basco's face. 'That isn't allowed.'

Basco bent his head, his hands on his knees, his face pea green. The drums rolled again for Harlequin to enter.

'I can't,' moaned Basco. 'I can't do it. Forgive me. Anything but this. Death is preferable.'

'And death it will be for all of us if you don't get your backside on that stage!' shouted Citizen Aulard.

The audience, sensing something was wrong, began

clapping and whistling and shouting for Harlequin.

Citizen Aulard was about to stop the show when a large hand grabbed him from behind.

'No need to worry, guv,' a familiar voice said. 'It's covered.'

Têtu and Citizen Aulard spun round, open-mouthed, to see Didier standing there and beside him, Yann, already dressed as Harlequin. 'Sorry, it took longer than we thought,' said Didier, as Yann, putting on his mask, made his entrance to howls of delight.

Chapter Seven

Later, after the show, Yann sat in his dressing room among the clutter of clothes, wigs and make-up. He was exhausted. Didier, unlike him, had been able to go straight to bed. Yann had had to keep going. He was dozing when he was woken by Citizen Aulard and Têtu, Iago perched on the dwarf's shoulder.

'That was very close. Too close,' said Citizen Aulard. 'Basco nearly had a heart attack and as for Iago, he thought he was meat for *coq au vin*. What went wrong?'

'The weather, the road, not taking horses, not having enough safe houses. Shall I continue?' Yann sighed. 'Please, I'm tired. Can we talk about this tomorrow?'

Citizen Aulard patted him on the shoulder. 'Of course,' he said, turning to leave. He glanced back into the dressing room to see the dwarf sitting close to Yann and, not for the first time, felt like a foreigner in their private world.

Têtu waited for the door to close, waited for Yann to take off his make-up, waited until he had changed back into his clothes. When he had waited long enough, he took from his coat a bottle of wine, cheese, bread and boiled eggs, an apple, some nuts and two slices of cake. Yann couldn't help but smile, remembering how, when he was little, it was one of Têtu's great tricks to conjure food from thin air.

Finally, he produced two glasses and a knife.

'You must be hungry.' He spoke in Romany. It was Yann's mother tongue, the language they always spoke when they were alone together, the language of their souls.

Yann laughed. 'Têtu, I'm pleased to see you.'

'The same.'

'I thought you didn't like that parrot,' said Yann. Iago was perching now like some exotic hat on the dwarf's head.

'He has a very good nature and I had overlooked the fact that he is a remarkably wise bird.'

Iago, as if on cue, flew to sit on top of the mirror, a better vantage point from which to observe the conversation.

'Well, what on earth delayed you for so long?'

'*Vive la Révolution!*' squawked the parrot.

Têtu shrugged. 'I've started to teach him a few useful words,' he said by way of explanation.

Yann tipped back his chair and laughed.

451

'What really happened?' asked Têtu.

'The weather,' said Yann, his face serious. 'An attempted burglary at the château and a butcher having a heart attack.'

Têtu listened carefully to all Yann had to say – and all he didn't mention.

'Mr Tull is involved in the business of exporting stolen furniture to England, a very profitable little industry apparently.'

'Did you see him?'

'No,' said Yann, running his hands through his thick black hair. 'There's no doubt it's getting harder to get people out. The National Guard is on the alert. They seem to be everywhere, and people are so frightened they're willing to sell their grandmothers, or anything else they might own, to avoid being arrested.'

'I believe it will get worse,' replied Têtu. His face was grave. 'Yannick,' he asked, 'do you have your talisman?'

'How do you know about that?' asked Yann, wondering why he was ever surprised by all Têtu knew.

'Because I saw it around your neck a long time ago and I realise I have been fooling myself, imagining that you still have it.'

'I gave it to Sido,' said Yann. 'She needed it more than I do.'

Têtu got off his chair and started to walk up and down the dressing room.

'Stop it, Têtu,' said Yann. 'It is up to me what I do with it.'

Têtu looked worried, more worried than Yann

thought the situation demanded, and for a moment he felt a jolt as if he had missed something, though what, he wasn't sure.

'Tobias Cooper gave you the talisman.'

'Yes, how do you know that?'

'It is irrelevant, it is nothing. I know. It is the bora bora, the shell of the shells. The emblem of light, a charm against evil, an agent of great luck – and you gave it away?'

'I didn't give it away to *anyone*, I gave it to Sido. That makes all the difference.'

'You gave it to someone who is not of our blood, who will no doubt discard it as a trifle, a pretty bauble to be lost.'

'No,' said Yann, 'you don't know her. I do, and I know she would never let it go.'

'Yann, you need it. *You* are the one in danger, not Sido. It will protect you from the darkness.'

'Then she and the shell are my talismans. They will bring me good luck. Together they make me even stronger.'

Têtu sat down and let out a sigh. 'So much is wasted on the young,' he said. 'This will only break your heart ... my advice is to get the shell back and try to forget all about her.'

'No, Têtu, that is not how it is. With deep respect, this is nothing to do with you.'

'Do you think for a moment that the Laxtons would be glad to know of your feelings for her?'

'I don't know,' said Yann. 'That is between Sido and me.'

'What's between you? Some letters and the sea. Yann, this will never work! The Laxtons may hold radical views, but do you think they would relish the idea of their long-lost niece marrying a gypsy? She may not have a dowry, but I tell you this, she has a title that is over five hundred years old and that in itself is worth a fortune.'

'You're wrong,' he said, knowing full well that Têtu's reasoning was sound. 'The Laxtons treated me like a son.'

'You're blind!' interrupted Têtu. 'Can't you see this is madness? This is their niece we are talking about.'

'I love her,' said Yann flatly. 'What does anything else matter?'

'Yannick, let it go, I beg of you! Find another girl, someone who is—'

'What, Têtu?' said Yann angrily, 'Someone who is ... more of my class, more of my breeding?'

'Yes, a gypsy, why not?'

'Tell me about when you met my mother.'

'No, Yannick, no.'

'Yes, it is the same. You have always loved Anis. Do you think I don't know that? Why didn't you find someone else when she died?'

'It's different,' said Têtu, for once at a loss as to what to say.

'I don't believe that, neither do you. I am like you, Têtu, we were made to love only once. Even if I can never be with Sido, I will love no one else.'

454

Both were silent. Words hung between them. Yann had learned how to hide his thoughts from Têtu. He could feel the dwarf's frustration.

'You are your own man. I have to let it go, I see that,' said Têtu. He rose to leave.

'Wait,' said Yann. 'There is something. That first day of the September Massacre – when Kalliovski was torn to pieces by the mob.'

'Yes.'

'You said something that I have been thinking about a lot lately. You said that day the devil went walking, looking for one irredeemable soul to blow his fiery life into.'

Têtu nodded. 'It's an old gypsy tale.'

'Do you think he did go walking?'

'I don't know,' said Têtu, sitting down again.

'There is a story on the streets,' replied Yann.

'Which one? You hear all sorts of tales in the cafés of Paris. Shall I tell you one I hear quite often? About a corrupt corporal who found a silver blade from a toy guillotine hanging over his head? Shall I carry on?'

'No,' said Yann, refusing to catch his eye.

'I hope you are never stupid enough to do that again.'

'I told you it was a joke, nothing more. I thought he would keep quiet.'

'Hmm. In my bitter experience corrupt corporals tend never to keep quiet. The name has stuck like mud, and the odd thing is that every time someone escapes and no one can work out the rhyme or reason of it, they say it is the Silver Blade.'

'So I've heard. No, the story I'm talking about is the mysterious figure who is seen with his black dog in the Place de la Révolution. Some say he is real, others that he is a ghost. Some say he is the spirit of the Terror. Have you heard this story?'

'Yes,' Têtu said. His face remained motionless. What could he tell Yann? That he lived in dread of Kalliovski's resurrection and the power that would come with it?

'Didier was sure we were followed from Paris by a wolf,' said Yann. 'I saw its shadow. I felt it belonged to the darkness.'

'Why?'

'There were no threads of light, and it made me wonder: if the devil went walking, and took Kalliovski, what would have happened to Balthazar?'

'A good question. One I need to think about.' Têtu moved towards the door. He clicked his fingers, and Iago flew and landed once more on his shoulder.

'One other thing,' said Yann. 'I heard Anis's voice. I'm sure she was warning me.'

Tetu said nothing. He wanted this conversation to be over. It brought back memories of Anis. Her loss was a hole in his heart that time had forgotten to mend.

He said, more briskly than he meant, 'You need your talisman. Good night.'

Yann watched him leave and then turned to the mirror, where he saw propped against it a letter from Sido.

He broke the seal and read:

Those simple words "I love you" are the most precious gems I have ever been given.

I have not dared to believe that you could care for me or that your feelings could match mine. I felt it would be my secret, that I would never have the courage to tell you that I loved you with all my being.

When I arrived in London all those months ago I had never experienced a loss quite like that of being parted from you. Only in your shell did I find comfort. I would lay it on the palm of my hand and see it almost shimmer as I asked it if you were safe. It has a voice, soft, like a gentle wave lapping at the seashore; it always sings the same song: 'He must love you so much to have given away such a talisman, he must love you so much . . . . A lullaby to soothe my troubled heart.

What would I have done without your letters? Don't think I don't know what danger they put you in, but I have counted the days between them, been frustrated beyond belief when there wasn't anything from you and even my dear postman would look sad. Poor Mr Trippen, I think if he could have conjured a letter from thin air he would have done so.

There is no one else. Goodness knows what you have heard. It is true that my uncle and aunt have introduced me into society. I can tell you this: all I ever meet is empty-headed or vain young men. I feel like an automaton dressed up and wheeled out. My fault, I fear, for once again I have retreated into silence. There are no words I want to share with anyone but you.

Here my soul is imprisoned. Only you can set it free.

457

You have been with me in everything. And you will always be with me. You are my beginning, you will be my end; in the middle lies our future. I am with you in spirit, as I feel your spirit is with me. I will wait, Yann. You and only you have the key to my soul.

Je t'aime.
Sido

Chapter Eight

When Sido arrived eighteen months earlier, she found London a noisy old lady wheezing monstrous in all her smoke and fumes. With her mantle of twisting narrow streets oozing into the countryside, uncontained by city walls, she was so different from Paris that to begin with Sido felt bewildered.

She was further bewildered by her aunt and uncle's genuine love of her. Juliette had tears in her eyes when Sido first entered the drawing room in Queen Square for, as she told her, she looked almost identical to the beloved sister she had lost.

That was their only similarity, as Juliette soon discovered, for here was a young woman who possessed not only beauty but understanding that exceeded her years. In her aunt's eyes, Sido's gentleness made the cruelty of what she had suffered even more repugnant. The Laxtons felt very protective towards her. There was a vulnerability about Sido that Juliette thought came from neglect. Henry knew it had more to do with the atrocities she had witnessed in the Abbaye prison and the ordeal she had suffered at the hands of Kalliovski. He shuddered to think of the obscene marriage contract and what would have happened if Yann hadn't rescued her.

It had been Mr Trippen, Yann's old tutor, who, sensing Sido's feelings towards his former pupil, had encouraged her to write to him. That first letter had taken ages and when it was finally finished she felt it was stiff, awkward and childish. Her only hope was that Yann might see all the invisible words written between the lines, words her quill was too shy to shape. She had left it on the silver plate in the hall with all the other letters to be posted.

That afternoon Juliette and Sido sat in the drawing room, Juliette at her needlework, Sido reading, as the fire crackled in the grate and the clocks ticked gently.

Outside horses clip-clopped by and Sido, half dreaming, did not at first hear her aunt when she said, 'My dear, I hope you don't mind, but I took the liberty of removing the letter from the hall table.'

Sido was wide awake now.

'Here it is,' said Juliette, handing it back to her. 'Please don't think me rude, but it is really not safe to write to Yann.'

'I wanted to thank him,' said Sido, feeling her cheeks flame.

'My goodness,' said Juliette, 'it is a very good thing you didn't. If he were to receive a letter from an émigré, it could be used in evidence as proof that he was a counter-revolutionary or a spy. Isn't that dreadful?' She paused. 'Anyway, your uncle tells me that his role as Harlequin attracts quite enough letters from ardent young ladies.'

The very idea that she would be just one of Yann's many doting admirers appalled Sido. Mortified, she said, 'It is only that I have known him for some time.'

Juliette smiled. 'Of course, *ma cherie*. He must seem like a hero to you. But believe me when I say he would understand. I'm sure there are many young women in Paris bewitched by those dark eyes of his, don't you think?'

Sido wished the floor would open and swallow her whole. Was she another silly little girl, infatuated by a young man who had taken the liberty of stealing her heart and kissing her for it? She put the letter in the fire, watching it burn.

'It is for the best,' said her aunt.

———————◆———————

Sido's spirits over that first long, dull winter in London had been very low indeed. She did all that was required of her, but with little enthusiasm. She felt dead inside, a terrible melancholy hung over her like a London fog that nothing could lift. She was haunted by nightmares of Kalliovski, of his beetle-black carriage.

In these dreams she knows she is to be the Count's bride. She is in a huge domed chamber in which stands a macabre altar made from the dismembered bodies of the victims of the Abbaye massacre, their limbs protruding, their hands moving, their fingers twitching, blood dripping on to the floor. In front of the altar stand seven women, screaming through sewn-up lips:

'Calico and corpses.

'Damask and death.'

Kalliovski turns his waxen face to Sido, his red lips a wound. 'Don't let the blood stain your white, white dress, my dear.'

Every time she would wake, terrified, shaking, and light all the candles in the room.

Often she wouldn't sleep for fear of the nightmare. On those nights she would sit looking into the fire, her knees pulled up under her chin, her arms wrapped around her legs and think, what if she never saw Yann again? What then was the point to living? So much had happened since the time she had first woken to see him standing by her bed. The only consistent thing in her life, which had never failed her, was Yann. No one in London understood her. She was treated like a china doll, to be worshipped like a goddess, as one handsome dandy told her.

Concerned for her health, Juliette and Henry sought advice from the best doctors in London. All agreed that news of what was happening in France was to be kept to a minimum. Henry believed this to be balderdash. Sido possessed far too lively a mind to be unaware of events in Paris and it would be near impossible to spare her from such conversations as they had an open house for émigrés three times a week. At these gatherings Sido's spirits would perceptibly rise, especially when the Silver Blade was mentioned, as if instinctively she knew who they were talking about. Henry's diagnosis was altogether more astute. The real reason for Sido's unhappiness was her longing for Yann, but on that subject it was impossible to speak. It had been Yann's decision that Juliette should not be told the truth about what he did. Juliette had been devoted to him, and if she thought that he hadn't run away to be an actor, but was dancing with death, playing a dangerous role in the Revolution, she would have driven herself to distraction with worry. Henry agreed it was far better that she was allowed to think Yann was an ungrateful young man who had given up a golden opportunity to go to Cambridge.

Not for the first time, he was considering the wisdom of his decision. It was as clear as day, whether they liked it or not, his earnest and very beautiful young niece was in love with Yann.

It was in the New Year, at one of their English lessons, that Mr Trippen handed Sido a letter. Her surprise at seeing her name written on it nearly took her breath away.

'Do you know who it's from, my dear young lady?' asked Mr Trippen.

Sido felt her heart beat faster, felt her words freeze on her tongue.

'I believe the handwriting, if my eyes don't deceive me, is that of a young Hamlet,' said Mr Trippen.

'By Hamlet, you mean Yann?'

'I do indeed. Mr Margoza wrote to me to ask if I would make sure this was personally delivered to you here. He feels Mr and Mrs Laxton might not think it proper or wise for you to correspond with him. He also wrote that if you agree with them, then he won't write again.'

The expression that crossed Sido's face told Mr Trippen all he needed to know. Sido was in love with Yann, and he with her. Just as he had suspected.

'If you're worried about the safety of sending such a letter, all I need tell you is that Mr Margoza has arranged the whole thing. My task is by far the more pleasurable: to make sure it gets into your fair hand.'

'Thank you,' said Sido, and she smiled. 'I have never written a letter before. I tried and it sounded so stiff. Anyway, it ended in the fire.'

'Now, as for the writing of letters, one has to make a start. To that end, there is always the "Dear So-and-So" to rely on, but once that is said, an acre of white paper can be most off-putting.'

'That is where I was having trouble.'

'Be brave, as the great bard would say. Nothing can come of nothing. No good worrying too much about politeness and etiquette. My advice is to speak what's in your heart. Be yourself.'

So started the secret exchange of letters that made London bearable for Sido, made cloudy skies sunny, and gave her the greatest happiness she had ever known.

They wrote of everything and nothing; with each letter they ventured deeper, like two people wading out to sea, hoping when the time came they would know how to swim. After more than twelve months of correspondence Yann had finally written to tell her he loved her.

⬩────◆────⬩

In April 1794, Sido first saw the strange man. It happened after she had been at the Trippens. She had arrived to find the whole household in nothing short of uproar and Mrs Trippen in a terrible state.

'Mice is what's done it,' said Mrs Trippen, standing on a chair while her daughters were similarly arranged round the breakfast room, leaving the son and heir to try to catch the little thing.

'My dear enchanting girl,' she cried, 'we are waiting for Mr Trippen to return with the cat who resides on Drury Lane, known for its expertise with mice. In the meantime I suggest that you climb on the table.'

Sido, who had no fear of mice, went over to where the mouse in question was busily cleaning its whiskers, looking rather fat and unconcerned about humans on chairs. She remembered well the mice at the convent and one in particular she had become fond of. Bending down, she startled the creature by throwing her shawl over it and taking it outside.

Mr Trippen came striding in. 'I have Mr Tibbets!' he cried with gusto. The cat, a ginger tom, looked a vicious flea-ridden thing. Nevertheless he had a commanding presence, enough to revive Mrs Trippen's flagging spirits.

'We are indeed at sixes and sevens,' said Mr Trippen, taking Sido upstairs. 'It is unpardonable, I know, but mice are a very common problem, alas.'

Sido tried her best to keep a solemn face, but was quite defeated and burst out laughing. 'Oh, Mr Trippen, it doesn't matter. I believe they even had mice at Versailles!'

'You think so?'

'Yes.'

'Good,' he said. 'Now I know I am on a par with royalty, I feel somewhat better.'

After her lesson, Mr Trippen saw her, as always, to the door, where two footmen waited with a sedan chair to take her back to Queen Square. It was as she was leaving Maiden Lane that she first noticed him, a large man, his face hidden by a three-cornered hat. Although she couldn't see his features, there was something familiar about him and she had the decided impression that he was following her. She had returned home to Queen Square wondering whether to say anything to her uncle.

When she arrived, she heard her aunt calling for her and, going upstairs to the pretty first-floor drawing room, she found her sitting on a small sofa, surrounded by Yann's letters.

Sido's heart sank.

'May I ask,' said her aunt, 'what is the meaning of this? After you have been asked not to write to him?'

'Those are private letters,' said Sido, horrified to think

her aunt might have read them. 'They are addressed to me.'

'That is by the by.' Juliette sat stiff and upright. 'He writes to you in such an informal way. Is that how you address him?'

'Aunt, you have no right—'

'I do,' she interrupted. 'I am your guardian. I love you and I want what's best for you. This is folly. Yann is not an appropriate suitor for you. He has nothing, no title, no money. It would be an ill-advised and scandalous union. You have much to learn and are not acquainted with the ways of the world. This is merely a young girl's infatuation. It will pass, Sido.'

'No, aunt, it will not. I love him with all my being. I always have and I always will, no matter what. My love is steadfast. May I have my letters back?' Sido said coldly.

'You may not,' said Juliette. 'When Yann lived here we treated him as an equal, he was even offered a place at Cambridge. Did you know that? He could have amounted to someone. Instead he chose to squander the opportunites your uncle gave him and go back to Paris to become an actor.'

'Aunt, that is not—'

Juliette interrupted. 'I take it that Mr Trippen is your collaborator? He should have known better.'

Sido felt the injustice of this acutely.

Her aunt's voice softened. 'There are many eligible young men in London, who are already in love with you. My dear one, please, this is a most inadvisable liaison and must stop.'

467

Sido composed herself. 'Aunt,' she said, 'I don't want a marriage made in a bank vault, like my mother's. I will marry for love or not at all. I refuse to live a lie like she did.'

'What on earth do you mean by that?'

'My mother was in love with Armand de Villeduval. I am their child. The Marquis arranged with Count Kalliovski to have us all killed the day they tried to elope to England. Only I survived.'

Now it was Juliette's turn to be outraged. 'That is not true! That can't be true! My sister would never have—'

'I know it is the truth,' Sido said quietly. 'I have letters and documents to prove it. Yann found them and gave them to me. The letters my mother and Armand wrote to each other prove who my real father is. I also have the note from the Marquis asking the Count to arrange the accident. I will not be a puppet any more. What's in a name? And what value now does that name have? The only person who has ever loved me for who I am is Yann. He risked everything to rescue me. I would be dead if it were not for his bravery.'

Furious and unable to comprehend what she had just heard, Juliette ignored it. 'Can you imagine the scandal? A marquis's daughter marrying a gypsy boy, for that is what Yann is, a gypsy! Oh, didn't he tell you? A fine education and all he wants to do is waste his life on the stage. I refuse to let you ruin your life too.'

Sido fled from the room as Henry entered.

'What on earth's going on?' he said.

Juliette was sitting as stiff as a tree before the wind bows it. Doubling over, she burst into tears.

'I demand to know the truth,' she wept.

'About what?'

'Was my sister murdered?'

Henry, caught off guard, said calmly, 'Who told you that?'

'Sidonie.'

Henry sighed. Of course, he thought. It was inevitable.

Juliette looked up at him imploringly. 'I have a right to know the truth.'

'Yes,' he said, going over to her and taking her hand. 'I'm afraid she was. I had my suspicions when I went to France all those years ago after the accident. At least Sido is still with us. Let the dead rest easy.'

Juliette pulled her hand away and with a look of disgust on her face, said, 'Why did you never tell me this? How could you keep such a thing to yourself?'

'Because you were unwell and grief-stricken, and nothing was certain, not then. Not until the papers were discovered.'

'So you have seen my sister's letters?'

'Yes. But what are these letters?'

'They are love letters Yann has written to Sido,' said Juliette.

'Did Sido wish you to see them?'

'No, of course not,' said Juliette. 'They are so ... forward. They say things that shouldn't be said. Let me read you—'

469

'No,' he said abruptly. 'I will not hear them and you, madam, should not have read them.'

Never before had Juliette heard her husband address her so sternly.

'But Henry, this match—'

'Madam, you will stop interfering in matters that don't concern you.'

'Sido does concern me; she's my sister's child,' Juliette sobbed.

Henry went to the window. Standing below in the square was a man, his face well hidden by a three-cornered hat.

He took a deep breath to calm himself and turned back to his wife. 'When Yann came to live with us you were in favour of taking him in as an equal, to be part of our family, remember?'

'Yes, yes, I did, and I meant it. He was, after all, a young boy. We did the right thing by him and he let us down; we stayed true to our word.'

'As long as our word suited us,' said Henry bluntly.

'*Mon cheri*, surely you can see this is untenable? What kind of life would he and Sido have together? He is of inferior birth, of lowly rank. He is a gypsy. In France gypsies are thought of as vermin.'

Henry bristled with indignation at his wife's *petit-bourgeois* attitude. 'That to me,' he said, 'is the worst form of prejudice. Do you wish Sido to be like your sister, married to a man who doesn't love her? To some ridiculous handsome fop with a good eye for a horse and the indolence of too many idle years as an

470

émigré? Being buried alive might be preferable.'

'Are you determined to be unpleasant?'

'No, I'm not. But your argument can't go unchecked. Yann could well have chosen to go to Cambridge, to have taken the numerous opportunities we were more than prepared to give him, and then you would have forgotten his origins. Instead he went back to Paris and saved Sido, risked his life to get her out.'

'And now he is an actor! It was his choice to stay in France.'

Henry felt disappointed in Juliette. 'There are things I can't discuss, and this is one of them. But you should know that Paris is more perilous than ever.'

'What are you saying?'

'In a world turned upside down, we need heroes. There are not many who are prepared to risk everything. Don't you think their courage earns them the right to defy social conventions? I can assure you of this: Yann is worth a thousand foppish young men.'

'But you are not listening to me. All I am saying is that he is not a suitable husband for Sido.'

'You are in danger of sounding like a hypocrite, someone who had no intention of thinking Yann an equal, who was always going to see him as a gypsy boy. Were you just playing a game, like Marie Antoinette pretending to be a shepherdess?'

Juliette put her head in her hands. 'No, no ... perhaps.'

They were silent for a while.

'Give Sido back her letters,' Henry said. 'Make it up

471

with her. If Yann survives ...' He paused. 'Be kind to her.'

———————◆———————

Sido's thoughts were in chaos. Yann a gypsy! Suddenly she felt foolish and ignorant. Her aunt was right. She was a child when it came to the affairs of men. Had she heard correctly? A gypsy? Now she thought herself a blind fool. The talisman, his dark eyes, his ability to read her thoughts. Oh, dear Lord, this made her love for him even more impossible. She remembered with horror the stories about the Marquis's hunting parties, when he would boast that he had killed gypsies like crows and hung them in the trees. To think that by birth she was part of a society that saw such barbarity as its God-given right!

And then she remembered a grand ball in what seemed like another lifetime, given on the day she first met Yann, the day Kalliovski had killed the magician Topolain.

She had been standing on the stairs when she overheard a young woman talking about the time the Marquis had brought a fortune-teller to the house who had predicted that he would lose everything to the King of the Gypsies.

The thought lifted her spirits and getting off the bed she went to the window and opened the shutters. It was a cold rainy night; only a few people were out. Then, in the flare of a passing carriage lamp, she saw him again, looking up at her window. Sido quickly backed into the room, blowing out all the candles before she dared look once more into the square. No one was there. The stranger in the three-cornered hat had vanished.

Chapter Nine

Madame Loup said not a word when she was told her husband was dead, fearful lest she might let out a hallelujah by mistake. After all, she had prayed every day of her married life for just such a miracle as this. And slowly it dawned on her that at last she was free of the murderous thug who had as good as ruined her life.

'A tragedy. I hope they catch the aristos who've done this,' said a drunk, fighting to keep his distance from the floor.

'Guillotine the lot of them!' said her neighbour, Citizen Planchot, a pale fish-like creature who had always been terrified of the butcher, but felt the necessity of singing his praises now that he was dead. He was hoping he might be able to buy the business.

474

Madame Loup finally found her voice. 'Where is Anselm?'

'No one's seen him. We can only hope he's still alive,' said Citizen Planchot.

'The Spirit of the Revolution,' said the drunk, hoping to be invited in for more wine. 'He'll turn up.'

Like a bad penny, thought Madame Loup.

There being nothing to say, nothing to sell, and no wine she wished to share with anyone, she closed the shop for good. After that she would stand night and day by the window, studying the passers-by, listening to the sign of the iron pig swinging back and forth.

Neighbours believed her grief and devotion to her family kept her there, holding a vigil, waiting for Anselm to return.

But they were wrong. Very wrong indeed. She had never liked him, even as a baby. All that beauty had a stink of cruelty about it that made her sick. Anselm, as far as she was concerned, could go to hell.

———◆———

Citizen Planchot came every day to report to Madame Loup on how his search for Anselm was going. He had been to taverns and gambling dens, but had neither found nor heard a thing that would give him a clue as to where the lad could be. He had even gone to the police headquarters in the Hôtel de Ville, looked in at the city prisons and been down by the Drowned Man's Benches, slabs of stone beside the Seine where the luckless ones were fished from the river to be claimed or not as the case might be.

'Maybe he's been picked up and conscripted,' said Citizen Planchot, hoping now his neighbour might negotiate the sale of the shop.

Still Madame Loup waited by the window, coffin-cold and unconvinced that the devil's imp was dead.

Then she heard that Anselm had been seen and knew she had no choice but to leave the shop and leave it fast. To that end she invited Citizen Planchot round, and sitting at the kitchen table they came to an agreement. The business and the shop would be his, and Madame Loup would have enough money to return to Mallemort in Provence, her childhood home.

After he had gone she went upstairs to her clean sparse bedchamber and sat on the bed, sewing her new-found wealth into her best red calico petticoat. Packing a few possessions, she went back downstairs and looked round the shop for the last time. It was then she saw a figure in the gloom and her heart sank.

He appeared, to anyone who didn't know the true colour of his blood, the kind of young man to give your heart to, such were his angelic looks, those golden eyes, that sensuous mouth.

'Well, well,' he said. His words snaked towards her; she could feel the venom in them.

'Sold the business, I heard. Took it into that sawdust brain of yours to do something on your own, without consulting your son and heir.'

Madame Loup had been edging towards the door, but Anselm got there first.

'We can do this the civilised way, or the hard way.'

'I don't know what you mean,' she said. Under her red calico petticoat her knees began to shake.

'Oh, I think you do, Mother. I want my money.'

She opened her bag and showed him just a few *assignats* that she had kept back for the journey.

'You're making me angry, Mother,' said Anselm quietly. 'And you know what happens if you make me angry don't you, Mother? I want all the money, every last *sou*.'

Madame Loup backed away.

Anselm was in no hurry. He would get his money all right; that was not the point. The point would be the pleasure he would have in seeing her beg for mercy. He put his finger and thumb on her jaw and pushed her hard against the wall. He could feel her soft skin, tissue thin like parchment, in his grasp.

'You'd better be careful, Mother, that you don't end up with the rotten chicken meat.'

Madame Loup's face was turning blue.

'Now, I ask you again. Where's the money?'

Ever since Madame Loup had been married, she had imagined her own death as a door through which she knew escape from the final beating was possible, a place where her husband couldn't touch her. Now she worried that he might be waiting on the other side, ready to grab her. The thought was enough to make her fight with her last ounce of courage, for suddenly she knew what she wanted out of life, and that was to live without fear.

Her new-found strength excited Anselm. He liked resistance. But it was useless.

He could feel her pulse beating, knew that he only had to squeeze and the frayed thread of her life would be broken forever.

He watched emotionless as she gasped for air. Madame Loup's words were now no more than a desperate whisper; her bird-like hands had curled over, trying frantically to claw at him.

'Oh, sweet Mary, save me,' she begged, with what sounded like her last breath.

Anselm had never been worried by his conscience. His moral compass, for what it was worth, his father had stolen from him long ago. The urge to kill was powerful, irrepressible inside him as he squeezed tighter. Madame Loup's eyes rolled back in her head.

All Madame Loup could see was light. It shone brightly. The Virgin Mary, she felt sure, had come to take her home.

'Leave her be,' came a rough voice. 'Do you hear me? I have work for you, but there'll be nothing if you kill her.'

Involuntarily Anselm loosened his grip as he recognised the voice of Mr Tull.

'Let her go,' said Mr Tull again, talking to Anselm as he would to a dog. 'Let her go, you pathetic little puke-pot.'

Anselm let Madame Loup drop to the floor like a pile of rags.

Realising that she was alive and her protector,

whoever he was, looked like a man strong enough to hold Anselm back, she said in a whisper, 'Holy Mary, Mother of God, I tell you this, and it is the truth, you are no son of mine. I didn't bear you. You were left in a basket of stinking blood and guts. Even your real mother didn't want you. She was glad to be rid of her devil's child.'

Anselm rushed towards her once more, but Mr Tull had him by the collar.

'Save your breath to cool your porridge.'

'Go to the devil!'

As Mr Tull dragged him from the shop he was still screaming, 'I'm going to kill her!'

Madame Loup lay on the floor for a long time, gasping for breath, until her strength returned. She sat up and drank a glass of wine. She knew she had escaped Death by a cat's whisker. It would be many years before he came calling again, walking through fields of lavender to find her.

———◆———

'Well, I see the shop business ain't to your liking,' said Mr Tull, when they were seated in a café with a jug of wine in front of them. 'Calm down, you're going to need your wits.'

'Where've you been? I haven't seen you around for ages,' said Anselm, drumming his fingers wildly on the table, his foot tapping a chaotic rhythm on the floor.

'Away on business. It seems I got back just in time.'

Anslem wasn't listening. He leapt to his feet. 'Let me

finish her off; it's what she deserves. She owes me, she does.'

'By all means,' said Mr Tull. 'Go on, kill the old girl; it's no skin off my nose.'

Anselm was rearranging his scarf, ready to charge back to the butcher's shop.

'The only thing is, you wouldn't get to meet Count Kalliovski.'

His words had the desired effect.

'Oh,' said Mr Tull, lighting his pipe. 'You're interested, then?'

'Yes.'

Mr Tull leaned forward and grabbed Anselm by the throat. 'If,' he said, knowing exactly where to press to cause the most pain, 'you breathe a word of what you see tonight, you are a dead man and no mistake. You get my drift?'

Letting go, he poured a tumbler of wine. 'Have a drink. We've got a long night ahead of us.'

It was early evening when they reached the Place du Faubourg de Gloire. All that was left of the Bastille were a few stones and blackened earth.

'A place of secrets,' said Mr Tull.

'They say it's haunted by the spectre of the Terror made real,' said Anselm, remembering what he had been told in the whorehouse where he'd been staying.

'That wouldn't surprise me. But I think the Terror is real enough, with or without the spectre.'

'I've heard them say he has a big dog.'

'Oh, put a rag in it.'

They walked away from the Bastille, towards the Seine ferrymen who were packing up for the night.

'One last trip?' asked Mr Tull, bringing out a good handful of coins.

'For you,' said the ferryman, pushing his boat into the water, 'a pleasure.' He lit the lantern. 'Take you to La Taverne des Trois Pendus on the other side?'

Mr Tull nodded.

The brown water of the Seine lapped past. Until they reached the south bank the only other sound was the swish of the oars.

They crunched up the shore and climbed the wooden steps leading to the inn.

'Is this where we're meeting him?' asked Anselm.

'No.' Mr Tull was in no mood for talking. 'Sit down and shut up. I'll tell you when we need to go.'

At midnight Mr Tull shook Anselm awake and stood him up, taking in his appearance.

'You're a mess. You don't half stink too. What, you been sleeping in the gutter?'

'No,' said Anselm.

'Pull yourself together, make yourself look respectable. One other thing. Not one word about the robberies. If you say anything, you'll be a bag of bones.'

It had started to rain heavily by the time they arrived at their destination: a shop with a shuttered front. Above, in the murky window, hung three dimly lit red lanterns. The room inside was equally empty, with sawdust on the

481

floor and a scrubbed counter on which sat a large ledger. Somewhere in the distance a bell rang. A man appeared from behind a velvet curtain. He was dressed from head to toe in black.

'Serreto,' said Mr Tull. 'How are you?'

'As well as these topsy-turvy days allow.' He opened the ledger in front of him and wrote something down. Pointing his quill at Anselm he said, 'He knows the rules, does he?'

Mr Tull nodded. 'He's here on probation.'

'I see.'

Anselm had the feeling from the look Serreto gave him that he had just been measured for a coffin.

They were taken through the curtain into an ante-chamber lined with row upon row of cloaks and masks. Bunches of unlit torches stood in wicker baskets, waiting to be used. Mr Tull lit one and opened another door that led to a flight of stairs descending to the cellar – or so Anselm thought, yet the further they went the more he began to realise that no cellar could possibly be this deep. The stairs, made out of limestone, became narrower and spiralled, step after step, round and round. The light of Mr Tull's torch flickered, throwing shadows across the white stone walls, and still they kept going down without end.

The air began to smell musty and damp and finally they reached the very bottom. They were in a cavernous room that led to a tunnel, lit with torches as far as the eye could see.

'Are you ready?' said Mr Tull.

Anselm was quiet. Mr Tull turned to check his companion.

'A lot of people couldn't stand it down here,' he said, 'but you get used to it. You still with me?'

Anselm nodded, following Mr Tull into the labyrinth of tunnels. He took a deep breath of stale air and said out loud, 'This is a new beginning and nothing is going to stop me.'

'What did you say?' said Mr Tull, turning round.

'Just that I wanted ... I want to thank you.'

'For what?'

'For giving me this opportunity. I owe you, I do.'

Mr Tull walked on. 'Better hope that my master likes you.'

What he didn't say was: if he doesn't, you will never see the light of day again.

Chapter Ten

O f all the châteaux Anselm and his father had robbed over the past year, nothing compared to this.

The first chamber had a higher ceiling than the passageway they had walked through. Anselm later discovered that it was only a prelude to what lay beyond, a waiting room of sorts, a place to contemplate one's own mortality. If he had been able to read the motto above the door he might have been more worried: *Enter here if you dare and you fear not death.* The words, no more than a pattern to Anselm, didn't interest him. What fired his imagination were the painted walls which, though he didn't know it, depicted Dante's *Inferno*. The ceiling too had been decorated so it looked as if the chandelier had been spewed out of the mouth of the devil. Three golden bowls stood near the far end of the chamber, and flames like forked tongues flickered menacingly. He was enthralled by the idea that tonight he would meet the great man himself. The master, as Mr Tull called him. Count Kalliovski.

Mr Tull, unlike Anselm, seemed oblivious to his surroundings, as he paced to and fro, fiddling with his watch. Seeing Anselm studying the walls he hissed at him, 'Remember, not a word about our other business, understood?'

'Of course, Mr Tull. My lips are sealed.'

Mr Tull was beginning to have his doubts about bringing Anselm here. His lack of breeding showed. He looked what he was: nothing more than a pretty boy, a small-time crook from the Place du Carrousel.

'Stop staring at everything,' Mr Tull said tartly. 'Look at the floor if you're going to look anywhere.'

'Why?'

'Because I say so, and because there are eyes behind them there walls.'

Anselm spun round, examining everything with even more relish than before.

'Are you trying to show me up or what?' said Mr Tull through gritted teeth. 'Just stare at your bleeding shoes.'

A door opened and into the room came a man who looked as if his skin had been patched together. He had one white fish-eye, a dead pupil staring through what looked like a film of rancid milk. His good eye, green and eager, surveyed the room. He was taller than Mr Tull and in the pecking order of thugs there was no doubt who was the superior. Mr Tull seemed almost sheepish as he introduced Milkeye to Anselm.

Milkeye, ignoring the boy, said, 'My master will see you now.'

Anselm followed Mr Tull. Milkeye stopped him, his hand held out like a barricade.

'Not you, you stay.'

Anselm, seeing he had no alternative, waited until Milkeye returned and led him down a corridor ablaze with candles. Each was held in a skeleton hand which had been gold-leafed and decked in jewels so that light was caught in the brilliance of the gems and reflected across the walls in radiant sparks of colour. A way off he could hear water.

'Where's that coming from?' he asked.

'You don't speak. You don't ask questions. You do what you're told,' said Milkeye, pushing open a heavy iron door for Anselm to slip through. 'Now you wait until you're called for.'

There was a finality, like being locked in a prison cell, to the closing of the door. For a moment Anselm was disorientated. When his eyes adjusted, he could see walls covered in a mosaic of human bones, the design punctuated by skulls, their eye sockets inlaid with a myriad mirrors, so that he was surrounded by fragments of his own mindless image. It had a giddying effect.

When a similar door at the opposite end of the room swung open apparently of its own accord, to Anselm this was an invitation to investigate. Curiosity, the killer of cats, drove him ever onwards, regardless of the words above the threshold: *The point of no return*. The door led to a gallery beyond which he could hear voices. Slowly he slid snake-like across the wooden gantry floor towards the carved banisters. From there he looked down into a vast domed hall, its walls made from human bones stacked like logs, bare and yellowed. The ceiling blazed with a multitude of chandeliers made out of bones, lit with hundreds of candles. The floor was laid with slabs of stone, dipping slightly towards the centre where there appeared to be a small hole like a navel, stained brownish red.

Figures stood waiting, dressed in cloaks and masks. A chair hovered just off the ground, as if suspended on invisible wires.

Anselm lay welded to the spot as he heard boots click-clack across the stone floor below. A man faced the assembly, his back to the gantry. The gathering bowed deeply. He was immaculately dressed in black with red kid gloves, and wore no cloak or mask. Instinctively Anselm knew it was Count Kalliovski. The man turned and looked up as if he were aware of another's presence.

Now Anselm could see him clearly and he shuddered as he remembered once, long ago when he was still a child, having been taken to see the waxworks in a passage off the rue St-Jacques. This man looked as if he belonged more to the waxy, embalmed dead than the living.

'I am the Terror incarnate, the engine of fear, I am your end and your beginning. Your salvation lies in my power, as does your damnation. You are my inner circle. If anyone here betrays me they will never escape my wrath.'

The hall was graveyard silent.

'I, the bringer of darkness, will soon possess the power of light. That day I will rise from the ashes, a phoenix, to reign supreme.'

He walked to the chair and sat down. 'To the business in hand. Bring forth the Seven Sisters Macabre.'

Anselm was hypnotised. Seven beautifully dressed women glided into the chamber. They were youthful and elegant, their faces hidden from him. They too bowed before Kalliovski; then one by one they began to leave the ground to be suspended in mid air, just as his father had been. Slowly they spun and now he saw why they had been given their name. They were hideous apparitions, ghastly harpies.

The chair in which Kalliovski was sitting rose higher.

'I am the Master,' he said.

The Seven Sisters Macabre began to chant.

'Calico and corpses.'

'We have a traitor among us,' Kalliovski said.

'Damask and death.'

'All of you know the penalty for betrayal.'

'Velvet and violence,' hissed the Sisters Macabre.

'I call on Balthazar to reveal the spy in our midst.'

'Brocade and blood!' Their voices reached a crescendo.

There was a rustling of fabric as the cloaked and masked figures pushed further into the bones of the wall as if hoping they might disappear.

The silence that now took hold of the chamber had a sound, just as wine has a smell. It was the high-pitched scream of terror. And then suddenly Anselm heard the howl of a beast and a shadow, liquid as molten iron, flashed past.

Anselm felt the hair rise on the back of his neck. He buried his head in his arms, imagining the great black dog was coming for him. He was certain this was the same beast he'd seen at the Duc de Bourcy's estate, that the diabolical creature had followed him here and would smell him out.

Through screwed-up eyes he saw the beast sniff its way around the room before singling out one of the cloaked and masked figures. The poor man started to shake and his teeth chattered in fear. The hound leaped at him, pulling the mask from his face. The victim's screams were without echo, as if the walls were greedily swallowing the sound of misery; his cries for mercy lost in dead men's bones. He was torn to shreds like a rag doll, the floor ran red. The beast licked it clean, then with a deep growl turned and vanished from the chamber.

Kalliovski's voice made Anselm jump.

'Those foolish enough to speak about our activities will, like Levis Artois, find their lives cut short. Anyone here who feels the necessity to discuss what is said within these walls will go the same way.'

Anselm felt his insides turn to water as he was hoisted to his feet.

Milkeye said nothing as he led him away.

489

Kalliovski's living quarters were even more spectacular than the previous chambers. They had the luxury of windows, and Anselm almost forgot they were so far underground that there would be nothing to see. Yet through the windows were vistas of gardens, of gravel drives which looked real until he realised they had been painted, while an artificial sun shone into the chamber. He even recognised some of the furniture he and Mr Tull had taken from noble houses, now put to great effect.

As Anselm waited with Milkeye, Count Kalliovski entered the room followed by Mr Tull. The Count's waistcoat was embroidered with silver skulls and close up he was even more intimidating. Anselm stared transfixed. This man acted not in the rage of the moment like his father used to. He killed in cold blood.

Count Kalliovski stood, lost in thought, his back towards Anselm.

'Tell me, do you believe the Governor of the Universe created the world?'

The question was one to which Anselm had never given much thought, and he wasn't sure if he was expected to answer. He looked beseechingly at Mr Tull, who stared resolutely at his shoes.

Kalliovski turned to look at him. 'Well?'

Mr Tull nudged Anselm.

'Yes,' said Anselm uncertainly.

'I don't,' replied Kalliovski. 'I don't believe the Governor of the Universe had anything to do with it. It is purely by the power of chance that the world is here at all. What say you to that?'

Anselm was out of his depth. He had never been involved in this sort of conversation. If it was a test he felt certain he was going to fail.

'All I know about religion comes from my mother and she believes in God and all the saints. She believes in purgatory and hell.' He added, more to himself than anyone else, 'She thinks that's where I'm going.'

'And if I told you there are no such places,' asserted Count Kalliovski, 'that it is the Church's plot against the people, nothing more, what would you say?'

Anselm thought, that's what Pa believed. He was all for getting rid of the Church. He said if the Revolution hadn't banned it, he might not have been as free with his pig-killing knife and would have worried more about what might happen to him when he was dead.

He shrugged his shoulders. 'I don't know, but if it is by chance that the world is here, as you say, then maybe there's a good chance that hell exists too.'

To Anselm's great relief Count Kalliovski's reply had a hint of laughter in it, though his face remained waxwork smooth.

'You have potential,' he said. 'Would you like to work for me?'

'Yes,' said Anselm. His puppy-like enthusiasm made Mr Tull wince.

'When do I start?'

Kalliovski glanced at him.

Anselm felt something push down on his shoulders, an invisible force. His legs gave way under the pressure and he found himself on his knees.

'You will do what I say, or you will be killed, do you understand?'

Kalliovski inclined his hand in its red kid glove, a sign that Anselm was dismissed. Milkeye helped him up and took him from the chamber, leaving only Mr Tull.

From the window the artificial glow of golden afternoon light flooded into the room and the reassuring sound of birdsong could be heard from the cages hidden behind the painted flats.

'A nightingale,' said Kalliovski.

Mr Tull had been dreading this meeting. He had told himself repeatedly that if his master took Anselm on he would speak out. He was determined to ask if he might be allowed to retire.

'Now tell me about Sido de Villeduval.'

Mr Tull, hands behind his back, feet squarely apart, started. 'The Laxtons live in Queen Square, in Bloomsbury. The house is well-staffed and is a meeting place for many of the émigrés newly—'

'That interests me little. Tell me of the Marquise Sido.'

'She is well cared for by her aunt and uncle. They are keen that she should master English and to that end she has lessons with a Mr Trippen, an actor. She is taken to his house in Maiden Lane by sedan chair twice a week and is always accompanied by two servants. This same Mr Trippen taught Yann Margoza.'

Mr Tull, somewhat relieved that his other little enter-prise appeared to be undiscovered and feeling braver, said, 'I wonder if after this business I might be able to retire. It's just that . . .'

He didn't finish what he had to say, for Kalliovski's look of pure rage was enough to silence him.

'Once you work for me there is no retirement other than your own demise. You will await further instruc-tions. When the time is right you will bring Sido de Villeduval here. Until then you are dismissed.'

◄──◆──►

B ack in the shop, Mr Tull, feeling the weight of hell upon his shoulders, said to Milkeye, 'Balthazar seems even bigger than when I last saw him.'

Milkeye turned his one good eye on Tull. 'Our master knows what you do. He knows that you and the butcher and his boy had a very profitable sideline, don't think he doesn't.'

'I don't know what you're talking about,' said Mr Tull, an icy sweat breaking out on his forehead.

Milkeye laughed. 'You're walking on the edge, my friend. One false move and you will be Balthazar's next feast.'

Mr Tull had the decidedly uncomfortable feeling that his bones might already have been reserved for the design of a chandelier or mirror.

Milkeye followed him on to the street where Mr Tull breathed in the night air.

'Do you know why he still wants Sido de Villeduval?' he asked.

'If I were you I wouldn't want to know. I'll tell you this much: she's not all my master is after.' A slow smile spread over his face. The effect was even more gruesome than usual. 'The Marquise de Villeduval is only one part of his plan.'

'What do you mean?' said Mr Tull, feeling a shudder run down his spine.

Milkeye leaned forward, towering over him. 'This is much harder to come by – some say impossible, but such an indifferent word has never stopped the Count. He wants a key to a soul.'

Mr Tull looked down the rue des Couteaux with a longing to be gone from this madness and never return.

He thrust his shaking hands deep into his pockets. As he walked away he stumbled on a soft, unlikely thought. Under his breath he said, 'Heaven help her. Heaven help all of us.'

Chapter Eleven

The leather box containing the key sat waiting on Remon Quint's workbench. Even looking at it made his stomach churn. He regretted his lack of courage. He should have spoken out when he had the chance, told the man with the waxwork face and the poppy-red gloves that what he desired was impossible, that no man on earth had the power to make a key to a soul. Speak the truth and shame the devil! But he hadn't. Instead he had listened, believing at first this was merely a rich man's foible. After all, he'd worked with enough clients whose wealth was beyond the realms of most men's understanding.

Usually flattery persuaded them to see that what they had purchased was unique, yet he had the feeling that this man was in deadly earnest. Flattery would never satisfy his desire. He wanted a key to a soul and nothing else would do.

The keymaker looked around his shabby apartment: a bedchamber, a workroom and a small anteroom. These poky, lopsided chambers were all he could afford now. It was stiflingly hot; the smell of rubbish and rotten meat wafted through his open window. Today there was no breeze, just an unbearable, claustrophobic, sticky heat that made everyone irritable. Below he could hear the cobbler and his wife bickering. He went to the cupboard and took out a half-empty bottle and a stale loaf, poured himself a glass of wine, carefully replaced the cork, broke off a piece of bread and said grace, as he always did. For all his new-found poverty, he remained a pious man. He took a sip of the wine and grimaced. It was sour.

Before the Revolution, when the power of prayer was believed in, his prayers had been answered. He had owned a shop in the fashionable rue du Labon district, had a fine carriage and servants, wore elegant clothes and wigs and was known for his hospitality. And he could boast that he had dined with the King of Keymakers, Louis XVI, whose obsession was labyrinthine locks. Oh, how he had picked his brains to know their secret. Those were golden days.

He had entertained, held supper parties. When, with

the dessert, he would bring out a mahogany toy guillotine, fashionable at the time, his guests delighted in taking turns to put little dolls under the knife and watch the miniature executions. The streams of red fluid that burst from them were merely perfume, to be caught on the handkerchiefs of giggling ladies.

How foolish to think nothing would change. Now everything was lost, ankle deep in blood.

———◆———

The row between the cobbler and his wife had spilled into the courtyard. A man yelled at them from an upstairs window to shut up, otherwise they'd be for it.

Only a fool wouldn't know what was meant by that remark, thought the keymaker. In this dog-eat-dog world everyone was food for the Tribunal, the tumbril and the guillotine. No man's neck was safe.

The keymaker knew he was doomed. Maybe it would be best if he were arrested and taken to prison. His life was hanging by a thread, like a child's tooth. One yank and it would be gone. At least in prison, he thought, there would be old friends to reminisce with, and he would be free at last to say what was on his mind. It would make no difference. The guillotine would be waiting to embrace him whether he kept quiet or not. Instead here he was, at liberty, but lonely and wretched, plagued by voices in his head. This was Death's waiting room. Every time he heard a tread on the steps up to his apartment he told himself it was the Grim Reaper.

If only he'd had the wit to leave after the fall of the

Bastille as so many of his clients had done, conveniently forgetting to pay their bills. But he hadn't had the foresight to see what a revolution was capable of doing. He had agreed with those who were in favour of a constitutional monarchy. Once that was in place, the keymaker was sure it would be business as usual. In a time of such political upheaval, instead of keeping an eye on events, he had buried himself in his work and refused to read the signs. He couldn't bring himself to believe that Paris could fall so low.

The toy guillotine had turned out to be no laughing matter. Its life-size version had sliced the heads off his most valuable customers, the Convention confiscating their property so there was no possibility of claiming the monies he was owed.

He had been forced to close his shop. There hadn't been enough business to keep his fine house, his carriages or servants. He'd been told that his name was on a list of those suspected of having supplied the Duc d'Arlincourt with a lock for an iron chest in which pamphlets opposing the Republic had been discovered.

Since he had been informed of this, he believed every day to be his last.

Three weeks ago, in the middle of the night, he had woken to find an apparition in his apartment, an immaculately dressed man sitting in his chair, his eyes closed. The keymaker couldn't imagine what he was doing there, or whether or not he was dreaming, for the figure didn't look quite of this world. The raw scream hurt his throat as it made its embarrassed entrance into the room. The man in the chair opened his eyes. Dark and deadly, they were staring right through him.

'Citizen Quint,' said this stranger, getting up and holding out a red-kid-gloved hand. 'I have a commission for you.'

———◆———

He'd been given a month to create the impossible. He'd worked night and day, obliged to use a friend's furnace for the purpose. His whole life's work had gone into that one key. It was his masterpiece and in itself it held great beauty. He had kept the design simple. Cast in silver, as requested, the bow was a circle in which stood a man, held in the wheel of life. The column was elegant and the bit was cut in the shape of the Ace of Spades. In this, if in nothing else, he had the measure of the man who commissioned it. But a key to a soul? What could he say? That such a thing was beyond him? In a week's time the nocturnal visitor would return personally to collect it. The very thought of seeing him again had robbed the keymaker of his reason, made him dizzy, as if the walls of the apartment were closing in on him. If they got any closer he would be squashed like an insect.

Then the voice had started, a woman's voice, gentle but insistent.

'*The devil's own is on your trail. Run like the wind.*'

The words never changed. She never stopped, night and day, until the hinges of his reason loosened.

He staggered, clutching the sides of his head.

'Stop it,' he shouted. 'Stop it. I am not mad!'

Wide-eyed he looked at the door. Yes, that's what he needed, fresh air. He walked, then ran down the stairs. He had to get away. On the landing he bumped into the cobbler.

'Look where you're going,' said the cobbler, then seeing the state of him asked, 'You all right, citizen? You're not going out like that, are you? You haven't got your shoes on.'

Remon Quint saw nothing but the foot of the staircase. The voice in his head drowned the cobbler's words so that he appeared like a fish mouthing silently at him. Everything had slowed down. In the street he gasped for air, not knowing where he was or where he should be, and with the voice near shouting in his head it came to him what he must do. He had to drown out the sound. He walked like a man possessed; even the cuts in his stockinged feet didn't register. At the Pont Neuf he stood looking down into the brown stained water of the Seine, like a man about to savour the first sip of a longed-for cup of coffee.

———◆———

Basco had been on an errand for Citizen Aulard. The tumbrils trundled past him, filled with the living dead, a drumbeat following them to their mass grave, a footnote to be forgotten in the folds of history. He took his time walking back to the Circus of Follies, thinking how much Paris had changed since the heady days of the fall of the Bastille, when everything had seemed brand new, a clean page. Who would have imagined that the rest of the Revolution would be written in blood?

Citizens scurried past, heads down, terrified lest they be stopped, each believing the other to be a spy or an informer. Never had Basco known the city so starved of *joie de vivre*.

He was halfway across the Pont Neuf when he noticed a man without hat or shoes, and thought he was behaving strangely. But didn't everyone behave strangely these days?

Then he realised what Remon Quint was doing. As the keymaker climbed on to the parapet of the bridge Basco charged like a bull, desperate to get to him before it was too late. He saw him jump, heard a woman scream, saw an orange spill from her basket and roll away between the legs of passers-by. He grabbed at what he prayed wasn't thin air and found he had the keymaker dangling by his shirt.

'Let me go, please let me go. If you have any mercy, let me go.'

Basco had no intention of doing so. Another man came to his aid and together they pulled the keymaker back on to the bridge.

'I want to die,' he said.

The crowd was already parting to let three national guards through.

'Papers,' said one of the Bluecoats to Basco. 'Now.'

Basco, whose sense of his failure as an actor had been acute, thought little about outwitting the guard.

'My friend is very sick,' he said. 'He has a fever in the brain.'

'Papers,' repeated the guard, unimpressed.

Basco propped his new friend against the bridge as he struggled to find his documents.

The Bluecoat looked bored. Basco knew that bored officialdom was far more dangerous than occupied officialdom and these three were pushing for an arrest. Then a woman screamed.

'Stop that man! He's stolen my bread! Stop, he's a ratbag of a Royalist!'

The guards, having found something worthy of their attention, left Basco and rushed after the thief, swords and guns rattling.

Basco wasted no time. Heaving the keymaker up like a sack of potatoes, and not a very heavy sack at that, he headed back to the safety of the Circus of Follies.

Chapter Twelve

'**B**read and theatres, whatever next?' cried Citizen Aulard, his operatic eyebrows rising ever upwards as his face fell like a curtain. 'I am now expected to give free performances to distract the citizens of Paris from their rumbling stomachs. *Mort bleu!* In return for what? Worthless paper money!'

He stuffed his hands into his waistcoat pockets.

Têtu, sitting with Iago as usual perched on top of his head, said nothing.

'What a wretched morning. A member of the Committee of Public Safety paid us a visit, inspected the theatre and wrote copious notes. Did you know that *eau de nil* green is an aristocratic colour?'

He stared for a moment at the ceiling as if from it might come salvation.

'I've been ordered to repaint the auditorium. Please,'

he said tilting his head right back, 'tell me when this stupidity will end. So many people dead, the prisons fit to bursting and the scum of the streets now rule the country and want everything painted *bleu, blanc, rouge. Mort bleu!*'

'*Vive la Nation!*'

'Will you keep that parrot quiet? And that is another thing. *My* parrot, Iago. *My* parrot now seems to be your parrot and, what's more, is talking far too much.'

He let out a heartfelt sigh and carried on with his list of woes, which were many.

'Why do they have to fiddle with everything? Three days of every decade, in this new calendar. Do you understand it?'

Citizen Aulard continued, not waiting for an answer, 'No, it would be much better if they had kept the weeks, and just said that three days out of every ten we have to put on shows that will appeal to the empty stomachs of *sans-culottes,* to serve up a visual feast full of hot air and patriotic dribble. The other seven days we can do *The Harlequinade.*'

'This is very obliging of them,' said Têtu.

'How so?'

'Because it gives us three days when Yann and Didier won't be missed. They'll stand a better chance of getting to the coast and back again before the next show.'

'How long will all this go on for?' asked Citizen Aulard.

In truth the visit of the member of the Committee of Public Safety had made him realise just how vulnerable their operation was.

Quite what Têtu's answer would have been remained a mystery, for at that moment Basco and Yann entered the room. Between them they carried the semiconscious body of a shoeless middle-aged man.

Yann laid him on the day bed.

'I found him,' said Basco, by way of explanation, 'about to throw his life into the Seine.'

'Oh wonderful, just what we need! And of course you thought straight away, I know, Citizen Aulard has hardly anything to do, and nothing to hide; I will take him to the Circus of Follies.'

'No, no, Signor Aulard, it wasn't like that,' said Basco. 'He was in trouble, no papers, and I thought—'

Citizen Aulard brought his fist down on the desk. 'Heaven protect me from a thinking fencing master! What are we now? Home to every stray, barefoot citizen found perching on the Pont Neuf about to answer to his maker?'

'That was not in my thinking,' said Basco. 'Yann said I should bring him here. I'd only intended to give him some brandy and some of my mother's homespun wisdom, then take him back to wherever he lives.'

'And Yann, why did you bring him up here?'

'Because he has something on his mind that struck me as unusual.'

'Have we all gone mad?'

'That's hard to know,' said Yann. 'Still you don't often come across a shoeless man raving about how to make a key to a soul.'

'What?' said Citizen Aulard.

505

'Quiet,' said Têtu, 'he's coming round.'

Remon Quint sat up, looking the colour of the auditorium. He was completely at a loss as to how he came to be surrounded by a strange assortment of people, one of whom was a dwarf with a parrot on his head.

'Do you remember your name?' asked Têtu.

'Yes. Remon Quint.'

Citizen Aulard peered more closely at the man propping himself up on his day bed.

'No! Surely not the celebrated keymaker from the rue du Lapon?' He adjusted his spectacles. 'It cannot be. He is a very respected gentleman who wore, if my memory serves me well, the most handsome wigs and—'

'You know this man?' interrupted Têtu, with surprise.

'Well, I know of him. He is a supreme craftsman. Of course, I never could afford one of his keys or locks. His customers were kings and princes. It was said that Marie Antoinette and King George of England commissioned keys from him.'

'Thank you kindly, sir,' said the keymaker, 'but all that was in another age, alas, all gone, washed away by the Revolution.' He tried to stand. 'Forgive me, I have inconvenienced you long enough and ...' He stopped and stared in amazement at his stockinged feet as if they belonged to someone else. 'Where are my shoes?'

'You didn't have them on at the Pont Neuf,' said Basco.

'The Pont Neuf? What was I doing there?' He held the sides of his head.

'Shall I take you home?' asked Basco.

Remon Quint had round eyes in a large round head on a small neat body. He looked not unlike a stick balancing a ball. The memory of what he had been doing began to come back, and his eyes looked as if they were about to pop out of his head.

'I can't go back,' he said. 'The voice will return. This is the first time since *he* came that she's been silent.'

'Would you like to tell us what the voice said?' asked Têtu, handing him a cognac, and knowing what the answer would be.

'She never stopped. She said, over and over again, "The devil's own is on your trail. Run like the wind."'

Yann broke the silence that greeted his words.

'Anis,' he said.

'I t is an incredible story,' said Citizen Quint. 'Things like this don't happen, not to me. I am an ordinary man.'

Citizen Aulard said, 'We are all of a theatrical disposition here and when I tell you that nothing is beyond the realms of possibility, I say it to comfort you and give you the courage to speak.'

'You will think me mad, perhaps I am.'

'I think you are exhausted,' said Têtu, with such authority that the keymaker felt his mind settling itself on the solid ground of rational thought.

So he started his story and he told it well; when he had finished you could have heard a pin drop.

'Where is the key now?' Yann asked Remon Quint.

'On my workbench.' He stopped, took out his handkerchief and mopped his forehead. 'It's my finest work.'

───────◆───────

Yann set off across the Pont Neuf towards the rue de Rivoli. Here at the Pavillion de Marson was the noisome quarter of dingy houses intersected by narrow alleys which extended from the rue St-Honoré to the Place du Carrousel. He found the house just as the keymaker had described. It was a tall tenement building which looked as if it had been stretched upwards to accommodate all its inhabitants; it hummed with life like a beehive. Yann took his time and decided that it would be better observed from the café across the road, though when he entered the place the smell of unwashed flesh and smoke made him instantly regret his decision. Having taken a table he felt that to leave straight away would draw unwanted attention to himself. He peered through the steamed-up window. Sobriety was a foreign word to the collection of drunks and misfits in the café, all of whom had the look of those who have sacrificed their souls to the bottle. The floor was covered in a matting of filthy sawdust, solid in parts where no one had the strength, or the will, to sweep it away.

To the disgust of the waiter Yann ordered coffee. At the next table sat a man with a bright-red face. He was dressed in a worn cotton jacket which had seen better days and had a red cap on his head. He was in the middle of lecturing a citizeness who was only slightly less drunk than him. She at least wasn't slurring her words.

Yann watched the comings and goings of the building opposite, half-listening to their conversation.

'No, woman, the way to feed the people is simple. We should be able to serve up aristocratic meat.'

'What?' said the citizeness, sniffing. 'How aristocratic? I don't mind where the blooming cow comes from as long as I have something to eat.'

Yann wondered, if purgatory did exist, whether it would be a café like this.

'I tell you, woman, if the butcher Citizen Loup was still alive he would have done it, he would have sold meat from the guillotine.' The man stopped to yell at the waiter for more brandy.

'That's disgusting,' said the citizeness, spitting out her drink. 'That makes me sick to my guts!'

'Well, woman, this city is plagued by famine. It's one way those stuffed-up, good-for-nothing, greedy, inbred aristos can bring about equality. After all, they eat only the very best food, so they should taste good.'

'You are talking codswallop, you are.'

'All right then, would you prefer that we kill all the cats and dogs to eat instead?'

'That would be a daft thing to do.'

'Why? Cat and dog not to your taste?'

'No, all I mean is, if we did that, what would kill the rats?'

The *sans-culotte*, realising that he'd been got the better of, grunted. 'The trouble with you, woman, is that your brains don't work.' He turned to Yann for support. 'But

509

it doesn't matter, does it, because we're all going to be equal.'

'Equal in what?' asked Yann. 'For you say that you have a better brain than your companion, so if you're right, where is the equality?'

'Take no notice, citizen,' said the woman. 'It's just a bee in his bonnet. Equality? I can't see it myself.'

Yann asked, 'Have you heard the one about the king who made all men equal by the simple means of an iron table?'

'No. How?'

'Everyone who came to his kingdom was forced to lie on the iron table. If you were too short for it, your legs would be stretched on the rack; if you were too long for it, your legs would be chopped off to fit. That way the king could guarantee all men were equal.'

The man looked foxed. 'I don't understand.'

'Neither did anyone who had to lie on the iron table, but they all had to live with the crippling consequence.'

The woman burst out laughing.

'Are you a comedian?' she asked.

Yann drank up his coffee and paid his bill. 'No, I leave that to the likes of your friend here with his taste in meat.'

The citizen lurched to his feet. 'You're making fun of me. No one makes fun of me. I will show you equality and you too, woman, if you don't shut your trap.' He went to take a swing at Yann. Mysteriously, he missed his footing and fell flat on his face.

The waiter rushed forward as Yann, stepping over the

510

prostrate man, winked at the woman, who sat there chuckling.

Outside the sun hit the narrow street in intense strips of light. A queue for bread stretched all the way round the corner. A scuffle had started by the door of the baker's shop between two women who were fighting tooth and claw over a loaf of bread. The crowd, bored with waiting, goaded them on.

We have become a city of scavengers, thought Yann, as he slipped into a small, dark courtyard, an open mouth stinking of bad breath. A door led to wooden stairs which twisted and turned unevenly, his footsteps were the beat of a drum. The smell of animal fat, rotten vegetables, tobacco and tallow candles hung thick and sickly in the air. He heard a noise on the ground floor, a door opening and closing, an argument, a man's voice shouting. Above him, a quieter click, the kind of noise you make when you don't want to be heard. Someone was coming out of the keymaker's apartment. Yann pressed himself against the wall and caught a glimpse of a face he recognised glancing over the banister. If the owner of the milky eye had any vision in it he might have seen him, despite the gloom of the stairwell. He heard Milkeye start to walk down towards him.

Yann, knowing there was nowhere to conceal himself, acted quickly. Têtu always said the best place to hide is under the noses of those who want to find you.

He slumped to the floor, almost blocking the stairs, pulled his hat over his face and started muttering drunken patriotic drivel. Milkeye took no notice of him except to kick his legs aside so that he could pass, at which the drunk let out an expletive for having been so rudely disturbed. The sound of his voice spurred Milkeye to move with greater speed down the creaking steps, taking them two at a time. Yann heard the door close behind him. He waited to make sure Milkeye wasn't coming back before going into the keymaker's apartment.

The place had been ransacked, the key was gone. Yann stood among the wreckage feeling as if he had been punched in the chest. What a fool he had been. How many signs did he need before he acknowledged his worst fear? Now seeing Milkeye again he had no doubt: Kalliovski must still be alive. Not for the first time he wondered if luck was on his side. Perhaps Têtu was right. He needed the talisman. Ever since he'd heard the dog howling at the Duc de Bourcy's château, he'd known the spirit of Anis was trying to warn him. Again fate was gambling with his life.

He looked up at the tobacco-stained ceiling. 'Kalliovski,' he said out loud, 'let this be between you and me, no one else. Leave Sido be.'

He left the apartment. There was nothing to be done there. He looked down the stairwell to make sure the coast was clear. At the bottom a door opened.

'Who are you?' said a man, reaching out to stop Yann.

'What is it to you, citizen?'

'Everything. I know everything that goes on in this building.'

'Well, you don't, citizen, otherwise you would know

that Remon Quint's apartment has been burgled.'

'What's happening, Brutus?' came a female voice from inside.

'Burgled, then? Maybe I just caught the villain who did it,' said the man, grabbing hold of Yann's coat.

Often Yann saw people's minds as market stalls, all the thoughts in their heads put out on display. This shoemaker's mind, pickled in wine, was so simple that he knew exactly what he was thinking.

'You should take your hands off me, citizen,' said Yann, 'unless you want me to report you. I know you're still making shoes for the counter-revolutionaries.'

Rats scurry away into dark places when they hear footsteps and so did the shoemaker. At the words 'counter-revolutionaries' he disappeared.

Chapter Thirteen

T he banker Charles Cordell arrived at the theatre around midnight.

He was a tall, bespectacled man, with a broken buttress of a nose and grey eyes that looked as if they had stared at too many facts and figures, and found that nothing in life added up. In the early days of the Revolution he'd been one of its most ardent supporters, but long before the execution of Louis XVI, he realised it had become a monstrous excuse for cruelty. The clever talk, the velvet-tongued justification of such acts in the name of liberty, equality and fraternity, mattered little. The truth, as far as he was concerned, was far less palatable and altogether more basely human: vengeance, jealousy and greed.

Unlike many of his fellow Englishmen he had stayed in Paris when war with England had been declared. With a rabbit foot for good luck in his coat pocket he hadn't been arrested yet. But he had a feeling that time was not on his side.

He and Citizen Aulard were engrossed in conversation when Yann entered the room. Cordell paused, wondering if the candlelight were playing tricks. For a moment he could have sworn that Yann had a myriad of brightly coloured threads dancing all around him.

He closed his eyes and when he looked again they had gone. There was only the room, the candlelight and Yann. But then again, he thought, many strange things happen around this young man. It was as if he weaved between two worlds: this one, bloodsoaked and ruined, and another altogether more mysterious.

'Do you know the Silver Blade's reputation is growing in London? You are quite a hero in émigré society,' said Cordell.

'That sounds worrying,' said Têtu, close behind Yann. He was more than aware of the speculation, not only in London but in Paris, as to the identity of the Silver Blade.

'The good thing is that no one can quite remember who you are, or for that matter what you look like. Would it be presumptuous to ask how you do that?'

'Too much is made of it,' answered Yann. 'Where is Remon Quint?'

'Basco is sitting with him,' said Citizen Aulard. 'Citizen Quint is quiet. Sleep is the best remedy.'

'Did he say anything else about the key?' asked Yann.

'He genuinely believes that he is going to be killed the minute he hands over his masterpiece.'

'Why?' asked Cordell.

'Because he was commissioned to make a key to a soul.'

'And what on earth does that mean?' asked Citizen Aulard. 'Yes, you can have a key to a door, a key to a city, the keys of a kingdom, but never a key to the soul. Such a thing is impossible.' He puffed his cheeks, letting a 'put-put' noise out through his mouth and exclaimed, '*Mort bleu!* You are a rational man, Mr Cordell, you don't believe all this nonsense?'

There was silence, then Cordell asked, 'Where is this key?'

'He left it in his apartment,' said Yann, 'and it is no longer there. I saw Milkeye leaving; he'd ransacked the place. The key was commissioned by Count Kalliovski.'

The theatre manager sat down heavily in his seat. 'No, no! He was killed in the September Massacre. Please tell me he was killed.'

An awful idea dawned on him. 'Do you think Kalliovski and the so-called phantom who walks in the Place de la Révolution are one and the same?'

Yann didn't reply, for Cordell's thoughts worried him. 'What report?' he asked.

Cordell sighed. 'Nothing much escapes you, does it?'

'Forgive me, that was rude,' said Yann, 'but this report, whatever it is, is much on your mind.'

'Correct. I had a spy working for me and Laxton, here in Paris, whose brief was to infiltrate a secret society believed to be operating under the city. His dispatches

516

made intriguing reading indeed. The spy, a man by the name of Levis Artois, reported that the meetings took place in the catacombs, in a large domed cavernous room made entirely of human bones. A man known simply as the Master is the head of this organisation, a terrifying figure of demonic power.'

Cordell looked grave. 'The last message I received from Artois was to say that he was sending me a report with further information about the Master, and the names of several of his followers, many, he indicated, working in positions of high office, in the Convention and the Committee of Public Safety. Unfortunately, the report never reached me.'

'What happened?' asked Citizen Aulard.

'A body was fished out of the Seine about a week ago. There was little left to identify. He had been torn to pieces by a monstrous beast. But I suspect it was Artois.'

Têtu had been silent. Of all of them he understood the dreadful signficance of Cordell's story.

'Remon Quint should be escorted from Paris to London,' he said. 'I don't think it would be wise to leave him at Dieppe. If he is as important to Kalliovski as we believe, the Count will have his men waiting at the ports to find him. Yann should go with him all the way to London.'

'I suppose he could do that successfully while the theatre is being repainted,' said Citizen Aulard.

Yann's mind was whirling. London. He would be able to see Sido. Sido – at last.

517

He did his best to keep the excitement out of his voice. 'That will work.'

'Before we agree,' said Cordell, 'I have something to say and it must be said now. The situation in Paris is going to get worse. I have heard rumours that a proposal to accelerate the Terror is to be put forward to the Convention this month.'

'That is ridiculous—' said Citizen Aulard.

'Please,' interrupted Cordell. 'I want to know if you all wish to continue with assignments, or would you rather we disbanded now?'

'No,' said Yann firmly. 'We should go on. To stop now would be the coward's way.'

'Yannick,' said Têtu, 'consider Cordell's proposal. You have helped more than enough people to escape. Now is the time to return to England, to take up your place at Cambridge.'

Yann looked at Têtu, bewildered. 'Are you all right?'

'Yes, quite well. What do you think, Citizen Aulard?'

'Have I missed something? Because I don't understand your reasoning,' said the theatre manager, perplexed. 'This business has always been dangerous. If we were to close down now and vanish in the night we would be deserting many who need us. And why is Yann at more risk than before?'

'I was just testing your commitment, that's all.'

No, you weren't, thought Yann. You have seen the future.

I t was about one-thirty when the small meeting dispersed. Yann waited until he was alone with Têtu.

'Is Death walking with me?' he asked

'I wish you knew more of the gypsy ways, I wish I had taught you better.'

'Têtu, answer me.'

'But did I tell you that bridges are important? They straddle two worlds and you walk with ease between them, but do you spit into the water before you cross? All gypsies know they must do that, there is a saying: "I believe that by the bridge of Cin-Vat all good deeds will be rewarded and evil deeds punished." Whatever Kalliovski has done belongs to evil. It is a bridge too unstable to cross more than once. And I am frightened for you, Yannick, very frightened indeed.'

Tears welled in his eyes and Yann felt cold inside. He'd never seen Têtu like this.

'It will be all right,' he said reassuringly. 'Next time I will remember to spit.'

He rested his hand on Têtu's shoulder.

With a heavy heart Yann made his way to his attic home and climbed out on to the roof. He would often sit and look out over the sleeping city, at its ramshackle rooftops, its lopsided chimneypots, and church spires pointing into the night sky.

Shirkis. The Romany word for stars, birds of fire that only fly in darkness. He remembered Têtu used to sing to him when he was small.

And the moon, the lady of the heavens coming nightly,
certain in her coming o'er the meadow
just to feed her chickens.

And Yann thought, I am like a bird of fire. Free at last,
coming to tell you I love you, Sido, I love you.

Chapter Fourteen

It was another hot evening when the curtain rose on the last performance of *The Harlequinade* before the theatre was to close for repainting.

Remon Quint was better than he had been, but worry had eaten at him and his eyes had a hunted look. Even Didier, who had no ability to read minds, could see that this man was close to breaking point. They sat together under the stage waiting for Yann, the keymaker locking and unlocking his fingers.

When the curtain fell, the audience was in no mood to let Harlequin go. Flowers were thrown on the stage; from the balcony a woman declared her undying love for him. The curtain was lifted again and again, until finally it rested for the last time, its velvet folds still quivering as Yann made a sprint for the door and removing his mask, rushed to join Didier and the keymaker below stage. From the minute they descended the stone stairs leading to the catacombs, Yann was filled with foreboding. The keymaker was shaking.

'I'm not good in small spaces ... I ...'

'You have to trust us,' said Yann, but he was aware of a bad feeling that fogged his mind. As much as he tried to force it away, he knew it was not a good omen and omens were important to his gypsy soul. The keymaker looked almost wild with fright by the time they entered the catacombs.

'I can't do it,' he announced. 'I can't stand the idea of all that earth above me. All the weight of the buildings pressing down, all the bones of the dead ... all the worms ... I have to go back, I have to. I'm going to be buried alive down here, I know it.'

Yann gently held his arm and, his voice a lullaby, said quietly, 'Look at me.'

The keymaker stared at him and in those ebony eyes he found, as little Louis had before him, a stillness like calm water.

'Do you think he'll be all right?' asked Didier.

'I hope so.'

They set off, Yann in front, Didier at the rear, their lights swaying back and forth, gently illuminating the distance that lay ahead. Their plan was to reach the Chamber of Sighs then stop for a rest. Yann had named the vaulted cavern after the words painted neatly on the wall: *Life is a circle of sighs*. It was the first landmark he'd found in his search for a route out of the city.

They walked keeping their heads down. It was wet underfoot. The catacombs were given to weeping and this evening the tunnels wept. All that could be heard in this echo-less place was the splash of their shoes.

Yann couldn't shake off the feeling that something was wrong. He was sure they were being followed. He turned several times to confront the darkness, convinced he heard the panting of a great beast. He shone his light back the way they had come. He could see nothing, just the same empty tunnels. Didier too looked back.

'What is it?'

'Nothing,' said Yann, but he sensed something evil closing in.

At the Chamber of Sighs they rested and took water and food from their knapsacks. They always carried enough oil to keep the lamps lit for eight hours, for without light they would never find their way out again. Yann had long ago explored the Chamber of Sighs, a dead end that led nowhere, but was a good place to stretch after walking hunched up for so long. There was a stone bench and here they sat in silence.

The keymaker was eating and drinking like a sleepwalker, when suddenly he let out a terrifying scream which sent a chill through Yann's soul. On the wall opposite loomed the shadow of an enormous dog.

Remon Quint was in a frenzy. He darted into the darkness of the vaulted room with Didier and Yann in pursuit.

'He can't get far,' Yann was saying, but to their

amazement the keymaker disappeared. Yann was surprised to see a gap in what he had always thought was a solid wall. They found themselves in a large unmapped tunnel ablaze with the light of candles gripped in bony fingers, coated in dripping wax. There was neither hide nor hair of the keymaker.

'Where the hell are we?' asked Didier. 'What do we do?'

The sound of the dog's barking was loud and close.

'We should split up. You go that way, I'll go this, and I'll meet you back here. We have to find him.'

Yann drew his knife and made a cross on the wall. As he set off down the long hall, a rush of wind blew out all the candles, even extinguishing his oil lamp. Powerless in the dark, he was trying to relight his lantern when he heard a rustle of silk.

'Calico and corpses.'

An icy hand touched his.

'Sisters Macabre, is it you?' he asked the pitch-black, endless darkness.

Something snowflake soft stroked his face. Holding his nerve, he tried once more to relight his lantern. Every time, the flame would flicker and die.

'Damask and death.'

'Where are you?' he asked.

'Where we should be.

Where you belong.'

Finally the flame took and light spilled out, and to his great relief he could see.

'Tulle and truth.'

Before him stood the Seven Sisters Macabre, lined up against the wall of the chamber, as hideous to behold as they always had been, their faces powdered, their cheeks rouged, their skin patched, their lips sewn closed. At their throats the infamous red necklaces. Their voices came from inner ghosts. They moved towards him, their feet not touching the ground. They glided. Yet Yann could see no threads of light. How were they being worked?

'We knew we would see you again.

For you belong to us.'

Yann didn't move. Slowly they glided closer. He tried with all his willpower to take control of them, but he could not.

'We are not yours any more,' said one.

Their flesh smelled of dead lilies.

'What do you want?' asked Yann, as they began to whirl round him, their faces a blur, their skulls showing through their stitched, papery, translucent skin.

They spoke with one eerie voice: 'Your father is waiting, he has been waiting a long, long time.'

In that moment, that last moment when Yann's future still shone so full of promise, before fate turned his dreams to ashes, in those last seconds when loving Sido was still possible, Yann wished he had the power to stop the clocks.

His words tasted of clay. 'My father? He is dead.'

'Count Kalliovski is waiting to embrace you. You, his one and only son.'

No sooner were the words spoken than somewhere close by the monstrous dog howled.

'Your father doesn't like to be kept waiting,' whispered the Sisters Macabre.

Chapter Fifteen

Count Kalliovski's new toy, the head of the Marquis de Villeduval, sat on a small ebony table in its glass case. Kalliovski's passion, if not obsession, was the making of automata. He was striving to create a being without the inconvenience of a soul, and with each one of his creations he believed himself to be nearing his ambition. The Marquis was manipulated, like the Count's many other automata, by the dark threads. Today the head gazed at the long gallery, with its tall windows and the painted scenery of the gardens where the air was filled with bird-song, so like the vistas he had looked on in life. The Count sat in a wing-back chair, his legs stretched, his red kid gloves like a blazing spire before his mouth. Balthazar lay beside him, his huge head resting on his paws.

'Shall I tell you my plans, my mad friend?' said Kalliovski.

'Have you woken me to bore me with information that holds little fascination for me?'

'No, you cake stand of a head. I am here to tell you what designs I have on your daughter, remember her?'

'I have no daughter,' said the Marquis de Villeduval. 'I never had any children. I don't like them.'

'Then I will tell you what I intend for your niece, Sido de Villeduval.'

'I have no niece. I once knew a Sidonie, an exceptionally plain girl with a limp. Speak to yourself about her if you must. I am engaged in an altogether more amusing subject.'

Controlling his creation's speech afforded Kalliovski much pleasure. He sat back feeling all-powerful, delighted with this head of his. A thin smile crept across his face.

'I see nothing to merit such mirth,' said the Marquis de Villeduval. 'And, as I said, you are interrupting an interesting train of thought about snuffboxes.'

'Not shoe buckles, my dear Marquis?'

'What use is a shoe buckle to a severed head?'

Kalliovski's laughter rang throughout the long gallery.

'It matters little, I will tell you all the same. I have

forged a deal with the devil, and Sido will ensure its success. She will be my pretty little caged dove. I shall use her to lure me a falcon. And when I have him, I shall steal his soul and the threads of light will be mine. I've had a key made for that very purpose. What do you say to that, surveyor of snuffboxes?'

'My ears are stuffed with wax,' said the Marquis de Villeduval. 'I cannot hear you.'

'My dear demented sir, there is no escape from me. I told you long ago, just as I told Sido. I have no mercy. I show no mercy. I never forget what is owing to me, what belongs to me.'

The Marquis's spirit, a moth imprisoned inside the head, was fluttering at broken memories.

'You are like me,' he said. 'We are both quite mad.'

Kalliovski stared incredulously at his creation, who dared to speak of his own free will. In quiet rage he sent out the dark threads. Slowly, as if squeezing juice from an orange they robbed the Marquis of all independent speech. Quiet now, his eyes snapped tight shut.

'Oh, my dear foolish Marquis. What? Silent at last?' said Kalliovski, closing the door on the waxwork head. And he thought he saw one unorchestrated tear roll down the Marquis's puffy cheeks.

He rang the bell and Milkeye entered.

'Where is the keymaker?'

'Citizen Quint is in the workroom, master.'

'Then tonight it will begin. Send Anselm Loup to me.'

How many day or weeks Anselm had been in Kalliovski's wondrous domain he couldn't rightly say, nor did he much care, for as long as he was never asked to leave, he didn't mind. Every day he had been called to the long gallery to sit before his new master. And every day he found himself coming out of a trance and feeling different, as if the furniture of his mind had been shifted. His feelings, whatever they had been, for his adoptive father, the butcher Loup, were now replaced by a passionate devotion to Count Kalliovski.

Soon after this transfer of affection an idea came to Anselm, independent, or so it seemed, of all that his master had planted in the fertile plains of his uneducated mind. Perhaps he was Kalliovski's bastard son, for they had much in common, and hadn't he been abandoned at birth? As his master said, everything has a design, everyone a destiny.

The day Kalliovski put his long-awaited plan into action, Anselm arrived in his master's presence brimming with enthusiasm. He was much changed from the day when Mr Tull had first taken him there. His hair was coiffured, his skin shiny clean and his clothes tailored especially for him. He looked every inch a hero: blond hair, amber eyes, a slayer of dragons, a breaker of hearts.

The Count studied him and said, 'If you fail me in this assignment, it will be the last you are given as a living man.'

Anselm felt his throat tighten. He wouldn't fail.

530

'There is a small theatre company called the Circus of Follies. I want you to find out what goes on there,' said Kalliovski.

Anselm looked bewildered. The question 'How?' sat uncomfortable and unspoken on his lips.

'I suggest you capitalise on your assets, your looks. There is a girl, her name is Colombine, she is the leading actress. Through her you will find out all I need to know about the dwarf Têtu and, more importantly, Yann Margoza. Succeed in this and you will be my day, as I am the night.'

———————————◆———————————

That afternoon Anselm found himself once more in the rue des Couteaux, with only the vaguest of memories of where he had been, and an overwhelming desire to meet an actress called Colombine.

Chapter Sixteen

Têtu had been working late and knew something was wrong even before he saw Yann standing on the landing, his face white, his clothes covered in limestone chalk.

'What are you doing here? Where's Didier?' Têtu asked, darting a glance behind Yann. 'Is he with you?'

'No.'

'And Remon Quint?'

'I don't know.'

'What do you mean, you don't know? Are they safe?'

'Why did you never tell me the truth? All this time ... all those lies.'

Têtu was frightened by the look on Yann's face. 'What has happened, Yannick? Tell me now.'

'No, first you owe me the truth. Is Kalliovski my father?'

'Who did you hear that from?' Têtu's voice was less assured.

'My friend,' said Yann coldly, 'time is running out. I'm a fool to have trusted you. How many times did I ask you who my father was? And all you did was lie.'

'No, no, I didn't lie. He was a gypsy. I just didn't name him.'

'If I remember rightly, you told me my father was dead.'

'And again I didn't lie.'

'I suppose that depends on what you call the truth.'

'Every truth is just one man's story, Yannick. You can believe whatever story you want.'

Yann was shaking with rage. 'I don't want some fairy tale. I want the truth.'

'Tell me what has happened to the keymaker. I need to know,' said Têtu, with a rising sense of panic.

'I don't care. Does that surprise you? I don't care. Lord knows how angry I am. I've a mind to kill you, you whom I trusted completely. You whom I believed to be my friend, you whom I love. How could you do this to me? Why hadn't you the courage to say who my father was when I asked? It would have been better then, when there was nothing to lose—'

He stopped. A lump in his throat made speaking difficult. 'How do I live with this? How can I ever be with Sido, knowing what I know? Now my life hangs by this thread. The devil take you, I want the truth.'

Têtu went towards him.

'Don't touch me! Leave me be.'

'Listen, listen,' shouted Têtu, turning red in the face. 'Kalliovski originally came from Transylvania to France.

533

When I first met him in St Petersburg he was a poor young gypsy with a pack of cards and a hatred for his own kind.'

'You have told me before that Kalliovski was born a gypsy, but I don't know if I believe a word of it. That could be another lie. After all, Kalliovski killed our people for sport. How can I trust a word you say?'

'I have proof,' said Têtu.

'What proof?'

'I met his people. I knew his family.'

'When were you ever in Transylvania?'

'Yann, stop this!'

'No, I want to know. When were you ever in Transylvania?'

'When I owned a dancing bear.'

'A dancing bear? If I weren't so angry, I would be laughing.'

'"There are many earths on earth there be." You, a gypsy, know this, you have evidence of it in the gifts you were given. Look at what you can do. How many men can work the threads of light? Some would say that none can. Is that the truth? Yes, in a way, because few have the ability to see such threads. Tell me, does that mean they don't exist?'

'And this,' said Yann, feeling every nerve in his body on fire, 'is supposed to comfort me? Well, it doesn't.'

'Your mother believed the spirit of her gypsy bridegroom was in you, even if Kalliovski is your father by blood. In her eyes you were never his child. She told me you were the ghost child of her one and only true love, a gypsy called Manouche. If you wish to think of Kalliovski as your father, you will be giving him a power he has no right to—'

'I hate you for keeping the truth from me,' cried Yann. 'I despise you for it. When were you planning to tell me? Sometime? Never?' He punched the wall.

'You must try to calm down,' said Têtu. 'Go to London as planned. Tell Sido what has happened.'

Yann laughed, a hollow, dead sound. 'No wonder, Têtu, that you thought we should disband and I go back to England. Did you think this might all disappear, that I would never find out?'

Têtu was silent.

'How did my mother die? I think you told me . . . that's right, my *father* murdered her.'

'I understand how upset you are, but once you have thought about—'

'You could never in a lifetime understand how I feel.'

Yann slumped into a chair, his head in his hands.

'I never told you because I was worried that it would destroy you. I have brought you up since you were an infant. I have never seen even a shadow of Kalliovski in you. The more you have grown, the more I believed Anis was right; you are indeed the child of her lost love Manouche. She made me swear never to tell you, so that Kalliovski wouldn't have any power over you.'

Yann took a deep breath. 'By my father's hand, I am cursed for life.'

Têtu sighed. 'Don't go down that path, Yannick. You

535

have all before you.' He went over to the desk. 'This letter arrived today.'

Yann took the envelope and looked at Sido's writing. He handed the letter back.

'It's over,' he said. 'These letters are not safe. There will be no more.' He was shaking with rage. 'Do you think I don't know that Juliette Laxton is terrified of her niece being in love with a gypsy? Let alone the son of the monster who tried to abduct her.'

'Yann, please, I know I counselled you against this liaison but love is precious and it has given you so much strength. Think of what this will do to Sido.'

'By my father's hand, I am destroyed. What is left is nothing. Yes, it will break her heart. I now know how that feels – my heart is broken. But she will recover. Sooner or later, someone will tell her I am Kalliovski's son. The Laxtons will sigh with relief that their niece was saved from such an ill-advised liaison. One day she will meet a good man, marry, be happy, and tell her children how once a gypsy boy saved her life in the days of the French Revolution.'

'Yannick,' said Têtu. 'Go to London and see her.'

'What could Sido possibly say? That it changes nothing?' Yann got up and went towards the door. Têtu saw he was trembling. 'What is the point? There is nothing left.'

'Where are you going?'

'Here is another truth for you, Têtu. There are a lot of men out there who are the walking dead. Tonight I join them.'

'Don't let Kalliovski win,' said Têtu. 'He wants to destroy you as he destroyed your mother. Don't let this ruin your future. You're Manouche's ghost child. Kalliovski was born with hatred and jealousy at the very root of him, like a rotten tree. You don't have to be his poisoned fruit.'

Yann looked back at Têtu. He seemed suddenly even smaller, as if he had shrunk, and Yann felt himself to have grown too big for the room. He had become a giant in anger. He needed air.

'Where are you going?' asked Têtu again.

'To get drunk.'

Têtu watched him leave, tears streaming down his face. 'Anis, what should I do? Tell me, what should I do?'

Later that night Didier wearily made his way back into the theatre. He found Têtu sitting at Citizen Aulard's desk, his face tear-stained, looking as old as Time itself.

'Is Yann back?' Didier asked.

'Yes.'

Têtu poured them both a glass of cognac.

'Where's Remon Quint?'

'I don't know,' said Didier, moving his shoulders back and rolling his head around his neck. He was stiff all over. He took the glass. 'We lost him down there. I searched and searched, but I couldn't find him. It's not good, is it?'

537

'No.'

'I could go down again.'

'You will never find him. It's too late.'

'It can't be.'

'But it is,' said Têtu, knowing the keymaker was already beyond help. He could only hope that Yann had the strength for the battle ahead.

'I'm very sorry we failed Remon Quint,' said Didier gravely.

'So am I,' said Têtu.

'Where's Yann now?'

'Gone out.'

'That's unlike him.'

'Yes,' replied the dwarf.

In the Café du Coin the company of actors was celebrating its last performance. Colombine had just met a young man who seemed to be devoted to her. Tonight Anselm was capitalising on his newly discovered assets.

'Come on,' shouted Basco, 'give us another song.' And standing on a table Colombine sang, her voice not strong, but sweet with an innocence that she had never possessed.

Yann knew he had chosen the wrong place the minute he opened the door.

A stagehand rushed over.

'Yann,' he said, louder than he meant to. 'What has happened? Why are you back?'

Looking round the smoky room, Yann noticed

Colombine's latest conquest and instinctively sensed the darkness round him. Anselm glanced in Yann's direction and recognised him immediately. This was the young man who'd killed Pa.

Yann walked past the stagehand to the bar. 'I'm thirsty, that's all.'

Colombine, who had been lifted off the table, rushed over to him. Anselm watched closely. Her obvious interest in Yann made her more desirable.

Yann drank up, not wishing to stay longer than necessary. He wanted to find a bar where he would be guaranteed some peace.

'Don't leave. You've only just arrived,' said Colombine, sensing that something was wrong.

Ignoring her, he handed the barman a roll of *assignats*, then turned to the rest of the company and said, 'Well done, everybody. Have a drink on me.' And with that he was gone.

Colombine picked up her shawl to follow him.

'Where are you going?' asked Anselm, grabbing hold of her arm.

'Let go of me.'

'Not until you tell me where you're going.'

'That's none of your business. Take your hands off me.'

'What? A lovers' tiff already?' asked Pantalon.

Colombine shook her arm free, to see two white marks where Anselm's fingers had gripped her.

'Look what you've done!' she said, and slapped him hard.

Red, raw rage surged through Anselm. His fingers itched to break every bone in her body, a longing that was almost beyond his control.

Only a small voice inside his head willed him to be still.

Colombine flounced out of the café.

'Have another drink,' said Basco, putting his arm round Anselm. 'Take no notice, that one has broken more hearts than the guillotine has cut off heads.'

Yann meanwhile walked towards the Seine, his hands stuffed in his pockets. He crossed the Pont Neuf and reached the Café des Amis. The owner knew Yann well and was pleased to see him.

'Not many out tonight,' he said. 'We miss you. You don't come this way so often since you left the rue du Temple.'

Yann nodded, took a bottle over to the table by the window, sat down and poured himself a glass. Damn Têtu. Damn all the lies, damn the Revolution. Damn everything. He poured himself another drink. How can I live with this? Tell me that, Yann Margoza, son of Count Kalliovski?

He downed his drink in one gulp. If I've inherited anything from my father, I'd better hope that it's his ability to feel nothing. Keep on tipping this vinegary muck down and nothing is all I will ever feel. Nothing is all I will ever be.

Why him? I could cope with a coward, a traitor, a fool – but not Kalliovski.

Yann looked down at the bottom of his glass and refilled it.

What is it that Pantalon always says? 'Life is a bottle of wine. The art is to make it last and to know how to enjoy it.' I don't want it to last. The sooner the bottle is empty the better.

'Can I join you?'

He looked up to see Colombine.

'Why aren't you with the others?'

She slid down next to him. 'I thought you looked sad. And something has gone wrong, I could tell.'

He laughed. 'What about golden boy? Won't he be a bit fed up that you've gone?'

'He's nothing to me.'

'Does anybody mean anything to you?'

'Yes. You do,' she said, looking wistfully at him.

Yann finished his drink.

Anselm had left shortly after Colombine and followed her, knowing she would lead him to Yann Margoza. He couldn't care less about Colombine, except that he had been ordered to win her trust. That was easy. If he wanted her, she was his and he knew it. No, the challenge lay with Yann Margoza. He was everything Anselm longed to be. What if he could possess Yann's powers?

Through the window of the Café des Amis he watched Colombine and Yann for a few minutes. Then, sweat gleaming on his face, he went in and sat down with them.

'I am Anselm, citizen,' he said extending a hand to Yann.

Yann got up and walked unsteadily to the door. He turned towards them. 'Goodnight.'

Anselm tried to follow him, but Colombine pulled him back. If she couldn't have Yann, let him at least see what he was rejecting. She quickly kissed Anselm, whose eyes were fixed on Yann's retreating figure. He wanted to throw her off, to punish her for her cheek, but Kalliovski's words were an anchor in his stormy mind.

'Make the girl yours and the rest will follow.'

Anselm violently kissed her back.

Chapter Seventeen

Next morning Yann woke on the forest floor, his head thudding. He looked at the sky. The sun shone bright through the canopy of transparent leaves as if it were the emerald stained-glass window of a great cathedral. A choir of insects buzzed and the day was already warm. He felt in his pocket and found a coin. Having no idea which direction to take, he flipped it and let fate lead him.

His anger with himself, with everything, was the spur which kept him walking. He tried not to think of Sido, which proved impossible.

Leaves, he said to himself, watching one young leaf fall from an oak tree. Leaves for a while must think they own the skies, that they are close to heaven. When do they resign themselves to gravity? I am like a leaf.

I believed I owned the sky without realising that I'm destined to fall to the ground.

He noticed neither rain nor sun. His tangle of thoughts slowly unwound so that by the afternoon, he could feel enough to know he was hungry. He hunted rabbits and ate berries. At night, with a fire going and his food on a spit, he felt himself like the king of fools, the stars the painted roof of this wondrous palace he had found. He paid no attention to his route. If he saw a hamlet or smoke from a farmhouse chimney he made sure he took a large detour. If uncertain which way to go, he tossed a coin.

Days passed in this way until early one misty morning, emerging from a forest, he saw a gilded armchair left standing, its stuffing oozing out as if it had been mortally wounded, its dainty carved wooden legs bravely sunk into the carpet of leaves. Ivy had already wrapped around it, anchoring it to the earth.

Walking past it he came to a gravel drive. Several of the trees on either side were burned, their skeleton limbs outstretched like ancient timber that had been turned to stone by what they had witnessed, for all that remained of the château was rubble.

He meandered round outbuildings, through the empty stables down to the overgrown garden, to see flapping in the breeze a lady's dress, poised like a butterfly on a box hedge, its silver bows catching the first rays of warm sunlight. It fluttered, waiting for a gust of wind to free it, to take flight.

Why the chair and why the dress? Why, out of

everything that must have been here, had they alone survived?

As he turned to leave he spied a child's wooden horse lying on its side in a stream, one of its wheels occasionally turning. He found these three objects profoundly moving: small mysterious relics of lives destroyed. He lifted the wooden horse out of the water. All the paint had washed away from the side that had been in the stream, and he imagined this horse was once beloved of a child who had refused to leave it behind until it became a burden.

He freed the dress, light as gossamer, and it nearly fell to pieces in his hands. He took it and the wooden horse back to the armchair and left them there: an altarpiece to a vanquished world.

He carried on walking. By late afternoon he was grateful to come to a lake surrounded by cornfields. In the far distance a row of poplars cast long sleepy shadows. He sat contemplating the still waters before undressing and diving in, swimming lazily back and forth, as a moorhen, in ruffled indignation, took flight. Dragonflies skimmed the surface of the lily leaves, flashes of incandescent emerald and sapphire. He floated on his back, hypnotised by the sky, before emerging from the water and dressing.

He made his way through a cornfield dotted with dancing bright red poppies, rubies among the gold.

The air was filled with birds, and it came to him then and there, a revelation of sorts, and he said out loud, 'The love I have for Sido is not diminished by what has happened, or by who my parents were. It is stronger. Even if I can never see her again, never be with her, this much I know, a truth as bright and yellow as the corn, as red and passionate as the poppies: I have loved and been loved in return. I can find the strength to set her free. I can do this, for true love must have at its very soul the power to let go and to know that nothing is lost.'

Yann was crying. He realised he was not alone. A little way off he could see the figures of a man and a woman. They were brightly dressed as if going to a fete, their clothes rather old-fashioned in style. Why hadn't he noticed them before? The woman seemed so familiar.

By now the sun was setting and for a while he was blinded by its glare. The two figures were walking away from him towards the poplar trees and Yann knew he must speak to them. He called out and the man, stopping, waved. Yann heard him say quite clearly, 'Son, we are birds, we are free.'

Yann ran towards them, yearning to hear more. They waited, shimmering mirages, all golden they stood, hand in hand. In that moment the sun blinded him again. He blinked and they were gone.

Looking back the way he had come, he could see where the corn had bowed under his weight and that there were no tracks other than his. He lay down, exhausted, and it came to him that the man had spoken Romany, and he was reminded of Têtu's story of his mother and her bridegroom, of their wedding the day the soldiers came.

He woke feeling as if he must have been asleep for days, although it was still light, a perfect summer's evening; and thinking back to the couple in the corn-field, he decided they were nothing more than a dream.

Now there was peace within him, as if a tempest had passed. All the anger gone, still he asked himself: can I forgive Têtu? In the fading light he came to a graveyard and realised to his surprise that he had been there before. This was, if he were not mistaken, the Duc de Bourcy's land. Curious as well as hungry, he wondered whether in his dishevelled state he could show himself. Then, the thought of seeing the Duchess, of explaining, the thought of talking, of being civil, made his hunger seem less important.

He was turning back towards the woods when he glimpsed a light spilling from the kitchen door. He went closer.

On a bench outside sat an old man and a young woman whom Yann recognised as the children's nurse. The small table in front of them was spread with peas that they were busily podding into a copper pan.

He was debating with himself what to do, knowing that it was only hunger making him linger, when he heard the girl say, 'What do you think will become of our mistress?'

The old man looked despondent. Yann knew what he was thinking: unless they did something the Duchess would be sent to Paris and the guillotine.

Yann came out of the shadows. The old man grabbed hold of a hunting gun that was resting beside him.

'Please, I mean you no harm.' Yann held out his hands. 'I am unarmed.'

'Are you a deserter from the army?'

'No.'

'Are you a priest?'

'No. I came here in March, about two months ago, to help the Duke escape to England. Please put the gun down.'

The young woman looked at him. 'I remember him, Grandpa. He came with the big man. Are you all right, monsieur?'

'Yes. I have been walking. I came this way by chance. I am sorry to have frightened you. I was wondering if your mistress was at home.'

The old man still looked uncertain.

'There could be another man with him, Marie. This could be a trap.'

'I assure you it isn't.'

Reluctantly the old man said, 'We'd better go inside the château.'

The kitchen was neat and the table well scrubbed. In the light of the oil lamps, Yann caught sight of his reflection in the window and was shocked to see what a wild man of the woods he had become.

The old man, looking at him, said suspiciously, 'Are you sure this is the same man? I don't remember him. He looks like a vagabond to me. He smells of woodsmoke.'

'It's his eyes,' said Marie. 'I've never seen eyes like his.'

'When I was here there was an attempt to rob the

Duke, and a man died,' said Yann, to put the old man at his ease.

The old man let out a sigh as if he had been holding his breath all this while. 'I remember you now. You all went down to the dovecote. The Duchess ordered breakfast, but you just wanted a fast horse.'

'Correct.'

'Monsieur, forgive me, I owe you an apology. I have grown too fearful of late that we will be attacked. My name is Tarlepied. Are you hungry?'

'Ravenous.'

Marie, now busy at the stove, said, 'Sit, please, and I will make you something to eat.'

'These are dreadful days indeed,' said the old man. 'Farms are going to ruin; the land worked by people who know nothing of the soil, only politics. Fine words don't grow into corn.'

'Has the National Guard been here?' Yann asked, remembering the sea of furniture.

'No, monsieur, so far they have left us in peace. Everyone in the village is loyal to the de Bourcy family. The peasants here were all well looked after by the Duke. There is a growing resentment about the lack of food, the abolition of the Church. Many harbour a secret longing for the old regime.'

'Where is your mistress?'

Monsieur Tarlepied said nothing.

Marie looked at him. 'Grandpa, we should tell him.'

'It goes against the grain ... but the Duke would never forgive me ...' He sighed. 'Ten days ago our mistress

549

left to visit the Marquise de Valory. The Duchess was expected to return last week, but today we heard the most terrible news and I don't know what can be done. One of the Marquise de Valory's servants comes from our village and has been sent back to her family. She is a friend of my granddaughter.'

Marie brought an omelette and a bowl of peas to the table. The smell of fresh mint almost overpowered Yann.

'What my friend told me was in confidence, you understand,' she said. 'But you have helped the family before.' She took a deep breath. 'She said the Marquis de Valory had been taken to trial, found guilty and executed. On hearing of it, her mistress went into early labour, and after giving birth became very ill. A few days later the soldiers came to arrest her. She was so poorly. They hid her in the servants' quarters and the Duchess pretended to be the Marquise de Valory. She was taken to the prison at Chantilly. She was always a brave woman, my mistress.'

'Chantilly,' repeated Yann.

'Yes, the château has been made into a prison. Can anything be done?'

'I hope so,' said Yann.

───────◆───────

That night Yann bathed in a large tin bath and slept in a feather bed. He woke early. Monsieur Tarlepied arrived with breakfast and later shaved Yann, and opened the Duke's dressing room for him.

Yann selected a pair of breeches and a waistcoat that belonged to the days of dancing and grand balls, a shirt and a beautifully embroidered dressing gown, and took them down to the kitchen. He and Marie sat at the table altering the clothes so that the breeches looked like those worn by the National Guard.

By three o'clock, Yann was ready to leave. He stood at the door dressed in a waistcoat, shirt, breeches and dressing gown, a three-cornered hat with a tricolour pinned to it and a sash of office across his chest, his boots well worn and muddy.

The old man stared at him, foxed. 'Forgive me, monsieur,' he said, 'but I can't see how this is going to work. You look too eccentric.'

Yann lifted his shoulders back, stuck his chest out like a cockerel and in the thickest of Marseilles accents, which Monsieur Tarlepied could hardly understand, demanded to know why he addressed him as 'monsieur'. Wasn't he a patriot?

Marie, looking terrified at the transformation in Yann, backed away. 'Stop it, sir, you're frightening us.'

'Good,' said Yann, 'that's the effect I want to achieve. As for the clothes, I will explain that the waistcoat and the dressing gown have come from the Conciergerie, property of a prisoner who was guillotined, a reminder, if one was needed, of what we are fighting for: the freedom of this great country against the tyrannical claw of the past that all this brocade represents.'

It was late afternoon when Yann set off, riding the Duke's only remaining horse, a fine white stallion which had been loose in the fields and near gone wild. Yann whistled him to come, spoke Romany into his soft ears, and the great horse stood quietly as Yann mounted. Like Yann he had need of the wind beneath his hooves. Yann's unanswered question came back to him: should I forgive Têtu? And he was surprised by his own answer. Yes.

Chapter Eighteen

The grand château of Chantilly purported to be one of the finest specimens of Renaissance architecture. In the moonlight it looked like an enchanted castle, surrounded on all sides by a silvery moat, but its wrought-iron gates had been boarded up to stop any prisoner talking to the outside world. Yann arrived as he had planned, at midnight.

On the journey he had been thinking about how he was going to free the Duchess. He planned to use his new trick, one Têtu had taught him. Yann had spent months perfecting it.

Now he was here, he realised that only audacity would save him. He started shouting at the top of his lungs.

The old turnkey, gnarled like applewood and pickled in cider, came running, woken from a drunkard's dream, and with great effort pushed the gate open far enough to see who was causing such a rumpus.

What the turnkey saw, or thought he saw, standing at the gate were several young men on horseback, all rather oddly dressed.

'I am here from Paris. Take me to the governor. What's wrong with you, man? Stand straight when you talk to me.'

Yann handed him a letter, knowing the man couldn't read, which made him considerably easier to deal with. The turnkey saw on the paper a lot of squiggly lines that looked like the kind of official squiggly lines one might need to see the prison governor.

The gate ground open all the way and Yann was in.

'My horse needs feeding and watering. Did you hear me? Jump to it!'

Yann's voice was very loud, loud enough to waken the dead. It worked. Lights appeared at windows. Half-dressed, the guards came running.

'I want to see the governor of the prison now,' he demanded.

He was taken to see Citizen Notte.

The prison governor came reluctantly from his bed-chamber, wearing a dressing gown quite inferior to the one worn by this very handsome and assured young man.

Yann handed him the papers. He examined them carefully and all the while Yann's eyes never left him.

Citizen Notte put them down. 'All seems above aboard. Just the one prisoner, I see.'

'That is correct.'

The governor was staring at Yann.

'What is your name?'

'Socrates,' Yann replied.

'And what was it, citizen, before this new fashion to have Greek names?'

'The name of a saint that stinks of the old regime.'

Citizen Notte could see this earnest young man took his job very seriously indeed, and without an ounce of humour to lighten his load.

'Quite. Will you be wanting a bed for the night?'

'The Public Prosecutor's office never sleeps. This woman is wanted in court tomorrow in Paris. My duty is to get her there. I shall need a carriage.'

This came as a real blow. Carriages were valuable and scarce.

'You mean you didn't bring one?' said Citizen Notte, beginning to wake up. 'We are very short of such things. A farm cart, maybe?'

'No, it wouldn't get there fast enough.'

'I should tell you that we are understaffed. I suppose you will need a prison guard to accompany you as well?'

'Why? She is just one miserable woman.'

There was a knock on the door and a man entered. His eyes, too wide apart, had the look of a zealot, burning with fanatical passion. It was clear that mercy was not high on his list of priorities.

'This is my right-hand man, Citizen Marchand of the Revolutionary Army.'

Yann had seen his name in secret reports which Cordell had shown him. He knew that Marchand worked in confidence for the Committee of Public Safety and his ambition was to be transferred to Paris to work with Robespierre. Yann was more wary of Citizen Marchand than he was of the governor. For a start, he was stone-cold sober. And he took the papers from Citizen Notte before Yann had had a chance to work on him.

'What are these?' he demanded. 'There's nothing written here. What's your game? Who are you?'

Yann puffed himself up like a great cockerel. 'I am here on business for the Public Prosecutor's office.' He spoke slowly, concentrating on getting a hold on Marchand's mind.

Citizen Notte looked flustered and took back the papers to study them again. Visible relief spread over his face as he handed them to Yann.

'I hope there's nothing wrong with your eyes, citizen, for this is all correct. I am about to give orders for the woman to be brought down to the courtyard.'

Marchand snatched the papers from Yann and saw quite clearly the name of the prisoner. He looked momentarily uncertain; and yet there could be no denying this letter was from Fouquier-Tinville's office.

Yann could see how he was battling with his reason, as if doubt still threatened to get the better of him.

'Strange,' he murmured.

Yann knew he had him.

'No, what's strange, citizen, is that you questioned my word. I think certain friends at the Hôtel de Ville should know that.'

'I meant no offence,' said Marchand.

'Just get me the prisoner. I haven't got all night for these bourgeois pleasantries.'

Citizen Notte looked genuinely worried as he rang the bell, longing for this to be over, and for the young man and his prisoner to be gone.

A guard entered and spoke to Citizen Notte in a whisper.

'What is it?' said Marchand.

'There is a problem. The prisoner says she won't leave without the young girl who is sharing her cell.'

He looked at Yann, who knew exactly what he was expected to say: that they were to drag her out by her hair if necessary, he cared nothing for any attachment the traitor might have formed.

Instead he said, 'How old is she, citizen?'

The governor looked at the list. 'She is sixteen, sir. The whole family was arrested for hiding a priest. Her parents and older brother were guillotined last week.'

'Sounds to me as if she's guilty as hell. Better bring her along. They like all different ages on the scaffold.'

Ten minutes later a battered old carriage that looked and smelled as if it had been used as a henhouse was pulled into the courtyard, together with a tired-looking horse. Keeping his head low, Yann opened the carriage door to make sure he had the right prisoners.

'What's this?' shouted Yann, seeing the horse. 'This nag's good for nothing but glue. I have to be in Paris by the morning, not next week.'

There was a panic among the guards. Marchand suggested he should use his own horse.

'What?' said Yann. 'My horse is employed by the Republic to take me wherever I'm needed. It's not meant for pulling henhouses.'

Reluctantly Marchand led out a fine dapple grey.

'It's mine, I—'

Yann interrupted. 'What's yours is mine, citizen. Remember we are all one now.'

He waited as the old horse was unharnessed and Marchand's grey put in its place, then climbed up and took the reins. He had set off towards the gates with the Duke's horse tied to the back of the rickety vehicle when he heard Marchand call.

'Wait!'

Yann's heart sank. He could see the open road, he could smell freedom. He was so nearly there. He had a mad impulse to make a dash for it, to get away. That, he knew, would be suicide.

Marchand ran up to him. 'You will put in a good word for me?' he said. 'I am hoping to be transferred to Paris.'

'Again you waste my valuable time. Good morning to you, citizen,' said Yann, and he cracked his whip and set off.

The day had dawned by the time they came to a crossroads in the forest, and he took the carriage down an overgrown path as far as he could so that they were well hidden.

He opened the carriage door. The interior was coated with feathers, and perched on one of the upholstered seats was a hen that had obstinately refused to leave.

The Duchess was sitting in the opposite corner, the girl fast asleep, resting her head on her shoulder. Both had had their hair cut off so that what was left stuck up in tufts.

The hen seemed the most vocal of the three occupants. Yann grabbed it.

'May I ask why we have stopped?' said the Duchess, only glancing at her jailer. She was painfully thin.

'Maybe I wanted an egg for breakfast,' Yann said kindly. Still she refused to look at him.

The girl woke, sleepily taking in this apparition. Before her was a young man, extraordinarily dressed, with a hen under his arm.

'Are you going to kill it?'

Yann studied the hen. 'No,' he said. 'It looks like a good layer.' And he went off to put it in his saddlebag.

The two women climbed uncertainly out of the carriage. The Duchess looked around, wondering if this was going to be her end, to be slaughtered here in this wood. Seeing the girl was terrified, she said calmly, 'It is all right, Celeste.'

Yann came back with bread and a bottle of wine.

'This is for you, madame. Do you not recognise me?'

The Duchess finally looked at him, catching the smile in his dark eyes. Her face lit up with joy.

'Tell me I am not dreaming!'

She put her arms round the girl. 'There is no need to be frightened. This young gentleman is an old friend of mine.'

Yann bowed.

And the girl, looking at him, said, 'Does that mean we are saved?'

Chapter Nineteen

Yann arrived in Paris the day before *The Harlequinade* was due to re-open. He'd gone straight to the Hotel de Ville. There was one more thing he had to do.

The clerk whose business it was to draw up the names of the guillotined had had a busy morning. The previous day there had been a record harvest of heads, and in the enthusiasm to rid France of traitors and aristocrats names had become muddled. Now, his finger black with ink, he looked up wearily at the *sans-culotte* before him.

'Where are the documents?'

He peered over his smudged glasses and added three more names to the list, a thin smile curling like smoke across his face. Head bowed, tongue protruding, he wrote down the names, each one gloriously misspelled. Yann only bothered to correct him on one: the Duchesse de Bourcy. Her best chance of survival was to be dead to the authorities. The clerk dusted the ink and handed the paper to an officer to be posted outside.

'Good work, citizen,' said the clerk.

Only when that was done did Yann return to the Circus of Follies.

Citizeness Manou, seeing a *sans-culotte* with a three-cornered hat at the stage door, emerged from her sentry box in a cloud of smoky thunder and was taken aback to realise it was none other than Yann.

'Citizen Aulard is waiting in his office and I'm under strict instructions to send you up the minute I see you.'

Yann climbed the stairs to Citizen Aulard's office to find the theatre manager, Têtu and a young man he had never seen before. He was a year or two older than himself, had dark blond hair and a pleasing, handsome face, though Yann thought he looked as if he hadn't slept for days.

'There you are,' said Citizen Aulard, as Yann entered the room. 'Thank the Lord above, you're back. *The Harlequinade* opens tomorrow.'

'I know that,' said Yann.

Têtu knew from one look at Yann that he was, in part, forgiven.

'This is the Vicomte de Reignac,' he said. 'He was about to tell us how he came here. Please continue, Viscount.'

'Wait,' Yann interrupted, 'surely you were sent to us?'

'No,' said Têtu, 'the Viscount came to us through an unusual channel.'

'Yes, the priest who was hiding me made enquiries as

to the whereabouts of the Silver Blade, and was told they might know of him at the Circus of Follies,' said the Viscount.

'That's the part I don't like,' said Citizen Aulard. 'Not one little bit.'

'It's not important,' said Yann, recognising in this young man a sadness all too familiar, one he had seen so often in those who had lost loved ones. So much heartbreak. Paris was broken by grief.

The Vicomte de Reignac spoke quietly with a slight stammer. He had lost his father, his mother and his beloved fifteen-year-old sister. His father and sister had been taken to the guillotine three days previously.

'My mother and I escaped arrest. She insisted on going to the Place de la Révolution to be near them. I tried to stop her, but nothing would hold her back. She wanted to get as close to the tumbril as she could to touch the hem of my sister's dress.'

He stopped, fighting back tears.

'I watched my sister go up to the scaffold. One of the executioner's assistants pulled off the cap she wore and she flinched with the pain. They had cut off her long blonde hair. My mother let out a gasp and my sister, looking frantically into the crowd, called "*Maman!*" I knew there was nothing that could be done. I begged my mother to be quiet, but she was inconsolable. When my father went to the guillotine, she rushed towards the scaffold. I tried to stop her, but was held back by a man in the crowd. He said, "Monsieur, if you do anything you too will be caught. Get out of here while you can." I took no notice, but tried to get free. Again this stranger restrained me.'

'Who was he?' asked Têtu.

'I found out that he had known my parents. He was a priest who had taken Holy Communion with them and had listened to their confessions.'

'What happened next?' asked Citizen Aulard.

'They sentenced my mother then and there, without the inconvenience of a trial, for showing emotion for a traitor to liberty. They bound her hands, they cut off her hair. She looked almost happy. I think it was that that riled them. They tied her to the plank and then lifted the blade of the guillotine, leaving it suspended. The blood of my sister and my father fell like rain upon her and the crowd shouted abuse.'

He stopped, wiped his eyes and took a shuddering breath.

'After an hour, mercifully, the blade fell. I was saved that day by the priest. He hid me and told me about the legend of the Silver Blade. I can't stay with him; it's too dangerous. I need to get out of France.'

Citizen Aulard was shaken. 'What has happened? When did people become this cruel?'

'When Pandora opened her box,' said Têtu.

Yann put a hand on the young man's shoulder. 'You will be leaving very soon. You must rest now.'

'Thank you,' said the Vicomte de Reignac. 'May I ask when I will meet the Silver Blade?'

'You have met him.'

Têtu followed Yann outside and asked, 'Are you mad?

That was unwise, telling him who you are. Supposing—'

'Têtu,' said Yann, 'I am not sure who I am. Why shouldn't I be the Silver Blade? If I were you, I would say nothing more on the subject.'

Têtu shrugged his shoulders.

At the stage door Citizeness Manou said, 'Have you heard about Colombine, then?'

'No,' said Yann, stopping.

'She is now Citizeness Loup. Got married two days ago. Ah, they make a fine couple, but mind you, I don't call it proper. I mean, it wasn't done in a church and in my humble opinion, that doesn't count. Still, he looks like an angel, lucky girl.'

'Looks can be deceptive,' said Yann.

———◆———

Colombine turned up for rehearsal that afternoon. 'I hear congratulations are in order,' said Yann.

'Yes. Thanks,' she said, her voice sounding strained.

'It was very sudden.'

Colombine did her best to avoid looking at Yann.

'I suppose so,' she said.

'Are you all right?'

'Of course. Never happier.'

'Good. Well, I wish you both the best.'

'Thanks,' she said again, eager to be gone.

Pantalon came rushing up and caught Colombine by the arm. Yann noticed her wince.

'Pardon,' said Pantalon, 'I haven't hurt you, have I?'

'No, no.'

'Good. There is an hour of bliss before the curtain rises. Who wishes to join me at the café on the corner? Colombine, come on, let me buy you a drink.'

She glanced towards the stage door. 'I think I will rest, if you don't mind.'

Pantalon watched her leave and, turning to Yann, shrugged. 'She's not herself, have you noticed that?'

———◆———

At the opening performance of *The Harlequinade*, the Viscount appeared as an extra on the stage, for as Têtu had predicted the police decided to pay the newly opened theatre a visit. The Viscount was dressed as a young woman and looked every inch the part. Two of the gendarmerie stood watching from the wings, quite enchanted, blowing kisses and acting the fool until they were called away, neither knowing that they had been watching the very man they were searching for.

Afterwards, Yann sat in his dressing room removing his make-up, pleased to have got through the show.

His thoughts were interrupted by the sound of raised voices. It appeared to be an argument between Colombine and her new husband. Quite what was being said Yann wasn't sure, although Colombine's voice grew shriller until it became a cry as something fell on the floor with a deafening thud.

Yann got up and went along the corridor to Colombine's dressing room. Without knocking he went in, to see her crumpled in the corner, and Anselm standing over her.

'Get out,' said Anselm. 'This is between me and her. Get out. It doesn't concern you.'

Yann pinned him against the wall.

'Calm down. That is no way to treat your wife.'

'I can do what I bloody well please. She needs to learn some manners.'

'If you hit her again while you are in this theatre, you will answer to me. Do you understand?'

Yann let go of Anselm, wondering why it was he couldn't read this rat of a man's thoughts. It was as if somehow they'd been interfered with. As he turned to help Colombine to her feet, Anselm lifted a chair. Colombine tried to find her voice to warn Yann as it came hurtling down towards him, but the chair stopped short an inch from its target. Yann, without even turning round, clicked his fingers and sent it back the way it had come with such force that it smashed to pieces on Anselm's blond, cherub-like curls.

'I will kill you,' shouted Anselm, pulling a knife. Making a dash towards Yann he found that his feet were no longer on the ground. Instead he was hanging upside down, spinning like a child's top. He dropped the knife, which hung, caught in midair.

Citizeness Manou came to see what the commotion was about. As she helped Colombine from the room, Yann clicked his fingers again and Anselm fell unconscious to the floor.

Later that night, numbing his rage with cheap wine, his sides hurting, his head reeling, Anselm was aware of an unstoppable force entering the bar. Milkcye gripped him by the collar and dragged him to the Place de la Révolution. Only there did he let him go and, looking up, Anselm found himself face to face with Count Kalliovski. Balthazar was at his side.

'You have let me down,' said Kalliovski, his voice razor sharp. Balthazar growled.

'I can get the information, I can. I mean, I know that Yann Margoza works at the theatre and that the dwarf Têtu is there—'

'You're not very clever, are you? Do you think I don't know all that and more? What I needed was for you to become a part of the company, for the actress Colombine to feel that you would never betray her. Instead you beat your new wife.'

'I can do it.'

'You are nothing more than a common thug, a pretty bully boy. You bore me. All your kind bore me.' Kalliovski pushed his index finger into Anselm's cheek. For a moment he felt that his face was on fire.

'I can get her back. I can, honest I can. I know how and—'

Kalliovski's laughter resounded around the Place de la Révolution. 'What you know about women is nothing. You are ignorant. You are a slug, a miserable, slimy slug.

What, I wonder, did I see in you?' Kalliovski began to walk away.

'I will do anything, master, please!' shouted Anselm. 'Anything! Give me another chance!'

Kalliovski turned. 'You have a week. If you fail ... I need another chandelier, and your bones will fit my design beautifully. Or perhaps another talking head would be amusing. I haven't yet decided. Fail me, and you are dead. I have no mercy.'

Anselm shivered as he watched them all disappear into the night. Breathing heavily, he leaned against the winding cloth of the guillotine, relieved still to be alive. Something brushed against his legs and he stood suddenly upright, the hairs on the back of his neck prickling. He looked down to see rats, black as the plague, scuttling from under the scaffold, running between his legs, over his shoes, and a soundless scream, bone hard, caught in his throat. Terrified, he scurried away. The lugubrious shadow of the guillotine followed him.

At the theatre, Yann was still in his dressing room when Didier knocked on the door.

'I've been sent to fetch you. There's a real argy-bargy going on in the office. Cordell is here.'

'Wait, Didier,' said Yann, 'is there any news about Remon Quint?'

'None. I went down to the catacombs while you were

away, but I couldn't find that passage again. What do you think happened to him?'

'I don't know.' Yann sighed. 'But he had the smell of death upon him.'

'Is that another gypsy superstition?'

'I felt it the moment I first saw him. It never got any better.'

Didier shook his head. 'It's a bad business, that's for sure.'

'Where the devil have you been?' said Cordell, when Yann walked into the office.

'Downstairs.'

'No, I mean for the past week. What have you been doing?'

'Walking.'

'What were you thinking of? It was no time to take a grand tour, with Remon Quint missing. You were needed here, to help sort out this mess. And if you had been here we might have been able to save the Duchesse de Bourcy from the guillotine. But you weren't, you were rambling about the countryside. It's too late now. She and her friend the Marquise de Valory were both executed yesterday, along with Madame Picard's daughter Celeste, who was only fifteen years old.'

'Sixteen,' said Yann, 'and I am glad to hear it.'

Cordell hit the desk. 'That's preposterous, sir. What is wrong with you? Glad to hear it? Have you lost your mind?'

'No,' said Yann, 'but now they are all dead they might be able to live in relative peace.'

Cordell looked at Têtu and Citizen Aulard. His temper had suddenly evaporated. Yann was ill; that could be the only explanation.

'Maybe you've had too much sun. God knows what I'll write to the Duke. I gave him my word I would protect her.'

'Then tell him that his wife is in excellent health,' said Yann, 'that she suffered her ordeal with great courage. The only damage done is to her hair, which was cut off. And that the girl Celeste who shared the Duchess's cell is a delight, and thrilled to have exchanged a prison cell for the de Bourcy château. And no, I haven't lost my mind.'

Cordell's face was grave. 'Yann, I have the official reports. Do you wish to see them? They were all executed.'

'No, I've seen them already. After all, I wrote them.'

Citizen Aulard burst out laughing. Cordell looked completely stunned. A smile crossed Têtu's face.

'I came home past the Hôtel de Ville and they were very grateful to know that three more traitors had been sacrificed at the bloody altar. I made sure their names were posted. The governor of the prison at Chantilly will confirm that two of his prisoners were sent to the guillotine.'

'I think,' said Cordell quietly, 'I owe you an apology.'

'You owe me nothing,' said Yann. 'Write to the Duke and tell him there is life after death.'

Chapter Twenty

Auguste, Viscomte de Reignac, first met Sido de Villeduval at a summer ball. His arrival in London caused no end of a stir among the émigré society, for Auguste de Reignac belonged to that rare breed of aristocrats who not only held a bona fide title but, more remarkable still, had managed to escape France with their fortune intact.

Juliette had been delighted to see the effect her niece had on this handsome shy young man. Her beauty had already attracted many admirers, who treated her as if she were made of porcelain, a precious object to be treasured, worshipped. Sido had the feeling that she was nothing more than a pencil sketch, to be filled in and coloured to suit the needs of others, to be adored by the foppish young dandies who treated her like a lame Madonna. At balls, she was left to sit with whining, horse-faced ladies, whose dance cards were empty, and listen while their vicious tongues sliced and cut their prettier sisters.

Auguste de Reignac was different. He sat beside her and engaged her in intelligent conversation. He told her of his flight from Paris and how with the help of a young man named Yann Margoza he'd escaped and, as he talked, he noticed Sido's eyes brighten to a radiant blue.

She said, 'Yann rescued me too from Paris, at the beginning of the September Massacre.'

'Of course, forgive me, I didn't make the connection. Your father was the Marquis de Villeduval?'

'That is correct.'

'What a terrible ordeal you must have suffered. I heard that the Marquis was killed. Perhaps it was a mercy his mind had gone. I hope he was unaware of what was happening.'

'I pray so,' said Sido. 'And I heard about your family too. I am sorry.'

'I have decided to live,' said Auguste seriously. 'I think I must, as I have no idea why it should be me that is here, not my sister or ...' He stopped, the subject too painful for this garish ballroom. 'Would you kindly do me the honour of dancing with me?'

And Sido, who had too long waited for someone to ask her, didn't hesitate to say, 'Yes.'

That evening there were many frustrated young beaux who realised they'd missed a golden opportunity with the beautiful Marquise de Villeduval, who danced delightfully with an elegance of movement and an energy that lit up the room.

Going home in the carriage, Juliette had been quietly thrilled with Sido, and felt that at last Yann Margoza would be replaced in her affections by this altogether more suitable young man.

Next day Juliette invited Auguste to dine. The drawing room at Queen Square that evening was full, as it often was, with émigrés newly arrived in London, and others who had been in exile far longer and were now beginning to wonder if they would ever be able to return home.

As soon as Juliette was engrossed in conversation with the Duc de Bourcy, Sido asked Auguste to tell her more about his escape.

'We went out of Paris through the catacombs. Yann took me all the way to Le Havre, and didn't leave until he was certain I was safe,' Auguste said. 'Have you ever seen him perform on stage?'

'Once, when I was younger. He was a magician's assistant then. Have you?'

'I was on stage at the Circus of Follies. I took the role of a market seller and Harlequin came on, upset the stall to a great deal of laughter, and then without touching anything – and I mean anything – he put each and every piece back on the stall. I was told to stay silent, whatever I did, but that if he asked a question I was to move my mouth. I did, and – this is the oddest part – out of it came words as if I were speaking, though I said nothing.'

Auguste de Reignac had gone home that evening full of fine food and wine, and in love with the most enchanting pair of blue eyes.

The day after the supper party Sido received a letter from Yann, and nothing could have prepared her for what he had to say. She opened it, disappointed to find only one sheet, and with so few words. Not suspecting anything to be wrong, she read:

Dear Sido,

Please forgive me for taking so long to write to you. What I have to tell you I say with a heavy heart.

Sido, we can never be together. It is and always has been an impossible situation, a dream. It would take more than a revolution before a Marquis's daughter and a gypsy would be allowed to marry. For that is my origin, as I am certain by now you will have been told.

Please burn my letters. If you remember me at all I hope it will be with affection. We will never meet again, and I wish you all the happiness in the world. You deserve a better man than me.

Once again I ask you to forgive me for any injury I may have caused you.

Do not dwell on the past. Live for the future.
Yann

Sido couldn't breathe. She read the letter again, the room spinning, the world disintegrating under her feet. Could love just vanish? One day it was everything, the next gone, like a passing fever? Was that how love took men?

Her knees gave way and she crumpled to the floor. His words were stones in her heart.

Oh Lord, don't let our love turn to ashes, don't let it be an illusion. Yann is my rock, my strength, he gives meaning to my life. To him I'm not just a puppet made to dance for the delight of others. His love makes me whole, his love makes me free ... his love ... I thought he loved me.

How often have I dreamed of us living far away where no one would know our history, no one would judge us? Of Yann sitting with our children in front of the fire, telling them a fairy tale of how his magic saved their mama from the wicked Count Kalliovski, how he smuggled her out of a gated city. We would have grown old together ...

Like the broken banks of a river in flood, she felt her soul swept away by grief. She sat hunched on the floor, her arms wrapped round her body, rocking with pain. She could hear voices downstairs, the clocks in the hall ticking, outside a street seller shouting his wares, and another sound, the echo of unbearable loneliness that stretched before her for all eternity.

Her trembling hands took the talisman from around her neck, leaving her naked, bereft. Now there was nothing to protect her. She wrote:

It is returned safely to you but you still have my heart and my soul.

T hat afternoon, Sido went to see Mr Trippen, taking her letter with her. From the drawing-room window Juliette watched her get into a sedan chair and vaguely noticed a man in a three-cornered hat setting off after it.

Juliette had for weeks tried to persuade Henry that Sido's English lessons with Mr Trippen should stop and that he couldn't be trusted, not after his irresponsible behaviour regarding the letters.

'Fiddlesticks,' Henry had said. 'A load of tosh, and, my dear, you know it. It does the girl good to have a change of scenery, and her English is much improved. The lessons will continue.'

'And the letters?' Juliette had added.

'Leave that to me.'

Henry had said nothing to Mr Trippen on the matter, and the letters had gone back and forth between the two lovers without any more interruption.

N ow Mr Trippen stood by the empty fireplace in his battered housecoat and red hat with a tassel, and read the letter Sido had shown him.

'I don't know what to do,' she said.

'My dear, enchanting lady,' said Mr Trippen, 'tell me

you have done nothing reckless. The seas of emotion can so capsize young love.'

'I want to send back the talisman, you know, the shell Yann gave me. I have wrapped it up and—'

'I think that is most unwise,' said Mr Trippen.

Sido knew it was, but if Yann loved her no more then in all truth she couldn't wear it. Tears threatened to overcome her. She said, as lightly as her voice would allow, 'That's because you are an old sentimentalist.'

'No, it is because it is a very important talisman. As to this letter, Hamlet's lines do not ring true. He has not stopped loving you, and the fact he is a gypsy would never have deterred either of you from being together. Or would it?' he said, looking at Sido's pale face.

'No.'

'Trippen smells something rotten in the state of Denmark and you, my dear, are to be no Ophelia. That way madness lies. In my humble but well-considered opinion something dark is troubling our Hamlet. The question, and the question is always king, my dear, is what is it that he is not saying?'

Sido's thoughts that rainy day were in turmoil as the sedan chair took her back to Queen Square. How, she wondered, shall I cope with a broken heart? How shall I manage when my soul is dying? All Sido wanted to do was lie in a corner, curled up like a cat, and let time roll over her, instead of which she had to find the strength to hide her feelings.

What could she do now? All she possessed was a title. She had no money, and she couldn't go on living with her aunt and uncle indefinitely. Perhaps she could be a governess? Oh, dear God, there were already enough French women of noble birth in her position, who were now obliged to earn their livings. The newspapers were filled with advertisements.

Or she could marry. She knew that if she wasn't betrothed by the end of this season her aunt would be bitterly disappointed. Juliette was certain that Auguste would soon ask for her hand in marriage. Could she do that? Marry a man she didn't love, for grand carriages and pretty dresses, for security against poverty? Many a young woman would tell her she was greatly privileged to have the chance. For Auguste was gentle, kind – and not elderly. Still, without love, it made everything a folly. She would never make him happy, and she knew she would never love him as she loved Yann.

That evening at supper she listened to her aunt discourse endlessly on the merits of marriage and the finer details of the Viscomte de Reignac's fortune. Sido noticed that Henry, like her, was silent on the matter.

The next day Auguste came on the pretext of bringing Sido a book by Burke, *Reflections on the Revolution in France*.

'I thought you would be interested in it,' he said, as they sat in the drawing room.

'We are planning a picnic on Hampstead Heath for the day after tomorrow if the weather holds,' Juliette said. 'We would be delighted to have your company.'

'Alas, madame, I cannot. I am leaving London.'

'Where are you going?'

'To America.'

'But that is so far away.'

f'I agree, but I own land in Boston and need to see that my interests are secure. I can assure you I shall be back here soon. In fact, nothing would keep me away.'

Sido felt a rising sense of panic as she saw her aunt get up to leave.

'Where are you going, aunt?' she said, a little too urgently.

'I am sure, my dear, that you two have quite enough to talk about without my company. Viscount, shall I order some tea for you?'

———◆———

Alone in the drawing room with the ticking clocks, Sido, terrified that Auguste was going to propose, said quickly, 'Don't, we are such good friends, and ...'

'I – I insist,' he stammered. 'I know you don't love me, but I am in love with you and I want you to be my wife. It would be enough just to have you with me.'

'No – oh, you deserve so much more than that. You must find love.'

He took Sido's hand. 'I would settle for your companionship, for your wit, intelligence and charm. I would be happy.'

'No, no,' said Sido. 'What about passion? Surely there must be passion?'

'It is a fleeting thing. I could live without it and perhaps – in time – you would come to love me.'

She turned away. 'I couldn't live without passion. It's what makes us soar. And I refuse to think of you not finding that in your life.' She laughed. 'I tell you, when you do, you will wonder how we could ever have had this conversation.'

He took her hand. 'Please don't say "no". Don't turn me away. Think about my proposal. I sail in two days and I'm willing to wait until my return.'

'No ... I love ...' She stopped.

'Yann Margoza,' he said slowly.

'How do you know?'

'I would be a fool not to see it, the way your eyes light up when we talk of him. So tell me – is there any hope? Or am I just dreaming with my eyes open?'

'I like you very much as a friend.'

'Then that is a start, some would say a good start.'

'I know I would never make you happy, and you who have been through such pain deserve to be loved, and I am certain that you will find it.'

Auguste took her hand and kissed it. 'Then, *ma chère Marquise*, say no more, I understand. After all, I owe Yann my life. He is a lucky man to have won your heart. I will always be your friend. I hope our friendship, at least, may continue?'

'Yes, by all means, yes.'

'You have chosen a very fine man indeed. I hope he realises how fortunate he is.'

She watched him go, heard the front door click shut

and saw Juliette standing in the hall, a look of disbelief on her face.

———•———

Two days later Auguste de Reignac sailed for America, by which time Juliette could hardly bring herself to speak to Sido, so furious was she that her niece should wilfully turn down a proposal of marriage, a proposal that would have set her up as a woman of means with property in France and America.

Again Henry regretted he had not told Juliette the truth about Yann, but now was not the time. The situation in Paris was deteriorating and he had received a report from Cordell confirming the truth of the unwelcome rumour that Count Kalliovski appeared to be alive and active. Henry, sitting in his office looking out over the square, was grateful for one thing: Sido was safe in London.

Chapter Twenty-One

It happened just as Sido was leaving Mr Trippen's house in Maiden Lane. The maid, Betsy, had her hand on the latch of the front door when Mr Trippen called from the landing.

'Wait, dear girl, before you go. You nearly forgot this.' And he held out the talisman.

'I thought,' said Sido, 'you had sent it back to Yann as I asked.'

'No. I think he wouldn't want that. You must keep it safely on you.' He opened the catch and gently hung it round her neck.

Afterwards he was pleased he'd done it. In fact it was the only thing that brought him any comfort. For when Betsy did open the door, two armed men were standing there with handkerchiefs concealing their faces and their hats pulled down. Behind them the sedan chair lay on its side with the Laxtons' two footmen out cold.

One thug grabbed Sido by the arm and Mr Trippen, without thinking, went into battle. He heard a loud bang, smelled burning flesh and thought nothing of it.

'Let her go! Take your hands off her!'

Sido was lifted bodily and carried away. Mr Trippen, by now feeling as if he were made of air rather than flesh and blood, fell to the ground.

Betsy watched, ashen faced and stone-statue still as Sido was dragged down Maiden Lane to where a very smart berlin stood, its windows blacked out. She saw Sido bundled in to it and then the carriage disappeared from view.

All Sido could think of as the carriage drove off at speed was that her abductors had killed Mr Trippen. As she tried in the dark to open the door she became aware of someone sitting on the seat opposite.

Only when the man lit his clay pipe, the flame illuminating his face, did she recognise him.

'You've got more spark about you than I expected,' said Mr Tull.

'You have killed Mr Trippen.'

'The old fool should have minded his own business, instead of acting the hero.' Mr Tull laughed. 'As for you, if you don't do as you're told, miss, you'll end up as dead meat. Do I make myself quite clear?'

It was early evening when they came to the courtyard of The Travellers' Arms. It was busy and the arrival of one more coach, even with blackened windows, went almost unnoticed. Sido was bundled up the wooden steps that led to a gantry off which Mr Tull had arranged for two rooms. He locked Sido in the first room while he went to see about food, for Mr Tull was ruled by the needs of his stomach.

Sido looked hopelessly at the miserable furnishings: ponderous chairs and a small robust desk. Bored travellers, no doubt waiting for the packet to France, had carved their names on its surface. She turned the key, not expecting any good fortune, but found there a pot of nearly dried ink, some broken quills, and a few sheets of clean paper. It wasn't until then that it struck her that this was her last opportunity to tell anyone what had befallen her. The nibs and the thickness of the ink made writing difficult.

I am alive. I am at an inn near the coast and fear I am to be to returned to France. Mr Tull kidnapped me, his man shot Mr Trippen.

She addressed it to Mr Laxton and propped it behind a painting of a galleon at sea, which hung on the wall above the desk. She wished she had said more, but her reason was so clouded by the fear of being caught she could hardly think straight. To her horror, she noticed an ink stain on her finger, and hurriedly licked and rubbed at it until the stain looked as if it had been there for some time. She had managed to lock the desk and to slip the key through a crack in the floorboards, when she heard the door being unlocked and Mr Tull came in, a napkin tied round his neck, his mouth full. He snapped his fingers and two servants dressed in black entered, one carrying a silver goblet.

'Drink this,' he said.

'What is it?' demanded Sido, determined to show no fear.

Mr Tull smiled, or at least that was the impression he gave, though he looked less than pleased to have his order questioned.

'Drink.'

'Not unless I know what's in—'

Mr Tull pulled the napkin from round his neck and threw it on the floor in disgust.

'Do as you're told, my girl.'

'I insist you tell me what's in it,' Sido repeated.

She suddenly felt belligerent, knowing it was her only power, and she refused to let the feeling go. Mr Tull turned on his heel and left the room. Sido thought for a moment that she might have won, but then he came back carrying a metal funnel.

'Hold her head back,' he commanded the servants.

Sido was pushed, fighting, into the armchair. She struggled, biting Mr Tull hard on the hand. She could taste blood. He hit her across the face and for a moment she blacked out.

'Hold her!'

Sido's jaw was prised open and the funnel pushed down her throat. Gagging but unable to resist, she swallowed the bitter-tasting liquid.

She remembered trying to get up and Mr Tull shouting, 'Give her some more.'

And again she was held down.

Then nothing, just a dark abyss.

Chapter Twenty-Two

P oor Citizen Aulard found the plays he had been instructed to put on, full of patriotic drivel, almost too hard to bear.

'I tell you, Têtu, it was a travesty last night. You should have seen the nonsense. The minute the play started, this man in the audience stood up and said he had written a song and could he sing it. Never have you heard such sentimental rubbish from a Frenchman. After that, what need of the play? Everyone started to sing and shout and march upon the stage like barbarians. I could have wept.'

Têtu brought out cheese and a loaf of bread and put them on the theatre manager's desk. Citizen Aulard's eyes lit up.

'Hunger, my friend, doesn't help,' said Têtu kindly. 'What will happen tonight?' he asked, producing two glasses and a bottle of wine.

Citizen Aulard raised his hands in the air. 'More of the same,' he said, then added, 'I have been thinking.'

'A dangerous thing, my friend, at a time like this.'

'Maybe, but let me tell you: if we survive the Reign of Terror, I don't wish to stay in France. I never thought I would live to say that. Perhaps I've become a gypsy in my old age. Still, I have a mind to go and take my chances in the New World, in America. There, Têtu, we could put on real magic performances. What I'm proposing is that we should be partners.'

Têtu laughed. 'Better that you asked me for some gypsy luck, for that is what you need, not a partner.'

Iago squawked. 'I've seen you where you never were ...'

'Quiet,' shouted Citizen Aulard. 'That bird is getting on my nerves.'

'One day you will be grateful you have a parrot. Anyway, it is a line from a gypsy poem. Shall I tell you it?' And without waiting for a reply Têtu continued:

> 'I've seen you where you never were
> And where you never be.
> And yet within that very place
> You can be seen by me.
> For to tell what they do not know
> Is the art of the Romany.'

Citizen Aulard laughed. 'I thought I would end my days with a beautiful actress by my side. Instead I find a daft dwarf, who I am too fond of to be parted from.'

Têtu smiled. 'The New World might well appeal to my restless feet, that is if we get out of this alive, but I am not certain that Yann would want to come.'

Citizen Aulard sighed. He had been avoiding this topic of conversation, for something was very wrong with Yann. Gone was his calm good sense, his cool head.

'Explain to me what has happened to him. Ever since we lost Remon Quint he is a changed man.'

'I know,' said Têtu.

'I have been told,' said Citizen Aulard, 'that silver blades are again being found after someone has escaped. It is madness, there is enough talk already. If he goes on like this, he will be ...' He drew his finger across his neck. 'What is he trying to do? Get himself killed and us too in the process?'

Têtu went to the door and looked out.

'What is it?' asked Aulard.

'Nothing. I thought I heard something.'

'You see, we are all jumping like circus fleas. Yann must be stopped.' Citizen Aulard looked thoughtfully at Têtu.

'I've seen you where you never were ...' repeated the parrot.

'There is an explanation for Yann's behaviour, and I am not sure what to do,' said Têtu.

'That is most unlike you.'

'Yann has stumbled on a secret that I have done my best to conceal from him, for his own sake.'

'Already I don't like the sound of this.'

'It is hard to explain, but in our world the spirits play as great a role as the living. Yann's mother, Anis, believed that his spirit father was her lost love, Manouche. She never wanted him to know the identity of his real father.'

Citizen Aulard took a sip of wine. 'Come, it can't be so terrible—'

'One day I will tell you the whole story,' interrupted Têtu. 'It is Kalliovski.'

Wine sprayed in a fountain from the startled theatre manager's mouth. He started coughing.

'Kalliovski? No, no, tell me I have misheard. All the angels in heaven and hell! Tell me I have misheard!'

Outside the door, Anselm was lurking in the shadows. He'd come up from the stage door on an errand for Citizeness Manou. He was eager for any excuse to listen in on the theatre manager's conversations. Like a magpie he collected gems of information and took them back to his master. He listened intently in the dust-filled silence, unable to believe what he was hearing.

Anselm, like many before him, had fallen under the Count's spell, and he was sure the dwarf spoke nothing but poisonous lies. It was not possible that Yann Margoza was his master's son. He had convinced himself that he was the rightful heir to the Kalliovski crown. Anselm walked slowly down the stairs to the stage door. Everything had turned red, vivid, bright red. He wanted to kill someone, it didn't matter whom, just someone.

'Well,' said Citizeness Manou, 'what did he say?'

'What?' said Anselm.

'I sent you up there to give Citizen Aulard a message, and you forgot, didn't you?' She shuffled out of her sentry box, wheezing and panting. Pushing past him, she said, 'As usual I have to do everything myself round here.'

Anselm, lost in a blind fury, didn't answer. He left the theatre and, crossing the square, went to the Café du Coin where he sat shaking with rage, mulling over what he would do. He knew he would only find peace by killing. In the past a chicken would have satisfied him, but not now. Now he needed something more than a scrawny neck.

He saw Citizeness Manou leaving the theatre. She stopped to adjust her cap and set off, a long, thin quiff of smoke following her. Anselm felt his fingers tingle. Getting up, he paid and left.

Walking behind Citizeness Manou, keeping to the shadows, he waited to pounce. Then he saw his opportunity. An alleyway with a dead end and Citizeness Manou so obligingly stopping at the corner to relight her pipe.

Before she could even take in the face of her attacker, she found herself at the end of the alley where two cats were fighting over a fishbone. The stench of human waste and rotten meat made her gag.

'What the hell—?'

He had his hands tight round her neck and a feeling of all-encompassing power filled him with excitement. This is what he should have done to Mother. He watched Manou's face turn blue, her eyes nearly popping out of her head. He felt her last tobacco breath leave her body. As her tongue flopped from her mouth, he let her body drop to the ground.

Later, much later, Anselm felt calm as he sat with a glass of wine studying his pretty wife, whom he loathed. At any other time, listening to her incessant chatter would have made him long to hit her.

'A penny for them,' she said, looking at him in the mirror.

'They ain't worth that much, and I don't think you will listen.'

'Anselm, I love you. I know you never meant to hurt me.'

'I can't forgive myself,' said Anselm. 'I love you too and I'm just terrified of losing you.'

'What do you mean?'

'I have a bad feeling. I've heard rumours.'

'What rumours?'

'I don't know ... I shouldn't say anything.'

'Tell me,' she said, putting her arms round him.

'Well, I have heard that Yann Margoza is a gypsy and so is Têtu. Did you know that?'

Now he had Colombine's full attention. 'That would explain that funny language they talk together.'

'What I've been told is, Yann works for a man who lives in the catacombs. They are all in it together, double-dealing the clients and selling them back to the Tribunal.'

'No, that's not true.'

'Think about it.'

Colombine thought for a long time. Yann was

becoming reckless. And there was that funny business with the keymaker. Looking up at the cherubic face of her husband, she said, 'Perhaps you're right.'

'I know I am,' said Anselm, with more passion than he had ever shown for her. 'I think we're all in grave danger. We've got to turn Yann Margoza in, let the Commune know he's the Silver Blade. If you were to do that, we would be able to have a life together. Isn't that what you want?'

'I can't, Anselm. I can't do that, it's—'

'What?' he said, feeling his rage rise again.

What Colombine saw, or thought she saw, was Anselm trembling with passion for her and it did her pride good. He truly loved her.

She went up to him and he turned and kissed her. She was taken aback by the strength of his longing. She felt shaken by that kiss. Love made her feel reckless.

Afterwards, as he escorted her to the theatre, he said, squeezing her hand tightly, 'You've made the right decision, you won't regret it. We will do it together.'

The shocking news that evening was that Citizeness Manou had been murdered. Yann was absent, on an assignment. Everyone else was cast into despair.

Pantalon said what the rest of the company was thinking. 'Who would have done such a terrible thing? Isn't there enough killing in this city?'

'I think it was Yann who killed her,' Anselm whispered to Colombine. 'She knew too much.'

Chapter Twenty-Three

I n Sido's dream she hears her name being called. Walking down a woodland path she comes to a clearing. There sits an old gypsy woman who wears many skirts of moss, of mists, of snows. In front of her is a small fire on which a kettle bubbles, its lid chattering merrily to the boiling water.

The old woman speaks with a voice that is the rustling of leaves. She calls to the spirits of the forest and, down each of the seven paths which lead into the clearing, silvery ghosts appear.

The old woman says, 'Yann Margoza, Sido de Vil-leduval is not a gypsy. Why is she here?'

Then she sees him standing beside the old woman, looking older than she remembers. A tiny silver thread begins spinning towards him from the shell hanging at her neck.

'Because I love her. She is the key to my soul; without her I am powerless. She has the shell, the *baro seroeske sharkuni*, the shell of the shells. Only a true gypsy soul could benefit from its power. It will keep her safe.'

The old woman turns to face Sido. In those fathomless eyes Sido sees the road unfolding and knows her journey is about to begin.

When Sido woke, her limbs ached, her eyelids fluttered against sleep and she wondered if she were back in the Marquis's château, for through blurry vision she saw a canary sitting in an elaborate birdcage, singing. Slowly the chamber came into focus and, to her horror, she saw that the walls were lined with bones overlaid with gold leaf. Was she dreaming? She sat up suddenly, her head throbbing. At the end of her bed were three women servants, dressed in black.

'Where am I?'

They said nothing, but came forward and forcibly led Sido towards a bath in the middle of the room. She tried to pull free, but the women possessed uncanny strength.

'Where am I?' she asked again.

They took no notice of anything she said, just washed and dried her, then stood her naked before a long mirror while a fine powder was blown on her until her skin had turned china-doll white. A gown of watered silk was placed over a corset and petticoats. Her hair was dressed and decorated with flowers. She saw herself disappear in the mirror.

A man came in. His face was covered in scars, like a map of a city you would never wish to visit. He had one milky eye.

'Come with me,' he said.

She followed him down a corridor lined with brittle bones, still not certain if this were real or part of a kaleidoscope of dreams. She had the shell. What was the shell called? She thought if she could remember that she would be safe. It came to her: *baro seroeske sharkuni*, that was it, and walking down the haunted hall with its finger-bone lanterns blazing, she said the words over and over again, a prayer to keep her safe. Milkeye stopped at a large, imposing door on which was written:

The dance to the hollow drum of time is done.
Here then be death's domain.

The doors opened to reveal a long room. On one side were mirrors framed in bones. She saw chandeliers, also made of bones, candles burning, and skulls strung together and festooned across the ceiling. On the other side of the room, there were windows, blessed windows.

Outside, moonlight flickered on water. She turned away from the windows and caught her reflection in the many mirrors. She was unrecognisable, a ghost.

The doors at the other end of the room opened and in walked Count Kalliovski, followed by seven women. He was taller than she remembered and much changed, his skin cadaverous, like waxwork rather than flesh and blood, his hair black as tar. As always, he was immaculately dressed, in a fitted black cutaway coat. He wore white lace at his neck and red kid gloves.

A living nightmare, the sight of him revolted her. His raven-black, dead eyes stared straight through her. Nothing human was left in him. She felt that she was in the presence of great evil.

He took her hand and she tried to pull away, but it was held fast in his rigor mortis grip, and raising it to his frozen lips he kissed her palm.

'I hope you find everything to your liking.' He clicked his fingers and the seven women, whose feet appeared not to touch the ground, came forward. 'May I introduce the Seven Sisters Macabre?'

They curtsied.

Sido stared at these horrendous apparitions and trembled. Their eyes were like glass, their skin stitched upon their faces, their mouths sewn tight shut.

When Sido had last found herself with this monster, silence had been her only power over him. Seeing the muted mouths of the Sisters Macabre, she understood that now her survival lay in words.

'I have a gift for you, one that will complement your beauty,' said Count Kalliovski, and he handed Sido a jewel case. She opened it, and saw rubies lying there on black velvet. They made her think of blood, and she was certain this was the prelude to her death.

'Your chain first,' said the Count. 'Allow me.'

'No,' said Sido, her hand reaching up to her throat, touching the shell.

The Count leaned towards her, then, as if snagged on

a thorn bush, he stepped back and indicated to Milkeye to remove the chain. Milkeye had no more success than his master.

Only at that moment did Sido comprehend the extraordinary nature of the talisman and, gathering her strength, she said, 'This is worth more to me than all your rubies.'

'It is a shell, a mere trinket. These rubies once belonged to Marie Antoinette.'

'Your wealth is dust beside this shell.' Every word she said made her feel a little less afraid.

Kalliovski's expression changed, or rather, since his face was incapable of such a thing, it was as if a thunderous cloud were passing overhead. His granite eyes glinted with pure malice.

'Yann Margoza gave me this talisman,' she said, as if his name itself were a magic spell that might ward off evil.

'Have you wondered why Yann Margoza hasn't come to rescue you? Could it be that he no longer loves you?'

Sido bit the inside of her lip. She mustn't think about that.

'You see, he is my son. Perhaps he has taken after his father, for love corrupts, destroys and ruins. I prefer evil. It is cleaner, has a certain honesty to it – and the devil is always so obliging.'

'Your son,' she said, and now she was falling, falling.

'Yes, didn't you know that? Oh dear, did he forget to mention it?'

'Yann is of Romany blood. You cannot be his father.'

'But I am – and he is.'

Sido instinctively clung to the shell, which glowed, warm and comforting. The light shining from it grew blindingly bright and filled the room.

Kalliovski turned away. 'Take her back to her chamber,' he said to Milkeye.

To the Seven Sisters Macabre he said, 'You are all dismissed.'

Like a gaggle of geese they flew at the door, eager to be gone.

Once more in her chamber, Sido sat on her bed. What had Kalliovski said? That Yann was his son? It could not be. Not Yann, not her Yann.

The three harpies arrived to undress her. Exhausted, she sat in a plain linen shift, as if, having completed one dance with the devil, she were allowed to sit out the next.

In the long gallery, Kalliovski paced. How could he have been so weak as to let himself be caught off guard by a shell, a talisman? Did she know what she had round her neck? Had she any idea of the power of the *baro seroeske sharkuni*? His gambler's instinct had been correct. Yann was in love with her. But to entrust to her such a talisman, the shell of the shells, given only to great shamans and gypsy kings . . . he would never have been parted from it.

No, he thought bitterly, because I was not worthy of the shell of the shells. I was only worth my mother's curse. And the son I never wanted possesses what I would give my fortune for, the threads of light.

He could feel rage bubbling under the surface of his waxen skin, and another emotion, belonging to the living, so long foreign to him that it shocked him: jealousy. As he found the word he thought he heard laughter.

He looked down the long gallery. Nobody was there. He had convinced himself that his mind was playing tricks when Anis appeared, standing before him in all her beauty, the Madonna of the Road.

Emotions were other men's seas; he could walk on water, never needing to plumb the depths. Anis threatened the perfect void of his being.

She came close, her hand outstretched, and touched his waxen face.

'Dead man's skin,' she said. 'Do you not know that the devil always keeps the high, wild cards for himself? You will never win at his table. Look, my murderer, at what lies at your feet.'

Kalliovski stared down to see that the floor had become transparent, like an enormous dragonfly wing, and from under its iridescent surface he could see the faces of his many victims, their eyes open, staring up at him. He may have silenced the Sisters Macabre, but nothing could quieten the bodies in the grave of his conscience. He tried to move away, but Anis held him fast, forcing him to look.

A crack in the nothingness of a hollow man is a very dangerous thing, for it lets in the past and the worm of memory.

'Where is your companion?' asked Anis. 'Where is Balthazar? He who never judged you, who never found you wanting? Who accepted all you did ... except for one thing.'

'What thing?'

'Forbidding him to go with the ferryman when Death came walking.' She smiled. 'A cruel trick, to make him live in limbo. He is another of your victims.' She was in front of him, behind him, beside him, passing through him.

'Stop it, stop it!' shouted Kalliovski. The mirrors showed a multitude of his own reflections.

'Do you remember the story of the devil's dog? Tell me, how does it go, my killer?'

Giving way to a seething rage, Kalliovski picked up the jewel case and flung it at a mirror. It cracked so that he was reflected in many parts, and in none of them was he whole.

The splintered apparition of his other self spoke. 'You are a dead man. I am the remains of any good that was ever in you. I am you the moment before you murdered Anis, when all roads were yours to travel, when you could have made the circle whole.'

'You are nothing but a figment of my imagination!'

'I am all there is left of you,' continued the apparition. 'I am a small part. You belong to the grave, you are made from a dead man's bones.'

Kalliovski, holding tightly to his very being, saw the apparition fade as he heard Anis sing, 'We are birds, we are free.'

'No, no!' he shouted.

When Milkeye returned to the chamber, he found his master bent double, his hands over his ears.

Citizen Frenet and his second-in-command, Citizen Gabet, were on guard that night at the St-Denis gate. They were not young and both, if they were honest, missed their beds. They'd managed to stay awake by playing cards and talking. Citizen Frenet was a fervent *sans-culotte*, passionate about the Revolution and the Republic. Citizen Gabet had been a little less so since the awful business of his wife's niece, who two weeks previously had been taken to the guillotine on a trumped-up charge of conspiracy. It had frightened him, making him realise no one was safe. Frenet had little sympathy. In his eyes the Committee of Public Safety could do no wrong.

'They would do me a great favour,' he joked, 'if they guillotined my wife. Now, that would be a service to the nation. I wouldn't miss her.'

Their conversation switched to the news they had had of a colleague who had been tricked by the Silver Blade. He had had the audacity to rescue someone from the prison of La Plessis right under the guard's nose. The guard had been sent to the guillotine for his carelessness, swearing he'd been shown all the correct papers.

'Do you know what gave him away?'

'No.'

'A silver blade from a child's toy guillotine. It was left hanging right above his head. I tell you,' said Citizen Frenet, 'if the Silver Blade were to come this way with a blank piece of paper and say it was a bona fide document, I would have him and no mistake.'

'I agree,' said Citizen Gabet. 'I wonder if this Silver Blade ain't a bit of a myth, made up to hide slovenly practices.'

'You could have a point. And all that nonsense about how it's always left hanging somewhere out of reach. I tell you, it sounds fishy.'

It was then that both men nearly jumped out of their skins. Peering through the yellowed window into the smoke-filled room was a ghastly, toothless old hag.

Citizen Frenet, seeing her, grabbed hold of his pistol

and went outside. The old hag was not alone; she had a friend with her who looked in an even worse way than the toothless one.

'What are you doing here? You know the penalty for being out after curfew. I'll have you arrested. Now, push off!'

Gabet joined his colleague at the door.

'We should arrest them. No messing around.'

The toothless one began to cough. She came closer and the smell of death on her made both guards back away.

'We've been in the Place de la Révolution,' she said, spitting out her words. 'Watched the scum of France lose their heads. See this blood here on my petticoat? Fresh today, it is. That's the blood of a nobleman.'

'Enough,' said Citizen Gabet, who knew full well what these ghastly old witches got up to, knitting at the foot of the guillotine.

'Hear that, sister, they're going to arrest us. That's kind of them, ain't it?'

Citizen Gabet noticed with alarm that her scrawny sister seemed to be on the point of fainting. The old hag grabbed her and held her upright.

'She's been sick, that's why we weren't here earlier. Been throwing up all evening. Now she has a little rash. Go on, show these citizens that rash you've got.' And the old hag made to lift her sister's skirt.

That was enough for Citizen Frenet. He knew if she had smallpox she would be infectious. Gabet, thinking the same, went to open the gate.

'Don't you want to see our documents?' said the tooth-less hag, and she licked her fingers and pulled the papers from her skirt.

Frenet could not bring himself to touch them, in case he too would be taken sick.

'Be gone, both of you.'

'Well, I would have thought with all them stories of the Silver Blade,' said the toothless hag, 'you might like to—'

'Get the hell out of here. Go before I change my mind.'

'As you please.'

The two guards watched as, painfully slowly, they made their way into the countryside.

Back in the guardhouse, Citizen Frenet, lifting the cognac bottle, poured some over his fingers. Citizen Gabet did the same.

'A precaution against infection,' he said, and taking a mouthful from the bottle, he caught a glimmer of something silver glinting in the candlelight. The liquid ran down the side of his mouth.

'Hey, hey, don't waste it. That's good stuff.'

Gabet pointed upwards.

The colour drained from their faces.

'How the hell did that get—' Frenet rushed outside to the gate. The road was empty. He returned to the guardhouse.

'We'd better get it down. And let's agree not to tell a soul that we've been duped by the Silver Blade.'

The two old hags, having rid themselves in a convenient barn of their stinking costumes, emerged as Yann Margoza and a Monsieur Bille, a terrified wigmaker from Paris, who had needed almost no make-up, since fear had made the poor man look like death.

'You did well,' said Yann kindly. 'At least, my friend, you didn't faint.'

Poor Monsieur Bille was speechless. All he could do was nod. Only when Yann handed him over to a trusted bargeman at Port du Gravier did the wigmaker recover his sense of humour.

Yann returned to Paris later that night, sure he was being followed. Once again he sensed Balthazar close on his heels. Then he caught sight of him in the moonlight, through some beech trees. He was monstrously large.

What is it he wants from me? Yann asked himself. The great beast slowly raised his head and stared straight at him. Yann's blood ran cold. Once he had spoken to the soul of the hound, but Balthazar no longer had the eyes of a dog. Those brown orbs of love and devotion had been replaced by human eyes. Yann had no words that would touch him.

Then the beast was gone.

With a jolt Yann remembered the story of the devil's dog, and knew that the spirit of *beng*, the evil one, was out walking. He trembled for himself; he trembled for Paris.

He was relieved to be back in the city once more. Still trying to shake off the image of those human eyes, it came to him that it wasn't Balthazar who was evil, but his master.

He felt overcome by pity for the dog and for all those caught up in this bloodbath. Pity for those never to be remembered: the curtain-maker, pleased to dress the tall windows of Versailles; the hosier, whose silk stockings the King wore to his death; the tax collector, who brought in the revenue; the banker who sent money abroad to an émigré client. Pity the seamstress who sewed the Queen's hems; the butcher who hoarded, the wife who whispered a confession to a priest. Pity France. What a sorrowful city Paris had become. And spare some pity for yourself, Yann. Perhaps Têtu was right. It would have been better if I had never known about Kalliovski, for the knowledge is a cancer that has eaten its way into my soul.

That night, as with many nights when he wasn't on stage, he felt lost. He had put away all Sido's letters and would not allow himself to look at them. He had thought of burning them, but the idea of never seeing even her words again made him unbearably sad. As usual he sought comfort at the café on the square.

Têtu had witnessed Yann's descent into deep melancholy and was powerless to help. Everything he suggested, Yann rejected. He disregarded Têtu's carefully laid plans for escapes, choosing instead to go about things in his own idiosyncratic way. If a priest knew where to find the Silver Blade, it would not be long before the authorities managed to work it out. It was as if Yann wanted to be caught. Even faithful Didier, who would have followed him to hell and back, was bewildered by the change in him. The only person who benefited was Anselm. For if Yann had been his old self, Anselm would never again have had access to the theatre, but somehow he had taken over Citizeness Manou's job, and Yann made no protest.

Têtu had waited anxiously for Yann at the theatre. He needed time alone with him; there was news that he didn't want to tell him publicly. But Yann had avoided him, as he often did these days. Têtu found him seated with Pantalon at the middle table, engrossed in a card game. Anselm was watching with Colombine, whose arms were wrapped round his neck. She was wearing a small pair of guillotine earrings, which were all the fashion in Paris.

Têtu pushed his way to the table. 'I need to speak to you, Yannick.'

'Not now, I'm on a winning streak. Look what I inherited from my father. Good at cards. The Jack of Diamonds, that's me.'

'Yann, please, now. It's urgent.'

'No, Têtu, leave me alone.'

'Why don't you talk French, you two,' said Colombine, 'instead of that gibberish none of us can understand. Anyway, what language is it you're speaking?'

Têtu ignored her. His presence began to irritate Yann.

'Go away, Têtu. It can wait till the morning. There, I win.'

'This afternoon I saw Cordell. Serious news has arrived posthaste from London—'

'Damn it,' said Pantalon. 'Another hand?'

What Têtu had to say couldn't wait.

'Last week Sido was abducted. There was no note, no trace left behind.'

Yann found that he had lost his appetite for cards and wine. Sobriety hit him abruptly in the face.

'Who ...?' He swallowed. '... How did it happen?'

'She was leaving Mr Trippen's. He was shot trying to save her.'

'Is he ... dead?'

'No. The doctors believe he will recover. The Laxtons expected a ransom note, but then they had word that she had been found.'

'Thank God,' said Yann. 'Is she all right?'

'Her body was recovered from one of the ponds on Hampstead Heath. It had been in the water, they think, for a week.'

Yann could no longer hear any voices, only the drum of blood beating in his ears. Had everything stopped? He couldn't breathe.

Têtu saw the brightly coloured threads that danced around Yann fade before his eyes, as the young man staggered to his feet, his face bloodless.

'What is it?' said Colombine, looking frightened. '*Chéri*, speak to me! What's wrong with you?'

He pushed past Colombine, knocking over the card table.

'Hey,' shouted Pantalon, 'that was a winning hand.'

Yann, gasping for air like a drowning man, made it out on to the street before he spewed up half his insides.

Têtu was talking to him, and yet he heard nothing. He felt Têtu put something in his jacket pocket . . . but he was falling, falling, and had a long way to go. Sick to his soul, he stumbled into the night, so lost he hardly knew where he was going. Sido's death stripped Yann of his powers; the threads of light had gone, disappeared from his vision. He was blind.

He went down to the Seine and sat on an upturned boat. Tonight they could arrest him, he didn't care. They could guillotine him, he didn't care. He would willingly lay his head on the block, as if it were a feather pillow. How could he go on living if there was no Sido? Without her, time had stopped. She would always remain in yesterday, and he felt Paris wrap itself around him, a city of the broken embracing a broken man.

I want Sido to be alive. I want to hold her. To love her, to tell her the truth. I want to have lain with her, to have been beloved of her, always. And in that I would have known I was blessed upon this earth. The luckiest of men.

At dawn, Paris was almost quiet as if she were holding her breath, the city trembling at what the new day might bring. In its watery light Yann found something in his pocket. It was an envelope.

He opened it, pulled out a letter and straightened it. The words danced away from him until he made them stay still long enough to read.

I have something that I wish to tell you.

I couldn't live like this all my life, a doll in a dolls' house. I long for adventure, I long to be free, I want to ride with you across moors, through forests. I want to travel with you across the seas. I don't want a painted ceiling in a bedroom, I want the stars, I want to lie with you on the mossy grass in fields of poppies, in haylofts of gold, to be with you always. I am not a marquis's daughter, Yann. I was born the wrong side of an unhappy marriage. What use is a title? I give it away. There. Anyone can have this iron cage full of prejudice and privilege. I want to be plain Madame Margoza. That has a freedom to it, that has wind in its sails.

Never, ever, Yann, tell me that your being a gypsy

would stop me loving you. I too have a gypsy soul. I am yours and only yours.

Sido

Yann felt as if he had been mortally wounded by his own hand, his own folly. This was the letter he'd given back to Têtu, unread. He thought of what Sido had received from him in return, his short letter cutting her off from him.

And now it was too late.

'I must go to London,' he said out loud, as if emerging from a fog. His words sounded awkward, his tongue heavy as lead. He never wanted to talk to anyone ever again if he couldn't talk to Sido. And by the waters of the Seine he wept.

———— ·◆· ————

Didier had been out since dawn looking for him. Now, having as good as scoured Paris, he decided to go back to the Circus of Follies.

The barman at the café on the corner was sweeping out the sawdust, the tables and chairs stacked in the morning sunlight.

'Citizen,' he called to Didier, 'have you found him?'

Didier shook his head. The barman brought him coffee.

Didier drank it and was about to leave when the

barman said, 'It looks as if Citizen Aulard has the inspectors in again.'

Didier, thinking nothing of it, entered the theatre by the stage door. He'd started up the stairs to Citizen Aulard's office when, too late, he saw five National Guardsmen on the landing, their pistols cocked. He turned to run when two more armed guards stood up in the concierge's sentry box, their weapons aimed straight at him. Didier was chained and taken on to the stage. The rest of the company, including Anselm, was there, surrounded by soldiers.

'Is that everyone?' said the sergeant, catching Anselm's eye. The look that passed between them didn't escape Didier's notice.

Didier, a giant of a man and stronger by the power of ten when angry, rushed at Anselm and with one punch hit him halfway across the stage. The guards descended on him like wasps on jam, but even in chains, Didier knocked three of them unconscious before the sergeant restored order by firing his pistol at the ceiling.

'You've broken my nose,' whined Anselm. Then seeing everyone's sharp eyes on him, including Colombine's, he said, 'Don't look at me, she's in on it too.'

'Quiet, not another word,' said the sergeant.

While Anselm and Colombine were taken away separately, the sergeant said, 'You are all under arrest. All of you are suspects. Things might go better if you tell us which of your company goes by the name of the Silver Blade.'

Silence.

'I ask you again, and this will be the last time. Which of you is the Silver Blade?'

And again no one said a word.

'To the Conciergerie with the lot of you.'

<hr />

The barman at the corner café on the square stared open-mouthed in horror to see nearly all his regular customers from the Circus of Follies chained together and loaded on to the waiting wagons like sheep.

'Oh, these are the days of murder and mourning,' he muttered miserably to himself.

The only two persons missing from this sorry band were Têtu and Basco.

'Where are they?' asked Didier.

'Têtu went to see Cordell,' whispered Citizen Aulard. 'Basco accompanied him.' Iago was perched on his shoulder.

'Good.'

'Cordell wanted to see you, too. Oh, God, what's going to happen to us?'

'I would have thought,' said Didier, avoiding the subject, 'that you'd have left the parrot behind.'

'So would I, but Iago was adamant.'

Didier looked at the cart carrying Anselm and Col-ombine. What we do for love, he thought. Still, he would have imagined Colombine to have had more sense than

616

to fall for that thug. He turned his back on them and instead watched the city he loved roll slowly past, saying a long farewell to his freedom. By the time the turrets of the Conciergerie came into view the sky had turned ominously black, the air laden with the approaching storm.

In the past, when there was still justice in France, this palace had been its seat. But justice had long been banished, and the palace was home to the dreaded Revolutionary Tribunal and its tyrannical ruler, the hatchet-man of the Convention, Fouquier-Tinville. It contained within its weather-stained stone walls one of the most notorious prisons in Paris. The sight of those infamous gates sent a ripple of fear through the whole company. This was where Marie Antoinette had been imprisoned; through these gates Danton had been taken in a tumbril on his way to execution. The list was growing, day by day, of the great and the good who had been sacrificed to the pernicious new ruler of France – the guillotine.

It was not surprising, then, that the company was trembling as they stepped from the wagons. Pantalon was a sorry sight, make-up running, knees knocking, as he and the rest were unceremoniously prodded and pushed, unable to hear themselves think above the barking of the dogs. They were ushered through more gates and doors which clanged shut and locked behind them, then down a long stone corridor, to be left waiting on a bench in a sunless place whose walls seemed to sweat tears.

Opposite was a small room, and through the filthy glass they could see the prison governor seated in his armchair in front of a wooden table. Above and below, a tangle of sounds reverberated: the turn of a key, the echo of footsteps, the cries of a prisoner, laughter and the clang of a bell. All were separated by impenetrable silence, and still they waited. Tick . . . tock. Tick . . . tock. Time imprisoned here was thin and whispery, its beat almost lost in the dungeons.

The prison governor seemed not to have noticed the new arrivals, or that one of them had a parrot on his head, for never once did he bother to look in their direction. Only a rat appeared interested in them, sniffing the air before scurrying under the bench. Colombine let out a gasp.

'Quiet,' boomed the guard. His dog looked hungry and mean, ready to tear to pieces anyone who crossed him.

'You there,' said a turnkey, breaking the silence, pointing at Anselm, 'the governor is waiting.'

A few minutes later Anselm came out, and avoiding all eye contact, walked to the end of the corridor where a door, unlit and unseen by those left seated, opened. Then he was gone.

Colombine was next to be summoned, followed by Pantalon, and after a short interview each was taken out through the door at the end of the corridor. This routine went on until only Citizen Aulard and Didier were left.

'Do you think they betrayed us?' asked Citizen Aulard gloomily.

What had saved Yann from returning to the theatre that fateful morning was exhaustion. It had finally overcome him, and he had curled up and slept under a tarpaulin in the bottom of a broken boat. He had woken with a start around midday and for a moment, one blissful moment, all looked right with the world. Then he remembered.

Slowly he made his way back to the Place de Manon.

'At least,' said the barman, his hand on Yann's sleeve, 'you have been spared. I feel terrible.'

Yann looked at him, bewildered.

'I mean, I didn't know,' continued the barman, making no sense whatsoever.

'Know what?' asked Yann.

The barman pulled him inside the café.

'I didn't know the National Guards were in there waiting to arrest everyone. Early this morning they took all the members of the Circus of Follies away in tumbrils to the Conciergerie.'

What have I done? thought Yann. I have let so many people down.

'I heard,' said the barman, 'that they think they've caught the Silver Blade.'

Chapter Twenty-Six

S ido was wearing a heavily embroidered gown, her hair was dressed high on her head, and sprinkled with diamonds. The shell was still resting safely at her neck. In the mirror she saw someone else, someone completely detached from herself.

Milkeye escorted her into the dining chamber where the candles were all alight and the long table laid as if for many guests, decorated with bowls of sugared fruit and silver vases of lilies. The blooms were fleshlike, their smell heady.

Sido was wondering who would be joining them when she noticed, in the centre of the table, a strange cake stand. What delicacy was hidden behind the frosted glass, she couldn't imagine.

Kalliovski not so much entered the room as materialised, seated at the end of the table. With him was

Balthazar. Sido was taken aback to see the size of the dog. There was no doubt he was more like a huge wolf of almost mythical proportions. And his terrifying eyes were all too human. He snarled, revealing a mouthful of pointed teeth, and Sido noticed that Kalliovski held the dog tightly on a chain.

They sat together in silence, Kalliovski studying her closely until Sido, unable to stand his gaze any longer, asked, 'You are expecting other guests?'

'All my many friends,' he replied.

Still no one came. He clicked his fingers and Milkeye poured champagne for her, and her alone, and served her tasteless morsels of food. Kalliovski watched. He neither drank nor ate, but then, addressing Milkeye, he said, 'The Marquis de Villeduval might like to join us.'

Sido stopped eating and watched in horror as the frosted glass of the cake stand was pulled back to reveal the Marquis's lifelike head. She stood up, knocking over her champagne. The delicate, fluted glass shattered on the stone floor.

She ran to the door. Milkeye barred her exit.

'You always were so clumsy, Sidonie,' said the head of the Marquis, 'and I see that there is little improvement.'

Sido closed her eyes and put her hands over her ears. She willed the room to disappear. Milkeye held the chair for her to be reseated.

The Marquis said, 'And you still have that irritating limp, Sidonie.'

Sido had lost her voice. She was shaking.

The head sniffed in the exact same way the Marquis used to. Everything about him seemed so real. This was the devil's work.

On Kalliovski's orders, Milkeye lifted up the contraption and moved it closer to her.

'I knew things were coming to a pretty pass when ladies stopped wearing corsets,' said the severed head of the Marquis.

'He is, you must agree,' said Kalliovski, 'a lot more entertaining – and much less expensive – now he is dead.'

'Stop it!' shouted Sido. 'Stop this charade. What do you want of me? You have done enough. You have ruined our family, had the Marquis killed – what more do you want?'

'That is a little exaggerated. I once wanted you for my bride and if you had done as you were bid, I would be a different man. No, instead, you ran away. I told you I never forget.'

'He has no mercy. He shows no mercy,' said the Marquis's head.

Sido rose to her feet and, regardless of Milkeye, refused to sit down again. 'I will not stay here. I would rather go to the guillotine than stay here.'

'There is no need to over-excite yourself. Such drama. I always remembered you as so silent, so interesting. Give me the shell and you shall have your freedom.' Kalliovski spoke with calculated precision.

'May your soul burn in hell!'

'The Marquis always was very wrong about you, wasn't

he?' said Kalliovski. 'A foolish man. If you've had enough to eat, let me show you something.'

He came closer and the temperature in the room grew colder. Sido shivered. The red glove stroked her face and she flinched. He took her hand and led her to a room adjoining the dining chamber.

'Here are my guests.'

On several benches stood rows of heads. On the shelves above were glass jars containing organs. Artificial limbs hung from the ceiling.

'This,' said Kalliovski, 'is where I make my automata. I have a choice of heads from the guillotine, for I don't forget my friends. I have death masks taken of those I knew so that they may keep me company. This one is Remon Quint, the renowned keymaker.'

'Why are you showing me these obscenities?'

'Because if you don't give me the shell, I will be forced to take more drastic measures, and if those measures result in your death, so be it. As an automaton you will be more beautiful, I think, than the Sisters Macabre, and you will keep me company for all eternity. I might make you my bride after all.'

Sido backed away as Kalliovski addressed the head of the keymaker. 'Such a pity you couldn't dine with us tonight,' he said.

Remon Quint's eyes opened.

'Citizen Quint, may I introduce you to the Marquise Sidonie de Villeduval. Tell her what you've made for me.'

'A key.'

'Tell her what kind of key.'

'A key to a soul.'

'Such a key is impossible,' said Sido.

Kalliovski's laughter, like the drone of bees, travelled around the chamber, his words stinging her. 'Nothing is impossible. Citizen Quint, tell her whose soul it is the key to.'

'Yann Margoza's,' said the keymaker.

Kalliovski clicked his fingers and the heavy eyelids of Remon Quint closed abruptly.

Sido shuddered. 'The shell would never belong to such a one as you.'

'Consider my offer, for I will not make it again. Take her back to her chamber.'

———————◆———————

M r Tull, accompanied by Anselm, waited in the long gallery for his master. Anselm was tapping his foot, looking more restless and disturbed than Tull had ever seen him.

Mr Tull was feeling nervous too. For all his assiduous planning, the kidnapping of Sido de Villeduval hadn't turned out well, no, indeed it hadn't.

'He wasn't my father, was he?' said Anselm, turning on Mr Tull.

'Who wasn't?'

'The butcher Loup. He wasn't.'

'Don't ask me, I don't know. He said he was.'

'He was a liar, he only said that to protect the master.'

'What are you on about? You've been down here a bit too long. Sent your brain mushy, has it?'

'You see, I know. I know the very truth of truths.'

'Good for you,' said Mr Tull, thinking once again that the boy seemed a bit odd.

'It's Count Kalliovski.'

'What is?' said Mr Tull. 'You've lost me there.'

Anselm's foot was now tapping a frenzied beat. 'No, I mean, I am Kalliovski's son.'

'Look, could you stop fidgeting? You've been drinking, haven't you?'

'No. I just know I'm the devil's son.'

'Well, that ain't a lie,' said Mr Tull. 'He has a few, so I'm told.'

'No, you see, you don't understand. I am the master's one and only son,' said Anselm, grabbing Mr Tull by his coat.

'Get off me! What the hell is wrong with you? You're talking absolute gibberish. Bloody Frenchman!'

They both turned and jumped to see Kalliovski sitting in a wing-back chair, listening to them.

'Anselm,' he said, 'wait outside.'

Anselm, suddenly calm, did as he was told without a word.

'You have let me down,' said Kalliovski as the door closed.

'No, master, it wasn't my fault. I did everything to the letter, but I wasn't to know they would find a body in the Hampstead pond, and that some buffoon would think it was Sido de Villeduval.'

Kalliovski sat looking at him. 'Then you had better find another way to bring Yann Margoza to me.'

'I have, I've got a plan. Anselm has already put it into action.'

'This does not reassure me,' said Kalliovski, as he slowly peeled off one of his red kid gloves.

Mesmerised, Mr Tull could not look away. He felt an insane urge to burst out laughing when he saw that the hand was just like any other man's. Slowly Kalliovski took off the second red, bright-red, poppy-red glove to reveal his other hand. A skeleton hand. He beckoned Mr Tull, spinning sticky threads of darkness from his fingers. Mr Tull moved closer and his screams choked in his throat as the skeleton hand almost throttled him to death.

'Do not fail me if you ever wish to grow cabbages in Kent.'

'I won't. I've got a plan,' gasped Mr Tull.

Next to see his master was Anselm.

'So, you think you are my son?' said Kalliovski. 'What makes you believe you could ever belong to me?'

Anselm felt his words, knife sharp, cutting through his reason. 'I was left in—'

'A basket of stinking animal entrails. But that doesn't make you my son. No, you see, you are a common murderer. Take the killing of Citizeness Manou. You kill like a coward, full of rage. Rage will be your undoing. I have never murdered anyone in anger.' As he said it, he thought he heard Anis laughing. 'Anger is an emotion that is useless unless properly controlled. It will destroy you.'

'I know I am—'

'Know? You don't know anything. You understand even less,' said Kalliovski. 'If you can bring me the shell from Sido de Villeduval's neck, then perhaps I will find some use for you. If you fail me in this . . .' Kalliovski was now beside him, his breath coffin stale. 'If you fail me, however hard you try to disappear, know this: I will find you. Were I you, I wouldn't trust my own shadow.'

Sido found herself once more dressed in a plain linen gown. This time the dance had nearly defeated her. Curled on the bed, her knees pulled up tightly towards her chest, she felt her courage ebb. The shadows were closing in and she knew she was completely alone. How long would this torture go on before Kalliovski decided to murder her? She closed her eyes against the inevitable and, for a moment she wasn't sure if she were asleep or awake, for when she opened them a woman was sitting beside her. Her clothes were colourful and bright; she was dressed as for some strange fete. Her hair was jet black, she had dark eyes, high cheekbones and a full mouth, and in that face Sido saw someone she recognised.

'I am Anis,' said the woman, 'mother of Yann. Come, I have something to show you.'

She held Sido's hand as the walls of bone faded and were replaced by a deep mist. When it cleared, they were walking over the rooftops of Paris and then down into a dark courtyard where the tumbrils waited to take the condemned to die.

Sido turned to look at Anis and said, 'What are we doing here? This is the Conciergerie.'

Anis put her finger to her lips as like two ghosts they drifted down the cold corridors. The smells and noises of the prison brought back memories of the Abbaye and filled Sido with dread. Now they were in a tiny cell and there, lying on a narrow bed, was a young man.

'No,' said Sido, 'no! What is Yann doing here? Tell me this is not so, tell me this hasn't happened.'

'This is now, and his end will be tomorrow, but for you.'

'I don't understand. You talk in riddles.'

'Go to him.'

Sido sat beside him. He looked through her and said to the air, 'Sido.'

'I am here.'

'He can't hear you,' said Anis, 'and he can't see you.

He is broken by the knowledge of who he believes his father to be. I would never have had him learn of it. It is this knowledge that makes him think you will love him no more.'

'That is not so. Why can't I tell him? Yann . . .'

'Come.'

'No, wait. I must tell him . . .'

She felt Anis's hand in hers and once more they were travelling, this time out of the city over tree tops to where, in a woodland clearing, a young man stood laughing among a group of gypsies. Sido wondered if this too were Yann, for he looked so like him.

'This is Manouche,' said Anis. 'This is the man I love. He is Yann's spirit father.'

Then Sido saw soldiers coming through the trees, saw bright flashes from their muskets.

'Warn them,' Sido shouted. 'Why don't they run? We must help them!'

'This is the past. What has been done is done. No tomorrows can unpick history.'

The guns fired again. The acrid smoke cleared and all was quiet, all were dead.

Once more Anis took Sido's hand and they rose higher to see scorched earth in the clearing below them. In the burned trees hung the bodies of the gypsies, like broken birds of paradise.

In the room of bone once more, Sido longed to hold fast to Anis so that she might never leave her. She felt Anis's fingers, velvet soft, touch her face as she whispered, as if in prayer:

'That is the shell of the shells he gave thee.
You are blessed, he loves thee much.
Don't be afraid, stand up.
He is within you as I am beside you,
You are one with us.
Yann is Manouche's ghost child. Don't lose faith.'

And she kissed her in the middle of her forehead and was gone.

The sleep that followed was deep and peaceful. Sido woke to find an angel in her room; his golden hair, his amber eyes so luminous that she wondered if she were still dreaming. She sat up knowing, as if Anis were whispering to her, that this was no angel. This was death's seducer.

Anselm, for once, was at a loss, for never before had he seen a creature more beautiful than himself.

'My master wants to know if you will give him the shell.' His voice was almost a whisper.

'No,' said Sido.

'My master says he will have it from you whether you are dead or alive.'

The memory of Anis's words gave her courage. 'Leave me be and tell your master my answer is still no.'

Anselm couldn't understand why he felt no anger. Usually by now such obstinancy would have been enough to rouse the red dragon in him, but looking into Sido's blue eyes he felt almost at peace, the voices in his head quietened, the flame beneath the cauldron of his fury spent.

He tried again, hoping to ignite something in himself that would make it possible to take hold of her and pull the shell from her neck. He went closer. It would be so easy, and then Kalliovski would embrace him as his son.

Sido stood up. For a moment he wasn't quite sure what had happened, for she began to fade away in front of his eyes. All he could see was a blinding light coming from the shell and it felt like the sun burning him.

Try as he might, he could get no closer and the light was so strong. He knew he was defeated and turning, he ran like the devil's own wind from the room. Outside, Milkeye watched him go and knew he wouldn't be returning.

Kalliovski, looking out of his window on to his artificial garden, was told of Anselm's failure.

'A pity. Sido leaves me no alternative,' he said.

Behind him stood the Seven Sisters and, from one glass eye of each, a tear rolled without permission down their dead skin faces.

'So,' said Kalliovski, 'there will be another to keep us company.'

He rose and, hauling on Balthazar's heavy chain, said to him, 'You may have the first and the last taste of her innocent beauty, that is my gift to you.'

At Sido's chamber, Kalliovski removed his poppy-red glove. From his skeleton finger tips, skeins of black threads hungrily searched out the lock in the iron door. At a signal from his master, Milkeye opened the leather case containing Remon Quint's key. The dark threads seemed to devour it as they pushed it into the lock. The door opened. Kalliovski freed Balthazar from his spiked collar and let the ravenous hound in, swiftly closing the door behind him. Sido's scream filled the air. As he walked away, his red-heeled boots clicking on the stone, he heard the howl of a hungry dog.

Chapter Twenty-Eight

'W hat is your name?' The prison governor looked down the list.

'Yann Margoza.'

He had been caught as he was leaving the café. He had no will to fight. In a strange way he was relieved that at last it was over. Death finally had hold of him.

'Well, now, isn't that interesting? And they tell me you're the Silver Blade. Are you?'

'There is no such person,' said Yann. 'It's a myth.'

'I agree. I wouldn't have believed it unless I'd been told,' said the governor, leaning back in the armchair. 'I always imagined the Silver Blade to be older and to be an Englishman.'

Yann stayed silent. He didn't feel that anything he had to say would make the situation any better.

The prisoner governor laughed. 'There I was, fishing for trout, when I went and caught myself the biggest pike in the river.'

He turned to the theatre manager. 'You have never heard of the Silver Blade either?'

Citizen Aulard shook his head, hoping to goodness Iago would keep quiet. Lord knows what Têtu had taught him to say.

'I would make the most of all that head-shaking while you still have one,' the governor said, pen in hand.

Yann concentrated hard on him; the pain was like burning rods pushing through his eyes. He knew his powers were nearly too weak to catch the governer's mind, full as it was with confused indictments.

The governor signed the paper before him and called for a turnkey. 'This one is to be taken to the Luxembourg prison.'

Citizen Aulard was completely baffled by what had just happened. The Luxembourg meant a chance of survival, whereas to remain at the Conciergerie was certain death. He was about to say something when the parrot squawked, '*Vive la Nation!*'

'That's a very talented bird you have there,' said the prison governor, indicating to the turnkey to take Citizen Aulard away.

He returned to the matter in hand. 'As for you, Citizen Margoza, and you, Citizen Didier, you two are under arrest on the serious charge of being counter-revolutionaries and working against this great and glorious Republic. Both of you will be sent for trial.' He nodded to the guard. 'Take them away.'

They walked along the dimly lit corridor, passing rows

of cells where the cries of anguished men could be heard.

In the last glimpse that Yann had of the outside world, the skies opened and rain splashed upon the cobbles, puffs of dust rising with the water. Citizen Aulard was standing in a wagon, soaking wet, looking more like a martyred saint than ever. Iago, on the other hand, his head held high, looked like a hero of the cause.

Yann was separated from Didier and escorted by three guards into a small cubicle, the floor of which was covered in hair. The barber, obviously drunk, stood swaying, a filthy leather apron tied round his waist. Yann struggled as he was pushed down in the chair, knowing what was to come.

'Cut it off,' said his guard.

'Will all the ladies be weeping?' the barber enquired, as he went to work.

Still Yann said nothing as the scissors cut irregular chunks off his hair. Chop, chop, chop. A foretaste of the blade to come.

'Makes it easier,' said the barber. He took a swig of wine from the bottle next to his instruments on the table. 'As I was saying, it makes it easier for the blade of the guillotine to cut through the flesh and bone.'

Yann was locked in a small cell containing a bed and a pail, which smelled as if it hadn't been emptied since the last occupant left.

Thunder started to rumble and lightning illuminated his cell. Lying on the hard wooden bed, he thought, tonight is my last night on earth, tomorrow my life will be over and I care little.

Yet he felt uneasy, not about his own death, no ... and in one flash of lightning it came to him. What if the body found in a Hampstead pond wasn't Sido's? Where was she? He sat upright. It was as if Sido were with him, beside him, giving him the answer. He was a fool not to have thought of it before, a dunce, a numbskull! And now he was caught, locked away in one of the most notorious prisons in France.

If she were alive, the only man who would have taken her was Count Kalliovski.

———◆———

A t about three in the morning, the grille in the iron door to Yann's cell slid open. He heard a guard ask, 'Is this the one?' Then, 'How do you want to do it?'

The door opened and Yann tried to see the threads of light. If he could make them work again he could escape. He looked from one prison guard to the other, but could only read their thoughts, a jumble which gave him no clues. Two more burst into the cell, pinning him down while his mouth was wrenched open and foul-tasting liquid was poured down his throat. Yann's eyes felt heavy and almost immediately his limbs seemed to fill with lead, his vision dissolved like ink in water, and he heard a crash, a curse, and smelled what must have been the spilled contents of the pail. The stench, as good as smelling salts, revived him, before more liquid was forced down his throat. He gagged. Lightning lit up the cell, and Milkeye's face loomed monster large over him, then all went black.

———◆———

Yann woke. His mouth was dry, his head hurt, his face was cut and bruised. He was lying on a damp stone floor in a vaulted chamber, the walls lined with human bones. It took a moment for the room to stop spinning, for him to find his feet. Now he was wide awake and, like a cat sensing danger, he took in his surroundings, looking for a way out. At one end of the chamber there was a door, while at the other side were two smaller doors under a wooden gantry. He could smell a familiar mustiness, which no amount of incense could hide. He knew he was under the city. Suddenly the chamber became ice cold.

He turned to face his fear and understood then that there is no greater devil than the fiend we invent for ourselves.

Had he really lost his powers because of this living waxwork? Let a man that was neither of the grave nor of life ruin his future? He thought back to when he had seen Kalliovski on the Pont Neuf before the mob claimed him. At least then he was made of flesh and blood. Now he bore merely a passing resemblance to the man he had once been. He was still immaculately dressed, his face waxen smooth, his hair powdered, and his eyes shining with an insect intensity. But they were the eyes of a dead man.

Yann watched Kalliovski pull off one of his red kid

gloves to reveal a skeleton hand. From his waistcoat pocket he took out a long silver chain at the end of which was a key. Idly he began to swing it back and forth.

'This is the key I commissioned Remon Quint to make. Do you know what it is the key to?'

'No,' said Yann.

'It is the key to your soul.'

Yann's laughter sounded like fresh water in a desert. 'You're mad if you think such a thing is possible! Quite mad, deluded by your own desire.'

'No,' said Kalliovski quietly. 'I am in earnest. If you show me the secret of the threads of light, I will give you back your soul.'

'I don't need your key to own my soul.'

'Don't you understand? I have Sido de Villeduval. I will give her her freedom, let you take her out of the catacombs, if you give me the secret of the threads of light.'

Yann felt a surge of strength. At last he was close to her. He would not fail. His words were measured. 'You, more than I, should know it is not mine to give away. It is within me, as is my heart and soul. The devil duped you. You are the one in chains.'

Kalliovski pointed his skeleton finger at Yann. For a moment Yann could not think what he was doing: then he saw dark sticky threads snake their way towards him. They wrapped themselves round his waist, lifting him towards the vaulted bare-boned ceiling.

Kalliovski released the dark threads and Yann tumbled

like a falling star on to the unforgiving floor.

'So, you have lost your powers,' said the Count. 'I should have known as much. What a pity. I was looking forward to a duel. My powers will never leave me. Unlike yours, they don't toss and turn on a sea of emotions. And there I was thinking that they might be something to master. You are not worthy to be my son.'

Yann became aware of a figure in the chamber, the woman he had seen in the field, all golden. He heard her laughing and knew Kalliovski heard her too.

'You are not my father,' said Yann, knowing that he was at last speaking the truth and feeling freedom in that knowledge. 'I am a ghost child. Listen, my mother is still laughing. Take me to Sido.'

'Certainly, but she is dead. You see, I asked her courteously for the talisman, but, as I said, she has a wilful streak. Or perhaps it was for love of you that she refused to relinquish it. I offered her Marie Antoinette's ruby necklace in exchange and still ... There was no alternative. I had to put Balthazar in with her, and he has an insatiable appetite for human flesh. No doubt he is licking her bones clean as we speak.'

'I don't believe you,' said Yann, knowing that if he showed any emotion all would be lost.

'It doesn't matter whether you believe me or not. If she's dead I will make her whole again. I have that power. She will be my finest automaton yet.'

Kalliovski clapped his hands.

'You shall see for yourself.'

Milkeye appeared and led Yann along a corridor, lined

with skeleton hands holding dripping candles.

At the door to Sido's chamber, the dog's barking, wild and furious, was deafening. Once more Kalliovski sent out the dark threads, turning the key slowly in the lock. Yann, his heart beating fast, felt he was standing on the very edge of his existence. If she was dead, he knew he had no soul to fight for.

He didn't flinch as the door creaked open. At first, all he could see was Balthazar, his troubled eyes all too human. The rest of the room was hidden by his bulk.

Yann could hear his thoughts: I have waited. Where have you been? I called for you and you didn't come, I followed you and you didn't see me.

It wasn't Yann who backed away, it was the master and his servant. Count Kalliovski, with a rattle and a clang, slammed the door shut. Yann was in the room with Balthazar.

And then there was silence except for Balthazar's panting. He stayed where he was until, hearing his master's red heels retreat down the corridor, he moved further into the chamber towards a bed where he lay down at Sido's feet.

She stood there, the tamer of wolves, in a white linen shift, her dark hair curled around her shoulders, her blue eyes shining like a cloudless day. Yann was filled with a wondrous relief. She was alive, unharmed. From the shell at her neck threads of light danced, spinning towards him, reeling him in. She shimmered as her hand touched his and, as he wrapped her in his arms, he felt the softness of her skin and the warmth of her body, made of the flesh and blood of mortality. He found her sweet mouth; her kiss sent a jolt right through him. The threads of light had returned to their master.

He whispered, 'Sido, if we get out of this, will you forgive ...?'

She kissed him. 'Balthazar and I have been waiting for you. He has been waiting a long, long time.'

Yann looked into the face of the great beast and began to talk to him as once, long ago, he had talked to him in the library at the Marquis de Villeduval's château.

And the great dog listened. The great dog spoke. Yann understood.

Standing, he held Sido once more to him. She smelled of the future, a perfume filled with the promise of life and days to come.

Chapter Twenty-Nine

It was the dog's size that undid Kalliovski. He could ignore Balthazar's human eyes, but this ... this tore at the worn fabric of his sanity. Memories, butchered and disjointed, came back to him: of a caravan, a baby crying, of Balthazar, his brown eyes devoted, of Anis telling him of the two roads she'd seen on his palm. He knew all too well the danger of letting light into rooms where no light has been. It illuminated images from a life he would rather not revisit. A grief was engulfing him, finding the cracks and fissures, tearing at the seams of his existence.

What was happening to him? A story, fragments of an old gypsy tale, jostled in his head: The day the devil went walking, looking for one irredeemable soul to blow his fiery life into. How did it go? He should remember. 'And he called to the devil's dog and the devil's dog said, "Master, I am here to take you …" '

'Stop it, stop it! Silence! Why isn't there silence?'

Milkeye looked at his master. He'd never seen him like this before. Kalliovski pulled off his red glove and stared at his skeleton hand as if expecting it to turn to dust.

'If I had the threads of light I would be whole again, complete. I must have the threads of light.'

Balthazar's howl, low and long, rumbled like thunder through the echo-less chambers. A warning from the mouth of hell.

'He's coming for me. He's coming for me. I must stop him.'

There was a deafening sound as if a battering ram were knocking down the door. Kalliovski did his best to concentrate on the dark threads and nothing else, but still there was the endless noise in his head, like the chattering teeth of the keymaker before he was killed.

Then all was eerily quiet and Kalliovski knew Yann's threads of light had defeated the keymaker's masterpiece. He heard the iron claws approach and Balthazar, magnificent, majestic, walked in, head held high, Sido and Yann in his wake. Kalliovski stood straight, determined that this must be his victory. He had planned it all and this hour had been purchased by him. As Balthazar stared at his master, unblinking, he threw out the dark threads.

'Stop it, stop it,' shouted Kalliovski. 'Quiet! Silence! Don't look at me!'

The threads snaked towards Balthazar and plaiting themselves together, formed a hangman's knot round his neck. The great dog's gaze never left his master. Kalliovski's laughter filled the chamber and he pulled with all his might, tighter and tighter, forcing open the monstrous mouth. No more would men be killed by those jaws. Still the dog stared with knowing eyes while the dark threads cut into his coal-black fur. Then his huge paws slid, and he lay on the ground, his countenance ghastly, his tongue lolling, his blank eyes accusing the master who had slain him. Inky liquid oozed from between his steely teeth. The enormous beast was no more.

'You thought you could outwit me,' said Kalliovski, his reason teetering on the brink of madness. 'I will be all powerful, I will have the light and the dark, I will have my revenge. Take off the talisman.'

As Yann took the shell from Sido's neck he was illuminated, made radiant by the power of the *baro seroeske sharkuni*. He held it out to Kalliovski.

'No!' Kalliovski bellowed, nearly blinded as the light grew stronger, encompassing Sido. 'Stand away from her or I will kill her, like I killed . . .' He stopped, pierced by the sharp bee sting of a memory. How did the story go? The devil's dog . . . what was it Anis had told him when she had seen his future, all those years ago? Two roads, one light, one dark . . .

'Like you killed my mother? You will not take Sido from me.'

'You cannot stop me. You do not have the power or the intelligence. I see nothing of myself in you.'

'And I thank Anis for that. You have no hold over me. I am certain of my powers. I will not be dragged into your darkness.' Then Yann said, in Romany, 'You know your end.'

He walked towards Kalliovski holding the shell as he would a shield. He stopped, and kneeling, laid the shell on Balthazar's body. As it touched him, the floor began to ripple, the centre became a whirling vortex. Yann caught hold of Sido as the great dog was sucked down, down, down into the abyss.

Breaking the doom-filled silence that followed, Yann said, 'Shall I tell you the story of the devil's dog?'

'What use have I for stories?'

'Every man who is foolish enough to do a deal with the devil is given a dog,' said Yann, as the threads of light began to dance from him. 'The dog at first is his companion, but it grows with every evil deed his master does until it's of a size to take him down to meet the lord of the underworld.'

Once again came a flicker on the flintstone of Kalliovski's mind, igniting a memory so bright, so intense that it seemed to wound him fatally.

'She told me that story,' he said. 'I thought she loved me. Anis told me that story.'

Suddenly filled with rage, he threw the threads of darkness towards Yann. They fell, impotent, to the floor.

Thunder rolled from the bottom of the earth, as if

Hell's orchestra was tuning up, shaking the great chamber and rattling the walls of bone.

The floor began to ripple beneath Kalliovski as from the vortex rose the distant sound of Lucifer's anvil, and the panting of a great beast. Balthazar reappeared, quite transformed. His coat was burning flames of fury, his eyes the colour of hot coals, his mouth dripping with molten saliva, scorching the ground.

Too late, Kalliovski remembered. 'No, go back,' he screamed, 'I didn't call for you!'

'But the devil did,' said Yann.

Again Kalliovski threw the dark threads but they were no defence against such a force as this. Balthazar clamped his jaws on the screaming figure of Kalliovski. In the intense heat Kalliovski's face began to melt, the dark threads, flowing like Medusa's hair, trailed behind him as he was dragged down.

The devil's dog, the hound of hell, had come to take his master home.

Kalliovski's screams were drowned by the singing of the Seven Sisters Macabre, their ethereal voices ringing out:

'Damask and death.

Velvet and violence.

Brocade and blood.'

Still he fought with all that was left of his strength. His skeleton arm appeared, his hand clutched at Milkeye's ankle. Like a madman he tried to kick himself free of his master, but to no avail. He was pulled closer and closer to the edge. As he stood tottering on the brink, one of the Seven Sisters Macabre pushed him over.

The floor started to whirl again.

Yann held on tightly to Sido as the bony walls began to crumble. He knew they had to escape before the whole edifice collapsed.

One of the Sisters put a hand out to stop him. 'Only you can free us,' she whispered. 'Your survival depends on it.'

'What must I do?'

'Call Balthazar.'

Yann whistled for the dog, fearful that he was too late.

Then Balthazer emerged, no longer a monster, but the ghost of the puppy he had once been. Wagging his tail, he leaped up at Yann, and then jumped with joy at each of the Seven Sisters Macabre. Out of their battered and tortured carcasses emerged the ghosts of seven beautiful women, at long last set free, at long last at peace.

'Come with us,' they beckoned.

Yann was conscious of a blinding light. Then he and Sido were in a meadow full of poppies, the Seven Sisters running through the tall grasses, laughing, chasing Balthazar towards the poplar trees.

Their voices sang out 'We are birds, we are free . . .'

———◆———

Yann had no memory of how he got back to the theatre. It was Basco, who seeing what he thought were two ghosts, raised the alarm. Têtu came running down the stairs, a sword in his hand, to see Yann and Sido, covered in dust. At Sido's neck was the shell of the shells.

———◆———

T hat July morning a building in the rue des Couteaux collapsed into the catacombs. It had happened before; no doubt it would happen again. This time the disaster took only one shop. No one was quite sure how many were buried in the rubble. It was days later that they found the body of Serreto.

Chapter Thirty

D idier couldn't stand the noise of the prison. All night long it sounded like some grotesque engine fuelled by fear. It gurgled, its belly rumbling, as if it were by degrees digesting its inmates. Just when he felt he had the measure of the infernal racket he was wrong-footed by the voice of a woman singing. Her song rose, to be caught like a butterfly in an iron net.

In his windowless cell with no light, all Didier had for company were these voices. He sat upright on the edge of his wooden bed refusing sleep. It wasn't worth it; after all he would be sent to his eternal rest soon enough.

At six in the morning, his cell was beginning to feel hot and airless. The iron grille in the door slid open and a clerk with ink-stained fingers pushed through a piece of paper with his indictment.

'Your trial's this afternoon.'

Didier didn't bother to try to read it. He knew it was his death sentence.

The grille in the door still being open, he shouted for a guard. A man came limping, dragging his leg behind him. He had a kinder face than his fellow jailers.

'What is it, citizen?'

Didier handed him some money.

'Can you find out what's happened to a young man by the name of Yann Margoza? He was arrested with me last night.'

'Keep your money,' said the guard, and Didier thought he was going to walk away. Instead he said, 'Yann Margoza? That name rings a bell. I once came across a lad with that name, working with a dwarf, if I remember correctly?'

'Perhaps. Why?' replied Didier, seeing a ray of hope. 'Do you know him?'

'Yes and no. He never said his name, but afterwards, I made enquiries.'

'After what?'

'It was in the great winter of 'eighty-nine. Back then I was a coachman. I worked for the Vicomtesse de Lisle. I gave a lad and a dwarf a lift back to Paris from the old de Villeduval estate. Saved my life, that boy did. I often wonder what happened to them two. Honourable. Not a word you can use much these days, but that's what those two gypsies were. Honourable.'

'That's Yann Margoza all right. How did he save your life?'

'The horses took fright on an icy road. Fireworks made them bolt. I thought we'd had it. The lad climbed down from the carriage, as bold as brass, and managed to mount one of the horses. He whispered into their ears, and blow me down if they didn't come to a halt. Yes, I tell you, I'd be a dead man if it weren't for Yann Margoza.'

'Will you find out if he's here?' asked Didier.

'Leave it with me. My name's Dufort.'

At half-past two the door to Didier's cell was opened. He was taken through the wicket gates to a courtyard where fourteen prisoners were already walking up and down, a rag, tag and bobtail collection of men. Ten were young wags, well dressed and well fed. They swanked around, bolstering themselves with fighting talk, each telling the other that he was innocent.

'I am a true revolutionary,' said one.

'We'll be in Moët's Tavern before the day is done,' said another.

'I shall be in my mistress's arms before the night is through,' said a third.

Didier, always an observer, watched as one of their party boasted of what he would do when called before the Public Prosecutor.

'After all,' he added, 'it was I who designed the playing cards for the Republic.'

The three priests took no notice of the young dilettantes. Neither did a man who looked mad, his beard white, almost down to his feet, with bits of straw and food in it, his clothes torn and tattered.

Didier breathed in the fresh air, tilting up his head, drawing down the sky. The prison courtyard was surrounded on all sides by the Conciergerie walls and the gothic towers of the Palace of Justice, yet he could see a cockade of white sky high above, and he watched the swallows swooping, wishing with all his being that he too might sprout wings and fly.

———◆———

Later that morning Didier, chained to his fellow prisoners, waited in the corridor. Fifteen prisoners in all, to be seen by the judge in small groups. Didier, his back against the stone wall, waited for the first five to come out.

Dufort sidled up to him. 'He's not here.'

'But he must be,' said Didier.

'A man took him away last night. Where to, they wouldn't say.'

Dufort was interrupted by the sergeant. 'What are you doing, talking to the prisoner?'

Dufort stood to attention. He sighed, looking along the line of men left waiting to be sent for trial. Were any of them guilty? He thought back to the days when he had worked for the Viscountess. She would turn in her grave if she could see her old Dufort a guard in this most notorious of prisons. True, she was mean, stingy, and her monkey had been a pest, yet for all that, when she died, just after the fall of the Bastille, she had left him her house to look after. As long as her monkey lived longer than four years the house would be his. That was almost five years ago and the monkey was still alive.

Dufort was a decent man. He wondered if Yann had been transferred to another prison, or already sent to the guillotine. If that were the case he could at least do something to help the lad's friend.

Watching the sergeant walk away, he once more went up to Didier. 'Where's the dwarf?'

'At the Circus of Follies in the Place de Manon.'

<hr />

Dufort had managed to get an hour off a day, pleading the needs of a child in his care. What he didn't say was that the child was a monkey. He liked to keep an eye on the Viscount, as he called him, even though his wife was just as capable. He made a detour to the Place de Manon, arriving at the theatre, out of breath, to find it apparently abandoned. He knocked on the stage door anyway. At last it was opened by Têtu, a huge sword in his hand.

'I'm a friend. I mean you no harm. I come from the Conciergerie. Didier told me where to find you. Please, we need to talk. My name is Dufort. I was a coachman for the Vicomtesse de Lisle.'

Têtu looked at him, uncertain.

'Do you remember? I gave you a lift to Paris from the de Villeduval chateau, in the winter before the fall of the Bastille?'

Têtu was still studying him. 'Yes,' he said slowly. 'I remember you.'

'Yann Margoza saved my life that night and I want to repay the debt. Is there anything I can do to help you?'

'We need somewhere to hide.'

'I have a house that no one will search and is safe.' He leaned forward. 'It's the residence of the late Viscountess.'

Têtu put down the sword and shook Dufort's hand.

Yann appeared at the top of the stairs.

Dufort nodded. 'Come with me,' he said.

Didier was in the last batch of accused to be sent before the judge, who was an imposing sight, severe in his black hat and cloak with his dark hair and eyebrows.

'You,' said the judge to the designer of cards, 'you have a brother who is an aristocrat and an émigré.'

'No, no, sir, I have no brother,' replied the young man, seeing a glimmer of hope. There had, after all, been a misunderstanding. 'I am an only child. I live with my mother, a widow.'

'Quiet!' boomed the judge. 'As I said, you have a brother and a father who are both émigrés and who have escaped to London, working for the British government.'

The young man looked dumbfounded. 'No, no, that's not—'

'Quiet!' shouted the judge, turning his attention to the next prisoner.

Didier had decided to say nothing. There was no justice here.

'Well, mooncalf, what have you to say in your defence?' said the judge. 'You've been denounced as a traitor and a spy.'

Seeing that Didier wasn't in the mood to argue his case, the judge moved on with relish to the poor man with the long white beard.

'Name?'

'The Duc de—'

The judge didn't even let him finish.

All the men were found guilty as charged.

Chapter Thirty-One

B asco, beside himself, was hardly aware of anything as he walked blindly along the street.

He as good as jumped out of his skin when someone grabbed his sleeve, and a man in a battered hat said, 'Slow down, my friend.'

'Yann,' said Basco. 'Oh, thank goodness.'

Yann put his finger to his lips.

'What has happened to Didier?'

'He was found guilty along with fourteen others. He has been condemned to death. They are taking him to the Place du Trône. We must do something.'

'What about Citizen Aulard?'

'He's not on today's list,' said Basco.

Yann and Basco mingled with the jeering crowd across the Pont au Change, then through the rue de la Coutellerie to the Faubourg St-Antoine. It had been Robespierre who had ordered the removal of the guillotine from the Place de la Révolution to the Place du Trône.

His excuse for its removal was that it would waken the sleepier parts of Paris to the true meaning of the terror. Those on the executioner's tumbril had a longer, slower journey in which to contemplate the injustice of their sentences.

***

Didier, staring down from the cart, was unaware of his friends in the sea of faces. He stood taller than the rest of his companions in the tumbril. Next to him was a girl who reminded Didier of a young deer, fresh-faced, her whole life before her and about to be cut short. He heard her sob and say a 'Hail Mary' under her breath.

'I'm frightened,' she whispered. 'They took my mother and I can't see which cart she's in.'

'Give the lady your seat,' Didier said to the man sitting next to him.

'What's the point,' he replied. 'We're all dead.'

'Listen to me. Look at that crowd. You know why they're jeering?'

'The same reason I jeered when I went to see the guillotine. They're grateful it's not them.'

'Yes,' said Didier, 'and did you shout louder when you saw a man stumble, when a woman pissed herself?'

'For my sins, I did.'

'And did you feel humbled when a man walked with his head held high and showed courage?'

'Yes.'

'Then hold your head high, be proud that for the

moment it's still connected to your body, and for the sake of this young terrified girl, be a man.'

The procession continued its agonisingly slow journey and when they reached the rue du Faubourg St-Antoine, in sight of the Bastille, Didier looked up to see the sky darkening.

Yann and Basco had so far failed to attract his attention, and Yann was beginning to think that saving Didier might be beyond him, for the crowd was clumped together, a wall that seemed impossible to break through.

Suddenly the sky turned black, pitch black. The gods were angry. Thunder rolled over Paris, Zeus sent lightning to rend the sky and rain fell in huge gobbets, giant spit balls that bounced and burst in small puddles. The mob, frightened by the power of the elements, hurried for shelter in doorways and shop fronts. Only Yann stood in the rain, soaking wet. Taking off his hat, his face illuminated as lightning flashed through the sky, he opened his long pale coat, which in the eerie light was incandescent, like butterfly wings.

Didier saw him then, silver in the storm, like an avenging angel, and his spirits rose.

Balling his huge hand into a fist he tipped back his head. 'I knew he wouldn't let me down. I knew it!' He turned to the girl. 'Don't give up hope. Keep praying.'

The rain was still falling by the time the guillotine came into view. The stalwarts of the scaffold did not care about the weather, as long as heads fell as well. They had claimed their seats, waiting for the drama to begin.

The girl's cries could be heard loud and clear above

the din of the storm as she called for her mother.

The guards, soaked through, took their places round the tumbrils. The executioner and his two attendants examined their human cargo. The executioner enjoyed making the most of their misery, for the crowd fed off the drama of these executions. The girl was exactly the kind of rosy plum he liked to begin with. He ordered the guard to pull her out. As she clung to Didier the guard wrenched her away. Didier had tears in his eye and a lump of fury in his throat. He would willingly kill all the guards, and the executioner.

'Be brave,' he said, as the girl was taken screaming from him.

A woman's voice cried, 'Odette, where is my Odette?'

'*Maman!* Don't let me die!' the girl screamed, 'Help me, someone, help me!'

'Come on,' said the guard. 'Let's get this young aristo executed. Bring the mother, let her watch.'

Didier shouted to Yann, 'Don't worry about me, save her!'

Basco eased himself closer to the tumbrils as the girl was brutally dragged to the scaffold, screaming, fighting and kicking for all she was worth.

'Let's see,' one of the old hags shouted.

The executioner tore off her hat.

'Oh, she's a piece of liquorice if ever I saw one!' shouted one of her companions.

The girl, still sobbing, was tied to the plank.

The drums started to roll. The blade fell, to the screams of the mother and the cheers of the onlookers, then came to a shuddering halt, less than a metre above the girl's head.

Yann, throwing his voice across the boom of the thunder, shouted, 'Set the innocent free.'

The mob went silent, wondering what could have gone wrong.

Yann, his head aching, held tight the threads of light, keeping the silver blade fastened in midair.

Basco took his chance while the guards all had their heads turned towards the guillotine. He leaped on to the cart and cut the ropes tying Didier. Didier jumped down and, to a great cheer from the onlookers, pulled back the plank and untied the terrified girl. Yann could see that the guards were about to fire at Didier, and he threw threads of light round them, pinning them down as Didier hoisted the girl over his shoulder. Basco, still on the tumbril, cut the ropes of the other prisoners.

Only the executioner was free to examine his killing machine. Yann let go of the threads and the blade fell, too quickly for the executioner to remove his hand and in horror he stared at the stump, screaming in agony as his blood spurted over the knitting women.

In the chaos that followed, the prisoners clambered down the carts and ran to freedom. Some of the mob who tried to stop them found themselves pulled out of the crowd as if caught on a giant's fishing line, to be left hanging from the top of the guillotine like dead crows.

The mob was terrified. The old hags by the scaffold saw their knitting unravel. Hats flew off heads; swords fell out of their sheaths. The crowd began to disperse hurriedly. Was the Supreme Being sitting in judgement on them?

Rejoining Basco, Didier said, 'We'd best get Yann and be gone.'

Yann was so drunk with exhaustion that Didier had to prop him up.

'Is he all right?' said Basco.

'Yes. It takes its toll, working the threads of light,' said Didier, setting off towards the Circus of Follies.

'Not that way,' said Basco, 'Yann told me we should go to the house of a Citizen Dufort.'

'Dufort?' said Didier. 'Well, I never.'

'Têtu and Signorina Sido are there already,' said Basco.

***

It didn't take them all that long to find the house, well hidden behind a rusty gate in a deserted street. If they hadn't known better, they would have thought that it had been long abandoned.

Têtu came out to greet them, followed by Dufort, who took them into the kitchen where a meal was already laid and waiting.

'It's good to see you,' said Dufort to Didier.

'I didn't imagine . . .' He stopped. 'You're a good man, Dufort.'

'Tell us what happened,' said Têtu.

Didier started to relate the story.

Yann was beginning to feel more like himself. 'Têtu,' he asked, 'where is Sido?'

'Upstairs, sleeping.'

Yann left the merry party to go and find her.

The house was strangely preserved, wrapped up in huge dustsheets as if at any moment it would be brought back to life by tall-wigged, corseted women and elegant men.

Yann, uncertain of which way to go, spied a monkey in a wig and wearing full court dress. It jumped on to the shrouded furniture and sped towards him screeching, its teeth glimmering white, then stopped abruptly and banged on one of the doors in the corridor before running off.

As Yann watched it go, the door opened and there stood Sido. She threw her arms around him.

'Oh, thank goodness, you are safe.'

Whatever he had planned to say, to do, was lost the moment he saw her. He held her like a starving man and kissed her, not knowing how long it was since he had been this hungry, thinking it must have been years. He could feel her, feel her hunger as great as his. He knew then that there was an element beyond himself; a river, and he was weightless in its warm waters. He longed to understand its tides; pulled by its urgency, he was aware of the wave breaking, his whole being lost, drowning as it emerged breathless in another soul, knowing that this was the pull of the tide, this was the flow and the ebb, this was what love could do, transport you until you reached the sea, where the waves rise higher still, waiting, white-tipped and rolling. He was there and she was there and this was theirs and theirs alone, as if they were one, washed gently up on a longed-for distant shore, a land that would take a lifetime of togetherness to explore.

E arly next morning Anselm arrived in the rue de la Culture Ste-Catherine. Colombine had hoped never to see him again, after what had happened at the Conciergerie. He had been released along with the other actors, but everyone knew who was responsible for betraying Yann. Colombine had told Anselm that their marriage was over. Every one of the company had felt wretched and Colombine, returning home, was disgusted with herself for being duped into turning traitor. Now here he was again with a mad, demonic glint in his eyes. His clothes were torn, his neckcloth filthy, he stank of drink.

She wanted to slam the door in his face, but he barged past her.

'Aren't you pleased to see me?' he said. 'I've brought a friend with me, Mr Tull.'

Colombine took one look at the dishevelled figure and recoiled.

'Don't he look a picture?' said Anselm, rummaging around to see if there was anything to drink. Finding a half-finished bottle, he tipped it down his throat so fast that wine dripped from his chin on to his waistcoat.

He went to kiss Colombine. His breath reeked of rotten fish.

Colombine pushed him away. 'Get off me. I think you should leave and take that man with you.'

'That's not very nice. That's no way to treat me, is it, Mr Tull? And she's hurt your feelings, hasn't she?'

'Come on, Anselm, let's get out of here. Has she got any money?'

'You heard him. Have you?'

'No. I have nothing. Just leave, for goodness' sake.'

'You and me are in this together.'

'Get off me.'

'Oh no, Mr Tull. She's cross with her Anselm. What shall we do with her?'

'Get out, both of you.'

Anselm slapped her across the face. 'Now, that's not nice.' He pushed her up against the wall. 'Have you seen Yann Margoza?'

'He's in prison, awaiting trial, that's what I heard.'

'I wish that were so, but unfortunately you're wrong.

Don't worry, though, I'm going to kill him for what he's done, before the day is out. Oh dear, a tear. Look, Mr Tull, she's crying. Happy to see me at last.'

'Leave her,' said Mr Tull. 'We have bigger fish to catch.'

Anselm still held her. 'Give us a kiss for goodbye, and tell Yann Margoza I will be waiting for him at the theatre,' he said, and as Colombine turned her face from him, he punched her so hard it took her breath away.

She waited until they had gone before setting off in search of the only member of the theatre company she knew might not wholeheartedly shun her.

Basco, sitting in his usual place in the Café de Foy in the Palais-Royal, was caught up in the middle of a heated debate.

'I tell you,' said the waiter, 'Robespierre shot himself, that's what I've heard, trying to avoid the guillotine.'

'In the jaw? Why wouldn't he have done the job properly? No, I think someone took a shot at him, a member of the National Assembly.'

'Well, it don't matter,' said the barman. 'What matters is that he will be dead today without a trial, so I hear. They're moving the guilliotine back to the Place de la Révolution so that everyone can see the bastard die.'

'A tragedy,' said the *sans-culotte* sitting at the table opposite. 'A tragedy. France will be lost without him.' He stared into his glass. 'Robespierre was a great man, a priest, a philosopher. You agree, citizen, don't you?' he said, addressing Basco.

'No, I don't,' replied Basco. 'I don't. I think he's a

villain. I see nothing incorruptible about him. I see a villain who gets other men to carry out his murders.'

'How can you say that?' said the *sans-culotte*. 'He isn't responsible for what the Tribunal decides.'

'Do you want to fight? Do you? I am the great Basco!'

'Calm down, the pair of you,' said the waiter.

The *sans-culotte*, seeing that he might well have met his match, shrugged his shoulders and mumbled under his breath, 'You're wrong, the Republic will live to regret this day.' He headed for the door and nearly bumped into Colombine.

Basco, pleased to have won his point and still fired up with the need for a fight, felt in the mood for giving Colombine the rough edge of his tongue. He was about to set to when he noticed the beads of sweat on her ashen face.

His fury began to fade as gallantry overtook him.

'Are you all right? You don't look well.'

'I saw Anselm,' she said, having trouble speaking. It was hurting to breathe. 'I must have run too fast, I have a terrible stitch in my side. He's threatening to kill Yann ... please, we must do something! He says he'll wait for Yann at the theatre.'

Basco noticed a small purple stain on her dress. As she talked, it began to spread.

Colombine, glancing down, saw it too and moved her hand there, lifting it to find it covered in blood. She looked horrified.

'Where's that come from?' she said, her eyes flashing

in panic at the sudden realisation of what Anselm had done.

Basco gently laid her on the floor, took off his coat, and rolled it up for a pillow.

'Get a surgeon. Now, man!' he said to the waiter.

'Don't leave me,' said Colombine, clinging to his hand. 'I don't want to die, don't let me die.'

He pushed the hair out of her eyes.

'Shh, *bella ragazza*, it's all right.'

Colombine, with tears spilling down her cheeks, said, 'I did the right thing, coming here, didn't I?'

'Yes, *cara mia*. I will find him and tell him you came.'

She lifted her fingers towards his face. Then her voice fell away with her hand.

The surgeon arrived soon after, but he was too late. Colombine was already dead.

Basco, kneeling beside her, noticed that the surgeon had left his house wearing his slippers. Such a foolish thing, but the ordinariness of it was strangely comforting.

Outside, people were singing, celebrating the impending death of Robespierre. An impromptu band played. A man in an oddly old-fashioned hat went past, banging a child's drum and singing the Marseillaise. A lad shouted in at the doorway, 'This is a day to remember!'

Basco knew it was a day he would never forget. Crossing himself, he bent down and closed Colombine's eyes.

He pulled himself together. There was no time to be lost. He must find Yann.

———◆———

Yann lay in bed that late summer's morning, his limbs entwined with Sido's. He was lost to the season and the time of day. He became sleepily conscious when he heard someone tapping gently on the door. Careful not to wake Sido, he disentangled himself and pulling on his breeches went to the door.

'I'm sorry to disturb you,' said Têtu, 'but it's late.'

Yann pulled the door behind him.

'Colombine has been murdered.'

'By Anselm?' said Yann, saddened at the predictability of it.

Têtu nodded. 'She found Basco before she died. She was desperate to warn you that Anselm is out to kill you too. He told Colombine he would wait for you at the theatre.'

Yann went back into the room and gathered his clothes. Sido lay lost in dreams, all sleepy like a meadow on a hot summer's day. Bending over her, he kissed her softly.

'I love you,' he whispered.

Têtu was waiting at the top of the stone staircase as Yann quietly closed the chamber door.

'Didier should go with you,' said Têtu, as if he had been giving the matter considerable thought.

'No,' said Yann, 'this is something I need to do on my own.'

'It's too dangerous,' said Têtu, following Yann down the stairs into the large cool marble hall.

'I owe you an apology,' said Yann.

'You owe me nothing.'

'I want you to know this.'

'No, no, I don't need to know anything. I know it already.'

'Will you be quiet, you old cantankerous dwarf, and let me say my piece?'

Têtu crossed his arms and stared belligerently at the opposite wall.

Yann laughed. 'This is what I want you to know, just this and nothing more. I have a father, the best father I could ever have had; I have a friend, the best I could have had, and both these people are you, Têtu. It's because of you that I am who I am, and I would never have it differently.'

'Being in love can make a man quite sentimental, you know,' said Têtu curtly.

'I meant what I said.'

'Cordell has sent word that arrangements are being made to take Sido back to London with all speed. I am to take her to him today.'

'No,' said Yann firmly. 'You're taking her nowhere. She's staying with me. If Cordell wants to do anything, he can concentrate on getting Citizen Aulard out of prison. Do you understand?'

Têtu sighed. 'Yes. I understand perfectly that Sido's aunt would be beside herself with anger if she knew what her niece had been up to.'

670

Yann, unable to help himself, smiled. Regardless of Têtu's look of annoyance, he lifted him off his feet and kissed him on both cheeks. 'If anything happens to me, you will look after Sido? If she wants, take her with you and Citizen Aulard to America . . .'

'Put me down. What on earth has come over you?' said Têtu, battling with an irritating wave of emotion that was making him feel grumpy. 'Of course, and you know that.'

'And you are not to let Cordell make any arrangements.'

'I promise.'

'Good. Tell me, old gypsy, do I have death on me today?'

Têtu said nothing.

'I do, don't I?'

Têtu's face was grave as he nodded. 'Let's say he is close on your heels. Don't let him catch you, Yannick.'

'Look after her, you bad-tempered old dwarf.'

The shadows drew in around Yann as Têtu watched him go. He closed the door and saw Sido standing at the top of the stairs. Panic rose in him. The talisman. Where was the talismann?

Holding on to the bannisters, she came down and, as if she had read his mind said, 'It's all right, he has it safe on him.'

Citizen Aulard was freed from the Luxembourg prison the following day. He was quite baffled by the turn of events that had led to his safe delivery from the clutches of the Tribunal. He had Iago to thank for his new-found freedom, for the parrot had spent his entire time in prison rousing the inmates and prison officers alike with his patriotic fervour and his whistling of the Marseillaise. It became apparent to all that Citizen Aulard was a man of the moment, a man of the Revolution, for anyone who had spent so much time training a parrot to speak like this could only be innocent of all charges.

His release had happened so quickly that it had gone unnoticed by Basco, whose job it was to keep an eye on the day's lists of those who were to be taken to the guillotine.

So it was that Citizen Aulard and Iago returned to the theatre to find it deserted and, having not slept in ages, the good citizen lay down on his chaise longue, and both bird and man fell fast asleep.

Mr Tull, creeping into the theatre later that day, wasn't as set on the plan as Anselm. He was a man of limited imagination and couldn't see how it would be possible for Yann to teach Anselm those sort of tricks. After all, Anselm wasn't that bright. But whether he liked it or not, the lad had a point. They were broke, stony broke, for with the loss of his master went the loss of his income.

Mr Tull had never been that keen on theatres. Places like this gave him the creeps: too many things to hide behind, too many ghosts. He felt better killing a man out in the open, but Anselm was more than at home here. He knew exactly where to go and what he was looking for.

'Do you think he will come?' asked Mr Tull.

'Oh, he'll come all right.'

'Why?'

'Because I killed Colombine.'

At first Mr Tull wasn't sure he had heard right. 'No, you didn't. She was alive when we left her.'

Anselm, his face shining, said, 'I didn't work with Butcher Loup without learning where to put the knife in. Let's just say he'll come.'

'What's that noise?'

'Shush,' said Anselm.

They waited in a dark recess.

Citizen Aulard had woken and, thinking he heard voices, wandered down to the stage, hopeful of seeing Têtu. Instead, there before him, looking quite deranged, stood Anselm.

***

Yann had not been expecting anyone else at the theatre apart from Anselm. He walked on to the stage to find him with a pistol in his hand and a knife in his belt, his eyes flickering. Then he saw Mr Tull twisting Citizen Aulard's arm up his back and holding a gun to his head.

'If you do any of your magic tricks,' said Anselm, 'Mr Tull here will kill him. I mean it.'

'What is it you want with me?' asked Yann.

'What do you think? I want what's mine, to know how the threads of light work. You see,' said Anselm, coming closer, 'Count Kalliovski meant me to have the gift of the threads of light. He promised as much. It doesn't belong to you. Do you know why?'

Yann said nothing.

'Well, then, I'll tell you. Because I know I'm his son. He didn't realise it, but I know. I heard voices, they told

674

me it was so. They are telling me now. I am his rightful son and heir, not you.'

'Hold on a mo,' said Mr Tull, 'what are you rambling on about? He didn't have a son.'

'Shut up, Tull, I ain't speaking to you.'

'I was born with the gift,' said Yann slowly, all the time thinking how to get Citizen Aulard out of this alive. 'My magic belongs to the light.'

'I'm getting very angry,' said Anselm, 'aren't I, Mr Tull? He isn't hearing what I'm saying, is he?'

'That's right,' replied the old rogue, his eyes glued to his worrying erstwhile protégé.

Yann looked at Citizen Aulard and said calmly, 'I'm glad to see they released you.'

'I'm so sorry, I should have—'

'Shut your mouths,' said Anselm. 'Come on. Unless you tell me the secret of your magic, I'll kill him.'

'Let him go.'

Anselm burst out laughing. 'Got you now, haven't I?' He pulled back the trigger and pointed his weapon straight at Citizen Aulard's heart. 'His death will be your fault.'

Mr Tull, seeing what Anselm was about to do, yelled, 'Wait a minute – I'm holding him!'

'Well, don't,' shouted Anselm.

At that moment, as Mr Tull let go of Citizen Aulard, Iago flew on to the stage, straight at the startled Anselm. His pistol went off.

Yann saw the smoke, and for a fraction of a second relived the nightmare that had haunted him since boyhood, the moment the old magician Topolain had failed to catch the bullet. He concentrated all his powers and reached with his mind's eye for the missile.

Yann looked at his hand. It was covered in blood, but he had caught the bullet.

Citizen Aulard stumbled into the darkness backstage. As Anselm reloaded, Yann threw out the threads of light to catch the pistol, missing his target as Anselm darted up the stairs to the fly tower. There among the ropes and lanterns he looked down on the stage, took aim at Yann and fired. To his astonishment, his second bullet found its mark in Mr Tull's shoulder.

Yann followed Anselm up the fly tower. He flicked out the threads of light and, lifting him off his feet, hung him like a pendulum above the stage.

Mr Tull rose unsteadily, murder glittering in his eyes. He had had enough, more than enough of Anselm Loup. Seeing him hovering there, he knew what he was going to do.

'Get me down, Tull,' shouted Anselm.

Mr Tull pulled back the trigger and fired his pistol at Anselm's rotten heart.

———◆———

E very citizen in Paris would be able to tell you exactly where they were on the day of Robespierre's execution. Paris was in a holiday mood, the streets hummed with people, there was an air of excitement. The Terror was ending and France stood at the dawn of a new era.

The two lovers, oblivious to everything but each other,

walked, hand in hand, against the tide of the crowd.

At the Jardin du Luxembourg they strolled along a winding gravel path.

'Without the Revolution,' said Yann, as they sat under a grove of chestnut trees, 'we would never have been together and I wouldn't be able to ask you this. Will you marry me?'

Sido, her blue eyes shining, said, 'With all my heart, yes,'

'Even if your aunt and uncle don't give their consent?'

'Yes. As long as you promise me we won't have an ordinary life, and that whatever we do, we'll do it together.'

He laughed and, wrapping her in his arms, kissed her. 'It will be filled with adventures. This is the just the beginning, I promise.'

Chapter Thirty-Four

Henry Laxton sat in his study in Queen Square, having just finished reading the letters that had arrived that morning from Paris. Leaning back in his chair, he looked out of the study window at the sun-dappled leaves of the oak tree in the garden and remembered the day he had first seen Yann. Who would have thought then ...? Oh, well. Life is a strange affair.

Among the letters, one had finally arrived from The Travellers Arms. It was not, as the writer, a Mr Suter, reported, the cleanest of inns. Hence he believed that the letter he had found might have gone undiscovered for longer still, if it hadn't been for the fact that he had taken a room at the inn to recover from the effects of seasickness. Seeing the painting of the galleon upon a wild sea, he had turned the picture to face the wall. In doing so he dislodged Sido's letter. Being an honest man, Mr Suter had posted it, and he hoped that whatever the letter had to say, it hadn't arrived too late to be of use.

It contained a hurried and frightened note from Sido. A few weeks ago this note would have brought Henry comfort, but now the circumstances were well known to him and his wife. Poor Juliette had suffered badly, and her condition had not improved when she heard that her niece had no intention of returning to London before her wedding. A wedding that Juliette still believed to be ill-advised.

Now Cordell's letter outlined the situation perfectly. Regardless of any objections her aunt might have, Yann and Sido were to be married, and there would be another revolution if anyone tried stop them. He added that in his humble opinion Sido could do no better.

Were it not for Yann there would be many Frenchmen and women from all walks of life who would not be alive today.

He is a young man with a future, and I hope we can persuade him to employ his extraordinary talents and bravery on our behalf in the years to come.

To the matter of Mr Tull, Kalliovski's agent in London and Paris: he was arrested for the murder of Anselm Loup and sent to the guillotine four days after Robespierre, convicted as an English spy.

The next letter was from Yann.

Dear Mr Laxton,

I know very well that I am not the one Mrs Laxton would have desired for her niece and perhaps you too would have wanted someone better.

I have loved Sido since I first saw her all those years ago in the Marquis de Villeduval's château. I loved her before I knew what love was.

I know in my heart that I am a ghost child of my mother's one true love. His spirit is in me. My father, the father who raised me and deserves the name, is an extraordinary man named Têtu. I have so much for which to thank him: for the courage he has given me, the love that has surrounded me, and a feeling of home without the inconvenience of four walls.

I promise to look after Sido, to honour her, to love her. She is my soul, she is my life. We will walk together always.

Fortune smiles kindly on us. I pray that you will too.

Your blessing on our marriage would mean a great deal to us both.

It was a very humble and truthful letter and had moved Henry deeply.

The last one had again been from Sido.

My dear aunt and uncle,

I am sure by now you have been told that I am well

and happier than I have ever been. Yann, I know, has written to ask for your blessing and I hope with all my heart that you will be able to give it.

No doubt, Aunt, you are upset, and wish I was marrying someone of my own rank, but the man I am betrothed to is of noble birth. He was born to be King of the Gypsies.

We will go to America to start our married life, to begin again. I truly believe this is for the best. Têtu is coming with us, as is Monsieur Aulard, with a view to opening a theatre for magic.

Always your affectionate niece,
Sido

Henry was greatly relieved. In his heart of hearts he knew the young lovers would do well. Putting down his glasses, he looked up to see that tea was being served in the garden and felt somewhat sheepish. If he had been honest with Juliette, and told her Yann hadn't gone back to Paris to be an actor, if he had told her who the Silver Blade was, would she have fewer objections to the marriage?

Vane came into the room. 'Mrs Laxton is asking that you join her, sir.'

Henry stood up and, walking out into the garden, prepared to tell his wife an extraordinary story.

It was on a mellow September afternoon, as the mist once more clung like a lady's mantle to the earth and the air was filled with the smell of a passing summer, that the wedding of Yann Margoza and Sidonie de Villeduval took place in Normandy at the château of the Duchesse de Bourcy.

The long table in the dining room had been laid with the best silver and plate, and the candelabras lit so that the chamber had the quality of sun-filled honey as the guests filtered in.

Henry Laxton had chartered a private boat from Brighton to bring over Juliette, Mr Trippen, the Duc de Bourcy and his two sons. It had been an emotional reunion for everyone, each for different reasons.

Juliette, who had decided to put aside all her objections to the marriage, found herself humbled by the change in her niece and bewildered by her beauty.

Cordell had arranged for the actors from the Circus of Follies to be brought from Paris. Monsieur Aulard, sitting next to Têtu, was excited by the future. In two days' time, he, Têtu, and Monsieur and Madame Margoza would be sailing for New York. Oh, he thought, how the world has tumbled upside down to land on its feet again.

Didier was sitting with Dufort and the monkey, the Viscount, who was remarkably well behaved and well dressed. Basco was in his element talking to Juliette. Têtu, silently observing the proceedings, could see in the flickering light of the candles that the spirits were watching them. Anis, with Manouche by her side, was there to give her blessing.

The champagne flowed and, as the great doors opened and the little collection of musicans began to play, everyone stood, glasses raised.

'To Monsieur and Madame Margoza!'

Yann saw the threads of light spinning around them, all silvery, diamond, ruby bright, and knew that shadows were but passing clouds. Putting his hands to Sido's face he kissed her.

She said softly, 'We are birds ...'

Yann smiled. 'We are the children of the Revolution, we are free.'

Acknowledgments

I would like to thank Judith Elliott for her help in finishing the first draft. Thanks too, to the wonderful Jacky Batcman, who puts up with the vilest spelling mistakes and still manages to laugh, for her long-suffering patience during the many rewrites. There are, as she says, three ghost books from which this one has emerged.

My grateful thanks to Fiona Kennedy who helped shape the novel, pulling all the strands of the story together and weaving a better book; to Lauri Hornik at Dial Books for her continuing support; to my agent Rosemary Sandberg; and last but not least to the girl I met on a school visit who shyly asked, 'Please Miss, when will you write more romance – like Mr Rochester in *Jane Eyre*?'

I hope I understood the question. This book is my answer.

SG.

Also by Sally Gardner:

I, CORIANDER

I am Coriander Hobie.

I was born in the year of Our Lord 1643, the only child of Thomas and Eleanor Hobie, in our great house on the River Thames in London. Of my early years I remember only happiness. That was before I knew this world had such evil in it, and that my fate was to be locked up in a chest and left to die.

This is my story. This is my life.

'an extraordinarily beautiful and gripping tale, but what astonishes is Gardner's prose ... This is a classic new novel by an author who has written a rich fairytale for our times.'   *The Times*

DOUBLE SHADOW

'Once there was a girl who asked of her reflection, 'If all I have is fragments of memories and none of them fit together, tell me then, do I exist?''

In a bluebell wood stands a picture palace. Arnold Rubens built it to house an invention of his that could change the war torn world forever. It is to be given to his daughter, Amaryllis, on her seventeenth birthday.

But it's a present she doesn't want, and in it is a past she has to come to terms with and a boy whose name she can't remember.

Who knows what her past has been, or what the future might hold for Amaryllis, lost as she is in this place with no time?

'Sally Gardner's astonishing new novel for older teenagers The Double Shadow is intriguing, shocking and very funny. Gardner creates a cast of wonderful characters in rich, inventive and evocative prose.'

The Bookseller